TO BE FRANK

TO BE FRANK

A NOVEL

KEVAN CHRISTIE

First published in Great Britain in 2025 by
The Book Guild Ltd
Unit E2 Airfield Business Park,
Harrison Road, Market Harborough,
Leicestershire. LE16 7UL
Tel: 0116 2792299
www.bookguild.co.uk
Email: info@bookguild.co.uk

The manufacturer's authorised representative in the EU
for product safety is Authorised Rep Compliance Ltd,
71 Lower Baggot Street, Dublin D02 P593 Ireland (www.arccompliance.com)

This work is entirely fictitious and bears no resemblance to any persons living or dead.

Typeset in 11pt Minion Pro

Printed and bound by CPI Group (UK) Ltd, Croydon, CR0 4YY

ISBN 978 1835742 860

British Library Cataloguing in Publication Data.
A catalogue record for this book is available from the British Library.

For Margo

1

The day Frank Savage was called in to see the editor had started in typical fashion; nursing a mild hangover that merited grabbing a flat white and bacon roll.

He arrived at his office and had to ask the security guard, Ronnie, a borderline psycho, to let him through the electronic barrier as he'd forgotten his pass, again. Ronnie savoured his moment of glory and attempted to lecture Frank on matters pertaining to national security, before adding, 'Late one last night, Frank?' which he duly ignored.

'Just give me the pass, Ronnie.' He made his way up to the 7th floor in the lift, his mind drifting to a familiar "safe space" where he stomps Ronnie to death while wearing his Church's brogues and argyle socks by Burlington.

On arrival, Frank nipped into the canteen area to buy a can of fat Coke before swaggering through the open-plan newsroom shouting his daily greeting of 'I'm not dying for these bastards.' He finally came to rest at a bank of desks staffed by Tom, the foreign affairs correspondent who the company couldn't afford to send abroad; Carol, the health correspondent, a hypochondriac; and Martin, the transport correspondent, who cycled to work and had a fetish for Lycra. Two of the desks were empty as Peter, the business editor, was on long-term sick leave, and Ruth, the education correspondent who hated children, was covering the teacher's strike.

Plunkett, the assistant news editor, was already at his desk; a permanently raging, gammon-faced bloke with a fine head of red hair who loved Celtic FC and, therefore, all things remotely Celtic. He greeted Frank with a nod before shouting down the phone.

'We're not printing another story about the traffic signs in Leith Walk.' He hung up and turned to Frank. 'There's an email from the bosses saying they're looking for voluntary redundancies again. Planning to cut four from Editorial. Looks like they could be picking them from our pen this time.'

'More cuts?' Frank replied while flicking through the paper. 'We're down to the bare bones as it is. Do they think paying someone thirty grand a year makes them a high earner when inflation is rocketing? I'm past caring; I've been circling the drain for the last five years. If they want to get in a couple of fourteen-year-olds to write lists on the best place to grab a steak bake in Edinburgh, then so be it. The answer's Greggs. Anal-y-tics and digital clicks, that's all these fuckers care about, and they can shove their News Space of the Future up their arse... sideways. My legion of fans buys the paper to read the To Be Frank column on the bog and most of them don't own computers.'

'"Fans", that's a good one, Frank,' said Plunkett, the sarcasm dripping from his voice.

Frank considered his relationship with Plunkett to be like two hostages shackled together on a radiator. They were thrown together by chance and had no choice but to tolerate each other's foibles and ignore bad behaviour. Plunkett liked to holiday on remote Scottish islands and was forever championing the latest Gaelic supergroup or some teenager who played the fiddle and sang in a "real Scots" dialect, which, to Frank's untrained ear, sounded like a made-up language. Plunkett often asked Frank, 'Why do you hate Scotland?'

Frank browsed his emails and clicked on one from the deputy editor.

Hi, folks,

A huge week saw us smash our target by fourteen per cent. Without doubt the bionic penis story helped by notching up a fantastic 170,966 clicks. Top five stories copied below show a range of breaking news, sport and feature content.

Well done, give yourselves a giant pat on the back.

Alasdair Stewart (BA Hons)
Deputy Digital Editor News Content
Twitter: @futurenews

TRANENT MAN WITH BIONIC PENIS INUNDATED WITH DATE OFFERS:
170,966

STOCKBRIDGE DOG CAFÉ BRINGS IN THE POOCHES:
32,576

FRENCH SUPERMODEL WIFE OF HEARTS STAR IN LOVE WITH HAGGIS:
22,420

EX-FOOTBALL HOOLIGAN STARTS YOUTH THEATRE IN PORTOBELLO:
18,760

"TURKEY TEETH" LEFT ME LOOKING LIKE A GURNER, SAYS MUM-OF-FOUR:
14,600

Frank registered that his column addressing the issue of folk who leave "the big light" on in the living room hadn't made the top five, but his mind wandered to what it would be like to own a bionic cock. No doubt the embarrassment of having to buy Viagra over the counter in Boots did not apply if you had a metal tadger. It would be great if you just found Viagra lying near the railway tracks, next to the white dog shite, like torn pages of the nudie books Frank remembered fondly from his teenage years: *Razzle, Escort, Men Only*. The last time he was drunk in charge of a penis, he couldn't get it up. Erectile dysfunction: occupational hazard of the pisshead. Praise the Lord for Viagra, probably invented by a woman, along with bionic cocks.

A fresh email arrived from the editor.

> Hi, Frank.
> Could you pop into my office at 2pm for a quick catch-up?
> Richard
> Richard Bell (BA Hons)
> Digital Editor for News Content
> Twitter: @scoopmeister

Succinct and to the point, Frank thought, as he imagined bludgeoning Dick Bell-end to death with his giant bionic cock.

'I've to go and see Dick Bell-end at 2pm.'

Plunkett paused from shovelling Mini Cheddars into his mouth for a moment. 'I'm seeing him at 2.30pm. It'll just be to reassure us. I reckon there's at least two from Sport that'll get the bullet, and everyone knows the Business desk is a joke.'

Frank said, 'Nah, he hates me. He's an arse-licker who knows I should have been given the editor gig. We've tolerated each other for the last few years, and him marrying my ex-wife hasn't helped, but these corporate types are all the same – can't get off the tools quick enough. So, they head for the News desk and fail up the way, making decent reporters' lives a misery in the process. That's half the senior editorial staff in Scotland, right there.'

Plunkett replied with his mouth full, 'Cannae write bum on a wall, that's what you say, Frank.'

*

Richard Bell read Frank's latest column offering with the blinds down in his glass-panelled office where his door was never open. A collection of framed photographs took pride of place on his desk. These included Richard with various Scottish cultural icons of some renown including Sir Chris Hoy, Lorraine Kelly and Judy Murray. A picture of Richard with his one-time friend, mentor, and golf partner, (Sir) Fred Goodwin, lay in the bottom drawer of his desk.

He thought Frank had finally crossed the Rubicon in calling for all babies and dogs to be banned from cafés – evidence that his columns were becoming increasingly bonkers and out of touch. Richard saw an opportunity to put the final nail in the coffin of Frank's career. The inevitable complaints along with a social-media backlash would lead to Frank being "cancelled" with Richard having no choice but to sack his errant hack for the good of the paper, citing the column as evidence of declining mental health. He would claim that the columnist had gone rogue and filed straight to the page without getting his work checked, thus taking advantage of the lack of sub-editors whose numbers had dropped from twenty-three to three following the great weirdo sub cull of 2018. This would serve him right for never posting his columns on Twitter or Facebook where he enjoyed the grand total of six and eight followers/friends respectively and, unlike the rest of the staff, hadn't bothered to get a blue tick for verification. Add in his general attitude, penchant to shock and unwillingness to engage with the News Space of the Future initiative and voilà! No more Frank and his dinosaur ways.

He phoned Morag, his personal assistant, and asked her to send in Graeme, the column editor. Graeme – a man in his late forties past caring about his job, drank eleven cans of Diet Coke each day and hadn't tucked his shirt in once in the last five years – shuffled in to see his boss and sat down.

'Where are we with tomorrow's columns?' Richard asked.

'Nearly there, I've just finished checking Carol's and it's a decent piece about her own struggles with mental health, post-pandemic, and how increasing numbers of millennials are turning to wild swimming to help combat the stress of everyday living.'

'Sounds great. That's exactly the direction of travel that we're looking for and this should play well with our target audience; it hits the demographic and will generate a decent amount of digital traffic to the website. I'll be asking Carol to take a deep dive on wild swimming in the coming weeks. Excuse the pun.'

Graeme looked at the editor like he was a giant can of Diet Coke with tiny matchstick legs and clown's shoes.

'I tried wild swimming for the first time down at Portobello last week,' Richard said, bursting with pride. 'Really enjoyable, absolute buzz, great crowd of people.'

Graeme nodded, breaking into a rictus grin.

'Oh, and don't worry about Frank this week,' Richard added, avoiding eye contact. 'He's been working on a piece that I'm aware of and I'll make sure he files directly onto the page. Should save you a bit of time, what with deadlines being what they are.'

This seemed odd to Graeme, who normally worked in tandem with Frank and had lost count of the number of times he had to rein him in and protect the paper from copious complaints and potential libel claims.

'What's he writing about?' Graeme asked suspiciously.

'He's calling for the banning of babies and dogs from cafés; probably thinks it's a light-hearted, tongue-in-cheek piece that will strike a chord with our readers, but Frank is becoming a bit of a liability if truth be told. What do you think?'

Graeme imagined a red flash danger sign, thinking this was the last thing Frank should be writing about.

'Yip, sounds interesting,' he said.

'Do you think he is becoming a liability? The reason I ask is that upstairs are looking to cut staff.'

Graeme contemplated his own job security, then resorted to his usual stance of agreeing with everything the editor said.

'Liability, yes, I suppose he is a liability. I've spent a fair chunk of my working life cutting Frank's columns to save both him and the paper endless grief.'

Richard jumped on this with glee, seeking validity for his plan.

'Exactly, he always sails close to the line of what's acceptable in a family newspaper and is completely out of touch with our younger readers. I don't think too many people will be crying if Frank leaves. Do you own a dog by the way?'

Graeme clammed up and was now rubbing his thighs, eager to escape the office and head for the vending machine. He stood, slowly making his way towards the door whilst ignoring the editor's question on pet ownership.

*

Meanwhile, Frank spent the rest of the morning chatting with the younger reporters who worked for their sister paper. He thought he got on well with them but was wary of a couple who didn't get the cut of his jib. This was new territory for Frank, who had always considered himself the King of Banter – the KOB – but was starting to find that his sense of irony and general sarcasm was lost on certain people. Perhaps he had "Old Man Patter" and needed to polish his act. He'd heard mention of him having "no filter" and wondered if this was a good or bad thing. There was that time he'd offended the new starter, Eva, by proclaiming that fibromyalgia was a made-up illness, the same as "that ME", and she told him she suffered from both. Awkward. Generally, he tried to help younger members of staff but wouldn't go as far as to describe himself as a mentor as it sounded a bit creepy.

Frank already felt the need to escape the newsroom and decided to go for a lunchtime stroll through leafy Stockbridge to get his head together before his meeting with the boss. He lit up a Marlboro Red and made his way past the parents and their "miracle" offspring. The local primary school had scored heavily in the *Sunday Times* list of the 100 best state schools in Scotland. Frank counted seven Cocker Spaniels, three black Labradors and a French Bulldog, along with five Range Rovers, and pondered why all the dads seemed to be wearing the same jacket with "Rab" written on it. Surely, they weren't all called Rab. Frank wandered towards the mean streets of Comely Bank, peering in the front windows of the Georgian townhouses, catching a glimpse of artwork here and there. A crisp November morning, he could see the spire of Fettes College in the near distance, above the treetops in Inverleith Park, and felt blessed to live in such a beautiful city. A crashing sound of glass increased Frank's general state of anxiety and was playing havoc with his brain. It was bottle collection day in Stockbridge. Frank was amazed by the levels of consumption in the area and marvelled at the high standard of booze the posh folk had been guzzling behind closed doors. Not a can of Tennent's or bottle of Buckfast in sight – a decent effort from the pink chino brigade.

He decided to give his mate Gurkha Bobby a call to give him the bottle update and see if he was going to the pub tonight. *Is the Pope a paedophile?* he imagined Bobby replying. But, after a standard pat down of all pockets, he realised there was no mobile to hand. It was becoming the norm for him to leave home without his phone when nursing a hangover.

Frank contemplated nipping into the Bailie Bar for a swift half before meeting Dick Bell-end but didn't trust himself to leave. Still, he headed up Dean Street in the hope of spotting his dream car that was often parked there: the 1979 Rolls-Royce Silver Shadow Mk II in two-tone gold over metallic brown paint and West of England wool interior, complete with built-in eight-track player. He drooled over this car, imagining going for spin through East Lothian with French actress Isabelle Adjani in the passenger seat. They would stop for a cone at Luca's in Musselburgh as they made their way back to Edinburgh. She would choose a vanilla 99 with raspberry sauce and Frank would lovingly explain to Isabelle that it was called a 99 because the Italian ice-cream merchants who settled in Scotland named it after the King of Italy's elite bodyguard, which consisted of 99 men. At that point, Isabelle would stick her tongue in Frank's ear and grab his crotch, urging him to "hit the gas" so they could get home for seven hours of tantric sex.

His heart skipped a beat as he saw the Shadow parked outside the garage of a mews house with a homemade For Sale sign on it, stating "one careful owner" with an accompanying mobile number for interested parties. Frank felt a surge of longing before his head spun and he staggered, losing his composure for a few seconds. Isabelle Adjani's face briefly flashed before his eyes, then a 99 cone, as the 1970s whirled by in a blur. He was a keen student of the Shadow range and considered them to be the epitome of rock star cool, with *The Who* drummer, Keith Moon, and Elton John proud owners.

Quick maths. He reckoned it would go for somewhere in the region of forty thousand pounds. *Jesus*, thought Frank, that was miles out of his price range, which was nearer five thousand at a push. The phrase "mid-life crisis" crossed his mind before he tore the top off his fag packet and scribbled down the mobile number using the bookie's pencil he carried in the pocket of his Paul Smith blazer. He wanted that car so badly, but it seemed agonisingly out of reach. The 6.75 litre engine – or the "six and three-quarter" to those in the know – would guzzle the gas but Frank had read an article where someone had carried out an electrical conversion on a Shadow and said it was easy to do. He barely managed to cover his mortgage, had missed payments and was planning to use the remaining money from his tiny pension pot, which was mostly invested in Chinese Growth Funds, to help make a dent in the outstanding balance, but that was just juggling numbers. In short, he was a financial disaster, always had been. The divorce from Bridget hadn't helped and she eventually gave up trying to get money from him for their daughter, Katie, working on the premise that you can't get blood out of a stone. Frank's love of a punt had seen him invest in numerous surefire winners over the years, including a racehorse called Guinness, whose moment of glory was finishing fifth in a six-horse race at Kelso.

But the lure of the Shadow was too great not to let his mind fantasise about owning it. He hadn't driven for nigh on thirty years, since the ban for drink-driving round the roundabout at the Playhouse the wrong way to win a bet, but the thought of getting behind the wheel of this dream machine kept him awake at night.

Heading back into the office, he caught up with Graeme, who was drinking a can of Diet Coke at the lift.

'Hi, Graeme, sorry I was late with the column. I battered it out while nursing the mother of all hangovers; it's a bit bonkers and probably needs a few tweaks. You don't own a dog by any chance?'

Graeme gave Frank his usual bemused stare, which Frank always took for condescension.

'It's cool, Richard loves it.'

'Thank you, kind sir,' said Frank with a curtsey.

Graeme shrugged in the style of Alan Partridge and took a swig of his can before pressing the button for the 7th floor.

Back at his desk, Frank checked his emails – 564 unread from an inbox of twelve thousand – and clicked on an offer from one of his betting accounts. *You have £50 in free bets!* He made a mental note to give that his full attention later.

'Wish me luck,' he shouted to his colleagues before heading towards the editor's office. Blank stares, no response.

2

'Shut the door, Frank, and take a pew.'

Frank took a deep breath and concentrated on going in through the nose and out through the mouth, a trick he had picked up with Bridget at a Pilates class they had gone to in a bid to do "more stuff together". She filed for divorce a month later.

Richard shifted uneasily in his chair, before launching into his preamble. 'The reason I've brought you in is to have an informal chat about the direction of travel for Editorial when the News Space of the Future initiative gets up and running. Head office is planning a restructure of all departments with the aim of streamlining the content operation to make it more agile and robust. The emphasis will firmly shift towards the digital platforms, and I'll be appointing a new trends editor with a lifestyle bias, focusing on driving content across our titles and the wider group. We aim to increase our podcasts and video content tenfold, going forward.'

Frank glazed over as the editor continued his spiel.

'This will mean a degree of natural wastage, with voluntary redundancy on the table, which should mean no need for compulsory redundancies. We believe the optics on this will reflect our desire to move with the times in a modern Scotland where the emphasis is on inclusivity. That was the main takeaway that I took away from this week's brainstorming session in Cumbria.'

Frank had been thinking about people having afternoon sex on the carpets of Georgian townhouses when the word "takeaway" jolted him from his daydream and made him think of food. Chinese, fish supper or a kebab for tonight's tea?

'Is it true you're looking to get rid of four reporters?' said Frank.

'No decision has been taken on staff numbers.'

'Well, I can tell you for starters you don't need three sports guys reporting on the Hearts.'

'Like I said, no decisions will be taken until the consultation process has been completed, moving into the New Year.'

It only now dawned on Frank that staff would be getting made redundant just in time for Christmas. *It was always thus*, he thought. 'Surely I'm not in the firing line?' he said.

Richard bristled at being asked a direct question by an underling.

'That's one of the reasons I've asked you in for this informal chat. I want to gauge your thoughts on how things are progressing and how you see your role developing in the digital age.'

This wasn't Frank's first rodeo, and he was well-versed in dealing with management. He considered Richard to be a Replicant like in the movie *Blade Runner*, an alien mimicking human emotion.

'I think things are going brilliantly. I have loads of new ideas that will keep me relevant and bring in the computer hits. This week's column is a bit controversial, and you're bound to get complaints, but I think I'm on the money with the sheer number of dogs and babies in cafés these days. You can't get a minute's peace.'

'Yes, I've seen that; it's punchy but also brings a bit of light-heartedness to a topic that most people won't have considered. You can file it straight onto the page. Don't worry, I'll handle any complaints.'

'Brilliant. So, you don't want any changes?' Frank asked.

'No, it's fine as it is; great work.'

Frank decided to strike while his iron was hot and reaffirm his creativity and overall importance to the paper.

'I also want to do a bit on mental health issues for middle-aged folk, touching on how no one tells you how to deal with dying parents, but also what happens if they live too long, and you need the money. Then there's the issue of older relatives always giving you shortbread and tablet at Christmastime, like they know it's basically crack cocaine and will slowly kill you, so they don't go near it. Seriously, Richard, when was the last time you saw an elderly person eating shortbread?'

Richard appeared to contemplate this for a moment. 'To be honest, it's not something I'm aware of.'

'The bastards are wise to it. I'm telling you.'

'Well,' said Richard, after an awkward pause, 'it's good that you're making the effort to provide more robust content.'

Frank noticed the editor liked to use the word "robust" a lot, like he thought it lent gravitas to everything he said. '*I had a robust wank while wearing my spectacles and holding my phone sideways.*'

'Look, I'd rather you just told me my job is safe and cut all this fannying about,' Frank said, knowing that any kind of direct approach was alien to his editor, the alien.

'The truth is I don't know, and nothing has been finalised.'

Frank coughed and managed to say 'Bollocks' at the same time, which Richard ignored but Frank considered a transferable skill.

'However,' Richard continued, laying the foundations, 'there are a couple of issues that have come to light that I want to flag up with you.'

'Oh aye, here we go,' Frank replied.

'I've had a complaint from the younger members of staff about some of your comments and general office banter. Some of these will make more sense to you than me but the use of the following terms or phrases is proving to be problematic.'

Richard stared at the list like he was holding a piece of dog shit in his hands.

'For instance, you saying that you've spent forty minutes on the cross-dresser when you've been at the gym has caused offence and has been raised as a red flag for possible homophobic-slash-transphobic behaviour.'

'That's bollocks,' Frank replied. 'I'm up to fifty minutes now and you can't just slash homophobic and transphobic behaviour to suit your needs. I've got a mental block about that and get my words muddled up – I obviously mean cross-trainer,' he lied.

'Okay, suppose I give you the benefit of the doubt. But what's this stuff about calling people "Yifters"? It's been flagged as potentially racist.'

Frank laughed and shook his head. 'That's what I call the staff doing shifts – "Yifters" after Yifter the Shifter. It's got nothing to do with race. Miruts Yifter was the Ethiopian runner who won a couple of golds at the Moscow Olympics back in 1980. You know, the one the Americans boycotted.'

Richard nodded sideways, then forwards and backwards.

'It doesn't really work if you're forced to explain it,' said Frank, rolling his eyes, 'but it's certainly not racist, just something I say to lighten the mood. Anyway, we've never had a person of colour anywhere near the paper in the twenty years I've been here. There's more chance of a woman getting *your* job than that happening.'

Richard picked up the list again and squinted at it, trying to focus. 'That's just two examples of things you say that could be construed as offensive. There's more: *Upstairs for thinking, downstairs for dancing; Away and throw shite at yourself; Couldn't write bum on a wall; I'm not dying for these bastards; Gout is the closest a man will get to childbirth...* Half of this is lost on me, Frank, but it's starting to offend people. I've also been told you've called Plunkett a "poster boy for diabetes", said you prefer funerals to weddings, described a female PR as "the bride of Chucky" and also claimed Boris Johnson and his entire family

14

should be shot so the bloodline is wiped out. You also said this about the Royal Family after the Queen died.'

Frank replied in a forlorn voice, 'You missed the bit about making them dig their own graves first.' He let out a deep groan; he didn't have the energy to explain the concept of the wind-up to Richard. Anyway, he knew where this was going and suspected some of the Replicants might want rid of him or at the very least had spoken about it. Frank realised that taken out of context, or even taken in context, a lot of what he said could offend some people, but what was so harmful about being offended? It wasn't life-threatening. He genuinely did prefer funerals to weddings but only because he liked hearing about people's lives.

'Look, Frank. I know how hard it can be for older members of staff to adapt in the digital age. I also realise things are trickier with our, erm, personal situation, but I like to think we've gotten on all right and kept it professional.'

Frank wanted to say, 'Keep my wife's name out your mouth,' Will Smith Oscar-style before slapping him, but Richard hadn't mentioned Bridget by name. Instead, he shrugged and said, 'Okay, I'll rein it in a bit.'

'Great, Frank, that's what I wanted to hear. You must realise a lot of your references are lost on our younger readers. Not everyone has heard of *The Specials* or *The World at War*.'

Frank thought about this for a second and was about to launch into his familiar tirade about how saying "I wasn't born then" does not give you a pass for not knowing who *The Beatles* are or that the Battle of Hastings was in 1066. But a wave of apathy washed over him, and his thoughts turned towards owning the Shadow, a cold pint of lager and a packet of dry-roasted peanuts.

Richard stood up to signify the meeting was over and accompanied Frank to the door of his office. 'Good man, you've taken this well. Just remember, the industry is getting younger – it's not personal.'

'It's strictly business,' Frank replied, before realising his movie reference to *The Godfather* would be lost on Richard who had just turned forty-five and would claim he wasn't born when the film came out.

Frank decided to knock off work early seeing as it was Friday, and his hangover was beginning to subside thus creating room for more bevvy. As he left the office building and walked out into the street, he called the Shadow's owner; a guy with a slight American twang who sounded like an old hippie. The hippie asked if he was a time-waster before enquiring why he wanted to own the car. Frank said he'd always loved the Roller and admired it regularly on his walks around Stockbridge. He told the hippie the iconic image of Joanna Lumley posing in front of a Shadow Mk II, wearing a bowler hat and holding an umbrella with a revolver tucked into her stockings, took pride of place in his living room.

'Ah, Joanna,' the hippie said. 'Lovely girl, was at school with one of my ex-wives, used to visit us at the castle in Aberdeenshire. I loved it up there after I came to Scotland via Canada in '68 to dodge the draft. Spent the year playing in the folk clubs. Sure beat the hell out of fighting Charlie during Tet. A large dram in one hand, a beautiful chick in the other.'

'Wow, that sounds amazing,' Frank replied, sounding like an instant fanboy.

Forty minutes later and with Frank barely getting a word in edgeways, they arranged to meet at the mews house in Dean Street on Sunday morning.

Frank waited at the bus stop for the number 42 to take him to his local pub, The Haddonfield Memorial in Portobello, where he knew the regular teatime crew would be gathering. His head raced with thoughts of possible redundancy mixed in with how he could raise the cash to own the Shadow, and the idea of no longer being a journalist depressed him. Surely they weren't daft enough to get rid of him, a man of letters, their star columnist. Although he moaned about the job, he still loved journalism and knew the To Be Frank column defined him and provided a sense of identity. But he was too long in the tooth to imagine that anyone gave a toss if, "worst-case scenario", he lost his job. You weren't allowed to offend anyone these days, he thought. Punk would never have got past first base if it was around now. Frank realised he preferred things the way they were in the previous century, and the advances in technology had happened too quickly in the last thirty years so that people were now, basically, stupider.

Too many members of staff belonged to what he called "the cult of praise" where they constantly complimented their colleagues. It seemed to him like insecurity, and he saw scant evidence of any talent: providing a list of ten shops that have disappeared from the high street is a Google search, not a skill. Frank had grown tired of the number of "blessed to work with such a talented group of people" messages that now appeared from his colleagues on social media and considered it an insincere and undignified practice.

This was always worse around the time of the Scottish Journalism Awards, from which he had not received a single nomination in twenty-odd years as a columnist. His yearly mantra following rejection was *you don't work to receive awards*. Paper medals. Even Tom had been nominated and Frank took this as a sign of decline, rejoicing in telling him, 'Well, if you hang around the barber's long enough, someone will give you a haircut.'

You wouldn't get a bunch of plumbers going on about their brilliant work colleagues. Jesus wept. '*Blessed to work with wee Jimmy, a fantastic human being with an immense talent for unclogging shite from the cludgie, who always gets the bacon-and-egg doublers in.*'

The bus crawled past the old Ramsay Technical College where he lived. He'd christened the dominating red-brick, former chocolate factory and college "the Texas Depository building" and often thought it would be a great place to pick off hipsters and their nippy wee dogs on the promenade.

Frank was going straight to the boozer, deciding that his need for alcohol outweighed the need to collect his mobile phone. He arrived at the "Hadd", marching through the door like a gunslinger entering a saloon to loud cheers. Just the tonic. The King of Banter was in the building. 'Am-stel standing,' Frank declared as Bella, the owner, a die-hard Goth and horror aficionado, who ran the pub with her daughter, Frances, poured him a pint of the Dutch medicine.

The usual suspects were on parade, standing at the bar waiting to greet him. The pub was full of familiar faces, a mix of hipsters (who, to Frank, all looked like lumberjacks) and locals who got on well enough until around the eight-pint mark. Frank nodded to a couple of old Mods and headed through the back to the "beer garden", a glorified smoking area with a couple of plastic chairs. A Space Invaders machine was on one side of the doorway, a Galaxian machine on the other. They were a big hit with the hipsters. He sparked up a Marlboro Red and took a deep drag. This was the golden hour – a buzzing pub, the first hit of nicotine and a cold pint, followed by another, then another six. That was the main course. Frank knew it would deteriorate later and he'd end up drinking strawberry daiquiris on his own while trying to read the papers with one of the pairs of reading glasses they kept in a box behind the bar. But for now, the loneliness was at bay.

Gurkha Bobby, to give him his full title, joined Frank for another fag, having waited the required ten minutes to allow his mate to decompress. Bobby also had a love for Joanna Lumley but not because of her sterling work with The Gurkha Welfare Trust. No, he loved the blonde bombshell for her role as Purdey in *The New Avengers* – something he and Frank had bonded over as nippers at primary school along with a love of ska music and The Jam.

'All right, Frank?'

Frank came towards Bobby and gave him a big hug. He was seeking a bit of reassurance and, although he didn't think he was in much danger of losing his job, a touch of sympathy and praise from his best mate was in order.

'The bastards at the paper are looking to cut staff and they're wanting to kick some of the deadwood into the long grass. Not a bad idea, if you ask me; some of the correspondents have been phoning it in for years.'

Bobby took a step back. 'Well, you'll be fine, Frank. You're the best thing in that rag.'

Frank took a large drag on his cigarette and a gulp of his pint. 'Too kind, Bobby, but I have to at least consider the possibility that they're trying to send me to the garden centre or the supermarket tills. That would put me in the shit financially as the redundancy payment would be no more than the minimum, around thirty miserable grand, barely put a dent in my debt mountain and I'd likely splash it on a fancy car.'

'Is it that Dick Bell-end fanny? He better had not be behind this,' Bobby warned, clenching his fists.

'Well, he's the one firing the bullets, but the money men are driving it. Natural wastage, they'll call it; some bollocks about legacy staff.'

Bobby gave him a quizzical look. 'Surely that's ageist, Frank?'

'Well, I don't know about that, Bobby, but it's certainly Frankist.'

'Do you want me to kidnap his dog? I don't mind teaching the bastard a lesson. I'll come out of retirement. Hit him where it hurts, purloin the pooch.'

Frank thought about this for a moment and was genuinely touched that Bobby – who had previous for dog snatching in a row with an ex-girlfriend but had since sought treatment – would do this for him.

'That's really kind, but we'll keep the chloroform on hold for now.'

From there, the night ran its usual course, as Frank had predicted. He held court for a bit, telling anyone who'd listen that Roger Moore was the best Bond, why two serves should be scrapped in tennis (slows the game down), why Buckingham Palace should be turned into a giant Wetherspoons and his plans to open an adult-only café on Portobello promenade with no babies or dogs allowed. None of the regulars bit as these were familiar Frank tropes.

Throughout the night, the teatime crew began to disperse; some saying goodbye and others disappearing into thin air. Around midnight, with one hour to go until closing time, Frank found himself alone at the bar, having refused Bobby's offer of a Chinese from the takeaway on the high street. He ordered a white Russian, which Bella painstakingly prepared, and entered a debate with him about whether Michael Myers from the *Halloween* movies could take Freddy Krueger in a square go. They decided on a score draw before Bella ordered Frank to go home.

He made his way along the high street where the Christmas decorations had appeared, staggering slightly and bumping into the odd car, playing dodgems. The pubs were closing, doors half shut as punters drained their pints while a police car sat with its lights out. Frank shuffled his way along till he reached the last pub, The Portobello Arms, known to the locals as "Star Wars". He walked past, the usual racket of karaoke and folk refusing to drink up.

A group of smokers had gathered in a circle with their vaping groupies stood on the outside. One of the guys, who Frank recognised but couldn't remember his name, offered him a cigarette.

'Nah, it's all right, mate. I've been smoking like a Beagle all night,' he replied.

He peered through the steaming window and saw a man holding court and ordering drinks for the "last of the Mohicans" gathered round the bar. The guy had an old-fashioned flick hairstyle with an undercut, beloved by football casuals and soul boys alike. Frank had worn a similar style in the mid-eighties, which, come to think of it, was the last time he'd seen anyone sporting this 'do. The man was familiar – the way he carried himself; a "to the manor born" wide-o but much older and jail pale, despite the sunbed tan, with the waxy pallor of the hardened criminal. Then the man turned his head and Frank saw the scar down the right cheekbone.

'No way,' Frank cried. 'It can't be… Brewster.'

Frank thought he was hallucinating and started feeling dizzy as the bile rose up in his throat. He moved round to the side of the pub and knew he was going to spew. The feeling of swallowing sandpaper engulfed him as the first wave of yellow liquid poured out his mouth, then his nose and possibly his eyes.

He went back to the steamy window to confirm the sighting of Brewster, but the lights were off, and the pub had emptied. Frank banged on the door. 'Brewster, I know you're in there. Brewster, you murdering bastard.'

Frank leant against the pub door like a Couch to 5k runner trying to get their breath back as his head cleared. He finally made it home and managed to get his key in the door after fifteen attempts. His Nokia was on the sofa, looking like it'd had a nice day to itself. He attempted to read his texts then hit the voice message button. His daughter's voice filled the room.

'Hi, Dad. It's Naomi. I'm coming to Edinburgh tomorrow and wondered if you could meet me at Waverley Station. I need your help.'

3

N aomi was relieved to get the *no bother, love* text back from her dad at two o'clock in the morning. She imagined him checking his phone once a day and not really knowing how to use it, but she appreciated he'd replied.

Boarding the train at King's Cross, she felt the knot in her stomach slacken but the lingering cramps that caused her no end of grief were still present, gnawing away in the background. It was good to be heading out of London and away from the madness that had engulfed her in the last fortnight.

Naomi had told Tanya at the club that she needed a break, to get away and clear her head, without going into too much detail or mentioning that she wouldn't be back. Tanya was good as gold letting her go and it left her with the illusion of control, even though Naomi was at least five levels above in the organisation.

The combination of Prem ballers with their South London entourages, the teenage offspring of Russian gangsters, bit-part Saudi royals and 'Ndrangheta affiliates was getting out of hand. A gun had been pulled in the VIP area of Disco Italo on Sunday night and the new bouncer had been "disappeared" after letting unsanctioned dealers into the club. Sure, there had been threats before, but this was the first time Rudy, the owner, had been given an Osman warning by the Met and that lot from Peckham had nothing to lose. Half the punters who turned up at the club now were wearing jogging bottoms. All right, they cost eight hundred quid but they're still jobby-catchers with elasticated bottoms, mate. Picking beautiful girls for rich reprobates provided cover while she did her real job – money laundering on a laptop from home after the Wise One had spotted her talent for numbers. But Naomi was now starting to feel like a pimp, and deciding how to monetise the layout of the tables in a nightclub for maximum coin bored her rigid. The Wise One's offer to go up to Edinburgh and keep an eye on the Syndicate's new operation, which was her brainchild, appealed and she jumped at the chance to live in Portobello for "as long as it takes".

The only downside was lying to her dad about what she did for a living, and this made her feel a bit grubby. It wasn't like Frank had been a model father and they struggled to keep in touch, but he didn't deserve the deceit. Naomi squared this away by vowing that she would never put him or the rest of her family in harm's way and would come clean when the time was right.

She gazed out the window and placed her right foot through the strap of the Louis Vuitton holdall under her seat, the one that held her electric toothbrush, underwear, a couple of tops, five hundred thousand pounds of Syndicate money and her Glock 43. A woman about her age with a baby in tow sat down at a table for four and Naomi smiled at them both, feeling a slight pang of longing in her stomach, that she quickly told to "do one".

The waiter came around with the coffee, and she unwrapped the complimentary shortbread that you got in first class. A nice touch. Naomi was just getting settled when two men barged into the carriage, steaming drunk at eight in the morning, carrying their six-packs of wife-beater lager.

'*Bollocks*,' Naomi said to herself, while being thankful she'd had the good sense to book a single seat with a little table. This was the last thing she needed, a couple of lairy gits causing havoc as she was getting ready to read her book, *Farewell, My Lovely* by Raymond Chandler. They plonked themselves down at the same table as the Madonna with Child and proceeded to assault the poor woman's eardrums with a series of inane questions along with a running commentary of their every movement up until that point.

'Had a few before we got on at King's Cross. Can't beat an away day with my boy. Here's a quid for the little 'un.'

A father and son team; Daddy Beater wearing a little West Ham badge on his jacket, and Baby Beater sporting the obligatory Clone Island jumper to go with his soon-to-be pish-stained jogging bottoms. Cans cracked open, one was offered to the mum, who politely declined.

Naomi heard snippets of chat referring to 'running them back in my day,' sprinkled with copious references to the Old Bill and 'Geordie twats.' It dawned on her that West Ham were playing Newcastle, and this pair were heading up early and fancied a bit of free hospitality in the posh seats. Bastards were bringing shame on her club.

Naomi managed to get one of the little headphones into her ear, but Daddy Beater caught her eye before she could insert the other.

'All right, darling, got the day off from pushing the trolley?'

Naomi let that slide, pretending she hadn't heard him.

'Must have won a competition to sit in the posh seats.'

Again, Naomi ignored him.

'Fucking elephant washers.'

Naomi heard that and took a deep breath. She turned around and stared him down. Thankfully, the catering trolley arrived, causing a welcome distraction. However, that only provided temporary respite, with Baby Beater taking it upon himself to order more cans, then turn the music up on his mobile so the whole carriage was treated to a hardcore techno mix. Naomi sat there quietly raging, taking comfort from the fact they would be getting off at Newcastle, although that would be a long couple of hours.

The ticket collector made his way round as the rest of the passengers braced themselves for the inevitable confrontation. He wearily eyed the carry-out, then asked the men for their tickets. Smugly, and with an air of entitlement that would put a minor Royal to shame, Daddy Beater brought out a couple of briefs before proudly declaring, 'Weekend upgrade.' The ticket inspector stared incredulously at the tickets before giving a slight shake of his head and handing them back. He apologetically told Daddy Beater to keep the noise down as other passengers had complained and this was met with cordial respect for the rank.

'Of course, sir, no problem at all. My son and I are going to watch our beloved West Ham United and will be getting off at Newcastle in the frozen north.'

The ticket inspector beamed proudly. 'I'm a West Ham man myself, lads. Forty years man and boy. Up the Irons.'

This was met with a cheer from the Beaters that awoke the sleeping baby, who launched into a crying solo with intermittent bouts of screaming. Naomi sunk deeper into her seat, cursing the train company for their weekend upgrade policy that she'd taken advantage of on numerous occasions. Putting down her book, she reflected on what the Wise One had said. He'd told the Syndicate he considered Edinburgh an "open city" that was ripe for takeover with minimum fuss, and although the London firms had never bothered expanding that far north, things were about to change. With the financial regulators concentrating on Londongrad and the City's reputation as the "money laundering capital of the world", it made sense to broaden horizons. Naomi described the sleepy seaside town of Portobello as Edinburgh's Brighton; this had certainly appealed to the Wise One, who was sold on her vision.

The train stopped at Durham and a bunch of Toon Army fans got on. A well-heeled group of four older men wearing traditional football scarves and expensive overcoats sat down near the Beaters, who were past the point of no return, having drunk their weight in cooking lager. What the Newcastle fans took for a bit of banter quickly escalated with Dad Beater calling them "northern monkeys", which Baby Beater took as his cue to get in the face of the octogenarians looking to enjoy a glass of white wine on their jaunt up the road.

Naomi seethed until she could take no more. These bastards had ruined her journey and everyone else's. She dialled a number on the burner phone and gave the recipient the bullet points before making her way towards Daddy Beater, tapping him on the shoulder.

'This is for you, mate.'

Daddy Beater looked confused while she stood, arm outstretched, waiting for him to take the phone. The carriage went silent, pretending not to watch as Daddy Beater took the mobile, listening intently like his life depended on it, then nodding furiously before turning a whiter shade of pale and handing the burner back to Naomi. He grabbed Baby Beater by the scruff of the neck and told him to shut his mouth.

'We're going,' he said to his son, grabbing a couple of cans and shoving him down the carriage through the automatic doors to stand in the corridor, their new home for the remainder of their journey.

Five minutes later, ashen-faced and remarkably sober, Daddy Beater with sullen teenager in tow came back through to apologise first to Naomi, then to the Madonna with Child, then to the octogenarians, finally addressing everyone in first class. Naomi thought, *There's making an arse of yourself, then there's this,* as he started his speech.

'Ladies and gentlemen, I'd just like to say on behalf of my son and me that I'm truly sorry for our behaviour on the journey up from London. I… I mean we, didn't mean to cause offence and we deeply regret the distress and discomfort that we put you through. As a token of our goodwill, I've given two hundred pounds to the trolley people so that everyone can enjoy a drink on us. Thanks for listening and sorry again.' He gave Baby Beater a nudge.

Baby Beater, looking down at his feet, added, 'Like what my old fella said, I'm deeply sorry and saddened by our behaviour. Sorry, it won't ever happen again. Sorry.'

Half the passengers had taken a sudden interest in the Durham countryside while the other half tried hard to contain their laughter. The leader of the octogenarians, who had more than a passing resemblance to Terence Stamp, nodded his approval before saying, 'Okay, lads, off you fuck now,' to cheers from his fellow travellers.

Naomi gazed out the window, basking in the quietness that had engulfed the carriage, with time and Newcastle flying by as the train made its way over the bridge at Berwick-upon-Tweed and into Scotland. This trip was all about seeing her family and sussing out the lay of the land for a move to Edinburgh. She'd made a flying visit for reconnaissance purposes last year, staying at the Balmoral during the Festival, and spent a nice night with her half-sister, Katie, without her dad knowing. She was also looking forward to catching up with her grandmother, Rita, and seeing her grandad. But most of all Naomi wanted to spend time with Frank. The last time she'd seen her father was around five years ago when he'd come down to London for a weekend that turned into an epic bender. They'd discussed Naomi's mother, Maxine, a talented singer who'd toured with several top bands in the eighties. Naomi was just five years old when Frank told her that her mum was in heaven, and she'd gone to live with her Aunty Jane, who brought her up in a strict, God-fearing household.

She was following Frank's columns, which made her laugh but also cringe in equal measure. Despite being set in his ways, Naomi sought her dad's advice and needed a bit of parenting, hoping he could smooth the way for her to rent a decent place and integrate into the local community. Well, integrating herself into the local community to exploit them for the purposes of money laundering, but hopefully that was only temporary and the desire for a quieter life was the longer-term goal. She just had to lie to her old boy and move a bit of cash around to get there, but Naomi was used to living a lie.

The train hurtled through East Lothian with Arthur's Seat in the distance. Naomi recognised Musselburgh and watched the haar coming in from the Firth of Forth as they sped through Portobello, heading past the revamped Meadowbank Stadium, which no longer looked like a relic from the Cold War. The driver slowed down to a crawl as the train approached Waverley Station.

Naomi made ready to get off, hugging the holdall as the sense of anticipation built and the knot in her stomach returned, before grabbing a couple of shortbread packets from the empty tables. A present for her dad.

4

Frank lay in bed and tried to open his eyes, but his eyelids weren't responding. He felt like he'd suffered a serious head injury after being knocked out by Mike Tyson, spent a month on life support, survived, but had then been hit by a bus on his first day out of hospital and now had permanent concussion as a result. A throbbing sensation in his left calf which felt hot to touch convinced him of a deep vein thrombosis, so he reached for the aspirin to break up the blood clot. There was also a niggling pain in his big toe, and he feared the dreaded gout could be "coming soon to a cinema near you". Frank had once worked out that he'd lost approximately three years of his life to these types of hangovers and today would move him closer to year four. A flashback to white Russians, vomit on his shoes and a football hooligan with a flick hairdo.

He thought about his younger brother, Michael, as he always did when hungover and felt sad – what a waste. The pain of losing Michael seemed to be getting worse the older Frank got; a hollow feeling that never went away. He still had the odd dream about the wee man and cherished those but felt total despair at not being able to talk to him.

The dry boke started to rise in his throat as he sat down to pee, something their dad had taught them to do as children. This was preferable to the stand-and-spray method favoured by most men where half the urine lands on the bathroom floor.

It took Bridget a while to get used to her husband sitting down to pee, which wasn't on the "top five list of sexy things about my husband", but the upside was the toilet seat was always down.

Frank tried to brush his teeth but gagged again as soon as he put the toothbrush in his mouth, reaching for the mouthwash, which mercifully didn't contain alcohol, as that was the last thing he needed but the first thing he wanted.

Had he really seen Brewster last night, or was he hallucinating? He felt the anger rise through his shoulders, down his arms and into his clenched fists. Checking his phone, Frank saw it was 10am and was glad that he still had a bit of time before he met Naomi. What a nick he was in. Only thing for it: a bacon and black pudding doubler, with strong coffee and a double/Scottish/German/Belgian/Empire biscuit – call them what you like – for afters. *Black pudding: food of the gods,* Frank thought, placing Michael and Bridget into the compartment marked "for another day" in his marinating brain.

He headed along Portobello High Street and popped into the local shop to buy a paper so he could read his column. Frank normally spent Saturday mornings at home but had decided he was going to walk along the prom to clear his head a bit before going into Fusion Brew for his roll and biscuit. They charged like a wounded bull in there, but he wanted a treat. Sheila behind the counter gave him her usual, 'It'll take you all week to read that' spiel before examining the weekend edition of the paper for the price. She then scolded him, adding, 'Three pound twenty? What a rip-off.' A version of this exchange had gone on every Saturday for the last decade.

'What are you writing about this time?' she said with the usual scorn.

Frank had to think before he remembered the aberration he had filed. 'Oh, just a wee thing about the number of dogs and babies you see in cafés these days.'

This seemed to touch a raw nerve with Sheila. 'I would never dream of taking my poodle into a café, Frank. A lot of folk don't like dogs and I know poodles aren't everyone's cup of tea. It's not fair. Whatever happened to tying your dog up outside? It's like the dogs get priority now and the same can be said for the bairns. Us old folk don't get a look-in; used to be "show respect for your elders" but that's gone out the window.'

Frank stood back in awe of Sheila. She'd hit the nail on the head as far as he was concerned. 'You've hit the nail on the head as far as I'm concerned. You're a queen, Sheila; in fact, that's what I'm going to call you from now on: Queen Sheila.'

Sheila shook her head. 'You've had your mouth dressed, son. I can smell the drink coming out your pores.'

Frank took this as his cue to dip the shoulder and make a sharp exit. 'Have a great weekend, Queen Sheila. Keep the change.'

She replied, 'Righto, Carnegie.'

He headed along the prom, gazing across to Fife and remembering how he used to run along it with Bobby, in their prime, and they would joke about being prepared in case Argentina invaded Porty in revenge for the Falklands. It was a cold and dreary day, the kind Frank loved – a good day for drinking oneself into oblivion.

He shook his head at the number of dogs on the beach, with some folk having up to four, and very few on a lead. He'd often thought the dogs were working a number on the humans, treating them as marks by giving them the old puppy eyes in return for three square meals a day and a mug who'll pick up their shite. Frank dreamt of turning the "dog beach" section into a minefield with bits of fur and paw flying everywhere but checked himself for taking that "too far". This obsession with dogs had to end. No doubt a psychoanalyst would have a field day, telling him it was masking the underlying issue. But it was really the owners Frank had a problem with. A woman he was on nodding terms with came towards him with her French Bulldog in tow. Frank had always found that breed of dog ridiculous and had written about them in the column.

'Bastard!' she shouted at him. 'Think you're fucking smart. My Luna is worth ten of you, Savage. Stick to writing about golf and drink, ya prick.'

Frank made to defend himself. 'I beg your pardon, madam,' before realising she was in no mood for banter and quickened his stride. He continued walking along the prom but felt on edge as dog walkers and parents pushing buggies were giving him dirty looks. To compound the misery, his big toe was now throbbing along with his calf and felt like it had a hungry crab attached. *Le goutte est arriveé.* He would have to dig out the Crocs for comfort, to hell with fashion crimes, it was worth the stick.

A jogger wearing tube socks and a headband ran past, giving him the peace sign.

'Nice work with the column, man.'

Frank checked his phone and noticed he had three missed calls from Bobby, along with a pile of text messages. He clicked on one of the messages from Bella. Three laughing emojis in the first message, followed by *Congratulations, you mad bastard, you've really done it this time. xxx.*

Frank scrolled on: *Watch out for the Yummy Mummies. See you in The Hadd on Sunday afternoon. Life is a rollercoaster... Bella.*

Frank called Bobby in a state of panic. He picked up on the first ring.

'Frank, what have you written?' Bobby said. 'There's a social media pile-on going on; half of them want your nuts on a platter and the other half are calling you a hero.'

Frank held the phone away from his face and peered at it, wishing these things had never been invented. 'For feck's sake, Bobby. I haven't even read the thing, and I can barely remember writing it. My head is splitting, my foot is throbbing and all I want is a black pudding roll, a German biscuit and two flat whites.'

'You can't call them German biscuits,' Bobby said.

'Are you sure? I don't care what they're called, Bobby – German, Empire, Belgian – all I know is there's a wee jelly tot with my name on it sitting on some shortbread covered in icing.'

'Where are you?' Bobby enquired.

'I'm on the prom about to head into Fusion Brew.'

'Okay, I'll meet you in ten, order me an Americano.'

He walked up to the café and joined the small line of people waiting to be seated. It was hoachin' and Frank winced at the posh parents giving a running commentary of their child's every move.

'Dashiell, put the ball in the basket.'

Bet half of them hadn't even read Hammett. Was there no way of turning the volume down on these arseholes for full "picture no sound" effect?

Eventually Frank was seated at a table for two next to the bogs and beside a group of women with four dogs; two Cocker Spaniels, a Miniature Schnauzer and a Labradoodle that might have been a Cockapoo. Counting dogs again. He kept his head down and looked at the front page of the paper with a plug for his column that had a picture of a black Labrador puppy, and a baby in a buggy adorned with two red crosses and the word "cancelled".

'Jesus wept,' Frank muttered to himself as the sweat poured out his forehead, as it dawned on him that Dick Bell-end had stitched him up good and proper. *Touché, Bell-end, never thought you had it in you.*

The waiter came over and he ordered his doubler with a flat white and an Americano for Bobby. He asked the guy if they had any German biscuits and was met with a blank stare.

'Perhaps you call them Belgian biscuits or Empire biscuits. Maybe double biscuits? You know the ones covered in icing, with a wee jelly tot on top.'

The dead-eyed waiter said he'd ask at the counter, but Frank detected an element of lip service in his reply. He headed to the loo. Sitting down to pee, he noticed a sticker that said: *Seahorses ARE horses, hotdogs ARE dogs, there is NO debate.* Frank contemplated this and decided he needed to make his own version proclaiming *German biscuits ARE biscuits.*

On his return to the table, he realised the paper had gone for a walk and was now being pored over by the dog walkers at the next table.

'Excuse me, can I have my paper back?'

The women, who looked like angry primary school teachers, all stared at him, then back at the paper, then at him, then back at the paper, then at him, then back at the paper. *Here we go,* Frank thought, wanting to grab the paper which the self-proclaimed leader of the group was clutching with white knuckles.

'Is that you?' she said, pointing to his byline picture that was taken a good fifteen years ago.

'Moi?' Frank replied, after looking behind him, then pointing to his chest.

'Are you him? Did you write this drivel?' she said, as the dogs turned to stare.

'Yes, I believe so, the offending article is indeed mine,' Frank said, not knowing why he was now talking like an extra from *Brideshead Revisited*. He desperately wanted to get started on his black pudding and bacon doubler.

'Have you any idea how offensive this is… to EVERYONE?' she bellowed, pointing to the headline that read – *NO BABIES, NO DOGS, NO LATTES.* Frank stared at it in horror; an ill-advised play on the post-war *NO IRISH, NO BLACKS, NO DOGS* slogans. *At least they got the bit about the dogs right,* he pondered, playing for time.

'I don't write the headlines, and that piece wasn't supposed to go in like that. I'm truly sorry if you find it offensive. Keep the paper. Do any of you know if this place does German biscuits?' he added by way of deflection.

'I don't think they're called German biscuits any more.

Anyway, a biscuit is the last thing you need. Are you going to print an apology?' the headteacher barked.

'Probably but it's not up to me,' Frank replied apologetically, employing his best SS guard defence while letting the fat-shaming slide.

'Well, we're from What Women Want, and we're already at loggerheads with your rag of a paper. This is the last straw. I can tell you none of us call our dogs fur babies – that's a bloody insult. We'll be contacting your editor for a full retraction. Not just a line squirrelled away on page two next to the shipping forecast. This is pure clickbait.'

Frank had heard the term "clickbait" mentioned in the office but wasn't sure if it was a good or bad thing. At that point, they were distracted by a kerfuffle at the cake counter. Three angry student-types were arguing with the staff who were trying to block them from approaching Frank's tormentors. They were shouting, 'Fuck you, TERFS', at the women and accusing them of putting transphobic stickers up in the toilets.

Frank welcomed this as it took the pressure off him, before one of the students, with pink hair, lobbed a plastic bottle of water at their table, which clipped him on the ear before bouncing off the Cocker Spaniel's head. The dog yelped, then let out a pathetic whine.

The leader of the What Women Wanters bounded over to the offending protester and decked them with a belter of a right hook. Mayhem ensued, with the Cockapoo challenging the Labradoodle to a square go for the best cross-breed in show title, as soya lattes flew in all directions and hummus rained down on the Fusion Brew regs. Frank dived to catch a piece of caramel shortbread that he dipped into his coffee. *Not quite a German biscuit but it'll do,* he thought. He decided it was time for a sharp exit just as Bobby appeared with two police officers behind him.

They looked back and saw one of the dog walkers face down in a plate of poached eggs with avocado and feta smash on sourdough, as the staff and officers struggled to apprehend a student who had blood pouring from their septum piercing.

'Fuck a duck,' Bobby cried. 'It's like World War Three in there. Did someone read your column?'

Frank shouted, 'Let's get the fuck out of Dodge.'

They walked back along the promenade towards a bench, where Frank collapsed in a heap.

'Jesus wept, Frank. What made you write that shite?'

'Funny shite, Bobby.'

'Granted, parts of it were funny,' Bobby replied.

Frank contemplated Bobby's question as it hadn't occurred to him why he wrote the piece in the first place.

'It's just stream of consciousness bollocks that came out when I was drunk the other night. I thought it was about time I wrote something controversial as the online figures for the column are terrible and that's all I could think of. It's hard coming up with new ideas every week; you get one day of respite, then they're asking you what you're writing about next week. It's like water torture. The columns that do well are all personal stuff – self-indulgent crap about your drink problem and struggles with mental health. There's a piece about wild swimming in today that'll get double the hits I get. Do you remember when swimming in the sea was just called swimming? There was nothing wild about it.'

Bobby laughed. 'At least you never wrote about that trans stuff, Frank. That's what they were fighting about back there.'

'I'm not that daft, Bobby. I know when to stay in my lane. No one, and I mean no one, wants to hear from a gout-riddled, middle-aged white guy on that subject.'

Bobby put his arm round Frank's shoulder. 'Look, mucker. I don't understand how things work these days either but throwing your tuppence in without giving it a proper thought is madness. I know you don't mean what you say half the time, but the keyboard warriors will have a field day with this adult-only café malarkey.

And you won't get many readers who'll say, "Oh, Frank must be hungover again, let's give him a pass this week".

Frank let out a big sigh, then started laughing. 'Did you see those protesters throwing that chickpea paste at the walls?'

'Aye. I'm only hummus, of flesh and blood I'm made,' Bobby said, shoulders shaking as he chuckled.

They both laughed and gazed out over the water, looking for Argies as Frank opened the paper to finally read his column.

To Be Frank – Column #343

Today, dear readers, I am launching a one-man crusade to have all babies and dogs banned from cafés. We need to wrestle back control from these Apostles of Satan, these Angels of the Devil who roam amongst us guarded by the Beasts of Revelation. The future of humanity and flat whites is at stake here.

For God's sake, repent!

It was the American comedian W.C. Fields who said, "Never work with children or animals," an oft-misunderstood warning against both parties stealing the show. I am reminded of this on my twice weekly stroll along the promenade where I frequent the local café that has sourced the superfood black pudding that I like to eat on a well-fired roll with a smidgeon of butter.

Now I wouldn't dream of going in there plonking my cassette recorder on the table and playing *The Best of Chimpanzees Screaming Vol 2*, but that would sound like sacred choir music compared to the noise of a baby screeching while its mother orders a pint of caffè latte and a pint of caffè latte to go, while treating us all to a running commentary of junior's every move.

The owners of said café think nothing of relieving me of a tenner for a bang average cup of joe and a filled roll while turning a blind eye to the immersive crèche experience with buggy assault course going on in the background. Never mind that, on any given Monday, the place resembles best in show at Crufts, with a mind-boggling array of Cockapoos, Labradoodles, the obligatory black Labs and something called a French Bulldog that looks like it should be wearing high heels, smoking Gitanes and applying its trade down the docks.

I do not consider myself an unreasonable man, something you, my dear readers, can testify to, but in the words of mod revivalists, Secret Affair – "this is the time for action".

I am therefore starting a petition for adult-only cafés.

In the meantime, I suggest that babies in buggies and dogs – or "fur babies" as annoying owners like to call them – are left outside of any establishment where adults are trying to get a minute's peace to dip their German biscuit in their coffee. Perhaps the dogs could watch over them, thus killing two birds with one stone.

The genie is out of the bottle, the rabbit is out of the hat, and the dog is well and truly in the manger.

No babies or dogs were harmed in the writing of this column.

5

Frank had nipped home and was now wearing pink Crocs, cheap shades, a navy overcoat and jogging bottoms as he met Naomi on the platform at Waverley Station. She looked tired as he gave her a massive bear hug. Naomi stood back, beaming, giving her old man the once-over.

'What in God's earth are you wearing, Dad?'

He explained how the "old Brussel sprout" was giving him bother, hence the Crocs, and made to pick up her holdall.

'Leave it, Dad, I'm a big girl now and can manage this myself.'

They both made their way up the ramp and squinted to see the iconic view of Edinburgh Castle, blocked by a giant Ferris wheel in the foreground.

'Blackpool,' Frank declared, telling her the shades were required in December as he was trying to keep incognito given the stooshie about the column, even though as a rule he was opposed to Scottish people wearing any form of sunglasses.

'Here, Dad, I got you some shortbread.'

'The key to my heart attack,' Frank replied, before shoving it in his pocket and hailing a taxi.

Naomi had told him that she wanted to chill and just watch some old films or crap on the telly, and Frank said he'd make them homemade soup and toasted cheese. She had read his column online and was keeping him abreast of all the comments on Twitter where it was trending under #Banthebabies. Although

Naomi found the piece funny, there was little doubt that it was offensive. Surprisingly, there were as many people coming out in support of what Frank was saying as there were those calling for his head. But it was clear her father hadn't really thought things through on this one and it fell into the "rant" category.

Frank was delighted to see his daughter and made a promise to himself to take things slowly and not bombard her with questions the way his mother always did with him. He loved Rita but had brought in a *four question only* rule, with her having to wait till he answered one question before she could ask him another. Frank's aim was to cut down on repetition and reduce the general levels of anxiety he felt around his parents. Harsh but fair. It was hard enough hearing his mum constantly bang on about people he'd never heard of or couldn't remember. 'Do you remember Shona who worked with me in Goldbergs? She's got cancer. Her husband was a pilot, and he died from motor neurone disease last year.'

He felt like every conversation was about illness, putting this down to part of the aging process that was in the post for him. Frank would give one-word answers to the never-ending stream of questions often about the most mundane of arrangements, times, dates, etc. Then have a mild panic attack, followed by a strong desire to drink. He felt bad and had been told that all mothers were like this, but he was determined to give Naomi room to breathe.

They settled down on their respective sofas with bars of Fruit & Nut and Diet Cokes to watch *The Omen*. Frank remembered being allowed to watch it as a ten-year-old and had slept with the light on for three years afterwards. The scenes were ingrained in his mind; the nanny's suicide, 'Look at me, Damien, it's all for you,' and the priest getting impaled. Naomi fell asleep just before the *pièce de résistance* where the photographer gets decapitated and Frank paused the film, so she could watch it later.

'The things we do for our kids.' He chuckled to himself.

She hadn't said much since arriving but told him things were going well at work, something in finance, and she was up to oversee the restoration of the old Regency cinema on the high street. Frank told her the picture house held a special place in his heart, along with other notable Portobello landmarks from his childhood, like the modernist library, Daisy Park, the paddling pool on the promenade, and the saltwater swimming baths.

He remembered Naomi always being good with numbers and that had given her the opportunity to live and work in Edinburgh. Frank was delighted and would help find her accommodation but decided he would give his daughter time to rest before they discussed it further.

He gave her a wee nudge and said the spare room was ready. Naomi was dozy but gave him a big hug and said, 'I love you, Dad.'

Frank felt an overwhelming sense of sadness that he hadn't been there to watch her grow up and hadn't done enough to stop Maxine being exploited by that gangster Armstrong, the so-called Wise One. But it was undeniable that her Aunty Jane had done a fine job in raising Naomi after her mother's death and had instilled the right kind of values. He thought about Maxine but struggled to connect as it was so long ago, and the rawness of her passing had finally dissipated with the march of time.

Frank checked his text messages and saw he had thirty-five unread. One of these was from his editor telling him to see him *first thing on Tuesday morning, before news conference.*

He was filled with an impending sense of doom, convinced the axe was about to fall on his thirty-year journalism career. It dawned on him that he'd been royally set up by the editor – Richard had let the column go in unedited with the sole intention of using the fallout as an excuse to sack him. Frank worried that he'd get the boot on a trumped-up disobedience charge without receiving the pittance of a redundancy payment. Richard would deny telling him to "file straight onto the page". He decided on the spot that he was going to go in on Tuesday morning to tell the editor to shove the job up his arse, along with the money. He was done kowtowing to fucking eejits and if Richard got wide, he'd chin him.

Frank dreamt about spending a grand on lottery tickets that week or taking his pension pot and sticking it on black. He'd use some of the millions from his winnings to help Naomi convert the old Regency cinema building back into an independent picture house where he'd become the manager and run the whole of Roger Moore's back catalogue, including the non-Bond films. This was his passion project. He'd buy the Shadow and park it outside the cinema on the pavement, to send a message that Frank Savage *is* a player. He'd treat himself to more custom-made Savile Row suits and buy a house in the Grange or Merchiston next to JK Rowling or that Ian Rankin and he'd take over The Hadd and apply for a twenty-four-hour licence so he could drink in there whenever he liked, and Bella wouldn't be able to call last orders or throw him out.

A thought crossed his mind of an old contact from his crime reporting days. The Gypsy: a former bare-knuckle boxer with a talent for ultra-violence and a fondness for slicing the ears off people who owed him money. Frank dug out his moleskin notebooks and flicked through the coffee-stained pages until he found a mobile number and an address. He would pay a visit and ask for a loan while he sought out a publication that appreciated great writing and would give him a gig. The Gypsy owed him one and was bound to go easy on the vig as they got on well. After all, Frank wasn't his usual type of customer – no, he was a man of letters.

6

Frank woke early on Sunday morning and felt surprisingly bright and breezy. He brushed his teeth and only managed to boke once when the brush hit the back of his throat, which was something of a record; he normally gagged like a fledgling porn star. His mood darkened when he remembered that he'd been up for a pee three times during the night – a sure sign in Frank's mind that he had prostate cancer. He typed the words "prostate cancer" into his phone, scanned through the symptoms on the NHS website and decided he would call the doctor for an appointment. Grabbing his blood pressure machine, Frank put the Velcro strap on and tried to think pleasant thoughts that would calm him. He focused on the beach at Sitges, imagining a cool Mediterranean breeze brushing gently against his face. After a few seconds, the dial showed the reading as being 140/92, firmly in the Stage 2 hypertension ballpark. He waited a few seconds, took a couple of deep breaths and hit the start button again. This time, the image of him sitting at the wheel of the Shadow came to mind; 138/90, an improvement, that would do for now.

Hitting the deck and trying his best to give it twenty, he held his breath for the first fifteen press-ups, then shook like a leaf for the last five. He looked in on Naomi, who was sound asleep and hadn't unpacked the posh holdall lying at the side of her bed.

Frank went for a stroll along the prom ahead of his meeting with the hippie in Stockbridge, which he was looking forward to even if it was a bit too close to his work on a weekend. He returned home and made Naomi a full Scottish breakfast with Lorne sausage, black pudding and a tattie scone, which she loved. Then he showered and shaved before donning his Savile Row double-breasted, navy chalk-stripe suit with swooping lapels, broadened shoulders and a bit more room about the chest area. He'd had it tailor-made seven years ago after a win on the gee-gees and it still fit like a glove, given that his weight had now plateaued around the fourteen stone mark. He'd heard it described as a "dad body", but he knew the danger of underestimating old man strength and reckoned he could still find a knockout blow. Then he considered that a quick burst of physical exertion like being in a fight could lead to a heart attack and he thought about Tom at his work who recently had a stent fitted.

He put on his best white shirt and plain red tie by Thomas Pink, with matching pocket square, before stepping into black Church's brogues that had been spit 'n' polished to within an inch of their life. Frank sprayed some Eau Sauvage Extrême, his scent of choice since it first came out in 1984, handy for hiding the smell of drink. He strode to the living room and told Naomi that he was 'off to buy a Roller.'

'Bloody hell, Dad, you look amazing,' she said.

'We are the Mods, my dear. We are the Mods.'

Frank told the taxi driver to drop him off outside the mews house in Dean Street where the hippie was giving the Rolls-Royce a bit of TLC with a chamois leather. He certainly looked the part; a man in his early seventies with long flowing locks, trimmed goatee beard, wraparound flying scarf and a black velvet cowboy hat.

Frank got out and handed the driver a crisp twenty-pound note and told him to keep the change, which amounted to seventy-five pence, but the hippie wasn't to know that.

'Morning, sir,' Frank said a bit too loudly. 'She's an absolute beauty.'

The hippie gave Frank the once-over before extending his hand and bracelets in friendship.

'Please to meet you, man, the name's Falco. Nice suit.'

'Much obliged. Frank Savage.'

The two men quickly picked up where they had left off on the phone with Falco waxing lyrical about the Shadow and its metallic paint job and interior décor.

'Jump in; we'll take her for a spin down the coast to North Berwick,' Falco said, bringing a bunch of keys out of his pocket. 'Hey, I might even let you have a shot on the back roads.'

Frank beamed, then felt the need to pee, which he put down to excitement rather than anything medical.

'Sweet move,' he said in an American accent, which made Falco smile.

The roads were quiet, with the occasional "Sunday driver" going at a snail's pace as the Shadow glided through Portobello, along the bottom road through Musselburgh and the picturesque fishing village of Port Seton. Falco handled the car expertly and Frank was feeling every bit the pig in shit but couldn't understand why anyone would want rid of it.

'This car is absolutely fucking beautiful; why are you selling it?'

Falco gazed out the window, appearing to ignore his passenger's probing.

'We're taking the scenic route and have just driven through Port Seton. My friend, the artist John Bellany, was from there. I hung out with him in Berlin.'

Falco popped a cassette into the eight-track car stereo. The singer sounded like a pound-shop version of Bob Dylan and Frank realised it was Falco.

'Wow, this is great. Très Dylan with a hint of The Band,' he said, fawning over his new bestie.

'Born in the USA, my friend. Born in the USA,' Falco replied, before adding, 'I played with Bob on the island of Mustique and knew those dudes from The Band. Cool cats.'

He turned the volume down a notch, then returned to driving with one hand on the wheel, the other hanging loosely out the window.

'To answer your question, Frank, I'm finding the Shadow a bit too British for my liking. Sure, she's a fantastic lady but I'm harking back to my prairie roots. That's why I've pur-chased a couple of vintage Harley Hydra-Glides for me and my gal and parting ways with the Shadow. It's been a blast.'

They passed through Gullane, slowing to let a group of Sunday golfers dressed like Ronnie Corbett cross the road, and headed towards North Berwick. Frank was loving the glamour and imagined the Famous Five footballers from the Hibs glory days of the 1950s coming down to Gullane in their sports cars to play a round before dining in the Old Clubhouse.

By this point he was totally in love with the car, but didn't want to blow his chances by doing anything crass like talking about a price. The gout was killing him, and he now wished he'd worn his Crocs instead of the brogues, which felt like tiny coffins on his feet.

He was thinking about getting home and taking his blood pressure again, then buying beetroot juice to lower it, which was also good for the gout. Mercifully, the pain in his calf had subsided, so the aspirin had worked in breaking up the DVT for now.

Falco had moved on to talking about his time as a hash smuggler and how he still maintained contacts in Morocco, where he met the second of his four wives, and in Amsterdam where he recorded his eponymous album, *Songs from Falco's Big Chair*.

On the way back, Frank was allowed to drive. This was the moment of truth. He slipped into the driver's seat and admired the control panel before bringing out a pair of vintage leather crochet-back driving gloves out of his inside jacket pocket.

'Nice touch,' Falco said. 'Reminds me of the ones Peter Fonda wore in *Dirty Mary, Crazy Larry*.'

Frank laughed at this as he'd watched the film recently and had taken a shine to said driving gloves.

Falco adjusted his headband. 'I met Peter once. We dropped acid on the island of Ibiza where he was filming. What a trip.'

Frank slipped into first gear and promptly stalled. Too eager.

'Easy does it,' Falco advised. 'This one's a thoroughbred. Don't worry, I had my man give her the once-over yesterday, checked the oil level sensor and the ignition modules. If she gives you any trouble, you can always hit the fuel pump with a hammer. Works every time.'

Frank laughed nervously but was happy that things were moving in the direction of him owning the car. They passed Luca's on the way back through Musselburgh and Frank was about to share his Isabelle Adjani fantasy with Falco but thought better of it, as he'd likely say he had "made love to her on the island of Montserrat". Instead, he finally plucked up the courage to ask about a price.

Falco stalled. 'Easy, man, we'll talk about the scratch later. Let's pull in down by the promenade at Portobello and have a little smoke.'

Frank passed Joppa, soaking up the adulation the Shadow brought along the high street, taking a right turn towards the prom. He asked Falco if he liked Porty and his new hippie friend said he loved the place and his wife, the future ex-Mrs Falco, had gotten him involved in the youth theatre and community hub.

'I've played a couple of times at the Old Kirk, went down a storm. I'm thinking of playing the whole of *Songs from Falco's Big Chair*, which the younger crowd are hip to.'

Frank winced a little, as folk music was certainly not his thing and Falco's stuff was off the scale beardy bollocks, but he would do anything to own the Shadow and felt within touching distance. He pulled in near the prom and offered Falco a Marlboro Red.

'No thanks, man. I like them, but I've got something a little stronger for us.'

Falco brought out the largest hash pipe Frank had ever seen and proceeded to fill it with a brownie-green substance.

'Jesus wept. It's a bit early for heroin.'

Falco laughed. 'It's the finest kief, brother. Brought all the way from Morocco, the good shit. This will transport you into total Zen and take your mind off the gout.'

Frank hadn't banked on getting stoned but thought *What the hell;* if anything, it would take the edge off since the crabs were back nibbling at his throbbing big toe. Plus, he wanted to stay in the good books. He watched Falco handle the pipe and inhale like the pro he was. Frank waited anxiously for his turn, having not smoked a joint in a long time and being fully aware that this would be better gear than the stuff his postman used to shove through his letterbox at Ramsay Tech. Falco passed the pipe and Frank took in the smoke, holding it deep down until his lungs felt like they were about to burst.

'Easy, brother, nice and easy; let the herb do God's work.'

Frank laughed and said, 'Far out,' then immediately felt a little self-conscious. He'd forgotten about the whiteys he used to get when he smoked the wacky baccy and started to feel a little queasy, but that soon passed as his body went comfortably numb.

The two men stared over the Firth of Forth across the water to Fife, sharing a moment of stoned contemplation, as Frank caressed the ivory steering wheel of the Shadow. He didn't care how much Falco wanted for the car now. He was having this chariot of fire no matter what. Out of nowhere, there was a loud bang on the passenger side window that shook them out of their reverie.

'Jesus H Christ,' Falco cried as Frank looked across him to be met with the smiling face of the Ghost of Christmas Past, with a flick hairdo and a tan mark down the right side of its face.

'Brewster.'

Falco tried to hide the pipe, then made a fuss of rolling down the window.

'All right, chaps, nice day for it,' said Brewster.

'Hey, man, fancy meeting you here. We've just been for a spin in the Old Lady of English motoring,' Falco replied.

At that, he made to open the passenger door and gingerly got out. Frank, who by now was in the throes of an out-of-body experience, managed to open his door before falling onto the road.

'Frank, meet Brewster. Brewster, meet Frank.'

'Oh, we've met before, Falco. Frank and I go way back.'

Frank attempted a kind of nod greeting before a gurgling sound came out of his mouth.

'What's it been, fifteen years?' said Brewster.

Frank tried to formulate a response, but none came forthwith and everything around him seemed to have switched into magnificent technicolour. Brewster glared at Frank then was distracted by something to his left side that was making a howling sound. Frank peered round to see the cause of Brewster's consternation and saw a wolf that was straight from *Little Red Riding Hood* central casting, flashing its incisors.

'Down, Waffen! Down.'

Brewster's dog was called Waffen, which seemed a perfect fit for this killing machine. He walked round the back of the car, doing his best to avoid the German shepherd that Brewster was now calling Waffle, and the three men stood beside a garden wall that Frank had to sit on, or he'd fall over.

Frank managed to slur out, 'So how do you two gentlemen know each other?'

'Mr Brewster and I met through my wife at the Porty youth theatre that he founded,' Falco replied.

Frank cased Brewster from the wall. He was wearing a kind of corporate version of football hooligan attire that included a Paul & Shark jumper with patches on each shoulder and a bonus patch on the right elbow. Frank imagined Brewster getting a healthy kicking if he turned up for double history wearing that monstrosity in their school days. Brewster completed the look with a fresh-out-the-box, yet-to-be-christened pair of vintage Adidas Tobacco. He still fancied himself as a hard man and was adopting half a Liam Gallagher pose but couldn't quite pull it off as his right hand was wrapped firmly round the Nazi dog's lead.

'I only *helped* to start the theatre, Falco,' Brewster said with false modesty. 'I had a lot of support from the local community, and who knew there were so many out-of-work actors and artists living in good old Portobello, willing to donate their time and money to such a good cause? That reminds me, we've got the official opening next week. Shelby St. George, the actress, Hearts player Kyle Horsburgh and the Paralympian Caroline Decker are guests of honour but there'll be loads of other celebs there. The youth theatre is box office. You're both welcome to come along.'

Falco said, 'Yeah, man, in the words of the Four Tops, "I'll Be There".'

Frank was trying to engage his brain before he spoke, but the drugs had created a Berlin Wall between his frontal lobe and mouth. He eventually heard the words 'Must be a good earner' come tumbling out his mouth before he could catch them and shove them back in. Brewster gave him his best "out for the weekend" stare but Frank just smiled in a vacant manner.

'You still writing lies for the newspapers, Savage?' Brewster asked.

'I write my own column now; been off the crime beat for years. Which is probably why I haven't heard from you. What with paper and crayons being scarce in Saughton nick.'

It was Brewster's turn to smile.

'That was a long time ago, Savage. I'm reformed, pillar of society, doing my bit for the community, giving it back. Everything's out in the open air and people respect my honesty.'

The "former" hoolie now appeared to be weighing up the situation.

'So, Falco, are you going to sell me this beauty or what?' Brewster asked, pointing at the car.

Falco lovingly tapped the Shadow's roof. 'Well, Frank's in the driver's seat as it stands but I haven't made my mind up. There's a lot of interest, as you can imagine, with a filly this special.'

Brewster didn't take this well and jerked Waffle/Waffen's lead, causing the dog to snarl. Frank continued to smile as the munchkins inside his brain danced to the tune of "We've got the Roller, we've got the Roller; you've no, you've no," but he quickly realised he was counting his chickens before they hatched.

Brewster let his mask slip. 'I'll pay double what this joker and anyone else offers.'

Falco said, 'No, man, it's not all about the scratch. This lady needs a good home and some tender loving care. That's my main concern. Certainly not the cash money, and Frank tops the bills. For now.'

Brewster, realising he'd dropped his guard, tried to regain his composure.

'I was under the impression we had a gentleman's agreement, cash in hand straight away, and I'd certainly give her a good home, but if you want to sell to Savage, then that's your prerogative. I want her but trust me I'm not playing silly buggers. It's probably too old-fashioned for me anyway and a bit flash. I'm swaying towards a Tesla; do my bit for the environment. Electric is the future, and the council knows it. It suits you, Frank – a thing of the past, like newspapers.'

Falco looked to diffuse the tension and placate Brewster.

'Easy, man. Like I said, I haven't made my mind up. You're still in the frame.'

'All in good time.'

Frank still hadn't managed to wipe the smile off his face and gave out a little chuckle, but Brewster wasn't taking the bait any more.

'Okay, gentlemen, I best be heading off; Waffle here is needing fed.'

Frank, quick as a flash, said, 'I saw a couple of toddlers in Daisy Park.'

Brewster curled his lip. 'You better watch that tongue of yours, Savage, or someone may cut it out. Take care.'

Falco waved and Frank nodded, ignoring the threat, as Brewster sauntered towards the promenade with Waffen clearing a path for him.

Take care. Frank been around enough nutters to know the true meaning of that phrase. He resented these football casual types and the way they carried themselves like D-Day veterans, when to his mind they were just a bunch of dysfunctional radges who fought the Dundee Utility crew at the Battle of the Wellgate Shopping Centre in 1989.

Falco announced that he was going up Arthur's Seat for "some space" and to smoke more of the kief and would drop him off on the way.

'I'd rather sell it to you than that Brewster dude, but business is business. It's yours for forty thousand if you can come up with the money by Friday, otherwise I'll sell it to him for fifty, I guess. He gives me the creeps, bad vibes. What you see is not what you get with that guy.'

Frank nodded in agreement before Falco pried further. 'What's the deal with you and him?'

'It's a long story. We were at school together, played football together and have hated each other for years. He was also involved in my brother's death. I'll fill you in on the details over a beer some time.'

Falco knew to leave it and told Frank to call him when he had the money.

Frank headed to The Haddonfield where Bella was serving Bobby pints of lager, with the videotape of *Halloween* playing on the television, as was the custom on a Sunday afternoon. Bella didn't allow the football and anyone asking for a bit of Prem was given the shortest of shrifts.

'Sunday is for horror, end of,' she would proclaim, while sending disappointed young men with Turkey teeth on their way. She then proceeded to verbally tear Frank a new arsehole for writing, as she described it, "the biggest pile of shite I've ever read". Frank appeared sheepish but was secretly proud to have made it onto Bella's "biggest pile of shite" list. He told her about the Shadow and Bella quickly came around, after imagining herself being chauffeured around Porty in style.

Bobby said, 'I take it you're spunking your pension and any redundo payment on this then?'

'Correctamundo, my Nepalese friend. Life is for Livingston.'

'There'll no doubt be tears for souvenirs,' Bobby warned.

Frank pondered how he was going to pay for the Shadow and started to feel a clammy sensation in his chest. He made a note to self, to ask the doctor for a full cardiograph, as he ran through his options. Plan A was to cash in his pension, which was down to twenty-five thousand pounds the last time he looked and use part of his redundancy to cover the forty grand – that was if he avoided the sack. Of course, the "plan" was completely reckless and would leave him further in the shit, but Frank had made up his mind the Shadow would be his, no matter the cost. The problem was he only had five days to get his hands on the cash. Not long enough for the pension money or redundancy to come through. The thought of Brewster giving it the large one round Porty in the Shadow made Frank sick to his stomach. *Fuck it.*

He took out the bit of paper with The Gypsy's number on it and went outside to make the call. After going round the houses and speaking to three different people, he was eventually put through to the man. Frank got to the point quickly, skipping the pleasantries.

'It's Frank Savage. I'm needing a loan of money, possibly fifty grand. Can you make that happen?'

Silence. Finally, a reply. 'Come and see me tomorrow – 8am sharp.'

He went back inside, slid up next to Bobby and ordered a stiff drink to dampen his rising anxiety – about the car, his job and now, Brewster.

'Did you know Brewster is out and doing the rounds?'

Bobby looked concerned. 'Yip, I heard he's back in town, helping to run the youth theatre, with his sticky fingers in a few other pies. The hipsters have bought his reformed character – now a sculptor – giving it back to the community bollocks. There may be trouble ahead.'

Instead of bringing Frank's drink order, Bella uncorked a bottle of champagne and told them to 'Stop talking about that wanker' as they toasted Frank's soon-to-be new motor.

A couple of glasses in, the bubbles working their magic, Naomi phoned and told her dad that the column was still doing a roaring trade on social media and had been trending on Twitter for two days solid. None of this meant anything to Frank and merely served as a reminder that he had to see the editor, which he parked to one side as he ordered another bottle of champers. This was no time to be contemplating losing his job.

By this point, Bella was now on the other side of the bar and was taking it to 'Seshlehem and the Rivers of Swallyon' as she liked to shout when "letting her hair down" on a Sunday. The fact that she had shaved her head from the time Frances, who bore a striking resemblance to Frank, was born, and "the dad", a would-be Hells Angel from the Prestonpans Pirates, had fucked off, added to her sense of hilarity.

As the night wore on, Bella lectured Frank on the history of feminism and the struggles women had faced throughout the years in the face of patriarchal dominance before asking him if he fancied "coming back to mine for a shag". Frank and Bella had shared numerous sexual encounters over the years, so it was no surprise that he ended up back at hers after Frances, who Bella sometimes called Frankces to wind him up, had called last orders. They lurched into what the old warning notice at the swimming baths would describe as "heavy petting" before Bella told Frank to pour himself a drink as she was going to get changed. Frank pondered this for a moment, then decided Grey Goose vodka with Ribena mixer would make for a decent pre-coital aperitif.

Bella returned wearing her full *Elvira: Mistress of the Dark* ensemble that included thigh-high leather boots, a cleavage-enhancing bodice and a long black wig. Frank took a giant swig of the voddy 'n' Ribena, missing his mouth and pouring most of it down the front of his white shirt. 'Bastard.' He felt a rousing in his nether region as Bella's Elvira outfit always hit the spot and he thanked God and Falco for giving him another crack at the title. He kicked off the Crocs he was now wearing, having ditched the brogues in the pub, and dropped his suit trousers to reveal a bright-yellow pair of Calvin Klein underpants. Bella had pulled open the bodice and was now lying spreadeagled on her four-poster bed urging Frank to 'Take a bite of peach – down, boy!' she ordered.

Frank shouted, 'Anchors aweigh!' before heading to what he and Bella jokingly referred to as the "Rangers end". Bella didn't go in for any kind of fancy shaving down there, preferring to grow her garden wild. What Frank lacked in technique, he made up for in enthusiasm, licking away like a dog in heat, before she hoisted him up by the lugs, like she was lifting the European Cup.

It quickly dawned on him that the moment of penetration was upon them, and he urged his brain to send sexy signals to his cock, which was now doing a passable impression of a Wee Willie Winkie sausage. Bella was sounding the call to arms and Frank realised he didn't have time to run his wrists under the cold tap in a last-ditch bid to get the blood pumping.

'Come on my tits, come on my tits. I wank in churches. I wank in churches.'

Frank had never heard the 'I wank in churches' line before and considered it the mankiest thing ever to come out of Bella's mouth, and she had form. However, it had the desired effect of at least making him semi-hard as he managed to thrust his button mushroom into her for three strokes, which Frank considered a shag.

Bella quickly realised that, yet again, "Mr Lover Man" had alcohol-induced stage fright. 'Did you not take a Viagra?' she said accusingly.

'I never brought any with me. To be fair, getting my Nat King Cole was the last thing on my mind when I left the house this morning. Do you not have any?'

'Why the fuck do you think I'd have it? I'm not a deviant.'

Frank let that one hang in the air. 'What about that herbal shite you gave me once? Have you not got any of that?'

She shook her head as Frank sloped off the job, before declaring he was going out the back for a fag. Bella, who had ditched the Elvira outfit and was now wearing her ancient dressing grown and baffies, joined Frank, who was naked apart from his Crocs.

'Don't give me a hard time, Bella,' he pleaded.

'I wish,' she replied, not prepared to let him off the hook that easily.

Frank appeared genuinely distraught and flicked at his flaccid cock in disgust.

Bella felt the need to console him. 'It's okay, pal. But you should really try and drink less or at least carry the blue bullets with you in case of emergencies. You used to be a good ride.' They both laughed as she put the stove on to make them a coffee. Frank drained his cup, then told her that he best be off as he had a "big day" tomorrow.

'Keep out of churches, aye,' he said as a parting shot. The two friends hugged, and he felt blessed to know her, stepping out into the cold air and heading home.

7

Frank arrived at The Gypsy's compound near Loanhead on the outskirts of town at 8am sharp as instructed. He was hungover and felt the sweat pushing through his pores, adding to the clamminess that engulfed him like a dreich day in Portobello. He pushed a button and was buzzed into a courtyard. A sturdy youth with a fetching neck tattoo led him past a pig pen, heading towards a huge mobile home that consisted of two static caravans knocked together – the ultimate in trailer trash chic. They entered the "palace", which was decorated in a look that could be best described as lace curtain Irish meets *The Only Way is Essex*. A wooden *Love* sign was on the mantlepiece next to another wooden sign that proclaimed *Home*, in case The Gypsy forgot where he was.

'Frank Savage. A true friend to the Romani people,' The Gypsy roared, moving forwards to lock Frank in a bear hug that made him think he was genuinely being hugged by a bear. He caught a whiff of Aramis aftershave mixed in with stale sweat.

Frank was momentarily distracted by two American XL Bully dogs roaming freely in the kitchen.

'That's some beautiful dogs you've got there. What do you feed them on?'

The Gypsy, who stood six foot five inches in his stockinged feet, laughed menacingly. 'Mainly grannies, sometimes junkies and the odd grass. Satan is normally well behaved, but I must give

Hagler a regular beating or he'll go soft. I don't go overboard, like, just the odd dunt over the head with my shovel. Keep them keen.'

The Gypsy had professionally taken framed pictures throughout the mobile home of his adoring family – eight kids and, what appeared to be, at least three wives. Various action shots of them all in Dubai drinking champagne adorned with five-foot-high sparklers competed with boxing memorabilia and a truly gruesome framed photograph of the aftermath of a bare-knuckle fight in which The Gypsy, beaten to a pulp, was pointing one finger in the air to signify he'd won the contest.

They walked through the house to a garden area with a hot tub and extension that turned out to be a fully functioning boozer, with a vast array of gins on display, botanicals ranging from citrus peel to rose lavender, to the blood of fifteen slain virgins. A pool table, boxing arcade machine, pinball machine, original Wurlitzer jukebox and various pieces of sporting equipment and signed football shirts provided the décor. The Gypsy got down to business.

'So, you're needing some serious cash.'

Frank took this as his cue to expand on their telephone call and flesh out his request.

'I've got my eye on a motor, an absolute beauty. A 1979 Rolls-Royce Silver Shadow Mk II in two-tone gold over metallic brown.'

The Gypsy nodded approvingly. 'I take it that's Falco's car. It is, as you rightly point out, an absolute beauty. Thought about buying it myself; 6.75 litre engine – "six and three-quarter" as we like to call it. Had a couple of Rollers myself over the years – lovely motors.'

Frank relaxed. 'So, you know Falco?' he asked.

'Yeah, I've done a bit of business with him. Decent guy, just don't ask him to sing.'

Frank laughed a little too eagerly, thinking this Falco was a dark horse.

'Anyway,' The Gypsy said, 'fifty grand is a lot of dosh, Frank. You told me Falco wants forty for the Roller, which is a bit on the steep side but it's a sellers' market, and you want the other ten for, let me get this right... incidentals.'

'Yes, I thought if I'm going to borrow money it needs to be a one-off and I need a bit of loose cash to tide me over. Things aren't great at work,' Frank replied, then instantly regretted mentioning his job.

'Ah, the old newspaper game. I see no fucker is buying that rag. Are they paying you off or something? I read one of your columns – some shite about banning dogs from cafés. I hope you weren't referring to my beloved Satan or Hagler, Frank.'

'No, no, that was just a bit of fun. It's not to be taken seriously. Jesus, no. I only wrote that to get computer hits. That's what the journo game is all about these days.'

The Gypsy was enjoying seeing Frank squirm a little, playing cat and mouse, before finally relenting and cutting him some slack.

'I've no problem lending you the fifty grand, Frank. You're a good bloke and did us gypsies a solid with those stories you ran about the bent councillors trying to evict us from the site in Craigmillar.'

Frank smiled proudly. 'It was a privilege to defend the travelling community. They were out of order; Tory cunts looking for votes from the upper working class, performing their usual populist trick of picking on minorities and the disenfranchised. Preying on the poorest in society.'

The Gypsy stared hard at Frank, letting him stew in an uncomfortable silence before breaking into a sly grin.

'We're not that poor, Frank. James will get you the cash. You'll pay me back sixty grand over a year – that's five grand on the first of every month for twelve months and that's a very generous final offer.' The Gypsy spat on his hand before offering it to Frank. 'Don't make me take your ear off.'

8

Frank was running late on Tuesday morning, nursing a thumping second-day hangover, along with the usual aches and pains. He had taken his blood pressure after eating a banana and some porridge sprinkled with blueberries and almonds, but it still hovered around the 140/90 mark after five goes. The fact he'd been up for three sit-down pees during the night convinced him that, at the very least, he had an enlarged prostate, most likely cancer. He knew a guy in The Haddonfield, Alfie the postman, who'd had his prostate removed and was still drinking like a fish, so perhaps things weren't so bad. Frank dialled the number for the GP surgery, waited thirty minutes, which allowed him to take his blood pressure again, before they answered, and the receptionist said a nurse would phone him for a chat to decide if he could see a doctor.

They phoned while Frank was on the bus heading into the office. The passengers were treated to a virtuoso performance where he proceeded to blitzkrieg the nurse with a range of symptoms, including a detailed explanation of his nocturnal toilet habits. Just to be sure, he opened a second front on the poor woman, covering everything from the gout giving him gyp, to concerns about cholesterol levels and the very real possibility of Type 2 diabetes. She finally relented from questioning him further and booked Frank in for a 5pm appointment that day with Dr Khan.

By now, the gout was throbbing and Frank couldn't wait to get to the office and change into the orange Crocs that he kept in the bottom drawer of his desk, next to the Gentleman's Relish that he liked to smear on his oatcakes. He knew his lateness would piss Richard off, but he wasn't about to forego his morning ritual of grabbing a flat white and bacon roll from Roasters of Stockbridge. He ordered "the usual", then winced a little as the barista, who resembled a rank-and-file member of the Baader-Meinhof Gang, hit him with the dreaded words, 'I read your column.'

'Oh aye,' Frank said, knowing he wouldn't have to bother following this up with the obligatory "What do you think?" as that was clearly in the post.

'I loved it. Worst thing about this job is the posh parents who think it's okay to inflict their screaming offspring on everyone else, while they get their caffeine hit. I mean the kids are just an extension of themselves so it's no wonder they love them – they're loving themselves. I think you should run for First Minister. I'd vote for you, Frank.'

Frank was taken aback, grinning like a Cheshire Cat. 'Too kind, too kind,' he purred. 'I hadn't considered politics up until this point but now that you mention it, there are quite a few things I'd like to put right.' The Baader-Meinhoffer handed Frank his flat white and bacon roll with no sauce.

'Down with the pigs,' he said. 'Keep taking it to the man.'

Frank attempted a smile that was more like a grimace and whispered, 'Thank you.' Despite now being really late, with the morning news conference in full swing, he still found time for a quick fag while contemplating telling the editor to stick the job up his arse. He inhaled deeply, head pounding and organs marinating as he readied for a fight, walking past the advertising department, then sport, passing through the open-plan newsroom shouting his daily greeting of 'I'm not dying for these bastards.' Except this time, he noticed that instead of ignoring him, a sea of smirking faces mixed with the odd cold stare watched as he headed towards his desk. Frank laughed as he saw that a picture of a dog licking a baby had been placed over his computer screen.

'Hill-airy-arse,' he shouted.

Plunkett was shaking with laughter, while Carol and Tom appeared to be shaking with rage.

Plunkett said, 'You're late, Frank? Dick Bell-end is having kittens looking for you.'

'Fuck him,' Frank replied, while checking his mobile to see the four missed calls and three text messages from Morag, who was now goose-stepping towards him.

'Where have you been?' she barked.

'Er, sorry, Morag, the traffic was a nightmare, and the bus took ages.'

'Heard it. I suppose a dog ate your homework as well, Savage. Wait until after the news conference, then go and see Richard. I'll let him know you've arrived.'

Frank had grown accustomed to Morag speaking to him like this and quite liked it, wondering if she too had an Elvira costume. He thought if the paper goes tits up, she'd have a big career either as a doctor's receptionist or a prostate checker. But Frank and Morag went way back and got on well. He respected the fact that she was now on her fifth editor and had never slagged off any of them, preferring to play her cards close to her chest. Frank was sure she had signed some kind of Hippocratic Oath for PAs where they promised to serve whatever arsehole landed in the chair.

He sat down and tried to ignore Tom, who was chirping away in his ear about his Labradors being impeccably behaved in cafés. Frank blanked the white noise and checked his emails, clicking on the one with the weekend figures.

Hi folks,

A momentous weekend saw us smash our single page

view target by more than 250 per cent – a new record. This was largely down to the efforts of our esteemed columnist, Frank Savage, whose tongue-in-cheek column on banning babies and dogs from cafés proved a big hit with our online audience, racking up an incredible 1,655,218 views and driving traffic elsewhere on the site.

The previous best of 862,087 hits garnered for a single story after the Queen died has been nearly doubled with page views for a week bursting through the three million mark – uncharted waters for our publications.

Finally, the bionic penis has been pushed down the charts, recording a rather flaccid 125,002 page views.

Top five stories, copied below, show a range of columns, breaking news, sport and feature content.

Alasdair Stewart (BA Hons)
Deputy Digital Editor News Content
Twitter: @futurenews

NO BABIES, NO DOGS, NO LATTES:
1,655,218

DETECTIVES HUNT GORGIE SEX BEAST WITH "SUGAR PUFF" TEETH:
254,337

'YOU'LL HAVE HAD YOUR TEA' – MARCHMONT CAFÉ IN TIP RAMMY:
190,576

MISSING SCHOOL PUPIL FOUND LOCKED IN MUSEUM TOILET: 188,993

TRANENT MAN WITH BIONIC PENIS MEETS WOMAN OF HIS DREAMS:
125,002

Frank pretended to be "knocked for six" by the weekend figures, although he didn't understand them and had no idea how things would play out with the editor. There was bound to have been a shedload of complaints about his column, and he still didn't fancy his chances of survival given that Richard was weak as piss in the face of the slightest criticism, printing an apology for almost anything. Frank reckoned he liked having to print retractions, something any decent editor was loathe to do, and would have no hesitation in throwing any staff member under the bus to save his own skin. But they seemed pleased with the figures, and this could provide a lifeline. He saw the news editor and picture editor come out of the conference and went in to see Richard.

'Sorry I'm late, the traffic was a nightmare, and the bus was going backwards.'

Richard smiled and told him to sit down. 'Take a pew, Frank. Good weekend?'

'Certainly eventful. I've ordered a new car.'

Richard didn't respond as this was in danger of straying into small talk, human speak, something his Replicant brain struggled to comprehend. Frank noticed the weekend figures were projected on the giant computer screen.

Richard caught Frank looking at them. 'I was on a conference call with the chief executive of the group this morning and he's absolutely delighted with the response to your column. The rest of the board are impressed with the figures it's generated and, although a controversial and no doubt polarising subject, they see an opportunity for you.'

Frank was prepared for the old shit sandwich and could never really get his head round the obsession with traffic and digital hits. He noted that "polarising" was the new "word of the day" for the editorial staff, who were using it robustly.

Frank said, 'That's great. I knew it would fly. Our readers like to be challenged.'

Richard squirmed uneasily in his chair and pointed the remote control at the wall-mounted television while addressing Frank without looking at him.

'That's as may be. It was certainly robust and polarising, but it's really captured the zeitgeist in terms of audience engagement. Social media blew up over the weekend and the traffic has been off the scale. There's been a fair degree of blowback, and the optics look bad, but the chief exec wants me to absorb the criticism and we're not without our supporters in higher circles.'

Frank shrugged and felt the need for a coffee and a smoke to keep the blood pressure rate up.

Richard, speaking through clenched teeth, said, 'The boss man is delighted and has asked me to continue to give you free rein and take the shackles off completely. He appreciates the freedom I've given you and the way we've garnered your talent. So, it looks like that's the direction of travel we'll be going in for the short-to-medium term.'

'Is there any chance of you telling me what that means in English, or even entry level French?'

'We're looking for you to write more controversial stuff, Frank – anything you like; the more offensive, the better. Complete freedom. The thinking is it will drive traffic and we're miles away from any legacy journo ideas about objectivity and impartiality. The boss thinks you have what it takes to be a star columnist, a Scottish version of Clarkson, Piers, or Littlejohn. Increased profile. He sees you appearing on radio and television giving your tuppence ha'penny worth on current talking points but, crucially, setting the news agenda on social media with your column. What do you think?'

Frank beamed. 'Does this mean I can still call the Shifters… Yifters?'

'Absolutely, Frank. I'm glad we had our little chat but all of that can go on the back burner. You'll have pretty much carte blanche to do what you like, provided you keep kicking the arses of those clowns over at *The Scotsman* and *The Herald*.'

'So, I won't be getting my jotters?'

'No, you won't be made to take voluntary redundancy. Not that it was ever on the cards. In fact, there's a twenty per cent pay rise on the table for you as we speak.'

Frank pondered for a moment, looking at the list of top stories and smirking at the phrase "sugar puff teeth", as half his class at Leith Academy fell into the poor dental hygiene category. He also noticed the one about the stars set for the opening of the youth theatre in Portobello and realised the Brewster PR machine was in full swing.

'Make it thirty per cent and you've got a deal.'

Richard nodded enthusiastically and said he'd "clear it with the grown-ups".

Frank realised at that point he could have asked Richard for a gobble and he'd likely say yes.

'That's brilliant, Frank. I'm meeting with the head of the Scottish Broadcasting Collective to see about getting you a prime-time slot and the bosses are looking at running a billboard campaign across the country under the To Be Frank banner with an accompanying mugshot.'

Frank said he had a "face for the radio", to which Richard gave out his best false laugh.

'Right, I better be getting back to my desk, seeing as there's work to do.'

'Well done, Frank. I can't wait for your next column.'

Frank sat down at his desk and grunted at his colleagues, who were perched like buzzards on rooftops waiting for him to relay the details of his meeting with the editor. Ignoring them, he was now in a complete panic about how he would pay back The Gypsy at his extortionate rate and realised any chance of redundancy that would have come in handy was off the cards. He logged onto the staff pension hub and saw that his retirement pot was now sitting below the twenty grand mark and wouldn't even cover four months' payments. *Damn those risky funds*, he thought, then realised that plundering the tax-free element of his pension on his fifty-fifth birthday last year had been a bad move, seeing as he'd lost most of the cash at Cheltenham after treating himself to a fortnight in Sitges.

Frank thought about the fifty thousand pounds wrapped in clingfilm currently resting under his bed and contemplated phoning The Gypsy to say he'd made a mistake and hand the cash back. He tugged at his earlobes and quickly realised that wouldn't wash. The Gypsy had made it crystal clear that he wanted full payment of fifty thousand plus ten thousand interest over the course of a year; any attempt by Frank to renege on the handshake would have serious consequences.

If the worst came to the worst, he could sell the Shadow but likely wouldn't get his money back and would still be scrambling for a bit of cash, but at least this offered him a way out and provided a modicum of calm. He also planned to gamble some of the extra ten grand he'd borrowed for incidentals – the incidentals being the prize thoroughbreds he would back at this year's Cheltenham Festival.

Retirement now seemed like a pipe dream to Frank, who didn't fancy his chances of making it past sixty-five. In fact, if the grim reaper offered him another ten years, he'd snap its hand off. He had a vague notion of a side hustle where he hired out the Shadow for weddings and the like. He would get a natty chauffeur's outfit and chat to the bride and her father, putting their minds at ease, while telling them how he really preferred funerals.

He decided to go and see Graeme, who was drinking a can of Diet Coke and staring out the window. He put down the drink as Frank approached and smiled, then shook his head.

'Bonkers indeed,' Graeme said.

'I know, the world's gone mad. It's like that movie, *The Producers*. The worse the columns get, the more they like them,' Frank said.

Graeme asked him what he was going to write about next and Frank said he hadn't the foggiest.

Despite coming in late, Frank left work early to keep his GP appointment.

He arrived at the doctor's surgery, half a mile from Ramsay Tech, which was handy as Frank was never away from the place.

Sure, he got slagged off for being a hypochondriac but there was no way he was going to be one of those old-school Scottish guys who never went to the doctor, then dropped down dead two years after retiring during a domino flyer at the British Legion.

As far as Frank was concerned, Dr Khan was paid a fortune and should earn his money.

If that meant listening to his list of medical problems, each one a potential death-trap in Frank's own mind, then so be it. He didn't need to give his name at the desk as the receptionist knew it and his date of birth off by heart. He nodded and sat down in the waiting room, avoiding eye contact with the invalids and ignoring a small child who was galloping round like a show pony, egged on by a thirty-something dad wearing New Balance trainers and beige chinos. After twenty minutes of Frank playing blackjack on his phone and losing twenty quid, Dr Khan finally stuck his head round the door and shouted the battle cry, 'Frank Savage.'

'Hello, Frank, good to see you. It's been what? Three weeks?'

Frank ignored the sarcasm from Dr Khan, which he thought was a bit off, and thought he wouldn't speak to someone with a mental health problem like that.

'Hi, Dr Khan. I see the Arsenal aren't doing so well just now,' Frank replied, leaving a bit on the good doctor who was an avid Gooner. Dr Khan took a deep breath and got down to the business at hand.

'So, Frank, what's the problem this time? I see from the notes the nurse has left me that you've increased urination during the night, and this is causing you some concern.'

Frank launched into full Spud from *Trainspotting* interview mode.

'Yip, I've been peeing up to three times a night instead of getting up once, which I always call my "old man pee", but this is different. It's like the sensation of needing to pee, that wee tingly feeling is in my cock a lot. There's been no blood in my urine before you ask but I thought I better pay you a visit seeing as I'm now in my mid-fifties and haven't had my prostate checked. No one's stuck a rubber glove up my arse, at least not for a while.'

Dr Khan nodded, then said matter-of-factly, 'I'll book you in for a blood test first, then a prostate check-up. I see from the notes that you also have concerns about your blood pressure, cholesterol, potential diabetes Type 2, gout and a mole on your side that looks raised.'

Frank lifted up his shirt unprompted to show Dr Khan his mole. The doctor looked at it, before putting on a pair of rubber gloves for a closer examination.

'Has it bled or been inflamed and have you noticed it changing shape or colour?'

'No,' Frank replied, defaulting to his usual setting of feeling like he was wasting the doctor's time. 'I just thought I'd better get it checked out; it's been there a while and felt a bit bumpy.'

'When you say a while, how long do you mean exactly? When did you first notice it?'

Frank pretended to ponder the questions. 'Er, I suppose it's been there my whole life. I just thought it would be wise to flag it up. Does it look all right then?'

Dr Khan sought to reassure Frank like he always did.

'You did the right thing. It looks fine, if it hasn't changed shape and there's been no bleeding or inflammation. Keep an eye on it and contact us if anything noticeable occurs. I'll make a note for the nurse to perform a further blood test for cholesterol, uric acid levels in relation to your gout and we'll also check for diabetes.'

Frank was eager to show the doctor he wasn't dealing with a mere layman and was determined to make the best of his ten-minute consultation.

'I've started taking a yoghurt drink every day that's got plant sterols in it and is proven to reduce cholesterol.'

Dr Khan sighed. 'There's limited evidence these things work. It's more likely lifestyle changes like improving your diet. Quitting smoking and drinking will reduce cholesterol and provide you with immediate health benefits.'

Frank knew the doctor was having a sly dig as always about his smoking and drinking habits, but he didn't take the bait.

'Are you feeling anxious, Frank? Stress at work or in your personal life?'

Frank had gone from chatterbox to monosyllabic teenager in a heartbeat.

'Just the usual; work's work and that,' he mumbled.

'Okay, let's take your blood pressure, if you can roll up your sleeve, thanks.'

Frank felt a familiar panic as Dr Khan fixed the Velcro strap to his arm and the pressure tightened. He read the dial upside down, something he'd perfected over the years and felt sick as the reading showed 152/96.

'I think that's just white coat syndrome. It's normally around the 135/88 mark,' Frank lied, not wishing to be placed on any blood pressure meds.

Dr Khan, who had been through this ritual many times, repeated the procedure. This time, the dial showed 180/102 as Frank was now in the throes of a full-blown panic attack, sweating profusely with an overwhelming feeling of wanting to run away.

'Fuck, I'm having a heart attack. Jesus, this is it!'

Dr Khan sought to calm him down, placing his hands on Frank's shoulders and telling him to take deep breaths. This did the trick.

'You're right about the white coat syndrome, Frank, and it's common for blood pressure to be higher in a clinical setting. However, it is a cause for concern and I'm going to put you on medication that will lower it.'

Frank pleaded, 'Can I not just take a couple of weeks' readings on my machine at home, then give you the results? Please, Dr Khan.'

Dr Khan shook his head. 'We've tried that twice, Frank; the first time you did it for three days and the second time you stayed away from the surgery for six months. Something of a record for you, may I add.'

The panic subsided and Frank felt defeated, realising he'd fucked up his health so badly that he now had to take drugs just to keep his blood pressure down. Dr Khan talked him through the dosage but the usual burning question when it came to medication was at the front of Frank's mind; namely, *Can I drink alcohol on these?*

9

Naomi was distracted by the phone call from her GP that morning; they had got the results back from the laparoscopy and had found endometriosis tissue, which was no surprise. Naomi had suspected this, having consulted Dr Google hundreds of times after the period pains got so severe she had had to stop playing football.

She headed along the promenade towards Fusion Brew, dreading the "sit-down" with Brewster. This meeting had been arranged weeks in advance by the Syndicate, and the Wise One made it clear to her that she was to take no crap from the reformed soccer hooligan, pillar of the community, sculptor Nazi. The five hundred thousand pounds was to be handed over to Brewster, to be passed on to a couple of bent councillors who would ensure the cinema project was granted approval. This was the only bid in town after a property developer looking to convert the building into student flats was politely encouraged to withdraw their application.

Brewster had "persuaded" the councillors it was in their best interests to appoint a private equity firm to help fund the restoration, which would save some of the original Art Deco features and install modern cinema projection and sound equipment. Naomi decided there wasn't going to be a straightforward handover of the money with Brewster – that was too risky from her point of view. If anyone was going to get caught handling that amount of cash, it would have to be him. But she would make him jump through a couple of hoops to get his grubby paws on the dosh and she felt anxious at the prospect of pissing him off. She hated loose cannons; another thing she and the Wise One had in common, along with a love of figures and West Ham United FC.

She entered the café to find Brewster already seated with his dog beside him.

'What is it with cafés and dogs these days?' she muttered, thinking like her old man. 'Hello, you must be Brewster.'

Brewster gave out a little laugh as he eyed her up and down. 'Yip, that's me, this is Waffle, and you are?'

'Hello, Waffle. I'm Natalie.'

'Hi, Natalie, take a seat. I'm just about to order, can I get you anything?'

'Just a coffee, thanks.'

Naomi had decided she wasn't going to use her real name and Brewster needed to know the bare minimum.

'What coffee would you like, Natalie? A flat white, or maybe you'd prefer a caffè mocha?'

'Flat white's fine,' she said. Naomi felt her face flush momentarily but quickly managed to regain her composure. It had been a while since she'd encountered such blatant casual racism.

'Natalie, that's a nice name but a little difficult for Scottish people to say as they tend to miss out the second vowel and pronounce it, "Natlie".'

'Yeah,' she replied, in a non-committal tone.

'Anyway, how's Old London Town and Mr Armstrong?'

'You mean the Wise One, he's fine. This cinema project means a lot to him, and we have a lot invested up here. So, it'll be best for both of us if things run smoothly.'

Brewster nodded but clearly wasn't happy that she had scolded him for breaking protocol and using the Wise One's real last name, but she didn't care and was already hating him. The waiter came over to take their order.

'I'll have the full Scottish breakfast, an orange juice and a flat *white*,' Brewster said, while the waiter looked apologetically at Naomi.

So much for ladies first.

She said, 'I'll also have a flat white, and do you do any of those shortbread biscuits, you know the ones with the jelly tot on the top?'

'You mean a German biscuit,' Brewster interjected. 'Waffen – sorry, Waffle – loves them.'

The waiter replied, 'Yip, we do those, someone else was asking about them at the weekend, so there's clearly a demand. But I've heard them called a variety of things. We've decided on iced biscuit. So, it's a full Scottish breakfast, an orange juice and a flat white, and a flat white with an iced biscuit.'

Brewster grunted in reply, then turned back to Natalie. 'So, is this your first time in Scotland, Natalie?'

'No, I've got family up here.'

Brewster pondered this for a moment, squeezing his bottom lip with his tattooed right hand. 'Have you now. What, here in Edinburgh?'

'All over, some here, some in Glasgow, some in Dundee. Can we get down to business please? I'm not interested in geography.'

'All business; I like that, Natlie, because of course that's your real name.'

Naomi didn't care that he'd sussed her name was fake, as it was expected in their line of work, but now wished she'd picked Kitty or Candy, something a bit more exotic – exotic as in stripper. The name was her way of showing Brewster he wasn't that important in the big scheme of things and should stay in his lane.

Their order arrived and he started to tuck into his breakfast, feeding Waffle one of the sausages on his plate, which the dog swallowed without chewing. Brewster tried gleaning her for information, while at the same time blowing his own trumpet.

'This project with the old cinema is genius and will sit nicely alongside the youth theatre and women's football team that I've set up. Should secure a nice bit of funding. Ticks the box for the posh twats who have moved to Porty making it a trendy place to live. "Gentrification", that's the word. These marks go nuts for anything with the words "community, inclusive, diversity, space and hub" attached. They'll fucking pee themselves at the thought of an independent cinema on their doorstep.'

Naomi let him talk; she was well-versed in these types of conversations which always had the central theme of "What's in it for me?" running through them.

He said, 'I hope the Wise One and the Syndicate are fully aware of everything I've put in place for them up here. I've smoothed the way for a takeover of Edinburgh, or "Fake City" as I like to call it.'

Naomi could have said she was fully aware of everything he'd done for himself, having been given the skinny on Brewster from the Lafferty family in Glasgow. They had been watching his every move for the last three months including daily dog walks (no poop bags) and regular visits to his mother. He was also dealing on the side with a local gypsy family and had bought a couple of car washes as a side hustle that he was wide enough to think the bosses down south knew nothing about. But the main concern was the arrival in Edinburgh of two ex-paramilitaries, who were friends of Brewster and had been part of a UVF team specialising in murdering relatives of IRA men.

'Whose idea was the cinema project then?' he asked, with a mouthful of black pudding and egg running down his chin.

Naomi resisted the urge to tell him it was her brainchild, and that a similar plan was running on the south coast, which included a cinema, a kids soccer academy and a trampoline centre. That project had so far washed fifty million pounds of the Syndicate's hard-earned cash. Instead, she played things down. 'It's something we've been looking at for a long time; new opportunities to create a cash-flow funnel.' *Suitably vague*, Naomi thought to herself.

Brewster sussed she was holding out on him. He slurped his coffee. 'You must know something about Scottish Limited Partnerships then, and Community Right to Buy orders. There's a lot of legal loopholes that have had to be jumped through to secure a three million pound grant from the Scottish government.'

Naomi feigned ignorance but threw him a bone for now. 'I know nothing about all of that, but I do know it's easy to fiddle the number of cinemagoers and control the supply of refreshments, which is ideal.' She left out the bit about the Syndicate's long-term plans for a movie studio in Portobello and making inroads into television production.

Brewster, who had a piece of black pudding stuck to his chin like a bluebottle fly, stared at her with his beady little eyes. He said, 'Okay, what about the cash for the councillors? Have you got it with you, love?'

Naomi tensed as she prepared to make Brewster do star jumps.

'Here's a key to a black Toyota Auris that's parked at the Inverkeithing park and ride over in Fife.' She slipped it across the table. 'In the boot there's two plain black rucksacks, each one containing two hundred and fifty grand. That's the money you asked for to be dished out to the two councillors on the planning committee that you've got, as you say, in your pocket, to smooth the way for the cinema development. We've got all their details, including family members and where they live.'

Brewster attempted to take another slurp of his flat white, this time completely missing his mouth, as he fed Waffle a piece of bacon.

'A driver will pick you up at 1.30pm at the car park of the supermarket on the high street and take you to Inverkeithing.

You take the money out and put the key back in the boot. He'll take you back to that lock-up you use in Joppa for God knows what and you stash the money there, until such time as it's ready to be distributed. Got that?'

Brewster sat there with his mouth open, wondering how she knew about his beloved lock-up, before nodding his head and rubbing his eyes.

Naomi added, 'Okay, that gives you plenty time to finish your breakfast and take Waffen for a big shit. I hope you use the doggy bags.'

Brewster gave her an incredulous stare and Naomi had left him in no doubt where he stood in the pecking order.

'Fuck me. You don't mess about, hen, do you? What if I've got other plans for this afternoon? I might be doing something else at half-caste one.'

Naomi grimaced at his racist patter. 'Then you'll have to answer to the Wise One in person. He's planning to come to Edinburgh soon and this project is very close to his heart. Obviously, it would be in your best interests to "dae as yer telt",' she said.

The switch to broad Scots threw Brewster, who no longer looked like he was enjoying his breakfast.

'Okay, I get it, you're the boss. I'll go on your wee road trip to Fife. Scotland's Texas, banjo-land.'

Naomi dunked the iced biscuit into her flat white. 'You can get this. I'll be in touch.' She made to get up just as Gurkha Bobby walked into the café. He did a double take as he saw Naomi leave Brewster's table and immediately walked towards it with the aim of protecting her. Naomi put her finger to her lip, giving him the "wheesht" sign and left the café, followed by Bobby who tapped her on the shoulder.

'Are you all right, Naomi? What did that arsehole say to you?'

Naomi was taken aback at seeing him and was having to think on her feet.

She said, 'Who, that guy back there? He'd dropped a couple of empty doggy bags, and I was handing them back to him. I knew you'd think he was hassling me but that wasn't the case. Anyway, let's go for a wee walk along the prom. You don't want to go in that place. They charge a fortune.'

Bobby said, 'Aye, I was in there with your old man at the weekend. Carnage.'

Naomi scuttled away from Fusion Brew, forcing Bobby to follow her. She knew he could tell something was amiss, so quickly threaded her arm through his and stepped up the pace, marching into the biting wind. Glancing back after they were a bit away, she saw Brewster staring at them, with Waffle barking at a passing cyclist.

They walked up to Daisy Park away from the promenade. Bobby was waiting for Naomi to bring up Brewster, not wanting to instigate it himself. 'Do you know that guy back there then, Bobby?' she finally asked.

'Yeah, unfortunately. Your dad and me were at school with him. Brewster's his name. He was in the jail for a few years for attempted murder. A nasty piece of work; former football hooligan.'

Naomi, he couldn't help but think, did a show of looking surprised and innocent. 'God, he sounds like a right wrong'un. Did you and Dad have a fight with him or something?'

At that moment, Bobby felt the weight of the world on his shoulders. He wasn't sure Naomi knew about the circumstances surrounding her Uncle Michael's death, who she had never met, and didn't know if Frank had ever spoken to her about that night at the open-air pool.

Steering well clear of that issue, he said, 'Yeah, my love, we had a few run-ins with him over the years. Brewster was a bit of a sap at school and got bullied. Then, one day, he decided he'd had enough and made up his mind he'd be the one dishing out the beatings. He started going to karate and kickboxing, made himself a bit of a ninja, then got a taste for the violence when the whole football hooligan thing started, and he was running with the casuals.

'He was always a bit wary of your dad, though, as Frank could always handle himself but never went looking for trouble. Your dad saved Brewster from getting slashed in Leith one time, when the boys from the Fort were looking to play noughts and crosses on his ugly pus. He ended up hanging about with a bunch of Rangers thugs who ran a supporters bus from Haymarket. A nasty bunch of Orange bastards with a sprinkling of racism thrown into the mix and poof-bashing as a midweek hobby when the football wasn't on.'

'These casuals,' Naomi said, 'are they what you'd call "ultras" at the football now?'

'Nothing like them really, although some of their sons might be ultras. For a start, you wouldn't get any of these old hooligans banging a drum at the game or designing tifos, and their fashion sense was a bit different from the standard black hoodie. They looked more like the band Wham! or the tennis player Bjorn Borg, then they started dressing like golfers and gamekeepers. But I suppose all of this is a bit before your time.'

Naomi laughed. She said, 'I've heard of Wham! and I love George Michael. We get a lot of black hoodies at the nightclub that I sometimes work in, Stone Island, or Clone Island as we call it.'

They both sat in silence, watching a woman enter the park with a young child who was pointing at their bench. Bobby stood up, straightened his jacket and gave Naomi a peck on the cheek.

'Look after yourself, sweetheart,' he said, leaving her sitting on the park bench.

*

Brewster sat in the front seat of the red 2015 Ford Fiesta and cursed the Syndicate and their habit of using crap cars for every job. It was never a Porsche Cayenne or a Land Rover Vogue.

He'd tried to start a conversation with the designated driver, a big black guy called JJ, who just grunted and said, 'Dunno, I just drive' to his every question. Brewster finally asked him if he drove for Uber in his spare time, to which JJ slammed on the anchors and told him any more of that shite and he'd be walking to Inverkeithing.

'Feargal Sharkies think they run the show,' he murmured to himself, slinking back down into the passenger seat.

Brewster was uneasy heading over the Queensferry Crossing towards Fife and went over in his mind the meeting he'd had with "Natalie". Who was she and what was she doing with Gurkha Bobby? He was mates with Savage, who Brewster had run into the other day. These "blasts from the past" were becoming more frequent – everyone seemed to gravitate back to Portobello.

She had family up here, he remembered her saying. Maybe Bobby was her uncle; they were about the same shade, but then wasn't he from India or was it Pakistan?

He didn't like how Natalie had been wide and was thinking of ways to get back at her, but he'd have to bide his time as she obviously had Armstrong's ear. Wise One indeed.

He was getting old and sloppy. That twenty million pound shipment the feds seized in Antwerp had damaged his rep with the troops on the ground and he was on a yellow – one mistake away from a red and a one-way ticket to the boneyard.

Brewster fantasised about having Natalie tied up to a chair in his lock-up, duct tape covering her mouth while he told her, 'This is the last face you'll ever see,' as he sparked up the blowtorch, after stubbing out fags on the soles of her bare feet.

'Here, Natlie, meet Waffen,' he would say in the SS uniform that he bought online from the States. That was one he'd savour, torturing her while singing the old 'Um Bongo' tune from his teenage days.

Soon see how smart she is after half an hour with me.

Brewster knew the Syndicate would be watching his every

move and he'd have to box clever. The car washes were his way of future-proofing his earnings and might get him a warning, but he realised that, short-term, the key to survival was to keep himself useful to the Wise One, who he was yet to meet in person. He'd have to get on with this Natalie bitch as she was the contact for the cinema project, but he vowed not to take any more of her lip. The councillors were products of his hard graft and he'd be making sure Mr Armstrong was aware of that, when it came to handing out the Christmas bonuses.

The Ulster boys, hardened terrorists – who he'd brought over and christened the Two Billys after his favourite comedians, the Two Ronnies – were waiting patiently in the wings, but there was nothing funny about this pair. A key component of the long game, Brewster had planned to take over drug dealing in the capital. The Two Billys knew the score, having ventured into Edinburgh before, plying their wares in Wester Hailes and Sighthill around twenty years ago. Granted, setting a couple of local dealers on fire had taken things a little too far but they had cut their teeth slaughtering Catholics, or Taigs as they liked to call them, across the province. The Two Billys, who had fought the IRA, certainly had the know-how to deal with the Wise One and these London poofs who fancied themselves as the top dogs in the UK.

Brewster got out the car at the park and ride, saw the Toyota Auris, yet another crap car, and took the two rucksacks from its boot.

The journey back to Edinburgh was just as bad, with JJ ignoring him and refusing to be drawn into any kind of small talk, preferring instead to listen to Radio fucking 4 – a weirdo station if ever there was one. Brewster got dropped off near the lock-up and threw him a tenner as a tip. 'Get yerself a McDonald's, pal.'

10

Frank was now fair chuffed with his column offering that was doing a roaring trade online. The grown-ups in editorial were walking about with broad smiles and he was enjoying a day in the sun with his shit not stinking for once. The pay rise came in handy, and he'd had it backdated a couple of months, which meant he would be able to cover the first payment to The Gypsy due on New Year's Day. He was now the proud owner of the Shadow having paid Falco the forty grand and was feeling flush with an extra ten thousand pounds sitting under his bed.

A new byline picture had been taken for the online edition with him looking like a younger, more handsome version of the Irish actor, Brendan Gleeson – the one from *The Banshees of Inisherin,* who had chopped his fingers off because his mate was getting on his tits. Frank had occasionally felt like this with Bobby and was in no doubt the feeling was mutual. Perhaps he could lob off his gouty big toe.

Sure, there'd been a bit of controversy over the column, but a fair few punters were in favour of banning babies and dogs, with Frank gaining a new-found following among people who had both the Union Flag and the Israeli Flag on their Twitter profiles. A lot of the comments revolved around blaming the parents and dog owners for the behaviour of their respective charges.

On the other side of the debate were a lot of angry people who, in no particular order, called him a Nazi, a sadist, a paedophile, a gammon and a couple who compared him to the Child Catcher in *Chitty Chitty Bang Bang*. He was also called a yoon and a quisling, but that was nothing new.

A billboard campaign had now been launched and visitors to the capital were met with a giant picture of Frank's beaming coupon as they left Edinburgh Airport or boarded a train at Waverley Station, with the tagline *To Be Frank* prominently displayed. Plans were afoot for a series of these adverts, including a TV campaign that would run asking the question, "*What Would Frank Do?*" over the masthead of the paper. Frank thought back to the stick he'd got when the British Army ran the *To Be Frank, Join the Army* television advertising campaign back in the early nineties, where bored mates discuss what's become of their friend who is shown enjoying the adventurous side of life. But he doubted anyone would remember that.

He was a tad embarrassed by all the fuss but was thinking about the opportunities his brush with fame might afford him in terms of *Liaisons Dangereuses* with members of the opposite sex and was relishing the prospect of adoring fans dropping their Alan Whickers at the mere mention of his name. Clever, pale and interesting age-appropriate women, who looked like they worked in a library – that was his target market. Someone who might get one of his movie references, with a GSOH. Was that too much to ask? Probably.

The column fame and the Shadow had certainly put a spring in Frank's step, to the extent he was considering getting his teeth whitened. He seemed to be peeing less and was toying with the idea of employing a personal trainer, but that would likely entail him having to cut out the beer and the crisps. Frank loved Wotsits and considered cheese powder to be the crack cocaine of the crisp world. Dr Khan's medication had gradually started to bring Frank's blood pressure down and he was checking the machine daily to monitor the results. He now delighted in telling everyone in The Hadd he was cutting down on the bevvy and would make a big show of ordering a can of Guinness Draught Zero as his first drink before slyly switching to its stronger big brother. This was enough for an increasingly insufferable Frank to lord it over 'that bunch of alkies and dipsos.'

He did have the nagging feeling at the back of his mind that it would all end in tears, so it'd be wise to make hay while the sun shines. The effect of all of this was that his colleagues were now completely ignoring him, with Plunkett taking Frank's meteoric rise to the top of the digital hits league table particularly badly. Frank, of course, was loving this, having once asked Dick Bell-end for a pay rise only to be presented with a slew of data that showed he didn't generate enough traffic to the website and would therefore be getting the square root of fuck all. He thought it was harsh to solely judge someone's journalistic ability on the number of digital clicks they generated but had parked that thought now he was enjoying the fruits of his labours.

Frank smeared relish onto an oatcake and checked one of his online betting accounts as the editor approached.

'Hi guys,' Richard said, impersonating a holiday rep. 'How's our star columnist treating you all today; has he bought the cakes?'

Cakes and the buying thereof for any occasion was the nearest Dick Bell-end got to bonding with the staff. In his mind, there was nothing that a bag of jam doughnuts couldn't put right. No one looked up from their desk and Plunkett let out a low-level primal scream.

'Anyway, good news, Frank,' said Richard. 'I've been on to the producer of Scottish FM, who's a mate of mine, and they want you to go on the *Dial Deidre* show the week after next to talk about your columns. This is a great opportunity to raise your profile and engage with the target audience. Strike while the iron is red hot. Capture the zeitgeist. I won't ask you what the next one is about but I'm sure you've got another beauty tucked up your sleeve.'

Frank winced at the mention of *Dial Deidre* as he'd done his journalism training with Deidre McAllister many moons ago at Napier Technical College, where they'd enjoyed a brief fling that she ended. He knew she'd drag him over the coals, and he'd have to prepare a stout defence of the subject matter, employing tactics like not answering the question and running down the clock, like the politicians did. He was in at the deep end now.

Frank toyed with the idea of saying his columns weren't supposed to be taken seriously but he knew this would piss off the grown-ups at the paper as he realised absolutely no one in Scotland these days understood satire, or at least his version of it. The bosses were banking on him robustly defending his views, which, to Frank's mind, had the tiniest kernel of truth in them; that at least gave him something to cling on to. This would be easier than trying to argue the toss for something he was vehemently against but pretending to be in favour of. The "but I was only joking" card that had stood him so well throughout his life and career would have to stay in the pack. He was in unchartered waters and facing the prospect of having to defend his bonkers columns from here to eternity, at the mercy of social media and the easily offended. *Mind you*, Frank thought, *the likes of Piers Morgan and Jeremy Clarkson clearly don't believe half the shite they write about, and the public seem to know this. "Never complain, never explain". If it's good enough for the Queen Mother, then it's good enough for me.*

Frank decided there and then that he'd have to go all in if this celebrity columnist lark was going to work, giving him the chance to earn some proper poppy and, importantly, stay in the game. The good thing was people's attention spans were so short these days that the fallout from the columns would only last until the next one. Going by this logic, Frank surmised the secret was to keep churning them out.

He headed straight home after work; no stopping at The Haddonfield – part of his bid to drink less. Naomi had met Katie for lunch and had brought her back to see Frank. He was delighted to have both his daughters under the one roof and noticed they shared similar interests and had the same kind of banter. Katie was working as a buyer for a high-end fashion brand, having graduated in the summer. She was the double of Bridget; a real class act but, mercifully, a bit softer in temperament. The women took a sofa each and watched *Love Island* as Frank cleared away their plates.

Katie had mentioned to Naomi that the guy she shared a flat with in Stockbridge was due to move out in a fortnight and there was a spare room going. Naomi seemed delighted and was making all the right noises about moving in, but Frank noticed a wariness in her replies that Katie hadn't picked up on. A skilled actor himself, he recognised the subtle signs that something was playing on her mind. He would keep an eye on her to make sure everything was all right and perhaps have a fatherly chat. Frank hugged both his daughters, before telling them to turn the telly down and not to stay up too late gabbing.

11

Brewster had spent the best part of the morning at the sauna with a bored Eastern European sex worker who had been told to give him a "shot on the swings" free of charge. The Gypsy owned the establishment and had agreed to provide him with access to dealers based in Niddrie and Craigmillar. This was the bread and butter of the Syndicate's plans to take over the drugs trade in Edinburgh and launder the proceeds through their various enterprises, including the cinema project.

As Brewster sauntered down Broughton Street, he chuckled at the memory of his old haunt, which had provided him with plenty of sport in the form of gay men who he preyed upon as a nascent "poof-basher" back in the 1980s. He winced at the number of Pride flags flying now, with the new triangular bits added for the transgenders and assorted other weirdos, like picture frames on display in an art shop. *It wasn't like this in my day,* he thought, when the gay scene was confined to pubs like The Laughing Duck and the nightclub Fire Island on Princes Street. Still, he'd mellowed a bit since then and had adopted a bit more of a "live and let live" attitude through his involvement with the women's football team.

He had time to kill before his 4pm meeting with the councillor at the lock-up so decided to play the slots in the bookies. A bad idea; he was one hundred and fifty pounds down within twenty minutes, once again succumbing to the lure of the flashing lights. Feeling terrible with the gambling devil perched firmly on his shoulder, Brewster summoned up the strength to walk away from the machine. He decided to nip into the Barony Bar to have a pint and do a line of coke for old times' sake. He had drunk there a bit in the casual days and knew a few hooligans from around the area who followed the Hearts and had their own wee firm. Mercifully, the pub hadn't changed much at all, not like the once legendary Phoenix across the road, which looked a bit insipid and now went by another name. Brewster ordered a pint of lager and checked his phone. He had a text message from Billy One.

All set to go, boss. Got him at the lock-up. Look forward to the water sports.

Brewster suddenly felt the weight of the world on his shoulders; the thought of more mindless violence made him feel sick to the stomach. He was fed up having to play the psycho and hurt people. Getting old, he worried about dying alone with no one to just watch telly with and have a cup of tea. He was starting to fancy bus trips to the Lake District and thought it might be nice to go on a cruise with someone other than his mother.

Even the Nazi documentaries weren't doing it for him any more as he realised the likes of Hitler, Goebbels and Himmler were about as Aryan as Jesse Owens. The ongoing race riots down south playing nightly on the television were also pissing him off, with the so-called far right nothing more than a bunch of toothless jakeys, ransacking the bakers and thrift shops. Brewster had been thinking a lot about this white underclass, with their vaping and scratch cards. How their hatred of Muslims seemed to stem from their own sense of "loserdom". It irked him that so many of them were described as football hooligans as, in his own opinion, these cunts weren't fit to wear the Stone Island badge.

He was struggling to shift memories of the past; flashbacks to his childhood were becoming more frequent and had started to appear in glorious technicolour. Images of his half-brother, Glen, with blood pouring from his head kept jumping out at Brewster like a demented Jack-in-the-box. He thought about the hell he'd endured at the hands of his stepdad, Norrie, and how he missed his real father more than ever.

Back in the present, he sipped a pint as a feeling of emptiness washed over him and a pang of remorse settled in his belly. Brewster had never felt more alone. He cursed how he'd never had a girlfriend for more than three months and still felt a longing for Eva, the German chick who he'd met in Berlin five years ago. She had a degree in politics and sociology from Munich University and introduced him to the films of Leni Riefenstahl. They had got on great at first, the sex was good, and she found him funny. Brewster was smitten, wanted nothing more than to marry Eva, settle down and have kids.

That all changed when he pummelled a Turkish guy who he thought was "being wide" with an ashtray in their local. Turned out all he was doing was asking if a seat was free, but Brewster mistook the harshness in his accent for a threat. Eva ran for the hills after that, saying she didn't feel safe in his company and couldn't live with "an unpredictable, racist psychopath". She eventually blocked his calls after he texted three hundred times in one day, begging her to come back. He had made his choices but was starting to have regrets and was sick of being labelled a racist by the people he craved acceptance from. Nice people like the ones at the youth theatre, who lived happy, contented lives, without violence. He vowed to just keep shagging pros until he found a way to escape the Syndicate and finally settle down. That was the dream.

Brewster nipped to the loo and knocked out a couple of giant rockstar lines to lift his mood. He snorted the coke, looked in the mirror and pointed.

'Give yourself a fucking shake,' he said by way of a pep talk. On the way down to Joppa in the taxi, Brewster thought of all the money he was going to make through the partnership with the Londoners. He would rule Porty and rub it in the noses of the posh cunts and all the people he had grown up with who told him he'd amount to nothing. That was the motivation; to be the top dog, the *Übermensch*, as Norrie had taught him when they'd watched the Hitler documentaries together as his stepdad fed his pet python, which he regularly threatened to set on a terrified Brewster. If it was going to take a last flurry of violence, then so be it.

He arrived at the lock-up five minutes before Councillor Sneddon and was glad to see that everything was in place for the afternoon matinee. Brewster wanted this show over as quickly as possible.

The wee junkie was strapped to the weight bench with duct tape over his mouth. He'd taken a bit of a beating from the Two Billys but was still compos mentis and able to comprehend the sheer hell he was about to face.

Waffen was tied up in the corner enjoying a nice bit of rump steak and Brewster knew better than to pet his dog while he was eating. The animal added a sense of occasion to the proceedings, and would no doubt leave quite the impression on Councillor Sneddon, who rapped twice on the door of the lock-up as instructed.

'Hello, Councillor, in you come. We're a wee bit busy and the lads are just finishing up here,' Brewster said, acting the part.

The terrified councillor wandered in as Brewster put a firm hand on his back, leading him towards a desk underneath a giant Confederate flag. By now, the thugs had placed a cloth over the hapless drug addict's mouth and were pouring water over it.

'Hope you don't mind the show,' Brewster said. 'I've been watching a lot of execution videos and torture stuff from a few years back. Been meaning to try out the old waterboarding for a while, but the opportunity never arose.'

The councillor gripped the handles of the chair, afraid to

look round as the hapless victim writhed, with his sinus cavities and mouth full of water and his lungs in aspiration.

'That is until wee Deano here tried to get wide and bump us out of payment for the stash. So, it's the full room and waterboard treatment for him.'

He brought a rucksack onto the desk and pushed it towards the councillor.

'Here you go, Sneddon. Two hundred big ones as requested. Do your worst and make sure those clowns at the Historic Buildings in Scotland Partnership know the score.'

The councillor unzipped the rucksack and counted the bundles of cash.

'It's supposed to be two hundred and fifty grand. Looks like there's fifty thousand pounds missing here.'

Brewster gave him the Manson lamps and said nothing, letting the sounds of the water feature amplify the lock-up.

'There must be some mistake,' the councillor said.

'Nope. New arrangement. You're getting taxed fifty grand and if you've got a problem with that, I can get the lads here to fix you up with a pair of speedos and a snorkel.'

The councillor was speechless as Brewster left the desk and walked over to Waffen, giving him a big hug before grabbing the jug of water and pouring it over Deano's face.

'Does anyone know how long it takes to die from this waterboarding lark? There should be instructions for this.'

The Billys shrugged as Brewster laughed, masking his inner disgust.

'Okay, lads, that's enough. Looks like Deano here's had his fill. Take him back and dump him in the middle of the road so everyone can see what happens if they don't pay. Next time, it'll be his head on a stick.'

The two men dragged their now unconscious victim out of the lock-up and into a white van. Brewster returned to the desk and poured himself and the councillor large glasses of whisky.

'Look, Mr Sneddon of 101 Pinepark Terrace. You're doing well. Driving a nice Range Rover, wife has a horse, daughter has a pony. Those animals cost an arm and a hoof. So just treat the fifty grand as income tax, due to the cost-of-living crisis and inflation. I've got a lot of overheads, what with this place, and the lads won't work for minimum wage. You're buying peace of mind; a nice wee insurance policy. A good investment to make sure things go smoothly. Keeps you away from the boys there and the lock-up; means the ponies won't be going to the glue factory anytime soon. Capeesh?'

Councillor Sneddon gulped his whisky and spluttered. He nodded in agreement and took a deep breath.

'Don't worry, Mr Brewster, I totally understand. I can assure you that you'll have nothing to worry about in terms of me keeping up my end of the deal.'

Brewster helped the councillor to his feet, patting him on the shoulders while ruffling his hair.

'Good lad. That's the spirit. Don't let what you've seen today bother you. This is my world, not yours, and never the twain shall meet. I'll be in touch next week to make sure things are going swimmingly.'

The councillor got into his Range Rover and slowly pulled out of the lane, as tears streamed down his cheeks.

Brewster prepared for his next meeting with Councillor Kane. This time he had something special planned, designed to put the wind up the guy so he'd be left in no doubt who he was dealing with. He'd arranged for Kane to come to his house in leafy Joppa at 8pm where he'd hand him the two hundred thousand pounds and the bad news on the other fifty thousand. This gave Brewster a bit of time to kill, so he stuck on *Meet Me in St Louis*, the old Judy Garland musical that he loved. However, Judy wasn't doing the trick this time and bad memories of the punishment inflicted on him by Norrie were at the forefront of his mind. How his stepdad would punch him in the stomach before pinning him to the floor, stubbing cigarettes on his arms, then letting his hands wander. After the assaults, Norrie would play nice and give Brewster beer and fags, as they watched all kinds of video nasties together. He would preach about how the Jews controlled the money and how the UK was being inundated with Muslims who would outbreed the indigenous population and take control. He would play endless Nazi documentaries and tell the teenage Brewster how the Holocaust was a lie, perpetrated by the Jews and their friends in the media.

Brewster took another line of coke that led to grandiose thoughts about how he saw himself as a modern-day Arkan, the Serbian mobster who led his own militia made up of ex-Red Star Belgrade boys during the war in Yugoslavia. Brewster planned to establish contacts in Hungary and Croatia through a network of former football hooligans, who would dominate the drugs trade in Europe and obliterate anyone who stood in their way, especially those Italian Fenian bastards in the Mafia.

The doorbell rang and a driver delivered his takeaway chippy tea; a fish supper with a smoked sausage chaser and two battered rump steaks for Waffen. Brewster had the dog on a chain in his back garden, which was his pride and joy, full Astroturf and decking with state-of-the-art hot tub and garden furniture. The good stuff from Dobbies; none of that cheap shite. He'd installed an elaborate security system, with sensors and spotlights timed to go off at regular intervals, and a twelve-foot-high fence. The perimeter of his home had security cameras at regular intervals as a warning to would-be intruders to risk it at their peril. And, of course, Waffen was there to act as the last line of defence.

The dog was not best pleased as Brewster laid the rump steaks outside grabbing distance, threatening to yank the chain out of the wall. Waffen was now rabid at the game his owner was playing.

At 8pm on the dot, Brewster watched Councillor Kane arrive on the CCTV monitor that sat next to his eighty-five-inch television. He met him at the front door.

The councillor said, 'I take it you've got the money?' abandoning any attempt at small talk and getting straight down to business. This riled Brewster, who wasn't used to taking orders from anyone let alone a councillor in a sharp suit with an open-neck shirt, wearing those trainer/shoe hybrid things beloved by football managers and pundits alike.

'I've got the cash and there's a bit of bad news for you on that front. The Syndicate could only muster up two hundred grand. That's all they're prepared to pay at this stage of the proceedings. But you're doing well enough. I saw that Range Rover you pulled up in, same car as your pal, Sneddon. Do all the councillors drive them?'

Kane wasn't ready to back down in the face of this aging casual. 'That's not the deal. It's two hundred and fifty grand. That buys you my deciding vote as chair of the planning committee and your cinema projects get rubber-stamped.'

Brewster was getting fed up with this guy and contemplated gutting him there and then. Instead, he checked his watch and poured two large whiskies, opening the patio doors and signalling for the councillor to join him on the decking.

Brewster said, 'Look, you should take the two hundred grand; that's the only offer on the table and its bonus cash for you. Trust me, I work for serious people.'

Kane was furious. 'A deal's a deal. I'm not scared of you or your creepy pals. I'm from Muirhouse and I've dealt with plenty of arseholes in my time.'

'I bet you have,' Brewster replied, smirking.

The councillor wasn't giving up without a fight and Brewster admired his stubborn stupidity.

At that point, there was a noise coming from the bottom of the garden and Waffen started barking, moving into full attack mode, ready to pounce on any would-be intruder. Brewster and the councillor watched as a figure in a protective body suit with his arms exposed appeared to fall over the fence, landing with a thump on the lawn. Brewster stood up and clapped his hands in delight. 'Looks like the Michelin Man has arrived,' he said, before pressing a remote-control button that immediately freed Waffen from his chains. The German shepherd made a beeline for the intruder, who let out a piercing scream as the dog latched onto his right arm, which quickly started to resemble a half-eaten piece of corn on the cob. The victim, another drug addict unable to pay his debts, started convulsing.

'Get off me, get that thing off me. It's shredding my arm… aargh! Please, please, help me! Look what that beast has done to me. For God's sake, help me!'

Brewster shouted back at him, 'Don't worry about that, son. It's amazing what they can do with prosthetics these days. You'll be back at the ten-pin bowling in no time.'

At that point, the Two Billys appeared in full protective suits, this time with no body parts exposed.

'Magic, lads, this is brilliant. Love the suits. Well, your ones. I'm not so keen on his.'

Brewster shouted at Waffen to 'Leave' and the dog duly sprang to attention, arriving at its owner's side. The two hoods lifted the man up and carted him off to the van.

'Take the two hundred grand, councillor. It's the only deal you're getting.' Brewster handed the councillor the rucksack. 'Now be on your way. You'll be hearing from us in due course.'

Councillor Kane walked out the house to see the victim with the savaged arm lying in the back of a van. He stared straight ahead, beeping his car door open, then waited until he was well away before dialling the number he'd been given. Naomi answered on the first ring.

'It's just like you said. He gave me two hundred thousand pounds and kept the other fifty thousand.'

Naomi replied, 'Okay,' then hung up and smashed her phone into pieces.

To Be Frank - Column #344

Bring back the belt!

It has been brought to my attention, dear readers, that delinquency in Scotland's schools has reached epidemic proportions with attacks on teachers, spitting, sweary words, chewing gum and arson on the rise.

Two-score years have passed since the last hooligan was belted to within an inch of its life and it's high time we returned to the glory days.

The people need a champion, a hero to emerge, who will stand up in the face of spotty hordes, like the six-foot seven-inch Glaswegian PE teacher who, in 1978, thrashed thirty-two primary-school kids who had dared to enter the hallowed field of rugby sans full kit.

'What we do in life, echoes in eternity.'

Damn those pesky do-gooders at the European Court of Human Rights who meddled in our affairs after a couple of lily-livered parents complained about their miracle offspring getting the strap.

This outrage should have been nipped in the bud and I, for one, would have belted the parents as well.

Granted, hitting the bairns was a perk of the job for the teachers, along with the six weeks off in the summer and jam roly-poly on a Friday.

But it kept us kids on our toes and by God you had to be on your toes in the seventies and early eighties, folks.

Boys, for starters, had the "Golden Triangle of Paedophilia" to navigate in the shape of Cub Scouts, swimming club and juvenile football, where Akela and the like were waiting to pounce on the first show of weakness.

The girls didn't escape – they had gymnastics.

Then there was the violence that awaited you in the playground – people being "after you" and the glue-sniffers that you had to dodge.

No one had the time to be depressed.

Stealing apples, dust caps off car tyres and playing "tap-door-run" were our social media.

Teachers knew the score back then and understood their job was to crush the dreams of children, not make outlandish pronouncements like "the sky's the limit" and "you can be whatever you want to be".

Codswallop.

'It'll be the jail for you, Savage; mark my words and that's if you survive the Cubs.'

I hark back to my school days at Leith Academy and "inspirational" art teacher, Mr Dalgleish, who once sat beside me as I was drawing a house and said, 'Art's not for everyone, son.' A seminal moment. He also let us smoke in class to unwind and relieve stress.

Back then, only the crème de la crème went to university and degrees in "biz-ness", sports science, marketing and media studies were not a thing. No, for the rest of us it was the factory, the mines, the shipyards or steady employment as a bullet magnet with the army in Northern Ireland.

Christ, I never saw a banana until I was fourteen.

The brighter kids, with the requisite "O" Grades, headed for Standard Life or Scottish Widows, with a cheap mortgage, pension scheme, staff canteen and the chance to develop alcohol dependency after marrying Debbie from Accounts.

To Be Frank, dear readers, bringing back corporal punishment, be it the trusted Lochgelly Tawse or the cane as preferred by the

English, is the only thing standing between us and these modern-day Lords of the Flies.

Children used to be seen and not heard; a return to that era is long overdue.

12

rank headed to the radio station, having endured a fitful sleep, where he dreamt the *Dial Deidre* listeners were burning him alive like the policeman in *The Wicker Man*. His latest column was doing a roaring trade online and had topped the figures for the adults-only café debacle.

He stared out the window at the Christmas decorations and wondered what the joke about Edward Woodward was, that had the punchline, "Ewar Woowar", when the taxi driver recognised him.

'You're that boy, To Be Frank, eh?'

'Yes, that is me,' he answered, deciding on the spot that he was at least going to sound the part.

The driver launched into a spiel. 'I loved that thing you wrote about belting the bairns. I've ordered a Lochgelly Tawse on eBay. It cost forty-five quid, but that's money well spent if you ask me. My missus is going nuts, like, as our laddie is only three, but I told her it's an investment. If the wee runt's anything like his old man, then he'll need his backside tanned on a regular basis. Never did me any harm. I've got my own cab, two guys who drive for me and corporate hospitality at Tynecastle.'

Frank was gobsmacked, a wave of anxiety washed over him as he pictured a genie flying out of a bottle. 'Glad to be of service,' he said, before swiftly changing the subject. 'Do you by chance know that joke with the punchline "Ewar Woowar"? It's to do with Edward Woodward – you know, *The Equalizer* who also played the cop in *The Wicker Man*?'

The driver said, 'Aye, it's why does Edward Woodward have so many D's in his name? Cos if he didn't, he'd be called Ewar Woowar. It's a belter. Haven't heard that in ages.'

'Same here,' Frank replied, chuckling.

They arrived at the studio, and he told the driver to keep the two pounds change, having decided to up his tip game.

'You're a gentleman; wait till I tell the missus who I had in my taxi. Can't wait to read your next column, Frank. What's it about?'

'German biscuits,' Frank said, leaving the driver with a quizzical look on his glaikit pus.

Arriving outside the BBC studio, he nervously pressed the button and spoke into the intercom.

'Frank Savage here for *Dial Deidre*,' he whispered into it. A twenty-something assistant, wearing a Two Door Cinema Club T-shirt, escorted him through to a reception area, where pictures of Deidre and various other Scottish FM presenters adorned the walls.

'Can I get you a coffee?' they asked.

'Thanks, I could murder one.'

'How do you take it?'

'Up the arse,' Frank replied, then instantly regretted it. 'Sorry, my Tourette's is playing up today – must be nerves and I'm on medication for my blood pressure and the gout. Just black is fine with two sugars, thanks. Sorry.'

Pretending to have Tourette's instantly placated the assistant and Frank made a note to self to use this in the future. He drank his coffee but was a bit gutted there were no biscuits or a wee bit of tablet with it as he checked the betting app on his phone.

He had given up on preparing for his grilling, deciding he would take whatever punishment Deidre and the listeners were going to throw at him – in for a penny, in for a pound.

A producer appeared, wearing a better brand of vintage

nineties trainers than the assistant, to take Frank through to Deidre's office. She was all smiles as he entered.

'My oh my, Frank Savage. It's been a while; how the bloody hell are you, Frank?' she asked in a posh Kelvinside accent, moving forwards to give him the obligatory hug.

'You see it all, love. Sweet as a nut.'

Frank had automatically started speaking in a nasal tone familiar to residents of deepest, darkest Leith. He had always dumbed it down around Deidre.

'You've certainly lit the blue touch paper with your recent columns, Frank. Ban the babies and dogs but bring back child cruelty! What else have you got in your locker?'

'I was thinking about doing something on how they should make Botox compulsory on the NHS,' he replied.

Deidre let out a half-hearted chuckle but quickly got down to business. 'I take it you know the format of the show. I'll provide a bit of background to your Bring Back the Belt column, then introduce you. We'll have a gentle to and fro, then I'll open the lines to callers. The producer will try and weed out the nutters but that's easier said than done. You'll be on for around thirty minutes, but we can cut that or extend it depending on how it goes.'

'Marvellous,' Frank barked. He was trying to stay calm but felt his palms getting clammy and the faint throbbing in his big toe added to his general sense of malaise.

'It really is good to see you, Frank. You're looking well. I met Bridget the other day in Stockbridge for a coffee. We like to hook up at least once a month for a blether. She was telling me about her latest book hitting the *Sunday Times* bestseller list.'

Frank rubbed his eyes with thumb and forefinger, a telltale sign for wanting the ground to swallow him up. 'Oh aye, tell her I'm not asking for her.'

'Don't be bitter, Frank. It doesn't suit you.'

They made a bit of small talk about folk they knew in the industry and who was doing what to whom, and then Deidre asked, 'Are you going to the opening of the youth theatre in Portobello on Friday? I imagine you're invited now that you're quite the local celebrity. I'm sure the hipsters will welcome you with open arms, handing over their kids for you to belt.'

Frank looked blankly back at her, then recalled that Naomi had mentioned something about it. 'Aye, I think I might pop along. Children are the future and all that.'

They made their way to the studio and Frank awkwardly put the headphones on and watched as Deidre took charge.

'Morning, listeners. This year marks the fortieth anniversary of the European Court of Human Rights finding in favour of two Scottish mothers who took their case – arguing that their sons should not receive corporal punishment by way of the belt – all the way to Strasbourg. From the start of the 1982 spring term, no pupil in Strathclyde or Lothian was ever belted again. These brave women were spat at in the street, shunned by friends, had bricks thrown through their windows and front doors vandalised with graffiti. They were up against the majority of Scottish MPs who had voted down a bill to abolish corporal punishment, local councils and teachers themselves who considered the fearsome two- or three-tail leather Lochgelly tawse as a vital weapon in their armoury against unruly pupils.'

Deidre paused for effect, letting her preamble sink in with the listeners.

'We are joined by controversial newspaper columnist, Frank Savage, whose recent piece advocating bringing back the belt has become a major talking point, shining a light on the behaviour of young people in Scotland's schools and across the wider society.

'So, today we are asking, is it time for the return of corporal punishment?'

The intro played, followed by a traffic report, thus giving Frank time to catch his breath and say a quick Hail Mary. All too quickly, they were back on air.

'What was the thinking behind the column then, Frank?'

A pregnant pause followed as he tried to get some words out of a mouth that was now as dry as the Gobi Desert.

Finally, blurting out, 'Thanks for introducing me, Deidre, and can I just say it's great to be here. Like most of my writing, it's based on the sort of chats people have in pubs or around the water cooler, if you prefer.' Deidre passed Frank a glass of water.

He continued, 'Can I just say that I acknowledge the efforts of those brave mothers and fundamentally agree with the decision to ban the belt that was taken forty years ago. It was the right choice at the time as things were getting out of hand and pupils could be belted for literally anything. But times have changed, and there's now a creeping lack of respect towards teachers that is seeping into all aspects of life.' Frank paused for effect.

'I know a couple of teachers and they've told me the little bastards, er, sorry, the pupils are getting away with murder. They recite their so-called rights like mini backroom lawyers on the one hand, then cause mayhem on the other. Glued to their phones, half of them struggle to read and write.'

Deidre twiddled with a ballpoint, before gesturing with her hands for Frank to expand his argument.

'The situation in schools has gotten out of hand and the Scottish government, with their curriculum-for-excellence bollocks, are making it difficult for teachers, and the endless bureaucracy leaves them unable to carry out the basic function of the job, which is to teach.' Frank took a large gulp of water, managing to spill most of it down the front of his shirt. 'So, I decided it was high time I addressed the issue. Hence the Bring Back the Belt column.'

Frank started to blush and felt like his blood pressure was veering into stroke territory, but realised he had to stand his ground, not for the first time wishing he'd done more research into the subject.

Deidre, all business, came in with, 'Thanks, Frank, and can I just remind you that this is a family show and we're ten hours away from the watershed.' She let out a condescending laugh.

'Sorry for swearing,' Frank replied meekly, feeling like one of those nutjobs you meet in pubs who tell you in minute detail how they carved someone up, before apologising for "swearing in front of your burd".

'So, your evidence for this is largely anecdotal?' Deidre said accusingly.

Frank was briefly distracted by the producer crouching down on the floor beside him, then came back hard.

'Yes, largely anecdotal from the very people at the frontline in our nation's classrooms, which are turning into battlegrounds. There are a million teachers' chat groups online; one's called Life After Teaching, and it's got thousands of members. They're leaving in droves, running for the hills and most of it is down to pupil behaviour. That and the crap pay.'

'And you believe hitting the pupils is the answer?' Deidre said, itching for a fight.

'Look, the column is there to generate debate and it's certainly worked.' Frank sat back in his chair, but Deidre had the smell of blood in her nostrils and wasn't letting him off the hook.

'But Frank, you haven't answered the question. Do you or don't you think it's a good idea to belt the pupils?'

'Yes, I believe some of the wee shits definitely deserve a slap,' he snapped, instantly regretting the second swear.

'There we have it, you're in favour of corporal punishment, and can you please try to curb your language, Frank. You're already on a booking,' she scolded.

'Maybe I need belting,' he replied, then realised it sounded a bit pervy. Frank squirmed but was getting angry.

Deidre was now rubbing her hands in glee.

'So, what about your own children, Frank, did you hit them?'

He saw that one coming and had his answer oven ready.

'My daughters are now grown-up, strong, independent women and I never had cause to belt them. Lucky for me, they had fantastic mothers who instilled in them the right kind of values. Treat people with the dignity and respect we all deserve.'

He was glad Naomi had been playing that Destiny's Child song this morning as his answer was mostly based around the lyrics.

'Okay,' Deidre said, 'let's open this up to our listeners. First on the line is Bobby from Portobello. Hello, Bobby.'

'Hi, Deidre, can I just say I think your show is barrie.'

Frank grinned as he recognised the dulcet tones of the caller.

'Thanks, Bobby,' said Deidre, before adding, 'so where do you stand on this issue?'

'I'm two hundred per cent in agreement with Frank. I think the column is brilliant and finally someone's had the balls to speak the truth.' Deidre quickly reminded Bobby to watch his language before prodding him to continue.

'There are too many snowflakes out there who let the kids away with murder. I heard of one school where a pupil identifies as a giraffe. It used to be children should be seen and not heard but now it's a case of the dog wagging the tail or whatever that saying is.'

Deidre warned him, 'Now, now, Bobby, let's not stray into gender issues. Please stay on point here.'

Bobby replied, 'Aye, the belt. It's a short, sharp shock that deals with the problem there and then. No need for endless forms to be filled out before the guidance teacher steps in and says what we used to call bad behaviour is ADHD. And another thing, no one gets expelled from schools these days as the headmasters, or whatever they call them, are too worried about how the figures and that look.'

Deidre, taking back control, said, 'Okay, Bobby, you've covered quite a lot there. Let's bring in Frank.'

Frank took another gulp of water. 'Hello, Bobby, I'm glad you liked the column.'

Bobby said, 'I think you're a fucking legend, man.'

At that point, Deidre cut the call and Frank burst out laughing.

'Sorry, listeners, we've had to cut the last caller off – this is a family show and there's no place for bad language at this time of the morning.'

Frank gave her the thumbs-up sign.

Deidre decided it was time for the weather forecast. Off air, she filled Frank in on problem callers.

'I mean, some of them make good points but they haven't got the vocabulary. It's becoming more and more of a problem. Scottish people can't seem to talk for more than five seconds without swearing.'

'Good point, Deidre. You did the right thing cutting that daft cunt off.'

Frank was fair enjoying himself by this point and readied himself for the next caller.

'Okay, let's go back to the phone lines,' Deidre said. 'We have Bella from Edinburgh on line three. Go ahead, Bella.'

'Hi, Deidre, love the show. I'd just like to ask Frank Savage how he would like it if someone pulled down his trousers and decided to give him a smack?'

Frank blushed and felt a familiar stirring in his loins. 'Hello, Bella. No one is talking about smacking anyone on the bottom, other than you. If I had cut through a church cemetery like the teenage boy who sparked the campaign all those years ago, then I'd have expected to be punished for it. We can't have people treating sacred places like churches as their personal playgrounds now, can we?'

Deidre had a puzzled look on her face and jumped in. 'So, Bella, what you're saying is that you're *against* bringing back the belt?'

'Yes, Deidre, that's correct. I remember back to the seventies when I was at primary school and my mum always used to say that the teachers are belting kids who are already getting hit at home. That's always stuck with me.'

'Yes, that's a great point, Bella. A lot of the children who misbehave may have a degree of trauma in their home lives that manifests itself in the classroom.'

Frank nodded in agreement as Deidre was about to bring him back in, but Bella interjected.

'Don't get me wrong, if consenting adults want to dress up and involve themselves with mild forms of bondage and M&S... sorry, I mean S&M, then I don't see that there's anything wrong with that. It's a private matter—'

Deidre made a tap-tap sign before cutting Bella off. Frank roared with laughter and kicked out his leg in a reflex motion, connecting with the crouching producer's backside, sending them tumbling to the floor.

13

Frank had a feeling of dread in the pit of his stomach as he got ready for the grand opening of the Portobello Youth Theatre. Although he loved to hold court in The Haddonfield after a few pints with friends, any kind of organised social event that involved hugs and air kisses made him anxious. He knew he'd be heading into the lions' den but was determined not to bite if anyone wound him up and had made plans to imbibe his weight in cheap ethanol with a light dusting of Class A drugs and to hell with the health consequences.

He had agreed to chauffeur Bobby, Bella and Naomi to the town hall in the Shadow even if the trip was less than a mile – something he was looking forward to doing. He'd park the car round the back of the town hall and pick it up the next afternoon when his blood alcohol levels had returned to that of a normal human being and the Valium had brought him down from the coke.

The Savile Row double-breasted whistle was getting another airing, red tie with ivory pocket square *de rigueur*, and he'd decided to wear his grandad's old pinky ring as a finishing touch. Frank was confident he could pull the pinky ring off but was all too aware that any trinket placed on the wrong hand screamed "wanker" and there was a fine line between sartorial elegance and spiv on the make.

The event was set to be a veritable who's who of Scottish

celebrity Z-listers. Richard and Bridget would be there, along with Dial Deidre; Kyle Horsburgh, the footballer; Caroline Decker, the Paralympian; and the actor Shelby St. George, who Frank knew from their days at Leith Academy when she went by the name of Sharon Henderson or Hendo's wee sister – her brother being one of the school's top three bampots.

Frank practised his looking-interested face in the mirror as he tied a Windsor knot and attempted a smile that made ex-Prime Minister Gordon Brown's scare-the-bairns grin look sincere. He phoned Falco to make sure they'd be sorted for E's and Wizz and the aging hippie gave him the 'Roger that' reply. Frank knew his relationship with drugs was up there with his relationship with the demon drink but on this occasion felt the need for an out ball. He filled his hip flask with Talisker ten-year-old single malt, taking a healthy swig straight from the bottle for luck, which hit the spot. Naomi looked the part in the Celine safari dress in lightweight gabardine beige that Frank recognised as once belonging to her mother. A tug at the heartstrings.

Bobby and Bella arrived shortly after and they headed along the high street in the Roller with Bella sporting her best "eighties Goth on a hot day in Princes Street Gardens" look, insisting she was sitting in the front. Frank popped the Canadian import of The Specials' eight-track cartridge into the player as 'A Message to You, Rudy' blasted out and they all sang along in tribute to lead singer Terry Hall, who had not long passed away.

As they pulled up outside the town hall, a small group of protesters had gathered holding placards proclaiming *Frank needs a Savage Belting* and *Not In My Café* with his face plastered on both. A single protester wearing a *Frank is a Wank* T-shirt and green Santa hat stood out from the crowd. Frank recognised him as wee Fitzy, the epileptic Hibs supporter who drank in The Hadd and was obviously at the wind-up, making a mental note to chin him later.

'Jesus wept,' he said. 'They better not touch the Shadow.'

Bobby shouted, 'Fuck a duck, Frank,' while Naomi chuckled, and Bella said she agreed with Fitzy and would give him a free pint.

'This is no laughing matter,' Frank declared, fighting the urge to immediately find Falco and bang a couple of Calvin Kleins up his hooter.

A protestor banged on the Shadow as Frank rolled down the window. They screamed in his face, 'How would you like it if someone beat your children? Bastard!'

Frank pleaded to no avail. 'Look, I understand why you may have a problem with me but the car and the other people in it are entirely innocent.'

This was met with a hiss of boos and a round of vitriol that would strip paint from the walls, so he just shrugged and rolled up the window. One of them sat on the bonnet, but Frank kept on driving round to the back of the town hall and parked. He had a word with a couple of wiry security guards with thick Northern Irish accents, telling them to keep an eye on the Roller and watch the protestor sitting on the bonnet. The guards' eyes lit up at the prospect of a bit of the old ultraviolence.

'Dead on, big man. That's a lovely motor you've got there,' the guard said, before pointing to the protestor and telling them in no uncertain terms to leave.

Frank and party entered the hall and made a swift beeline for the makeshift bar, grabbing a couple of champagne flutes each from the waiters who were dressed as characters from *Alice in Wonderland*. People were turning round to stare at them, and Frank noticed a couple of people pointing. He was beginning to feel like the guy caught dipping the poppy tin and imagined the main event of the evening would see him in stocks being pelted with tomatoes by kids, at the same time as a parent administered forty lashes. *Just give me the rum and sodomy*, he thought.

At that point, Santa, or a former football hooligan dressed as Santa, shouted 'Ho! Ho! Ho!' Brewster was going all out to do his bit for the community and had even gone to the trouble of giving Waffen, who was back to his Sunday name of Waffle for the night, a luminous Christmas dog lead and matching Santa outfit, which Frank thought made the dog look like an even bigger tit than its owner. Hoolie Santa approached Frank and handed him one of the sherbet lollipops he was dishing out.

'Suck on that,' he said, in a most un-Santa-like manner.

Frank eyed Brewster from head to toe and shook his head. 'I've heard of Bad Santa, so you must be Really Bad Santa.'

Brewster motioned aggressively with his head towards Frank before snapping his heels and approaching the celebrity huddle. The group lapped up Brewster and Waffle, with Deidre and Shelby St. George hanging onto his every word.

Richard approached Frank.

'Hi, Frank, great to see you here engaging with the readers and doing your bit for the local community. This is our target market; affluent professionals all too keen to support community initiatives like the youth theatre right here in good old Portobello.'

Frank gave him a flaccid smile. 'I see you've brought my ex-wife with you.'

Richard looked back at Bridget for help, but she was busy downing champagne and talking to Naomi.

'Er, yeah, she was keen to come and lend her support. It's not often Porty is graced with a famous author and so many celebrities.'

'Did you see the protestors outside? They're here because of me, Richard. I've managed to unite warring factions in a way Pérez de Cuéllar could only dream of.'

'Yes, I did see a guy in a Santa hat wearing a T-shirt with your name on, but don't bother about that. Remember, there's no such thing as bad publicity and you've certainly stirred up debate. The main thing is the bosses are delighted with your contribution and digital traffic has gone through the roof. That's all down to you, Frank, with my robust support, of course. I've got your back on this.'

By this time, Frank was looking over his editor's shoulders and whooped in delight as Falco, resplendent in black suit with matching fedora, made his entrance like a hippie version of Laughing Lennie Cohen. Mrs Falco the fourth, who was a good thirty years his junior and fit as a butcher's dug, was hanging off his other arm – the one not holding the skull cane. Falco acknowledged Frank by lofting the cane, then bringing it down to touch his nose. Bingo. Frank told Richard he'd spotted someone who wanted to speak to him and made his excuses, leaving the editor turning round gobsmacked at the sight of Falco and the Russian gymnast. Falco gave Frank a big hug.

'Frank, meet Olga. Olga, this is Frank; the third careful owner of the Shadow.'

'Pleasure to meet you, Olga. Any wife of Falco's is a friend of mine.'

Olga gave him a hard stare, then smiled. He almost went for the kiss on the hand but gave himself a shake there and then.

'So, you're the famous columnist. I like what you wrote about belting the children. Little bastards.'

'Thanks, Olga, that's much appreciated,' Frank replied, then made a note to self: *never mess with Olga.*

Falco took Frank to one side as Olga sashayed off to grab them some champagne.

'I've got the stash, man, all ready for the interval. And I've got a little bit of our friend kief to take the edge off later after I've sung a number with the youth theatre choir. I'm going to do "Big Chair, Little Stool" – track four on *Songs from Falco's Big Chair.* Like I said, the kids are hip to it and Olga plays a mean glockenspiel, so she can accompany me.'

Frank attempted to take this breaking news in.

'Wow. What a buzz, man. I can't wait for that.'

Falco smiled. 'It's not quite Montreux in '73 when I played with Carole King, but it's cool to be asked. Give a bit back, you know. Let the proles see what they've been missing all these years.'

A drama teacher from the youth theatre who Frank thought he recognised as "dead girl floating in the Clyde" from an episode of *Taggart* was going round the bar area telling everyone to take their seats in a sing-song voice. Naomi and Bella ushered Frank towards the stage and plonked him down in the front row with Naomi on one side and his ex-wife on the other.

'Hi, Bridge. Nice night for it,' he said.

Bridget patted him on his left arm and said, 'This is cosy,' as Richard pretended to be engrossed in the programme. The lights dimmed and Frank strapped himself in for an hour-long cacophony of precocious theatre brats committing grand larceny on a string of show hits. "The Worst Pies in London" kicked off the fun, sung by the drama teacher dressed as Mrs Lovett from *Sweeney Todd*. Frank winced as Mrs I-Fucking-Hate-It proceeded to give it the full bhuna before segueing into "Tomorrow" from *Annie* and introduced the lead singer, who happened to be a child of colour, accompanied by a teenage "Daddy" Warbucks wearing a bald cap with two assistants. This went down a storm with the hip parents knocking back the cheap shampoo. Give yourselves a pat on the back. If musical theatre was bad, then musical theatre performed by a bunch of show-off kids who should be out playing "tap-door-run" was the stuff of nightmares.

Frank looked around for Falco, who was sitting three rows behind him with a pained look on his face and, catching his eye, gave him the nod to head for the toilets. They piled into one of two cubicles, not caring who was in the other, as Falco banged out a couple of rock-star lines on the cistern and handed Frank a rolled-up tenner.

'This is dreadful,' Frank said. Falco nodded while tilting his head back and rubbing cocaine on his teeth. Frank joked, '"Don't put your daughter on the stage, Mrs Worthington." She'll never work again. I'm so glad my ex kept my daughter away from that madness. Nightmare.'

Frank hoovered up a line and felt a power surge through his body, glad that his new friend had brought the good stuff off the rock.

Falco said anxiously, 'I need a bump before I hit the stage in the second half.'

The party was interrupted by a knock on the cubicle door and a Russian accent calling, 'Falco. Let me in. I know you are in there with the drugs.'

Falco whispered through gritted teeth, 'Keep it down, Olga, do you want the whole world to know?'

He gave Frank the thumbs up before opening the door, allowing her to squeeze into the cubicle. Falco laid out a line for Olga as she bent over the cistern Betty Boop style, which stirred something in Frank's borders and shading. A wave of happiness swept over him; he felt blessed to be in the town hall toilets at the grand opening of the Portobello Youth Theatre snorting a line with an old hippie and his Russian gymnast wife. Their karma was interrupted by a loud bang on the toilet door.

'Is that Mr Falco and Mr Savage, the esteemed journalist, writer of shite and proud owner of a Rolls-Royce Mk II Silver Shadow?' It was Brewster.

Falco said, 'Peace out, brother. There's nothing for you here.'

Frank decided he was keeping his trap shut. There was an eerie silence as the trio in the cubicle waited on the inevitable explosion of rage. It never came and there followed an awkward period where they all stood silently, wondering if Brewster had left. Olga opened the door and peered out to see dying-for-a-line Santa staring back at her. She quickly shut the door.

'That man he is still here.'

Falco sighed and opened the door, motioning for Brewster to come in and urging him to 'Hurry up' as he laid out the coke. Brewster, by now in his element, squeezed into the cubicle and took hold of the rolled-up tenner.

'My, this is sweet. All friends together,' he said, before theatrically snorting and shouting, 'Bingo!'

Frank, who was leaning back eyeing him up but also squashed against the wall, imagined headbutting his nemesis on the bridge of the nose but let it pass. They all left with Brewster telling Frank, 'After you.' He had a lingering feeling of dread that this was not going to end well. Then parked it.

Mercifully, the interval had arrived, giving the audience a moment's respite from the torture and the opportunity to pour as much alcohol down their throats as was humanly possible while nibbling on tiny little cheeseburgers wrapped in brioche buns. Frank and co grabbed some drinks, while Falco slipped round the side of the makeshift bar to nick a couple of bottles of champagne, and they headed round the back of the building for a smoke. The designated smoking area was rammed as hardened tobacco merchants mingled with the "Can I pinch one of those after a shandy" brigade, and a couple of kiddy vapers hid behind the Shadow. Frank thought The Kiddy Vapers was a good name for a band, then realised he was shouting this aloud due to being off his tits and at the stage of the evening where he was talking tripe to anyone who'd listen. Bella and Bobby approached.

'Have you been on the bingo, Savage?' Bobby asked accusingly. Frank nodded sideways, then forwards and backwards.

Bella added, 'Lucky bastard. Was it your new hippie bestie who gave you it? Has he got any for us? I don't think I can stand any more show tunes and the second half is shaping up to be worse than the first.'

Frank tried to empty his brain of words, but none came forthwith as he felt a level of numbness somewhere between wisdom tooth extraction jag and the spinal anaesthetic given at a private hospital for keyhole knee surgery. Damn, Falco's gear was good. He noticed Brewster talking to the security guards and pointing over to them but was past caring about that thug. Naomi came over and he gave her a by now customary big hug. Never one for the hugging game, Frank had started hugging everyone who came within a five-mile radius – a by-product of his new-found infamy. She stood back and studied him, sussing that he'd been on something.

'I love you, pal,' Frank said, like a teenager with a weekend camping ticket for T in the Park.

'I love you too, Dad.'

He gave her another hug and praised the work she was doing.

'I think it's brilliant something is being done to restore the old Porty and bring it back to the people. Something that doesn't involve opening another fucking café serving six different varieties of banana loaf. The old Regency cinema has lain derelict for years and it's a bloody A-listed building. A design classic to boot. I'm so proud of you, my love.'

Frank then muttered, 'Sorry for being a shite dad and an absent father.'

Naomi told him to forget all that as it was in the past, looking over his shoulder to continue her watching brief on Brewster, who still hadn't twigged that she and Frank were related.

The second half was about to start, and Frank took his seat next to Bridget, placing a hand on his ex-wife's thigh in what he imagined was a comedic style. Bridget gave him a sarcastic smile that screamed, "Really, Frank", before moving the offending paw. He was instantly overcome with regret for blowing their marriage but quickly parked that as he settled down to watch the show and glance furtively sideways at how beautiful she was. The lights dimmed and five milkmaids, including two boys with milk churns over their shoulders, started to sing, "Who Will Buy?" from the musical *Oliver!* and Frank swore he heard the audience groan. He tuned in to the lyrics as the kid playing Oliver appeared to sing directly to him.

Frank shouted, 'G'aun yerself, wee man.'

This was greeted with a mixture of tuts and hisses that were drowned out by guffaws coming from Bobby and Bella. A man and woman in the row behind tapped Frank on the shoulder, giving him pelters. Frank heard the words, 'belting, café, columnist' and 'arsehole', smiling benignly back at them, which had the undesired effect of increasing their rage. The guy, who was wearing combat shorts in the middle of winter, was now kicking the back of Frank's chair. He was about to get up and chin him when Bobby intervened and had a quick word in the chap's ear which instantly shut him up.

The drama teacher was back on stage to introduce Falco, talking to everyone like they were five years old.

'One and all, we have a special treat for you tonight. All the way from America in the good ole US of A, via Joppa, we have a musician who was a huge star back in the 1970s. This man has played with all the greats including John Denver, Bob Dylan and Carole King, although some of you under the age of forty may be too young to remember them. In fact, make that fifty. His name is Falco and he's going to play us a song from an album he made in 1976 called *Songs from Falco's Big Chair*. So please put your hands together and give a warm Porty welcome for… Falco!'

The audience applauded and Frank squinted to see Falco carried onto the stage in an actual big chair accompanied by a group of theatre kids and, of course, Olga.

'Ladies and gentle cats of Port-Oh-Bell-Oh. It gives me great pleasure to be here tonight, playing for your delectation with the lovely Olga on glockenspiel.'

Olga gave a little bow. Frank was pissing himself with laughter now and whooping like he was at the front of a Rolling Stones gig.

'This one's called, "Big Chair, Little Stool". Take it away.'

This was the cue for Olga to begin the glockenspiel intro with Falco struggling to get down off the big chair as a prelude to face-planking onto the wooden stage floor. The audience gasped as he shooed away Olga, who had run to help him, motioning for her to get back to glockenspiel duty. The crowd held their breath, waiting to see if Falco would beat the ten-count. He slowly staggered to his feet, wiping blood from his grazed face and scrambling for the black fedora. Falco found the hat, flicking it back on his head.

'Trippy, man,' he cried.

The audience cheered. He signalled to Olga to start the intro again and she banged the glockenspiel like Keith Moon in his pomp. After what seemed like an eternity, Falco, who had slipped twice on his own claret, burst into song.

'Got me a big chair, gonna sit out front there on the porch.
'Yeah, got ma big old chair, sipping ma whisky and watching them birds a-flying.
'Mama, she got herself a little stool, but Mama didn't raise no fool.
'Cats be like licking, flies be like sticking.
'But y'all be cool, be cool...'

Falco was surrounded by children wearing straw hats, gingham shirts and dungarees, who formed a horseshoe facing the audience and sang the chorus.

'Big chair, little stool, gotta learn the shit they don't teach you in school.
'Big chair, little stool, gotta learn the shit they don't teach you in school.
'Big chair, little stool, gotta learn the shit they don't teach you in school.'

The parents in the audience were horrified as Falco had changed the word "stuff" back to "shit" at the last minute, without gaining written parental consent or giving prior warning. By this stage, Frank was in pain from laughing and had jumped to his feet, clapping and shouting along to the chorus. After playing for approximately twelve minutes with five repeats of the offending chorus, Falco finally finished to the sound of no hands clapping apart from Frank, who was urging Bella and Bobby to their feet.

'Bravo! Bravo! Maestro! More! More!'

Naomi and Bridget simultaneously pulled Frank back down as Richard put his head in his hands. The final forty-five minutes of the night included a rousing rendition of 'Let it Go' from the Disney movie *Frozen* before the finale, which consisted of songs from the smash-hit musical *Mamma Mia!*

Frank, who was by now in Abba jail, got to the end by finishing off the rest of the Talisker in his hip flask, which he shared with Bridget and Naomi, much to the consternation of Richard. The show was brought to a close by two drag queens – Crystal Hips and Ally Fun – belting out "Dancing Queen" with the youth theatre dance troupe showing off their disco moves along with a mix of ballet, tap and Highland.

Frank headed outside for a smoke to find a downbeat Falco being consoled by Olga.

'I thought you were amazing, man,' Frank said. 'Don't worry about that lot in there – absolute bunch of heathens.'

Falco laughed and dabbed his bloody nose with a handkerchief. 'Too kind, brother, too kind.'

Olga, showing concern for her husband, said, 'I have told him to go to the hospital and have this checked but he doesn't want to.'

'I'm not discussing it any further, my queen. Falco don't do hospitals. I ain't at the mercy of the man.' He brought the packet of coke out of his pocket and showed it to Frank. 'Besides, we've still got this to get through.'

'Too right, the show must go on,' said Frank. 'I'll meet you in the cubicle in ten minutes when the toilets are a bit quieter.'

Frank dodged a couple of parents who were giving him the evils and said hello to Deidre, who was having a fly fag with Bridget.

'Hi, Deidre. Looks like half your listeners were in there tonight. You could get at least three shows based on what we've witnessed, with plenty of talking points. Tap-tap, curly-wurly cuckoo.'

Deidre looked at Frank with a mix of pity and disdain, but Bridget was smiling at him with her eyes just like old times. She said, 'Still a big Abba fan, Frank?'

Frank shook his head in disgust. 'There's a special place in hell reserved for them, alongside Annie Lennox. She's the fifth Abba.'

Frank offered them one of his Marlboro Reds, which they both declined, so he wandered off to meet Falco and Olga for another blast, noticing on the way that Brewster had his arm round Kyle the footballer and appeared to be offering him some fatherly advice.

'Keep your high balls low, son.'

He knocked on the toilet door and resumed the party with Falco, who had perked up, and Olga. No sooner had they finished a line each than there was another loud bang on the cubicle door. Brewster, looking for another freebie. Olga shouted, 'Fuck off,' which resulted in the door being kicked so hard that it came off its hinges. Brewster stood in front of them and threw a white powder at Frank which landed on his tie. Frank immediately dabbed it and took a taste of icing sugar. The three of them struggled to comprehend what was going on and a mildly panic-stricken Frank saw that one of the security guards was filming on his mobile phone while the other, who had Waffen on a lead, kept watch on the door.

'What the fuck are you doing, Brewster?' Frank said.

'Just capturing this moment for posterity, Savage. Keeping a public record of what Scotland's most famous columnist gets up to in his spare time.'

Frank went for him but was held back by Olga as Billy Two struggled to keep control of the German shepherd who was going berserk.

'I'll have you, Brewster,' Frank yelled. 'I swear it. I'll suck your eyes out.'

Brewster looked shocked but quickly regained his bravado when he realised Billy One was still filming. He said, 'This is in the public interest, Savage. Showing people that you and your friends here are nothing but coke-heads.'

The toilet door swung open and Bobby charged in, landing a peach of a right hook flush on Brewster's chin, which sent his Santa hat flying as he fell to the floor. Olga stepped forwards and booted Billy One in the balls, making a grab for the phone. Billy Two moved forwards with Waffen, who sank his teeth into Olga's thigh, causing her to lose her grip on the mobile. A game of telephone tennis ensued with the mobile changing hands three times before Billy One, who had taken a beating from Olga, bolted out the door with the phone. Falco, who had been watching proceedings up to that point, emerged regally from the cubicle and cracked Billy Two over the head with his skull cane. He went down in a heap, letting go of Waffen and joining Brewster who was rubbing his jaw and moaning. Falco commanded Waffen to 'Obey' while signalling with the cane and the dog let out a gentle whimper, then went silent by its new master's side. Falco brought the skull cane above his head and made to put Waffen's lights out but stopped it short by an inch as Brewster let out a blood-curdling scream. 'No! Not Waffen, not my dog.' He scrambled for the toilet door with Frank toe-banging him up the crack of his arse. A crowd including Bridget, Dick Bell-end, Naomi, Bella, all the Z-listers, pissed parents and terrified children had gathered to witness the carnage in the gents.

Frank walked out and wiped the white powder off his tie. He made for the door, followed by his entourage, knowing things would never be the same. Fitzy, who was still wearing the green Santa hat and *Frank is a Wank* T-shirt, appeared to be having a seizure triggered by the disco lights. Frank stepped over him and headed up the high street.

14

Brewster nursed his swollen jaw and damaged pride as he poured himself a bowl of Coco Pops and waited for them to turn the milk brown. He opened his notebook to jot down his to-do list for the festive period. He had one of those Bic four-colour pens but had only ever used three out of the four colours, refusing point-blank to write in "Fenian bastard green". Switching to red, he wrote:

> Waterboard, castrate, hammer nails into his eyes, then murder that cunt Gurkha Bobby.
> Decorate Christmas tree.
> Fuck up Savage.
> Buy ibuprofen, paracetamol, giant kitchen roll, duct tape, family-sized lasagne, raspberry-flavoured Magnum ice creams, shortbread for Christmas presents and doggy treats.
> Order machine for taking blood pressure.
> Find out how that Naomi bitch knows Savage.
> Get dodgy Fire Stick for TV.
> Pay the Two Billys for waterboarding, maiming junkies, car, etc.
> Check out pre-sale Stone Island gear at Harvey Nichols.
> Cut tits off mad Russian burd.

Tell window cleaner he's not getting paid (smudges).
Batter hippy bastard to death with his own cane.
Take Waffen back to dog therapist.
Buy tickets for Pet Shop Boys UK tour.

He swallowed two painkillers and thought again about all the beatings Norrie had inflicted on him. The bruises on his arms that he hid with long-sleeved T-shirts, wearing tracksuit bottoms so no one saw the fag burns on his thighs and having to avoid the showers after PE class at school. Norrie, a natural sadist, had been a workmate of Brewster's father, Gordon, at the printers. According to the police, he was the last person to see him alive after he fell into the water at Leith Docks and drowned. The pair had been drinking together all afternoon and into the night. He was taken in for questioning but the detectives, although suspicious, couldn't prove he was involved in Gordon's death, which was registered as "accidental". Norrie then sought to console Marjorie the grieving widow and one year later the pair were married, young Brewster gaining a "new dad" and a pet python, with a half-brother on the way.

Although the physical scars inflicted by Norrie had healed long ago, the mental ones were still at the forefront of Brewster's mind and there was no way he was going to allow Savage and his cronies to get away with humiliating him in public. No siree, he would hit Frank where it hurt the most. In his pocket. Brewster propped up a couple of cushions and lay back on the sofa gently petting Waffen. At least the dog didn't answer him back, unlike fucking humans.

15

Naomi had never seen her dad so low as they rounded
the corner to the town hall car park and saw the job
Brewster and his thugs had done on the Shadow. Battery
acid had been poured all over the driver's side and bonnet while
the passenger's side was spared the acid so the new paint job with
the words "*Savig Is Ay Peedayfil*" were prominently displayed.
The all-Ireland spelling bee champions had also smashed the
back windows and slashed the tyres.

Naomi took some relief from the car being undriveable, so
a still-drunk Frank wouldn't be able to take it the short distance
home. She consoled her dad, then phoned Bobby to explain the
situation, telling him to find a giant sheet like the type used by
painters and decorators to cover the Shadow. Bobby said he'd
arrange for his mechanic mate to come and tow the car to his
garage so they could assess the damage, with Naomi's main
concern being not to involve the police. Frank was now in full
"Don Corleone after they shot Sonny in *The Godfather*" mode.

'Look how they massacred my car.' He was crying tears of pure
vodka and patting the Shadow like it was a family pet, swearing
vengeance on Brewster. 'I'm going to kill that fucking "help the
janny" class idiot. I've had enough. I don't care any more. I'm
going to have that cardboard gangster's head on a platter.'

Naomi's mind raced as she weighed up the situation, trying
to deal with the immediate problem to hand, which was to get

her father out the way, before figuring the best way to deal with Brewster without jeopardising the cinema project. At least Bobby grasped the gravity of the situation, but he was another one who clearly wasn't going to let this lie and had now decided he was going to kidnap Brewster's dog. She told her dad he should go home and try to get some sleep, then had a word with Bobby, telling him to bring Bella, Falco and Olga to the house this afternoon for a crisis meeting.

Naomi needed to speak to the Wise One to explain the situation with Frank and Brewster while giving him assurances that she was in complete control. She quickly realised that speaking to her boss was a bad idea at this stage, as explaining that shitshow at the town hall would demonstrate the opposite of her being a safe pair of hands. She had a duty to get the lid back on things before they escalated and spiralled downwards. The Wise One would not be amused if he found out how Brewster was behaving, but Naomi also lived daily with the knowledge that she worked for criminals and had so far done a decent job of pretending she wasn't like them, while completely understanding their mindset.

The buck for Brewster stopped with her, for now anyway. She had been around the Syndicate long enough to know that everyone was disposable and could be "disappeared" at the drop of a hat if that proved to be the easiest solution to any problem that threatened the bottom line. It was always the money, never the principal. Uncle Ray taught her that on day one. Naomi was good at compartmentalising her thoughts and the one marked *you work for criminals* had been buried deep in the recesses of her mind, but recent events had pushed it high up the list for auditing and having to lie to her dad wasn't easy.

She decided to pay Brewster a visit, which he would no doubt be expecting after last night's events. His nose would be bothering him as to her relationship with Frank and she'd prepared a ready-made cover story to nip that one in the bud. It was also an opportunity to gauge his mood towards her dad while getting a handle on extracurricular activities involving the boys from across the water.

She prepared the prearranged "Bat-Signal" to meet Brewster in Daisy Park within the hour. Going to his home was a definite no-no as the police and possibly rival firms could be watching him. Naomi preferred to meet in the open air anyway and the thought of going to Brewster's Hammer House of Horror filled her with dread, as she shooed away thoughts of killing the thug. That wasn't her. She was a decent person who was just going through a transitional period and probably needed a career change, given that working for the UK's largest criminal network was proving a bit stressful. The Wise One was well into his seventies and wouldn't be around forever, so, at some point, she'd be able to get out, hopefully with a big bag of loot. Either that or they'd feed her to the pigs.

Naomi was starting to crave a quiet life, with a steady job and a normal phone, coming home to make herself dinner and watch Netflix. She'd get the endometriosis under control and sort out a form of contraception that might help ease the crippling pain. Regular trips to the gym and the odd night out with "the girls", whoever they may be. There may even be space for someone else and she'd come clean with her dad. But before all of that, she had to deal with Brewster.

Naomi was sitting in Daisy Park, which was covered in a thin blanket of white snow that reminded her of freshly laundered sheets. The bracing cold air pinched the skin and made her feel alive. This park was her favourite place in the world right now. She went there every day after long walks along the promenade and through Portobello to gather her thoughts and plan her next three moves to stay ahead of the game. Brewster was late but she wasn't bothered. Naomi was enjoying the moment of calm.

Her attention was drawn to the ornate drinking fountain, a memorial to Dr Hugh Dewar, who looked like a handsome, sharp-featured, clever Scotsman, typical of the period. He had lived from 1866–1914, which would make him forty-eight when he died. A bit young.

The plaque read: '*This fountain has been erected in remembrance of Dr Hugh Dewar, Portobello, by his grateful patients and numerous friends who deplore the loss in prime manhood of a kind friend and a skilled and beloved physician. His quiet charity was known to the needy. 1866–1914.*'

Naomi thought he must have been killed in the early days of World War I, perhaps tending to the wounded soldiers at the First Battle of the Marne. She'd enjoyed learning about the Great War at school. Intrigued, she googled him. The first thing that came up was an article with the headline *Monument to a Murderer* and the second was a detailed description of the death during childbirth of Jane Anderson, who died aged twenty-five in 1914. Naomi read both and it transpired the good doctor in "prime manhood" had somehow managed to pull out, almost intact, the fifteen-foot long mucous membrane lining of the maternal intestine after noticing a tube and remarking, "Here is something that should not be here". Eyewitnesses including Jane's mother watched as Dewar pulled out the tube in rolls over two yards long and placed it in a chamber pot. The subsequent autopsy found that Jane died in "great agony" three hours after the birth of her healthy son. The report in the *Journal of the Royal Society of Medicine* said that in the course of delivery, Dewar's forceps had punctured the posterior wall of the vagina, producing an acute rectovaginal fistula "large enough to admit the introduction of the hand". Dewar was later arrested, taken from Portobello to Edinburgh Central Police Office and charged with culpable homicide. He was found with a "considerable quantity of poison" but was admitted bail of one hundred and fifty pounds and returned to practice. With a pending trial and civil proceedings for criminal negligence, he was found dead from an "overdose of narcotic poison". He'd gone out on a high.

'*And they built him a fucking fountain,*' Naomi shouted to herself. What was it with Edinburgh and statues, monuments and plaques to horrendous white men? Bad enough with the slave traders, but drinking fountains to honour murdering halfwits? She considered this and thought about fundraising for an alternative plaque that would read: '*In memory of Dr Hugh Dewar, an imbecile who "accidentally" butchered a young mother to death by pulling out her innards. Enjoy the daisies if you can find any.*'

Naomi thought about her dad, another selfish man who was becoming a bit of a liability, then scolded herself for being so unkind. She did love him. It wasn't Frank's fault she'd become involved with the Syndicate, but Naomi had been thinking a lot about the past and was starting to resent his absence from her childhood. Normally black men got the bad rep for leaving but to her that was lazy racial stereotyping. The problem was men who pleased themselves, period, as the Yanks would say.

At that point, Brewster entered the *Daisy Park of Death* sans Waffen, who was probably still traumatised from last night's encounter with Falco. Naomi took great pleasure in seeing an ugly purple bruise on his chin.

'You're late,' she scolded.

'Fuck off,' he replied.

They both sat on the bench across from the fountain facing Dr Death. Brewster was wearing one of those designer parkas from North America that screamed "drug dealer".

Naomi opened the proceedings. 'That was some carry-on last night. I heard Frank Savage's Rolls-Royce was vandalised. Was that your handiwork?'

Brewster laughed, then stared quizzically at her. 'Nope. I hurt people, not cars.'

'Yeah, I can tell you're really hard,' Naomi replied, biting her bottom lip.

Brewster was kicking the snow and trying to appear nonchalant. 'How the fuck do you know Savage, anyway?'

Naomi never skipped a beat. 'He knew my mother. She was a singer in London, and he'd interviewed her for a magazine. A piece about black backing singers from the 1980s.' Naomi had decided to give him a kernel of information about Maxine, hoping that would pique his curiosity for now, but the chances are he would find out soon enough that Frank was her dad. Brewster was still trying to act cool and merely nodded but his beady eyes, like piss-holes in the snow, gave him away.

Ignoring his stare, Naomi continued. 'Savage could be useful to us in terms of providing publicity for the youth theatre, the women's football team and the cinema. It pays to keep journos onside.'

Immediately, this felt like an overreach, so she decided to turn the conversation around.

'More to the point. What's the deal with you and Savage? We can't have anything jeopardising our plans for Portobello, and fighting in toilets over cocaine, then pouring acid over a motor, is the opposite of flying under the radar and keeping a low profile.'

Brewster was clearly rattled but Naomi clocked that he didn't deny damaging the Shadow.

'Don't worry about Savage; I've got plans for him and his Paki mate.'

She stared at the Dr Dewar plaque, trying to shake the image of the skin being taken off a giant sausage, as the rage boiled up inside her.

'Leave it. You've had revenge, we need you to be professional. And dial down the casual racism. The Wise One is coming up for New Year and we don't want any local drama with things as delicately poised as they are. We must show him we're in control up here, that's in both our interests, and it doesn't pay to cause havoc, especially with high-profile columnists like Savage. How do the two of you know each other, anyway?'

Brewster shook his head and pulled the hood of his parka up and down like a sulky teenager. 'We were at school together, way back in the dim and distant past. We got on okay for a while and were kind of mates, but that quickly changed. Savage thinks I had something to do with his brother's death and he's hated me ever since.'

Naomi was shocked – Frank had never spoken much about her Uncle Michael's death, only saying that he'd died after a fall at the derelict open-air pool, with everyone else in the family suspecting suicide. She stayed silent, trying to make her face as neutral as possible.

Brewster stared across the park. 'He's written a load of shite about me over the years, trying to insinuate I was a paedophile and implying I was a grass. That gave me no end of grief in the jail.'

Now it was Naomi's turn to look cool as she prepared to casually ask the next question. 'And did you kill his brother?'

Brewster laughed, then said, 'No comment.'

Naomi strained every sinew to keep her anger at bay. She'd asked enough and he was bound to get suspicious if she probed further. Brewster switched back into hard-man mode.

'So, is there any point to this meeting or were you just dying to see me? Why have you got me out here in the freezing cold?'

Naomi felt the mobile in her raincoat pocket, the one with the voice recorder switched to "on". She said, 'Like I was saying earlier. We don't want any more grief with the locals. That comes from the top. It ends here.'

Brewster just sat there smirking, leaving Naomi in no doubt that things were certainly not going to end there. She was thinking on her feet now and wanted to probe him about the Belfast guys and find out if he was planning to make use of the mobile footage that appeared to show her dad doing coke.

'Who are those guys from Northern Ireland that you were with last night and why was one of them filming Savage and his mates in the toilets? You need to be careful if you're outsourcing Syndicate business.'

Brewster looked her up and down with contempt. 'Don't you worry about the boys. Good Protestants, very capable. I've known them for years. They know what side their bread's buttered, not like those North London ponces with their kippah caps. I thought it was wise to get a little bit of leverage on our good friend, Mr Savage. Call it an insurance policy. I've got friends in the media as well you know.'

He let that sink in with Naomi, but she wasn't impressed.

'The lads are helping me push gear and they've got local knowledge as they've been in Edinburgh before and know how soft it is. Believe me, these fellas can handle themselves.'

That was all the confirmation Naomi needed to convince her that Brewster was setting up his own firm and planning to go solo in the capital. It would bring him into conflict with the Syndicate, she would make sure of that, but he was clearly thinking the Wise One was vulnerable and could be taken out. The question was when.

She said, 'The Wise One is coming up for a visit around Hogmanay and wants to see us. You and I are to give him a full report on how the cinema project is progressing with the councillors and he wants to get a feel for the lie of the land. That's it, that's the meeting. Keep your head down. Last night was completely out of order and not acceptable.'

Brewster rubbed his sore chin but took the telling. Things were coming together nicely for him.

Back at Ramsay Tech, the crisis meeting was creating more of a crisis than dealing with one. Bobby was adamant that kidnapping Waffen was the way to proceed.

'I'm doing it; the sedative is ready and my contact at the dog and cat home has a kennel waiting. I want to hit Brewster where it hurts, go on the attack, give the dog a bone.'

Naomi rubbed her eyes, then massaged her temples. 'God give me strength.'

Olga, who had a bandage on her thigh where Waffen had sunk his teeth into her, was also in no mood for peace talks.

'I have to get a tetanus jab in my ass. That Santa bastard must pay. I will chop his balls off and take the head off this dog.'

Frank was still distraught, with the Shadow on life support, but the image of Olga getting a tetanus jab in her ass was providing him with temporary relief.

Bella, like Olga, thought the best solution was to tamper with Brewster's nut sack.

She shouted, 'Off with his balls! I heard he's only got one anyway, like Hitler, his hero.'

They all laughed before breaking into a chorus of, *'Brewster has only got one ball...'*

Falco, who was wearing full biker gear, banged his skull cane on the wooden floor and told everyone to 'Chill.'

Naomi decided to take charge.

'Kidnapping the dog is the dumbest thing I've heard in a long time, so bin that idea. We need to keep our heads down and wait for Brewster's next move. I reckon at some point he'll use the mobile footage to try and blackmail you, Dad, or he may offer it to the tabloids for cash through a third party. So, be prepared for him or one of his cronies to get in touch.'

Frank, who was starting to see sense through the fog in his brain, nodded in agreement.

He said, 'Brewster knows I won't play so he'll likely try and punt the footage or, at the very least, leak it online. I can deal with all of that. Naomi is right about keeping our heads down. Brewster is a pain in the arse and has wormed his way into the community, but it's only a matter of time before he royally fucks up. That's a guarantee, as sure as day follows night.'

Bella was still seeking payback. 'I agree with Bobby; we've all suffered at the hands of this bully and it's time to go on the offensive. Maybe not kidnapping his dog but certainly finding a way to smear him with the luvvies at the youth theatre. He needs to be exposed for the racist twat we all know he is.'

Naomi pleaded with the group. 'Look, none of us are gangsters. We're all just decent folk trying to get on with our weird and wonderful lives. This guy is bad news. Frank is right. He's been in jail before and is bound to be doing something illegal, drug dealing and, no doubt, heavy violence. He's already shown his hand as a blackmailer, into extortion. It's highly likely he'll come a cropper either with the police or he'll choose to mess with the wrong people.'

Falco, who until now hadn't said much, decided to speak up. 'I agree with Naomi and Frank. I don't like this Brewster cat at all. Just like the rest of you, I think the guy is one nasty piece of cheese. But we ain't vigilantes, at least I'm not. Olga here can get a bit fiery. Her great grandad died at Stalingrad, and she hates Nazis. I know the path of least resistance leads to crooked rivers and crooked men, but for now I vote we do nothing.'

Naomi raised her hand. 'I second that.'

Frank raised his hand. 'I third that.'

Bella raised her hand. 'I fourth that.'

Olga held up five fingers.

Bobby said, 'I'm nicking his dog.'

16

Richard struggled to open the packet of wasabi included in his favourite box of sushi – eight pounds fifty from the posh supermarket in Comely Bank – that he had for his lunch every Monday. He tried to bite it open with his teeth before phoning Morag, asking her to bring him in some scissors. Richard loved the wee black plastic fork folded in the box and the bits of ginger that he lovingly placed on top of the sushi, part of his weekly ritual along with the bottle of Belgian chocolate milk to wash it all down and the yoghurt pot with a separate compartment for the raspberry compote that he had for afters. Astronaut food. The whole experience reminded him of playing with his Action Man Polar Explorer as a child through to his early thirties, and the various accoutrements that came with it like tennis racket-shaped snowshoes, winter goggles, ration packs, a compass and utility belt. Morag came into his office, handed him the scissors without saying a word, then about-turned, gently shaking her head. He got back to work, surgically removing the tail piece from the end of a prawn that might have been a shrimp, placing it in a bit of kitchen roll to be taken to the bin marked "food waste". Richard clicked on the mobile footage sent to him from the email address brew1690ftp@hotmail.com and delicately tried to balance a block of white sticky rice on his tiny fork. He expanded the screen and watched as Frank stared back at him, covered in a white substance that appeared to be cocaine. He turned the sound up and could just about make out Frank saying, 'What the fuck are you doing, Brewster?' There followed a scene of absolute carnage with a chap who Richard recognised as Frank's friend launching a ferocious right-hander onto Mr Brewster's chin, sending him flying, to the sound of an angry dog barking off screen. At that point the footage went wobbly, with crackly sounds as the phone crashed to the toilet floor. It appeared to change hands several times, with the camera showing the ceiling, then the floor, then the dog, then Mr Brewster on the floor cradling his chin with blood pouring from his nose, then a Russian woman calling him a "fucking bastard" and that singer guy, Falco, holding a stick with a skull on the end above his head. Richard also heard the words, 'I'll suck your eyes out,' before the person holding the mobile phone ran out of the toilet, through the theatre towards the car park. The footage ended there.

Richard had been in the journo game long enough to know this short film was far from conclusive proof that his star columnist was a drug-taking deviant, given that the person holding the phone had managed to film the white powder landing on Frank's tie. No doubt this would be sorted in the editing before Mr Brewster sent this "gold dust to the tabloids" that he had alluded to in his email. Richard knew that his star columnist *was* a drug taker and certainly a deviant, but he was also a digital hit-making machine who had single-handedly dragged the paper out of the gutter. He saw that his phone was flashing, as the "Don't Stop Believin'" ringtone filled the room.

It was Brewster. 'Have you watched the video, Richard? I told you it was gold dust, and the tabloids will absolutely lap it up.'

The editor stalled for time. 'Yes, I watched it, and it certainly appears to show that some form of illegal substance is being taken.'

Brewster interjected. 'Surely that's enough to sack that fucking reprobate? He's toast, I'm telling you. Fucking toast.'

Richard sought and failed to diffuse the situation. 'Now let's not jump the gun here.'

'Jump the gun? Jump the gun! I've given you the gun, a big smoking one. Surely, you have to get rid?'

Richard, although a little bit scared of Mr Brewster, was fanatical about his digital hits and traffic to the website, to the point where Frank would have to get caught in the act of buggering a sheep for him to even consider a suspension let alone a sacking. And even if that were to happen, he could still see how his recently acquired star columnist getting filmed buggering a sheep could generate even more clicks. Win-win.

'I'm not sure it's proof enough, Mr Brewster. I mean, the film starts with the white powder being clearly thrown at Frank, then everything gets a bit shaky and is difficult to make out.'

Brewster went from calm, reasoned pillar of the community, willing to lend a hand at the local foodbank and help old people across the road, to *Scarface* final scene in the blink of an eye.

'Difficult to make out? Difficult to make out! He's covered in top-class Peruvian marching powder. In a fucking toilet cubicle at the opening of a fucking youth theatre. With a Russian prostitute, an American draft-dodging hippie, and a Paki – sorry, Pakistani – kitchen porter. Difficult to make out, my arse.'

Richard told Brewster that Bobby was from Nepal, not Pakistan, which seemed to rile him even more.

'Listen, you piece of journo shit. I don't give a monkey's what Paki country he's from. I was sucker-punched by one of his cronies and assaulted by Savage himself, who kicked me in the buttocks. I'm still struggling to sit down – my arse is killing me – and you're defending this reprobate. Un-be-fucking-lievable.'

Richard concentrated on his breathing, going in through the nose, out through the mouth, that he and Bridget were working on at the Pilates class she had started taking him to.

'Look, Mr Brewster,' he said, voice shaking. 'Frank Savage is certainly no friend of mine, but there are wider issues here.

I must consider the commercial interests of the organisation and, whether we like it or not, Savage is an asset for us at this time. Now, I'm not saying that won't change and obviously he'll be judged in the court of public opinion, but I don't think this footage, viewed on a standalone basis, is grounds enough for instant dismissal at this juncture. I will be speaking to Frank about this and will carry out my own robust investigation. Have you contacted the police?'

'I don't do police,' growled Brewster, 'I'm not a grass. You're a weakling. I should have known better than to come to you first, someone who takes sloppy seconds from Savage, scraps from the master's table. But don't you worry, mate. I've contacted the guy from *Daily News*, and they want to view the footage. No doubt they'll pay top doll-ah. Savage is finished. This will go virus or whatever they call it.'

He hung up, leaving Richard to get back to his sushi. The editor picked up his fork and noticed his hand was completely steady as he balanced a block of sticky white rice on it and smiled at the picture of him with Lorraine Kelly. A new email had dropped in his inbox from the deputy editor with the weekly page view figures.

Hi folks,

The hits just keep on coming!

Yet another momentous weekend saw us reach a key milestone in our online journey, with the editorial content team crashing through the four million weekly page view barrier.

Giant pats on the back all round and did I hear someone mention raspberry doughnuts? Shout-out to our esteemed columnist, Frank Savage, the Erling Haaland of online page views, for his robust Bring Back the Belt masterpiece. The bionic penis story has entered its third month and is still managing to stick rigidly to the top five.

I imagine Richard will have his hands full come awards season and that's in no small measure to the efforts of our dedicated team. We are all truly blessed to work with such a talented group of people. Top five stories, copied below, show a range of columns, breaking news, sport and feature content. Keep up the amazing work.

Alasdair Stewart (BA Hons)
Deputy Digital Editor News Content
Twitter: @futurenews

BRING BACK THE BELT! TO BE FRANK: 1,455,218
LOW ROAD TAKEN STAR IN FORT KINNAIRD ROAD RAGE RAMMY: 764,337
SAVAGE PROTESTS AT OPENING OF PORTY YOUTH THEATRE: 682,966
BAY CITY ROLLERS HOLOGRAM SET FOR ROSS BANDSTAND: 393,576
TRANENT MAN WITH BIONIC PENIS STOPPED AT AIRPORT: 154,011

Frank scanned the weekly figures and saw that he had broken the golden rule of journalism and was now becoming the story. Although there was no mention of Class A drugs, the *Savage Protests at Opening of Porty Youth Theatre* headline in his own paper left him in no doubt that the "looking after one of our own" mantras was not on the agenda when it came to the all-important digital clicks. Still, he thought, it could have been worse, like if he had a metal cock and couldn't pass through airport security.

There had been no word from Brewster, but Frank had an ominous feeling of a storm Brewstering and was starting to feel the crabs nibbling at his big toe – a sure sign that trouble was just around the corner. The damage to the Shadow was irreparable and although it could be driven again, it would always have the faint outline of "*Savig Is Ay Peedayfil*" on the passenger side and acid marks rendering it unsellable. This scuppered Frank's Plan B for paying back The Gypsy, which had been to sell the car if he struggled to meet the five grand monthly payments. He'd already phoned HR to tell them he wanted to encash his entire pension pot; at the very least that would cover the first few months and Frank reckoned he'd be earning a fortune by then as his career went stellar and the bets came in.

He thought about Naomi and how she was leaving Ramsay Tech between Christmas and New Year to move into one of Bella's flats at the bottom of Bath Street. Doing well for herself. A nice spot; Frank had spent most of his childhood down there playing at the amusements and eating quarter-pounds of sweets from Mrs Webber's. Soor plooms and Berwick cockles. He remembered the crazy golf and the paddling pool, playing football for Porty Thistle at the old Volta pitch and swimming in the saltwater at the baths, then him and Michael washing their hair with that pink carbolic soap before getting chips from the van with lashings of brown sauce.

Frank was letting his mind wander down the cobblestoned lanes of his seaside past. He reminisced about long summers spent at their granny's house in Regent Street which had a bohemian feel in the seventies, full of artists and models and was cool long before the present-day hipsters arrived. She ran it as a guest house and told him and Michael to keep an eye on the lodgers. Frank remembered one guy in particular who they thought was a spy. He watched BBC2, "the weirdo channel", and had a beard, therefore a slam-dunk – he was working for the Russians. What was the name of that old guy who swam in the freezing sea every day, towel under his arm, wore a blazer over his bare chest? Ned Barnie, that was him. A swimming teacher perhaps. Swam the English Channel – the first and oldest Scot to do it. The Porty folklore was coming at Frank thick and fast now but all too soon Michael flashed into his mind and thoughts of long summer days spent at the open-air pool, playing on the raft and whooping with delight at the wave machine, while praying no one had put chewing gum on the slides. Happy times that had left Frank with an aching sadness that seeped down into the pit of his belly. Michael slagging him because he thought

Portobello mushrooms were from Portobello and Frank teasing his wee brother for being scared to jump off the top diving board. Still too soon. Next month would be the anniversary of his brother's death and Frank felt the pain like an open wound. Fucking Brewster.

He made his way down to The Shore Bar and Restaurant in Leith for the annual newspaper columnist's bash. A raucous affair with decent grub, he was looking forward to revelling in his own success and rubbing it in a bit with the politics guys from *The Herald* and *The Scotsman*, trapped in their own version of *Groundhog Day*, writing the same five columns on a loop about Scottish Independence.

Quislings! Traitors! Yoons! Romans! Countrymen!

Pale, male and stale was something of an understatement at this night out with only two women invited, Maureen Bateman from the *Daily News* and Diane Harris from the *Mail*, who could both drink the men under the table and swore like troopers. He always thought it a bit sad that his female journo contemporaries had no choice but to adopt the attitude of having to be tougher than the men to exist in a male-dominated environment but he noticed how things were slowly changing for the better.

Frank rounded the corner at The Shore and saw Detective Inspector Bob Hope, an old contact from his tabloid days, walking towards him. He heard footsteps behind and saw two plain-clothes detectives leaning against the railings at the water's edge. Backup.

'Hello, Frank,' Bob said, extending his hand in friendship. 'Long time no see; I was wondering if I could have a quick word with you round at the station.'

Frank nodded but his mind raced towards Naomi and his friends, concerned for their safety.

'Is everything all right?'

DI Hope told Frank not to worry as he escorted him back round the corner towards Leith police station.

'Like I said, Frank, just a quick chat on a formal basis, then I'll give you the heads-up once we're outside. Shouldn't take too long and you can get on with your night out.'

Frank had a long-standing relationship with DI Hope going back to his days on the red top. They first met when Bob was a regular in The Haddonfield, working out of Portobello police station, and he'd enjoyed a brief fling with Bella. Frank had spotted early doors that Bob liked to be the man "in the know", had a fondness for the finer things and was taken in by the idea of having contacts in the media. A chance remark where Hope had asked Frank 'What's in it for me?' after dropping a titbit of information on a celebrity footballer being arrested for battering his girlfriend led to the beat bobby going on the reporter's unofficial payroll. Bob enjoyed a prolific run after that, earning a small fortune, providing information on stories ranging from a serial killer's past as a police cadet to a ring of top judges using rent boys for private parties in the New Town.

Frank entered the police station in Queen Charlotte Street, situated within the old town hall, having been there many times before on journo business and once for a "lie doon" after jumping naked into the Water of Leith to win yet another drunken bet with Bobby. DI Hope led him to an interview room where a brown folder was placed on a desk. The duty sergeant offered to stay but Hope said that wouldn't be necessary, telling him to bring them two cups of tea with two sugars in each.

'I'm sorry to bother you, Frank, but I want to run something by you that concerns your daughter.'

Frank was taken aback. 'Naomi? You want to talk to me about Naomi? I don't understand.'

DI Hope was giving it his usual respectful cop routine but Frank was anxious for him to cut to the chase and felt his face turn burning red.

'We've been watching your old friend Brewster, who's back in town as you know. I heard about your altercation with him at the opening of the youth theatre in Portobello the other night, but that's not why I've brought you in. Obviously, I know you and him have previous—'

Frank was rattled. 'Okay, spare me the preamble. What are the scores on the doors, Anthea?'

DI Hope opened the brown folder and brought out a classic police surveillance photograph of two people sitting on a bench. Naomi and Brewster. Frank knew this was taken at Daisy Park as he recognised the fountain for that doctor who killed the mother giving birth.

'I'll kill him,' Frank cried. 'What is that cunt doing harassing my daughter? And more to the point, what are you lot going to do about it?'

The sergeant came in with the cups of tea and a plate of dark chocolate digestive biscuits. This momentarily distracted Frank, who considered the dark chocolate digestive to be the numero uno in the biscuit world but preferred them to have been in the fridge and these weren't McVitie's. Cheap seats. DI Hope broke one of the imposter digestives in half before dunking it into his tea.

'Brewster is a person of interest to us, which should come as no surprise. The fact he appears to be meeting with Naomi puts her on our radar, but our main concern is for your daughter's safety. We don't know for sure if he was meeting her or just decided to sit there and try to chat her up. The surveillance team say it looked like they knew each other and spoke for about five minutes. So, the obvious question is why? And if that's the case, what were they talking about?'

He let that sink in as he reached for another biscuit and snapped it in two before continuing.

'This is just us doing a bit of due diligence, tying up loose ends. To mark your card, Frank, about the company your daughter might be keeping and to pick your brains to see if there's anything in this that we should be concerned about.'

Frank was shocked. There was a chance that Brewster and Naomi had met the other night, but he was too out his face to remember them speaking and he never saw them together. For once he was lost for words but knew whatever came out of his mouth next was crucial and his only concern was for his daughter's safety.

'Look, Bob, you're clutching at straws here. That's a picture of Naomi sitting on a bench, and I presume Brewster has sat beside her, not the other way about? I want you to have a word with that rodent and tell him to keep away from my daughter.'

Frank was desperate to get Bob out the police station and find out what the score really was with Naomi. He sensed his old compadre was holding back and sticking to the script in front of his fellow officers. He decided to play along with this charade of an interview.

'Look, Bob, my daughter works in finance; she's a high-flyer up from London to oversee the redevelopment of the old Regency picture house on Porty High Street. Private equity, that's what she does. Naomi's a women's footballer for Christ's sake, she's not into anything dodgy.'

DI Hope let that sink in, before adding, 'I loved that cinema. Saw my first film there. *The Green Berets* starring John Wayne.'

Frank smiled. 'Me and you both, Bob. I remember my old man taking me to see my first film there as well. *Snow White and the Seven Dwarfs*. But we had to leave as I cried at the Evil Queen.'

Bob shifted uneasily in his chair.

'Anyway, Frank. Now I'm not saying Naomi is wittingly involved in anything criminal and we know the private equity firm she works for is a legitimate enterprise or it certainly appears that way.'

Frank nodded in agreement.

'Look, Bob, this is out of order. My daughter is no criminal and doesn't associate with people like Brewster.'

Bob was all apologetic now.

'I'm sorry for bringing this up, Frank, and no one is inferring anything about Naomi. I just need to eliminate her from our inquiries. That's standard procedure.'

Frank played reasonable. 'I know, Bob. I know and I appreciate the heads-up. I really do. Now that I think about it, she may have been introduced to Brewster at the opening of the youth theatre. I know for a fact he's involved in that. So, their paths are bound to have crossed given they're both involved with community projects in Porty. But that's as far as it goes. Naomi's never mentioned him to me.'

Frank decided to leave a bit on the wily old fox. 'Look, Bob, this feels a bit racist. Brewster meets a woman of mixed ethnicity, so by implication she must be dodgy. Not great, Bob, not in the current climate or any other climate for that matter.'

DI Hope appeared flustered at the mention of race.

'Now, now, Frank. That's not the case at all; there's no need to be playing the race card. Sorry, I don't mean that. I mean there's no need to mention Naomi's skin colour, that's not a factor here. The force is focused on diversity and there's certainly no place for racism in modern-day Scotland.'

Frank relaxed, knowing he'd got him on the back foot and decided to throw the cop a bone.

He said, 'I'll have a word with her, suss out what the craic is with Brewster and report back to you. But I don't want any plod tracking my daughter, Bob. That's police harassment and you'll be hearing from my lawyer if I get the slightest whiff of Naomi being followed.'

Frank didn't have a lawyer but had always wanted to say that.

'Okay, Frank. Look, it's good to see you and I promise your daughter won't be bothered. I want Brewster back behind bars where he belongs and no doubt you feel the same. Come on, I'll walk you to the door.'

Once they were outside, Frank offered Bob a smoke, which he declined before guiding him round the corner away from the station.

'Okay, Bob. What's the score?'

Bob pulled the collar of his coat up as he furtively scanned the street.

'We're concerned that a major organised crime outfit called the Syndicate are muscling in on the drugs trade in Edinburgh. The boys from the Serious Crime Squad think they're using the cinema in Portobello to set up a money laundering operation. That put's Naomi in the frame, as it looks like the Syndicate have placed someone to help them revamp the Regency as a front while being run legitimately at the same time. The London mob are headed by your old friend, Ray Armstrong, aka the Wise One and have established links with Scottish criminals, namely Brewster.'

Frank was thinking on his feet as the wheels whirred in his mind. He did his best to maintain a straight poker face, despite being rocked to his core. What the fuck was Naomi doing? Was she working for Ray fucking Armstrong? Her "Uncle Ray". That bastard. A psychopath of the highest order who had preyed on Maxine.

'I'm not denying Naomi knew this Armstrong character, Bob, but that was way back when she was a kid. He was involved in her mother's singing career and would come round to our flat in Islington, but she won't have seen him for the best part of thirty years.'

Hope said nothing, giving Frank room to expand.

'I know you'll have done your homework, so none of this will be news to you, Bob, but you're putting two and two together and coming up with five. Remember, I'm not paying you – a public official – any more, so you don't have to embellish the tale here. Operation Elveden put an end to journos paying cops and none of this is for the papers.'

Frank knew he was being harsh but felt it was necessary to remind the detective of the leverage he held over him.

'You're out of order, Frank. That was a long time ago. I'm a detective inspector for Christ's sake and I'm giving you the skinny as a favour to a friend.'

Frank rubbed his forehead and felt his toe start to throb.

'I know and I appreciate the heads-up, Bob.'

'Look, Frank, I'm not saying Naomi is wittingly involved. It may well be she doesn't have a clue about the Syndicate and is being used. But her past with Armstrong is a wee bit too much of a coincidence and I hate fucking coincidences.'

Frank smiled wearily.

'I'll do a bit of digging. I don't want these bastards using Naomi. We need to nip this in the bud before Armstrong gets his tentacles onto her.'

Deep down, Frank knew it was too late.

He shook hands with Bob before heading round to The Shore, where he had a lot of catching up to do in the bevvy stakes.

17

To the early hours of Christmas morning and a tired, half-pissed Naomi was seeking to reassure her old man that she wasn't involved in anything remotely dodgy on the back of the tug Frank had gotten from DI Hope.

'I'll say it again, Dad. I met – sorry – bumped into that guy, Brewster, at Daisy Park. He had introduced himself at the opening of the youth theatre after handing me a lollipop while dressed as Santa, then boasted how he'd help set everything up with the theatre group and provide them with funding from a local charity. Then he waffled some shite about Portobello being an up-and-coming place and how he'd dragged himself out of the gutter to become a success story.'

She watched as her dad, now in full journo mode, paced the living room in his best Liberty of London dressing gown like a pound-shop Sherlock Holmes, sipping his brandy and stroking his chin.

'Tell me again what Brewster said about your work and the cinema project?'

Naomi sighed before pouring herself another large glass of wine and reaching for the After Eight mints.

'This Brewster character said that he knew I worked for the private equity firm involved with the restoration of the old cinema and would like to explore the possibility of a tie-in with the youth theatre, using the new venue to put on shows, including a pantomime. I've no idea how he knew I was involved in the Regency project before you ask. Like you always say, Dad, "Edinburgh is a fucking village".'

Frank barked, 'That fucker knows all about pantomimes.'

Naomi waited as her dad pretended to read one of the three Christmas cards he'd displayed across the mantlepiece with a piece of string in an attempt, along with decorating a tiny plastic tree, to make the place appear festive. After an age, he said, 'Okay, Naomi, but it all feels a bit smelly. The cinema thing and the youth theatre running in tandem with that bastard involved. It doesn't take a genius to work out there's potential for money laundering and God knows what else.'

Naomi made her face appear neutral, not wanting to give away any sign that her father had effectively nailed the whole Syndicate operation. Then she went on the attack.

'Look, Dad, my firm, Upton Park Wealth Management, are a FTSE 250 blue-chip company listed on the London Stock Exchange. We're not some two-bit fucking money laundering outfit. Look us up on the internet, we're a global conglomerate. I worked bloody hard to get that job, sweated to get my master's degree in mathematical sciences from Oxford – a place I fucking hated. Did shitty jobs in nightclubs, you name it. I remember how proud you were of me and now you're basically accusing me of being a criminal. It's not on, Frank.'

Naomi headed to the bathroom, slamming the door shut behind her. Sitting on the toilet, she ripped a piece of bog roll and put her head in her hands, ashamed of how easily the lies now rolled off her tongue. It was killing her inside trying to deceive Frank and it was becoming obvious he was too smart to fall for the cover story.

Back in the living room, Frank stared out the window of the flat down to the five-a-side football pitches that stood on the site of the old open-air pool. He had deliberately not mentioned the Wise One to Naomi during their earlier chat. The heads-up from

DI Hope had spooked him and he was in no doubt his daughter was in way over her head. He was trying to work out the best way to deal with the situation without compromising both his and her safety. Naomi slinked back through to the living room and Frank stood, arms outstretched, to give her a much-needed hug.

'You know I love you, Naomi.'

'I know, Dad,' she replied.

Frank collapsed in a heap on the sofa, with the weight of the world on his shoulders.

'I've never told you this, Naomi, but that racist, homophobic bastard, Brewster, was responsible for your Uncle Michael's death.'

He took a large swig of his brandy as the shock registered on his daughter's face. 'Yip, that bastard was there the night Michael died at the pool, him and his creepy football casual mates. They used to terrorise gay men up Calton Hill and around the toilets at London Road. "Poof-bashing", that's what they called it.'

Frank continued with tears in his eyes and clenched fists.

'Brewster had chased Michael along the prom before and was in the area the night he fell to his death. I know for a fact him and his cronies hung around the pool. Your uncle's death was registered as accidental, but I know in my bones that bastard caused it. Certainty. He was done with attempted murder of a gay man a few years later and that nails it for me. He killed Michael and now he's back in Portobello rubbing my nose in it.'

A couple of hours of fitful sleep later it had all been pushed aside for Christmas morning, with Frank handing out the presents and pouring the Buck's Fizz. Naomi whooped with delight as she ripped the paper off her present to reveal a digitally remastered, framed picture of her mother, Maxine. It was an action shot from her *Top of the Pops* days and she looked incredible.

'Here, open the rest of your presents,' Frank said.

She put down the Buck's Fizz to tear the paper off a parcel. A box of mint Matchmakers, which Frank described as "the damage", and a large bag of plain chocolate-covered Brazil nuts that she couldn't remember being on her Santa list.

'Thanks, Dad, these are my favourites.'

Moving on to the next gift, Naomi became the proud owner of a pair of posh slippers that her dad said were the "Rolls Royce of the baffie world".

Frank waited patiently as Naomi handed him his present in a little red pouch bag. Peering inside, a glint of gold caught his eye.

'You beauty,' he cried, pulling out a nine-carat gold, eighteen-inch, faceted Belcher chain and holding it in front of him before grabbing Naomi and giving her a massive bear hug. 'I've been wanting one of these for ages,' he shrieked in delight.

'I know,' Naomi said. 'I pay attention, Dad. I remember you telling me you had one back in the eighties because you wanted to look like your hero, Charlie Nicholas, and wore it over your Italian designer sweatshirts.'

Frank carefully pulled it over his giant bonce before admiring it in the mirror. 'This won't leave my neck, my love. They'll have to take my head off first.'

They poured themselves more champagne, not bothering with the fresh orange juice, and sat amongst the wrapping paper, both gazing out the window at the Firth of Forth and across to Fife in between staring at the picture of Maxine.

Frank had invited Bobby, Bella, Falco and Olga over, but Bobby had called earlier to say he was having to work at the Nepalese restaurant as the kitchen porter had called in sick. Frank told him to come over later and noticed a hesitancy in Bobby's voice that he found strange. They briefly spoke about the footage Brewster's henchman had taken in the toilets the other night, and Bobby told him, 'Don't worry, I've got plans for him.' This left Frank with a lingering sense of dread, compounded by his gut feeling that Naomi had been economical with the truth in their earlier discussions.

He parked those thoughts and got down to the serious business of preparing the Christmas dinner. A prize turkey had been ordered well in advance along with all the trimmings including cranberry sauce, which Frank considered the devil's work, sticking to his belief that fruit and meat did not belong on the same plate. He was something of a minimalist when it came to roast potatoes and ignored the raft of what he considered to be disinformation regarding the best way to cook them. He eschewed all talk of duck or goose fat, preferring to plough his own furrow. If truth be told, he was copying Michael Caine, who had claimed on Desert Island Discs that to make the "best roast potatoes in the world" meant boiling them first, then allowing them to marinate in cold extra-virgin olive oil, adding rosemary and sage leaves for extra flavour. If it was good enough for Harry Palmer, it was good enough for Frank Savage. But the magic dust was in the all-important shoogle you gave the potatoes (and they had to be Maris Piper) after a fifteen-minute parboil, adding butter and sea salt for good measure.

Bella arrived at noon with her homemade cheesecake that she described as "legendary" and two bottles of Grey Goose. They exchanged presents, with Frank receiving his customary dildo – this year, a fourteen-inch silver dragon one which he stuck in his dildo drawer alongside the thirty or so other rubber cocks she had bought him over the years. He had gotten her a box of Matchmakers and a large bag of chocolate Brazil nuts too, as well as a couple of pairs of Happy Feet socks. Bella said she was "made up".

Falco and Olga arrived with a bottle of twenty-five-year-old Macallan and Frank knew a monster sesh was in the offing. Falco was wearing a classic-cut tuxedo with shawl collar which Frank recognised as being by Dior, and Olga had gone for a double-breasted white suit – with nothing underneath – her hair slicked back like Brigitte Nielsen at the height of her married-to-Rocky fame.

Frank made a point of turning the sound down on King Charles's first Christmas speech as monarch, which triggered him and led to a ten-minute rant where he continually shouted, 'I knew his faither, I knew his faither' in between cries of 'Off with his head.' The turkey was delayed so they all decided to settle down and watch *The Sound of Music* before tucking into the gargantuan feast.

*

Brewster hit the red button on his new remote control, having acquired a dodgy Fire Stick that allowed him access to every channel under the sun for the princely sum of sweet fuck all. He planned to tape *The Sound of Music*, a film he loved, apart from the way the Nazis were portrayed, but he could always fast forward the bits he didn't like.

He'd hardly slept. The Ghost of Christmas Past paying him the annual visit in the shape of his half-brother, Glen. Brewster had relived this nightmare into the wee small hours of Christmas morning every year since he was thirteen. The images ingrained in his mind arriving on cue like Santa's reindeer.

He hadn't wanted to take Glen to the golf course. All he was looking for was a bit of peace and quiet to try out the new clubs he'd been given that morning by his mum and Norrie. Marjorie had gone to the trouble of wrapping them, but it was glaringly obvious to Brewster that his Christmas present was a half-set, bought from Maurice Pollock's at the bottom of Leith Walk. Glen started screaming and tugging at his big brother's arm, begging to go with the "big boys". Brewster relented, so the wee man was in, climbing through the hole in the railings at the council houses onto the second tee. They had the course to themselves on a mild Christmas Day with no snow.

Brewster had birdied 5th hole before choosing to hit his new nine-iron at the short par three. Couple of practice swings then the real thing. You could hear a pin drop as the teenager, by now oozing confidence, made to contort his torso round the hips to gain the necessary torque for the shot, just like the pro had taught him. He arched the club, keeping his head down and eyes on the ball. Instead of feeling the swoosh of air towards the trajectory, he felt a sickening thud, taking his eye off the ball to turn around just as the club, which should have been heading skywards with unrelenting force, met its immovable object. It was lodged in Glen's skull. A look of bemusement and sheer terror was etched on the child's face as Brewster used his strength to yank the club from his half-brother's head, sending a fountain of blood into the air before Glen turned pure white and keeled over.

Brewster had awoken to the sound of his own screaming. The image of the wee man on the life support machine, then his mother crying her heart out at the funeral as the six-year-old's mini coffin was brought in was playing on a reel in his head. That was only part one of the nightmare. Part two would see Norrie from that day onward make his life a living hell.

Brewster jumped in the shower to wash away the night sweats. He was picking up Marjorie, and they were heading to the Chinese restaurant in Lothian Road for a Christmas banquet – something they'd done every year since he was released from the nick. Marjorie had a particular fondness for their lemon chicken and Brewster loved how the owner gave him a big bag of barbecue spare ribs for Waffen, who would be waiting in the car seeing as the restaurant had a strict no dogs policy. Despite being a racist, Brewster liked Chinese food and, if pushed, would also admit to owning Soul II Soul's seminal 1989 album, *Club Classics Vol. One*, which he played in the spanking new Volvo Estate he had recently bought.

Brewster felt guilty for the stress he had put his mum through, becoming involved with the football casuals and the violence that ensued. Marjorie had always supported her son, did his washing and ironed his polo shirts with the little crocodile on the front, just the way he liked them. She had even bought him that book called the *Hitler Diaries* one Christmas, which he went crazy about as they turned out to be fake.

They arrived at the Chinese to be greeted by the owner, who knew to make a big fuss over Marjorie, giving them the best table in the house, miles away from the bogs. Brewster had invited the Two Billys along for the meal and they sat at the next table giving Marjorie space to enjoy a bit of quality time with her son. After the starters, the owner gave Brewster the barbeque spare ribs which he took out to Waffen. The dog went berserk, wolfing them down like the wolf he was, and Brewster loved to see him chewing on the bones.

For his main course, Brewster had ordered a whole aromatic crispy duck which the waiter presented to him and Marjorie before ceremoniously chopping it to pieces. He loved the accoutrements that came with the dish – the pancakes in the wooden bowl, the hoisin sauce, chopped spring onion and the way they served the cucumber impressed Brewster no end. He told the waiter to bring them knives and forks. Brewster had a theory that the only reason the Chinese used chopsticks was because they didn't have any steel to make cutlery.

'We'll be here all night if we use two wee shitty sticks,' he said.

Marjorie was having the time of her life, eating lemon chicken while her son lovingly prepared crispy duck pancakes. Brewster thought the order of a whole duck, accompanied by a bottle of the Peking Palace's best champagne, sent a message loud and clear. He was doing well for himself. He ordered the waiter to wrap the remains of the duck up for Waffen, who was getting really spoilt this year. For dessert, they ordered the ice cream; Brewster telling his mum, like he did every year, that "the Chinkys are shite at puddings".

Marjorie was in awe at the sophisticated gentleman he had become; well-travelled, smartly turned out, kind to animals, mothers, well, she could vouch for that, and now children, too. He had told her about his work with the youth theatre in Portobello and how he had helped get the girls' football team up and running. Marjorie thought her son had certainly turned his life around after falling in with the wrong crowd in his teenage years, and although she didn't approve of the gays, she had always thought Brewster had taken it too far by trying to murder one. Still, he'd served his time and was now seeking repentance through his actions.

The Peking Palace was including a karaoke in their Christmas party this year and Brewster was keen to get Marjorie involved as he knew she had a "cracking singing voice".

'No, son, no,' she half-heartedly protested as he urged her to take the mic. Marjorie finally relented and was desperate to get up there and sing for both her son and her supper. '"Danny Boy",' she told the waiter. 'But you don't have to put the words up on the telly, son. I know them off by heart.'

This went down like a lead balloon with the Two Billys at the next table who protested to Brewster that it was a "Fenian song". He swiftly put them right.

'It's not a fucking Fenian song; it was written by an Englishman and it's to the tune of "Londonderry Air" – that's Londonderry, not Derry, so, if anything, it's a fucking Proddie song. The Taigs stole it. Now shut your mouths and let my mother sing.'

Brewster told his mum to continue as the rest of the diners stared at their plates. Marjorie proceeded to belt out the first lines.

'*Oh, Danny boy, the pipes, the pipes are calling*
'*From glen to glen, and down the mountainside.*'

Brewster was welling up as the Two Billys looked on in disgust. Marjorie finished to strained applause. Billy One asked Brewster if his first name was Danny.

'My name is fucking Brewster. Okay? Brewster. One word: Brewster, like Madonna or Prince. Got that?'

Billy One murmured, 'Okay, Danny', but Brewster pretended not to hear him.

The coffee came as punters got up to sing Shania Twain, Ronan Keating, Take That and a mangled version of the Oasis hit, "Wonderwall", followed by the Two Billys belting out 'Penny Arcade' segueing into 'The Best'. Marjorie told her son that she'd love it if he got up and dedicated a number to her.

'That one you used to sing in your room, son, in your underpants before you went out on a Saturday night.'

Brewster thought his mother was pushing her luck but reluctantly got to his feet and took hold of the microphone.

'Pet Shop Boys, "It's a Sin", pal.' Brewster cleared his throat in preparation for his big number, then murdered the song, "treating" everyone in the restaurant to the longest five minutes of their lives.

A tearful Marjorie gave her son a big hug as the owner came round to congratulate Brewster on his performance, handing him the leftover duck for Waffen. Everyone in the place was reluctantly applauding and Brewster, chest filling with pride, took the applause, standing up to give a little bow, before heading out to feed the dog. Ten seconds elapsed before the door to the restaurant came flying open and a distressed Brewster came running in, shouting, 'Waffen's gone! Waffen's gone! Some bastard has smashed my car window and taken my dog.'

The drunk guy on the karaoke then decided to make the biggest mistake of his life, bursting into song without the need for any teleprompter.

'*How much is that doggy in the window?*
'*The one with the waggly...*'

Smash went the pint glass into the guy's face, claret and pieces of nostril everywhere – absolute carnage. The Two Billys escorted the singer from the premises pronto before anyone had time to digest the full extent of the horror, as Brewster and Marjorie headed down Lothian Road, through the Grassmarket, minus one dog and a back window.

'Fucking Savage,' Brewster shouted as he banged his hands on the steering wheel.

Marjorie told him to 'Mind his language' and was met with a swift, 'Shut the fuck up, Mum.'

Back at Ramsay Tech and the party was winding down. Falco had brought his guitar and was running through the standards, playing "American Pie" by Don McLean and telling everyone how he had helped Don with the lyrics.

Frank had nodded off contentedly, having eaten his weight in roast potatoes, and was now in the middle of a weird dream where Joanna Lumley, dressed as Purdey, was playing with a collection of dildos like they were dolls with faces drawn on wearing little knitted cardigans. He was woken from his slumber – just as Joanna was pretending that mama and papa dildo were attacking giant dragon dildo who was trying to eat baby dildo – by the sound of his phone beeping on the arm of his chair. Frank clicked on a message with an attachment from Bobby, who had so far been a no-show. It took him a while to digest the picture he was looking at, while attempting to shake the dream from his alcohol-addled brain. Bobby was giving it the thumbs-up pose with his new dog, that he appeared to have received as a Christmas present, and bizarrely the animal was wearing a canine version of an orange jumpsuit. Then it dawned on him that he had seen the beast before.

'Jesus wept,' he shouted. 'He's only gone and done it. The mad bastard has kidnapped Brewster's dog.'

18

Boxing Day began badly for Frank and went downhill from there. A Champions League knockout-stage hangover had left his head throbbing. He constantly felt dizzy, which he put down to a by-product of continuing to drink like a fish despite being on tablets for his blood pressure, which according to the latest reading taken that morning wasn't coming down. To top it all, his gout had flared up, making the wearing of his new Greggs the bakers Crocs – a present from his daughter, Katie – a must. But the last thing on his mind was looking like an arse as he made his way along the prom to the cat and dog home where Bobby was tending to Waffen. Just the four dog owners had accosted Frank on his journey of approximately 0.7 miles, two of them calling him a cunt, one trying to set his Jack Russell terrier on him and the other asking, 'Why do you hate dogs so much?' Frank had told the last guy that he didn't hate dogs, he just hated him, before telling him to "Fuck off or I'll suck your eyes out", which seemed to have the desired effect. *Merry Christmas.*

On arrival at the kennels, which were shut for the festive period, Frank gave the pre-arranged knock which was the password for Bobby to let him in. He rapped his knuckles on the door to the tune of 'Dee, dee, dee-dee-dee, dee-dee-dee-dee, Hibees!!'

'Jesus wept,' he cried, 'my mate is a feckin' eejit.' An age passed before the door opened ever so slightly and Bobby furtively appeared behind it, urging Frank to get in quickly, before peering out to check both ways that he hadn't been followed.

Bobby led him to the kennel that his mate had let him have, housing Waffen in what resembled a doggy prison. Waffen, with the sedative now fully worn off, was appearing relaxed and enjoying a nice bit of sirloin that Bobby had nicked from the restaurant. The animal certainly liked the finer things in life. Frank thought Waffen seemed content enough despite his ordeal and was treating the exile from his racist, Nazi, bampot owner like a holiday.

'Fuck's sake, Bobby, this is easily the stupidest thing you've ever done and that's a long list, my friend, a very long list, as long as your arm if truth be told.'

'At least I've done something, Frank. You lot had decided to do nothing other than let that bastard Brewster walk all over us as per usual. He was trying to ruin your career. That fiasco at the town hall, filming you covered in sherbet, then telling the whole of Porty he was going to the papers. And don't forget what he did to your beloved Shadow. He's gotten away with murder for years.'

Frank gave Bobby a hard stare for going there but soon got back to the matter in hand.

'Look, Bobby, I don't have a career. I write shite for a living and, despite wanting to keep under the radar, my employer and close friends have decided I've to sit not just above the radar but on top of it.'

Bobby fed Waffen, who he was now calling Waffle, a couple of doggy chews that the animal wolfed down. It appeared to Frank that his mate was rapidly becoming attached to the beast.

Bobby said, '"Under the radar", says the man wearing a pair of Greggs the bakers Crocs. You've never done anything under the radar in your life, Frank. Don't try and kid a kidder. Your ego is ginormous, and you've been loving the attention.'

Frank laughed as he thought of a comeback. 'Well, the devil

knows his own, Bobby, the devil knows his own. What's this latest dognapping if nothing more than a giant "look at me, look at me". You're on your own ego trip, my friend. One that involves kidnapping dogs and dressing them up in homemade orange jumpsuits.'

They both laughed at the absurdity of the situation, but Bobby was now well and truly starting to grate on Frank.

'What exactly are you going to do, Bobby? What's the plan? Because from where I'm standing, this looks like a clusterfuck of epic proportions. I mean, I know a dog is for life, not just for Christmas, but some other cunt's dog is not even for Christmas. You do know you could be looking at a seven stretch for dog theft? That's seven years spent with psychotic nutters who love nothing more in the whole wide world than their dogs. And you dognapped one of their own. That practically makes you a beast. But obviously, that's the least of *our* worries.'

Bobby opened the kennel, placing a bowl of fresh water inside for his new pet. 'I left a ransom note with a lock of Waffen's fur and his dog collar under Brewster's car windscreen this morning. Here, look, I took a picture of it.'

Bobby showed Frank a photo of the note which he'd compiled using different sizes of cut-out letters.

GiVe Us $5 GRanD
oR ThE dOG iS tOAst

'I just want to leave a bit on Brewster, you know, scare him a bit, hit him where it hurts, let him know we're here.'

Frank let out a sigh but felt drained and couldn't be arsed trying to work himself into a lather any more. He noted that Bobby had used the collective "us" instead of "me" in his ransom note, and for some reason had used a dollar sign instead of a pound sign, thus short-changing himself, but not by much given the current exchange rate.

'This ransom note is the icing on the cake of shite ideas, Bobby. You're not even doing this for the money. Christ only knows what you're all about. This is like some weird fetish where you kidnap a dog once every three years to feed a habit. It's a cry for help. I know I'm mental but you're in a worse nick. Knowing our luck, we'll have another *Shergar* on our hands after Brewster tells us to fuck off, then threatens to kill us; and he will try to kill us, Bobby. You know that, don't you? And it won't be a nice death either; it will be a nasty, horrible death, Bobby. A really nasty one, most likely involving us choking on our own cocks. Do you want to choke to death on your own cock, Bobby? Because I don't.'

'Look, Frank, I don't want to hurt this dog, even if it does belong to Brewster. I can dump him outside that prick's house tonight if you like, forget about the ransom money and I'll take the blame. I'm not scared of him.'

Frank grimaced like he'd been constipated for four days straight. 'That's the first sensible thing to come out of your lips, Bobby. You need to get the dog back to its owner pronto and we can deal with the fallout from there on in. But you certainly won't be owning up to anything. There's no need to. Everyone knows who the local dognapper is and he'll come for us anyway, most likely with those Northern Irish goons.'

Frank paced up and down Waffen's jailhouse corridor. 'I should come as well. Tomorrow morning. I'm thinking about 5am. We dump Waffen outside his house and leg it. The dog is bound to start barking and wake up the whole street.'

Bobby was having none of it. 'No way, Frank. This is my dog mess and I insist on clearing it up. I'll go alone. I can stick Waffle in the boot and give him more of the sedative before I dump him outside Brewster's house. That way he'll find the sleeping dog lying or the postman will.'

Frank made a half-hearted appeal to go on the mission again, but Bobby was adamant about flying solo. He made to leave as Bobby was patting his new friend, saying, 'Who's a good boy, Waffle? Who's a good boy?'

'Right, Bobby, I'm away home for a lie down before I visit my mum and dad. Hopefully I won't wake up. You need to keep your wits about you, Sonny Jim, and don't open the door to anyone even if they give the Hibees knock. Brewster will be on the warpath.'

Frank arrived back at Ramsay Tech to find Naomi slouching on the sofa watching *Chitty Chitty Bang Bang*, another film he hated. She asked him how things had gone with Bobby. Frank told his daughter that he was planning to hand the dog back tomorrow morning, calling Bobby a "fucking arsehole" with a liberal sprinkling of "daft and stupid bastard" thrown into the conversation for good measure.

Naomi absorbed the latest information, with an overpowering sense of dread, and realised she would need to step up to the plate or hand things over to the Wise One and let him deal with it. She tried her best not to wind Frank up any more. He had seemed distant since her last round of lies, so she just nodded her head and gave him one-word answers to rhetorical questions like, 'Does Bobby know what he's done here?'

Frank had arranged to pay his customary visit to see his parents on Boxing Day, something that always filled him with a sense of dread, turned up to eleven given the day's earlier events. He decided he was going to "fake it till you make it" for Naomi's sake, who to Frank's bemusement was looking forward to seeing her gran and grandad, even though he warned her that Arthur was losing his marbles and to be prepared for him getting her mixed up with someone else.

He told Naomi that he was away for a nap as an overwhelming feeling of despair pressed down on his shoulders and created a nagging sense of emptiness in his stomach. Black dog. How he wished Michael was here. He thought back to Boxing Days past and how Arthur took great pride in his quizzes. It had started with them all playing Trivial Pursuit back in 1982 after Frank had been given it as a present from his Aunty Margo. Frank, Bobby, Bella and Michael all played but were always too drunk to take the game seriously and the little pieces, that looked like Dairylea triangles, would get lost down the back of the couch or turn up swimming in a half-drunk glass of plonk alongside the fag butts. Arthur would lose the rag as he considered himself something of a quizmaster, boasting about how he often completed the *Daily Record* quick crossword or at least got down to one clue. That was until Frank ripped the piss out of him for being one letter short of completing it, with Arthur stuck on nine across, *Roman's Perhaps? (8)* and his dad staring blankly into space for the missing letter on *-talians*.

'Talians, what the fuck are talians?' he cried in despair.

Arthur was a member of the quiz team at the printer's he worked for and captain of the pool team.

The next year, 1983, the little pieces on the Trivial Pursuit board were binned and they just read out the questions. The year after that, they only read out the questions from the Entertainment category and by that point Arthur had taken the huff and was refusing to take part. He would sit in "Dad's chair" and call them all heathens, bemoaning how the "youth of today" knew nothing of the past, while randomly shouting out the Science and Nature questions, then pretending to know the answers, which he'd memorised. Frank had a creeping feeling that he might be turning into his dad.

He showered and shaved, then called a taxi to take them to the house in Leith Links where his parents still lived, with the nurse coming twice a week to help feed Arthur and take him to the toilet. Frank had decided to take a bottle of vodka with him and was thankful he'd made that decision as, on arrival, Arthur's opening gambit to Naomi consisted of him asking if her mother was black. His mum, Rita, however, was on better form, giving

Naomi a big hug and welcoming her into the home.

They tucked into yet another Christmas dinner, with Frank wincing as his mother placed a huge dollop of homemade bread sauce on the side of his plate, causing her son to boke dryly.

19

Naomi spent the time at her grandparents thinking of an excuse to leave and deal with the immediate problem to hand, namely how Brewster was going to react to his disappearing dog. Her stomach churned as she forced herself to get in the zone, so that she could focus on a holding strategy that would prevent extreme violence coming down on her father and his daft pal.

She nodded as Rita waffled on about how lovely Maxine was "before the drugs took hold" as her dad drowned himself in vodka and Arthur flitted between reminiscing about taking her to the paddling pool on Portobello promenade as a toddler and asking how long she'd known Frank.

Naomi was disturbed by the mention of her mother being on drugs, making a note to ask her father about this at a more convenient time. She kept visiting the bathroom to try and get Brewster on the burner phone, blaming a 'urine infection' which both Rita and Arthur could relate to. Finally, she got through and told him there was a kilo of cocaine that needed shifting quickly and arranged to meet him at his lock-up in Joppa at 5am tomorrow morning. Naomi said she'd bring the coke with her and had told Brewster it would be worth his while. Brewster had reluctantly agreed and told her to come alone to the lock-up.

'Christ knows why we have to meet at that godforsaken hour?' he said. There was no way Naomi was going there by herself and had already lined up security in the form of JJ, who was collecting the powder. She told him all he needed to know and said she would "see him all right" for the handers.

Naomi reckoned this elaborate distraction would give Bobby enough time to return Waffen to Brewster's house without the risk of him being caught red-handed. She had already decided to come clean about Frank being her dad and warn Brewster to stay away from him as this ongoing soap opera was bad for Syndicate business.

Naomi made her excuses in preparation for leaving, saying she felt 'rough as France,' not wanting to swear in front of her grandparents. It wasn't a lie as her stomach was bloated, and she hadn't been for a shit in three days courtesy of her new friend, "endo".

Frank said he was staying as he was well into the Grey Goose by this point and reckoned he needed to be drunk to deal with Bobby and his version of *Dog Day Afternoon* – or *Dog Day Early Morning* – and wasn't going home until he'd tanned the bottle.

Naomi went home and set the alarm for 4.30am when JJ would swing by and pick her up. She knew that sleep was but a pipe dream and had the ominous feeling of things coming to a head. The sense of shame she felt about lying to her dad and using him had become overpowering. It had all gotten a bit out of hand and she needed to switch back her focus to the Syndicate and the cinema project, which was a solid idea that would provide the foundation for years of steady income.

After a couple of hours of fitful sleep and a merciful trip to the loo, Naomi got ready to meet Brewster, reaching into her holdall and strapping the holster holding the Glock 43 over her shoulder. She prayed she would never have to use it. Naomi pushed the door to her dad's bedroom a fraction and saw that he was on top of his sheets, still fully clothed from the night before. She made sure he was still breathing before stealing one of his cigarettes to smoke while waiting for her lift.

Two draws into the cigarette, she stubbed it out as JJ flashed the lights on a powder-blue 1996 Fiat Panda that he described as his "latest whip". Naomi's first thought was he was too big for that car. They arrived at the lock-up to find Brewster standing outside playing what looked like a penny whistle and flicking his hair. The stress of losing Waffle had clearly taken its toll and he'd resorted to vaping; a faint whiff of blueberry with a hint of sour raspberry filled the cold morning sky. He did not look best pleased to see Naomi had arrived with company.

'What's all this pish? Are you going solo now, Natlie, or is it Naomi tonight?'

He sucked on the vape, then held it at arm's length like he'd just stuck a jobby in his mouth. 'Does the Wise One know you're punting his gear? I think we both know the answer to that one.'

Naomi was momentarily startled by him using her real name, then motioned to JJ, who walked up to Brewster and showed him the contents of the Glasgow Film Festival tote bag he was carrying.

She said, 'There's a nice taste in there for you, if you fucking behave.'

Brewster motioned for Naomi to join him in the lock-up. 'Just you; King Kong can stay in the motor.'

JJ smiled as Naomi told Brewster, 'He goes where I go.'

'Fair enough,' Brewster said, shrugging. 'Bring your pet monkey. I think it's time me and you had a little chat.'

Naomi sat down across from Brewster who had plonked himself behind his desk, picking up and staring at the framed photograph of Waffen that took pride of place alongside a picture of Marjorie, hair in a beehive, wearing National Health specs, with a microphone in her hand.

Brewster opened the bag and stuck a knife into the cocaine like he'd seen them do in the movies. He stuck a dab under his nose and cried, 'Good shit,' before asking Naomi if she wanted some.

'Do you want some? You want some?' he shouted out in an English accent like he was on the terraces at Millwall.

Naomi shook her head, then made ready to deliver her speech. 'Look, Brewster. I've been meaning to tell you—'

'That Frank Savage is your fucking dad,' he interrupted. 'Do you seriously think I didn't know that? Do you think I came up the Clyde on a bike?'

Naomi wriggled uneasily in her chair but wasn't surprised as she knew this moment had been coming. She said, 'It's "came up the Clyde in a banana boat", that's the saying. How can anyone come up the Clyde on a bike?'

Brewster chuckled with menace. 'Aye, you and him would know all about banana boats, right enough.'

JJ cracked his knuckles, which silenced him for a second. He recovered his composure, running the blade of the knife along his index finger like a Mexican bandit in a spaghetti Western before letting out a pathetic yelp as he accidentally drew blood, causing JJ to laugh then cough out the word, 'Wanker.' Brewster stuck his finger in his mouth, then searched for a plaster in a first-aid box he brought out from under the desk.

'It may have escaped your notice, but I am missing one rather large German shepherd. And if I find out that your father, the esteemed newspaper columnist, has anything to do with the disappearance of said German shepherd, then I will cut his cock off, right here in this very lock-up, and shove it down his big fat gob. In fact, if it was up to me, I'd have cut his rancid cock off the moment he used it to impregnate your dusky-hued mother.' Brewster broke into song.

Naomi took a deep breath and concentrated on not taking the bait.

Brewster smiled. 'Funny coincidence that your dad is best pals with a guy who has previous for stealing dogs.'

Naomi rubbed her shoulder under the Burberry raincoat and resisted the urge to blow his brains all over the mahogany desk. JJ was like a coiled spring, giving her the eye, waiting for the slightest of nods that would give him the signal to boot Brewster into next week, but it never came. Although she considered Brewster increasingly pathetic, he was still a dangerous prick.

'Okay, I should have come clean about Frank being my father. And I realise you and him have a bit of previous. But I didn't think it was germane to our business relationship.'

Brewster sighed. 'What's it got to do with the Germans?' he asked.

'Nothing. It's got nothing to do with Germans. I used the word "germane" in the context of you knowing Frank is my father and that very fact not having anything to do with our business here in Edinburgh.'

'I have no fucking idea what you're on about, love,' Brewster said, throwing his hands in the air.

'Look, forget it. It doesn't matter. What does matter is that your dog is being returned to your home as we speak.'

Naomi checked her watch and saw it was now after 5 in the am.

Brewster appeared to be ignoring her, instead concentrating on calling someone on his mobile. Naomi looked at JJ and shrugged.

'I said Bobby is returning your dog.'

Brewster put his finger to his lips, giving her the shush sign as he spoke into the phone. 'Great, so Waffen's fine and you've got the Paki. Magic, top work, there's a bonus for the pair of you. Ping me the pic.'

He stared at his phone, then howled, 'Ya fucking beauty!' before turning it round to show Naomi a picture of the Two Billys supporting Bobby with their arms round his shoulders, giving the thumbs-up sign. Bobby had blood coming out of his nose and was sporting a pair of black eyes.

Naomi registered her shock at the picture, then got angry.

'This is out of order, Brewster; you've overstepped the mark here. You better not fucking harm him any more and tell those goons to back off. I'll be having a word with the Wise One about all of this. It ends here.'

Brewster wasn't about to be lectured. 'Listen, you cunt. That bastard kidnapped my dog; he's your dad's best mate, so that makes your old boy guilty by association in my book. If anyone's out of order, it's that pair of arseholes. First, they assault me at the town hall. Then they conspire to kidnap my pride and joy, smashing my car window and nicking Waffen – sorry, Waffle – on Christmas fucking Day, when I'm out with my fucking mother.'

Naomi took this on board but wasn't about to concede anything.

'My dad had nothing to do with kidnapping your dog. I know you know Bobby is the local dognapper, so leave Frank out of this. You need to release Bobby pronto; no more silly games, Brewster, this is unprofessional bullshit.'

Brewster picked up his phone and clicked on the picture of Bobby, gloating now. 'I'll tell you what I'll do. Frank pays me ten thousand pounds – double the amount Bobby was originally looking for when he kidnapped Waffle – and I'll let the Paki go.'

Naomi said, 'He's Nepalese and you're not getting a cent.'

Brewster was adamant. 'Nah, your old boy must pay me retribution or Bobby goes. Swims with the fishes. It's as simple as that. I can't be seen to lose face. Imagine word gets out that I've let this slide. I'll have every drug dealer from The Inch to Wester Hailes taking liberties.'

He picked up the knife as JJ made to move towards him.

'Easy, tiger,' Brewster said. 'You've got him well trained, Natlie – sorry, Naomi.'

She told JJ to back off and he stood behind her.

Brewster smirked. 'I'll tell you what I'll do. I'll have Bobby call Frank and tell him to bring ten thousand pounds to my house at 8pm tonight, and if he does that, I'll free his mate. Deal?'

20

Frank got the call from Bobby early on Boxing Day morning, five minutes after he arrived at work for his festive shift. He saw his friend's name come up on the mobile and expected to be told that Waffen had been returned to his owner without fuss, with both dog and dognapper doing well. Instead, a sobbing Bobby laid it out for him.

'They've got me, Frank. Brewster and the Two Billys have got me. They want you to deliver ten grand to Brewster by 8pm tonight or they'll say I'm a goner, Frank.'

Frank, heart racing, marched through the newsroom looking to find a quiet space.

'Slower, Bobby, slower. What the fuck is going on? What do you mean they've got you?'

'I delivered Waffle back to Brewster as planned but the Irish guys grabbed me and dragged me into his garage. They gave me a bit of a doing, Frank, but I'm all right… for now.'

'I'll fucking kill him,' Frank shouted down the phone. 'Put that fucking prick on, put him on, Bobby.'

Frank heard Bobby tell someone, 'He wants a word with you,' and the next minute Brewster was on the line.

'Is that the esteemed columnist, Frank Savage? How the devil art thou, Frank?'

Frank booted a filing cabinet.

'Listen to me, you cunt. If you lay one more finger on Bobby, I'll come down there and torch the place. Do you hear me? I'll fucking torch the place.'

Silence followed by more silence. Then a blood-curling scream.

'Sorry, Frank. I got a bit distracted there,' Brewster said. 'Anyway. So, the situation thus far is I've kidnapped the dognapper and need you to pay a ransom for his release. I want ten grand – that's double what you and the Gurkha valued my Waffen's life at, so I think it's more than fair. You can drop the money off when you come down to torch the place this evening. 8pm sharp, or your mate goes in the dog. And Frank, don't even consider going to the police. Toodles, ciao for now.'

Frank put his head in his hands and shook it from side to side. In that moment, he experienced a strange feeling of not knowing who he was or why he was here. An odd sensation of being outside of himself looking in. His heart raced and the clamminess descended. Frank wanted to run. He picked up the phone and dialled 999, fearing he was about to die. Deep breaths, deep breaths, one, two, three… nine, ten. He was still alive. Frank hung up the phone, recognising yet another panic attack. How the fuck was he going to get ten grand by 8pm? Frank thought about leaving Bobby to his fate, which seemed like a ready-made solution. In fact, he might phone Brewster back and ask if he could give him a hand to murder the daft bastard. He now regretted having spent most of the ten grand extra he'd borrowed from The Gypsy for incidentals, which included a repair bill for the Shadow, some Christmas presents and the two grand he'd blown at the bookies. He reckoned at best he could pull together a miserable three grand, leaving him seven thousand pounds short.

To compound the problem, Frank was in the news editor's chair and would be working with Richard as part of a skeleton staff. He thought about asking Naomi if she had any money, but tapping his recently not so estranged daughter for ten g's wasn't exactly in keeping with his new dad persona. He contemplated asking Bridget before he remembered the endless fights they'd had about money and how much he paid her in the divorce settlement. Bad idea. In the meantime, Frank had to put together a news list which he would run through with Richard, thus eating into his valuable time. The news list consisted of plundering what was left of the so-called "Christmas box", where each reporter provided four stories of varying quality to be used over the festive fortnight. Frank had failed to hit the required par four last Christmas, filing two tales that could best be described as "utter pish" but had been given a pass this year so he could concentrate on racking up the digital hits through his columns.

He spoke to Plunkett, who was also working, and asked him to call round the department stores to get the final figures for the Boxing Day sales and put in calls to the emergency services to see if anything was occurring. Plunkett had brought in a box of Mars Celebrations and had come round to being Frank's mate again as they argued over which sweet was the best – Frank: Malteser Teasers, Plunkett: Snickers – while both agreeing that the little Bounty bar was for weirdos. The two sub-editors came in with homemade cakes and Frank decided he was going to the bookies at lunchtime to bet his last three grand on a horse he fancied in the King George VI Chase.

Plunkett, who was as close as Richard had to a friend in the industry, couldn't resist giving Frank the gossip on the latest company travails to stay afloat amid rumours of a pending takeover by a Swedish media giant that would put the News Space of the Future launch in jeopardy. They both agreed that a bunch of eco-friendly, right-on, media-savvy Scandies would waste no time in putting them both to bed, with the redundancy on offer being of the compulsory "You've no choice, pal" nature as opposed to the voluntary "We'd really like it if you left" option. Frank had heard it all before and normally switched off to this kind of media-talk bollocks, but Plunkett hit him with the old Jimmy Cricket, "And there's more..." catchphrase.

Plunkett, whose record for keeping a secret was ninety seconds, said, 'It's all gone Neil Diamond in the Bell household, Franco.'

"'Love on the Rocks'", Frank cried. 'I bet Bridget's started taking him to Pilates.'

Frank had taken to thinking about his ex-wife whenever he needed to go somewhere nice and escape in his mind to a better time and place. A better time and place, long before they started doing Pilates. No, this was a better time and place, in the early days, when they were getting to know each other, laughing at each other's jokes and having regular sex. But a combination of them living together, Frank's behaviour which became increasingly erratic and Bridget's rise to fame put a strain on their relationship. Frank knew he was the self-proclaimed King of Banter and therefore assumed Bridget would always laugh at his jokes, but he was also self-aware enough to know that hearing his patter on an endless loop could begin to grate. Or, as Bridget often put it, was "really fucking annoying".

Plunkett was warming to his subject and keen to maintain their "friendship" to stay in the star columnist's good books. He said, 'Dick Bell-end looks like a bag of shite, and this is a guy who irons his pants and socks. He's been sleeping on the sofa for weeks since Bridget booted him out the bed. He swore me to secrecy, Frank, but you know I can't keep a secret, especially when it's in the public interest.'

Frank said, 'Yip, you spill your guts like a Newhaven fishwife.'

'So, the latest is he wants them to go and see a marriage counsellor.'

'He's onto plums there. Once Bridget has made up her mind, there's no going back. Guaranteed.'

'I don't know why she ever got in toe with him, Frank; she must have really wanted to get back at you.'

He was always mystified as to how a woman as smart and beautiful as Bridget had chosen to get married to two losers like him, a self-inflicted loser, and Dick Bell-end, who Frank considered a born loser and therefore perhaps less of a loser seeing as he had no say in the matter. Bridget had made a fortune writing a series of so-called chick-lit novels. Her success coincided with divorcing Frank, citing his excessive drinking and general unreliability as key factors. It was only years later when he picked up one of her books, which was lying in a hotel lobby in Madrid, that he realised the central male character was based on him. An alcoholic waster, oozing toxic masculinity, who acts as the catalyst for change in the life of the main protagonist, forcing her to embark on a journey of self-discovery, travelling to India, before discovering she prefers women. Touché, Bridget.

Frank went into Richard's office. The editor had a napkin tucked into the collar of his shirt and was picking away at the remains of a Christmas dinner out of the Tupperware box.

'All right, boss?' Frank asked. 'How was your Christmas?' Richard took the napkin out of his shirt and noticeably gave himself a jolt of energy.

'Marvellous, Frank. Absolutely bloody marvellous and thank you for asking. Bridget, Katie and I had a lovely time at my mother's, where we tried roast goose instead of turkey this year for a change.'

'Wow,' said Frank. 'Did you do the cooking?'

Richard put on his best fake smile and beamed with pride. 'Yes, Frank. I took control on the Bell kitchen flight deck. Followed Gordon Ramsay's recipe to the letter and provided all the trimmings, cooked the roasters in goose fat as well, which went down a treat. Then we played the Genius edition of Trivial Pursuit.'

Frank now had his deepest suspicions confirmed: Christmas at Mama Bell's had been a nightmare.

Richard decided to pivot the conversation back to work matters. 'Good news, I've got you booked onto the BBC Scotland Hogmanay special. Your old friend, Deidre McAllister, is hosting this year and there's a variety of guests lined up including the Minister for Culture, Shelby St. George, Chic McGrain from eighties favourites Token Gesture and Kyle Horsburgh the footballer, who'll announce the launch of his gambling addiction charity. Texas, and Scots newcomers the Pictish Fairies will be playing in the studio. Then they're going to cut to Princes Street Gardens where a giant hologram of the Bay City Rollers, singing "Shang-A-Lang", will be beamed onto the Ross Bandstand shortly after the Bells.'

Frank's heart sank at the prospect of sharing a sofa with these rockets and he'd always hated the Rollers. He'd already planned the traditional all-day Hogmanay bevvy session in The Hadd and was looking forward to passing out on his sofa and missing "the Bells" like he'd done for the past five years. Now Richard was throwing a large spanner in the works, leaving him with the prospect of not just working on Hogmanay but entering a tartan version of Dante's *Inferno*.

Frank said, 'I had plans for Hogmanay.'

Richard gave that less than a moment's thought before hitting him with the sales pitch.

'They're prepared to pay you fifteen hundred pounds to appear and there's a free bar after you bring in the New Year. It's only a few hours' work, Frank, and I'll put you through for another five hundred pounds on expenses. I plan to go with Bridget, and Plunkett is also invited, so the paper will be well represented.'

Frank felt his heart pound as it dawned on him that he was due The Gypsy his first payment of five thousand pounds on New Year's Day, so the money would come in handy.

'What is it exactly that they want me to do?' he asked.

'You've just to sit on the sofa, Frank. Deidre will no doubt engage you in a bit of light small talk, get you to compliment the bands while interacting with the other guests. But of course, as far as we're concerned, you have free rein to give classic "To Be Frank" opinions; they'll be expecting a bit of that, within reason.'

Frank had a lingering feeling that he was being set up but had decided he was in for a penny. He said, 'Will they be talking to Bridget? I mean, she'd be a decent guest.'

Richard looked sheepish as he attempted to bat away any talk of their former/current wife. 'I don't know, Frank. Deidre might mention her presence, or they may ask her a few questions as part of the audience. She'd expect that. But Bridget is always a bit reluctant to do interviews.'

'Does she know I'm coming?'

'Of course. It was her idea to have you as a guest and she mentioned your name to Deidre, who also thought it might be "interesting" and could liven things up a bit, give the Hogmanay show an element of danger.

'Frank Savage and the Minister for Culture sharing a sofa. What could possibly go wrong?' Frank stroked his chin and smirked. 'I've slaughtered the Minister a few times in the column, and I've never understood a word to come of Chic McGrain's mouth, especially when he wanks on about Scottish Independence. Can I bring a couple of mates?'

'Yes. You can bring a couple of friends, but they must behave. We don't want a repeat of that fiasco at the opening of the youth theatre. That's caused me no end of grief.'

Frank winced at the mention of the debacle.

'Who's been giving you grief about that? I was badly set up.'

Richard immediately went on the defensive. 'It's nothing to worry about, Frank. I've dealt with everything, including the footage that was doing the rounds appearing to show you taking drugs. I had a visit from a Mr Brewster, who I believe you know. He was urging me to sack you, but I gave him short shrift and told him where to go.'

Frank looked at Richard in disgust. 'Don't call that racist piece of hooligan scum "Mr Brewster". His name is Brewster and he's a murdering bastard. You need to be a bit more careful about who you invite into your office, Richard.'

Richard stood his ground. 'Now, now, Frank, there's no need to take that tone. I told Mr Brewster – sorry, Brewster – that the allegations were completely unfounded, and I would defend you to the hilt. This Brewster chap seems to do a lot for the local community and we're running a piece in the New Year about how he's turned his life around. He's running a women's football team and is heavily involved in the youth theatre, with a keen interest in sculpting. I don't think he's the fellow you think he is, Frank.'

'Listen, Richard. You're being played. The guy is a murdering psychopath. I can't prove it, but I know he was involved in the death of my brother, Michael.'

Both men stared at each other in stony silence.

'And another thing, I'm not your fucking star columnist. You're encouraging me to write ever-increasing mad shite so that you can generate digital hits and show the grown-ups how you've turned this crumbling paper around. I'm a useful idiot, nothing more. That might keep the wolves from the door for a few months, but I think we both know that the game's up for so-called legacy media and I've heard rumours that we might be getting taken over... again.'

Frank felt glad to have gotten that off his chest as he was getting sick of his new-found fame and craved a quiet life, preferably with Bridget, in a cottage, in the Scottish Borders, at some point in the not-too-distant future.

'Your column is great, Frank, always has been. People love it and, yes, it's now doing brilliantly online. But we are onto something here and are really tapping into the zeitgeist.'

'My last column was about belting children,' Frank snapped.

Richard leant back in his chair and attempted to put his foot up on the table but missed as the chair wobbled and he nearly fell off. He managed to regain his composure and, at that moment, Frank felt a bit sorry for him.

'I'll not lie to you, Frank. We've had our ups and downs, but I love my work and I know you love being a journalist as well. I've defended you at every opportunity and that includes batting away pressure from the Scottish government and numerous charities to have you fired. If we are to be bought out, I'll be the first to go as they always sack the editor, but I've never enjoyed my job more than I am just now and a lot of that is down to you.'

Frank thought the editor was almost starting to sound human.

Richard continued, 'So, you've already filed your next piece about tourists at Hogmanay, which I love. What are your plans for the one after that, the first column of the New Year? We need to maintain the momentum, keep striking while the iron is hot.'

Frank pondered this for a minute, then it came to him in a flash. 'That's a no-brainer, Richard. I'm going to write about banning child mascots at the football. It's gotten completely out of hand. I counted twenty-four of the little shits at the recent televised Man Utd v Liverpool game including one for the referee and one for the match ball. The players couldn't move for kids. Absolute shambles.'

He got up and walked out, leaving the office door open and a speechless editor behind.

Frank spent lunchtime shovelling chunks of homemade lemon cake into his mouth while telling the sub-editors they were "through to the next round" in the style of Paul Hollywood. All of this was a welcome distraction from the "get ten grand or we'll kill your best mate" problem which he'd decided to now give his full attention, seeing as time was marching on. He made his way down the hill to the bookies in Stockbridge which was full of punters desperate to part with their Christmas cash. Frank looked scornfully at these mugs. He had a tip for the big race given to him by Bert on the Sports desk and decided he was going to put his last three grand on the six-year-old Irish mare, *Ruby Murray*. Frank ignored a couple of customers who recognised him and handed the teller his betting slip with a price of 10/3 marked on it. He joked that the horse was "hot stuff" with Bert who had joined him in staking his "life savings" on the mare. Frank caught a glimpse of Bert's slip and saw he'd bet ten pounds each way. Frank told him he'd bet fifty pounds on the nose and Bert shook his head, saying, 'Madness! Sheer madness.' This unsettled Frank, who felt a throbbing sensation in the back of his left calf and noted his DVT had returned. The race started and Frank settled in for the longest five minutes and roughly fifty-five seconds of his life with champion jockey Aiden O'Hanlon keeping *Ruby Murray* at the back of the field. Frank and Bert joined the other punters shouting at the screen as the 25/1 outsider *Thinks He's Erchie* took an eight-length lead widely described as a "rookie move".

'He'll die a death,' Frank declared, with Bert nodding sagely in agreement.

Both men watched as O'Hanlon skilfully steered *Ruby Murray* gently up the field. The horse looked like it had hardly broken a sweat and Frank whispered, 'This is in the bag,' thinking about the thirteen thousand pounds that would soon be nestling in his pocket. Problem solved. Him and Bobby would have a monster sesh tonight. The noise in the bookies was through the roof now as anxious punters willed their favourites towards the finishing line. O'Hanlon brought *Ruby Murray* to the outside of the field, like a stealth bomber about to unleash its deadly arsenal. To say this magnificent beast had more in the tank was something of an understatement. Frank half expected the horse to light up a Hamlet cigar as it jumped the last fence and strode majestically towards the finish line, leaving the field of hapless nags who looked like they belonged on Blackpool Pleasure Beach trailing in its slipstream.

Frank turned from the screen, preparing to make his way to the payout desk, when an almighty groan went up. He turned round to see O'Hanlon lying in a crumpled heap on the turf ten yards from the finishing line as *Ruby Murray* shot past the finishing post in record time. The punters who bet on the horse were shocked into stunned silence. This was Devon Loch all over again – the horse who fell in the final straight of the 1956 Grand National. Shouts of 'Stewards' inquiry!' rang out but Frank had seen this movie before and was certain his three g's would be staying in the bookies' pocket.

'Well, that's twenty quid down the drain,' Bert cried, looking to Frank for sympathy, who stood rooted to the spot staring at the screen. 'Stupid cunt,' he added, before explaining to Frank that O'Hanlon had decided to start his trademark victory salute, where he raises both hands in the air, and had fallen off when the horse reacted.

'I can't believe you put fifty quid on, Frank. Madness! Sheer madness.'

21

Frank arrived back at his desk a broken man. He knew there was only one solution to the problem and his priority was now to get his best mate back safely in one piece. He cursed himself for being so stupid and, grabbing another piece of lemon cake, headed through to an empty marketing department to make the call. The Gypsy picked up on the first ring.

'It's Frank. I need to borrow another ten grand.'

The Gypsy let out a little chuckle. 'When do you need the money?'

'Right away,' Frank replied.

'Okay, I'll get the kettle on and work on the terms of our loan agreement,' The Gypsy said, all business without a trace of menace. Frank thanked him, hung up, then felt a wave of nausea before running to the toilet for a spew. *Where the fuck did that come from?* Frank thought, peering down the pan to see chunks of lemon cake with bits of rind in them. Then he remembered the seven pieces he'd eaten with half a box of chocolates as a chaser. Still, at least he'd fed his diabetes. A more immediate problem was getting away from the office to visit The Gypsy and pick up the ten grand. Frank checked with Plunkett to see how the paper was coming along. Mercifully, tomorrow's edition was only going to be half the size with a standard splash about the Boxing Day sales. He nipped in to see Richard, telling him that he had to attend to a "family emergency".

'Is it serious?' Richard asked with genuine concern.

'My dad has fallen, and my mum needs a hand taking him to the hospital. That's all. Not life-threatening,' Frank replied, thinking on his feet.

'Of course, Frank, off you go. Plunkett can put the paper to bed. It's only a skeleton edition. No need to come back.'

This was what he wanted to hear. 'Thanks, Richard. That's very kind of you.'

Frank had a vague notion of Dick Bell-end perhaps mentioning something to Bridget about this, then he remembered what Plunkett had told him earlier about their marriage being on shaky ground.

He arrived at The Gypsy's compound on the outskirts of town and was buzzed in by the same stocky youth who now had his neck tattoo coloured in.

The Gypsy was lounging on his sofa eating a giant box of Ferrero Rocher chocolates, papers strewn everywhere.

'Come in, Frank. Here's a chocolate,' he said, lobbing one in Frank's direction which he failed to catch.

'Fucking butter fingers.' The Gypsy laughed before getting down to business.

'I know what you need this money for, Frank. There's nothing in this town I don't know about. Your wee pal Gurkha Bobby's been nicking dogs again except this time he chose the wrong fucking dog to kidnap. Brewster wants ten grand and, seeing as Bobby has sweet fuck all, he's decided you, his old friend from Leith Academy, are the one to foot the bill.'

Frank munched on the whole chocolate that he'd stuck in his mouth.

'Yip, that's pretty much the story,' he said, cupping his hand under his mouth to stop the tiny pieces of nuts falling onto the shag-pile rug. 'I thought long and hard about not paying him as Bobby has overstepped the mark here.'

The Gypsy shouted through to the other room.

'Róisín, can you come here?'

A woman, with the bluest eyes Frank had ever seen, came into the room holding a baby. She was at least twenty years younger than The Gypsy and stunningly beautiful.

'Couple of teas, love. Milk with two for me. How do you take it, Frank?'

'Just milk, thanks,' Frank replied.

'Frank, meet the missus. Róisín, this is Frank, the journalist who helped us out in Craigmillar. Mind I was telling you about him.'

Róisín smiled. 'Pleased to meet you, Frank,' she said, before heading off to make the tea.

The Gypsy stood up, his giant frame filling the room.

'So, I take it you've already blown the ten grand I gave you for… what did you call it again?'

'Incidentals,' Frank replied.

'Ah, that's right, in-ci-dentals,' The Gypsy repeated slowly. 'You're already due me fifty grand with ten grand interest, Frank, and now you want another ten and I still haven't received a penny back.'

'I realise how bad this looks and I'm sorry to ask but I've got nowhere else to go. I know what Brewster is capable of and I don't want Bobby to get hurt.'

The Gypsy cracked his knuckles as Róisín brought in the teas, swiftly setting the tray down on a leather pouffe.

'Brewster is a fucking Dinky toy. He knows I'm the better man and I rule this city. I've kicked his arse a few times and I wouldn't hesitate to do it again. But on this occasion, I'm taking his side. Stealing a man's dog…well, that's a death sentence, from where I'm standing. Anyone dared lay a finger on my Satan or Hagler and they'd be pig feed.'

Frank nodded in agreement, a quick convert to the gangster's code.

'I know he's bang out of order but Bobby's not right in the

head. Proper tap-tap, curly-wurly cuckoo. But he's my man and I've got his back.'

This had the desired effect of placating The Gypsy.

'Okay, here's what I'll do. You can walk out of here today with another ten grand and I won't harm a hair on your head.' Frank instinctively touched his head. 'But you've now borrowed sixty thousand pounds and the interest on that is thirty grand, so you now owe me ninety thousand pounds.'

Frank nodded furiously, just glad to have solved his immediate problem.

'I'll give you six months to pay that amount in full or it goes up another thirty grand and you'll owe one hundred and twenty grand. After that, I'll be looking to take your house and both your ears.'

He took the money to Brewster's house as instructed, on the dot at eight o'clock. Frank had flirted with the idea of getting DI Hope involved, then thought better of it. Something about the situation with Naomi wasn't sitting right and he didn't want the police getting involved until he got to the bottom of it. He'd also thought about taking his baseball bat and having it out with Brewster and the Orangemen but gave that a swerve. The throbbing in the left calf was getting worse, the gout was killing him, and his heart felt like it was thumping on the outside of his body. Frank had kept taking the blood pressure tablets Dr Khan had prescribed but his alcohol and tobacco intake had soared of late and, if anything, the blood pressure readings were rising. He badly wanted to slip into his comfy Crocs but decided on the next best thing, a pair of navy-blue New Balance 574s, now considered a classic but Frank's trainer of choice for the last thirty years. He peered into the Portobello Bookshop tote bag that contained the ten thousand pounds in crisp fifties as he pressed the buzzer on the massive security gate, prompting a blinding white light to come on at the house, followed by a dazzling array of smaller lights scattered at regular intervals on the surrounding wall.

'Blackpool Illuminations,' Frank shouted at the wooden gate that automatically slid open.

'Stop right there, Savage. One more step and your mate is a dead man.'

Frank looked up to the balcony and saw Brewster holding what appeared to be a karaoke microphone. He wondered if this arsehole was going to give him a song.

'I've got your fucking money. Now give me Bobby and we'll hit the road.'

'Not so easy, my fat friend,' Brewster replied, motioning for Frank to enter the house.

By this point, Frank was wishing he'd given this a bit more thought and planning. Going through that door meant there was a fifty-fifty chance he wouldn't come out, and given events earlier in the day he didn't fancy his chances.

'No way. I'm not coming in. You can fucking keep Bobby and use him for a pin cushion for all I care but I'm not giving you the money.'

There followed a period of silence, like a Mexican standoff, without the Mexicans, where Frank wondered if they'd forgotten about him. Then Brewster appeared with the Two Billys but still no sign of the Gurkha.

'You can have your mate back, Savage. He can talk for fucking Pakistan, India and Nepal, that cunt. Never shuts up. Joanna Lumley this, Joanna Lumley that, then it was on to The Specials and how there should only be one serve in tennis.'

Frank laughed nervously, then felt the anger starting to burn.

'I hope he's all right, for your sake, Brewster. You were always a fucking bully. Picking your victims and getting someone else to do your bidding for you. This time, it's the Irish Two Ronnies or whatever they're called.'

It took a moment for it to register with Billy One that Frank was taking the piss. Billy Two was oblivious.

'You better button your lip, boy,' Billy One warned. 'We've still got your mate.'

Brewster disappeared into the house and came back holding Waffen with a dishevelled Bobby shuffling behind. Frank handed over the tote bag as Bobby knelt to pet the dog and say his goodbyes.

'Fuck's sake, Bobby. Why don't you just join them?' Frank said, relieved to see that apart from the black eyes and swollen lip his mate appeared unharmed.

Brewster wasn't about to let them leave without a lecture.

'Listen, you pair of cunts. It ends here. All this shite must stop. I'm back in Porty and you're going to have to get used to seeing my ugly pus fucking everywhere. The posh pricks who live here now love me, and if they ever appoint a mayor, I'll be the prime candidate.'

Frank put his arm round Bobby and made to leave but Brewster couldn't help himself.

'Tell Naomi I said hi, Frank.'

Frank was off his mark like Usain Bolt. He launched himself at Brewster and connected with a perfect diving headbutt on the bridge of his nose. Brewster screamed in terror as a fountain of blood poured from his beak.

'Bastard! Get the bastard!' he shouted at the Billys, who stood frozen to the spot. Billy One was first to react, making to grab Frank, who smashed his elbow into the Orangeman's face, making a sickening crunching sound in the process.

Bobby decided now was a good time to get involved and booted Billy One in the balls.

'Have some of that, cunt,' he cried with glee.

Brewster shouted at Waffen to attack but the dog let out a whimper, not wanting to bite his new friend. A shot rang out as Billy Two fired in the air, then brought a swift end to proceedings by pointing his handgun at Frank's head.

'Do the cunt!' Billy One screamed. 'Fucking do him.'

'No! No!' Brewster screamed, regaining his composure as the blood poured out of his nose. 'Get out, get the fuck out,' he shouted, urging Frank and Bobby to leave.

Frank grabbed Bobby and headed into the street where they hailed a black cab, telling the driver to take them to Ramsay Tech. The two men sat in silence for the journey of less than two miles, with Frank throwing a crumpled tenner at the driver when they pulled up outside his flat. He fumbled to get his key in the door.

'Fuck me, Bobby, that was a close one. He would have shot us. No doubt about it.'

'Us?' Bobby replied. 'You were like a fucking Tasmanian devil back there.'

The last thing Frank remembered was seeing a blinding flash, then Michael's face as he pressed the lift button, before collapsing and passing out.

Michael

I remember the night my brother died like it was yesterday. It was bitterly cold, one of those evenings that Scottish people describe as being "too cold to snow", as I made my way back from the Café Royal bistro bar which we all called "upstairs at the Café Royal" or the "Café Royal up the stairs".

The Murrayfield Racers ice hockey team were in and a few rugby players from Heriot's having a late Christmas night out in the second week in January, which was a lively affair. I was drunk but not steaming, just topping up during that dead period in Edinburgh between New Year and the start of what was then the Five Nations Rugby when the city exploded back into life.

I was due to move down to London the following week to start a new job with Future Space *magazine as a features writer and was buzzing to get started, although people didn't say they were "buzzing" back in 1988.*

I had not long split up with my girlfriend, Bridget, and was thinking of giving her a call from the phone box in Leith Walk to ask if I could come down to Portobello for a "visit" but decided my need for a kebab was greater than my need for break-up sex, not that it was on the cards. We had split up after an argument about my drinking and it would have been rubbing salt into open wounds if I turned up pissed.

For reasons that would become clear, I remember the tiniest detail from the journey home to my house in Leith Links that fateful night. Every move would become ingrained in my mind; a photo album of misery that I could dig out whenever I felt the need to mentally self-harm. The smell of the roast potatoes that Ahmed put in with my kebab like he always did, and the taste of the chilli sauce on the meat combined with the folded flatbread. I had met a couple of guys I knew in the kebab house and the craic was flying. They were giving it the old "Chicken Curry YLT" gang shout and I told them they had the wrong takeaway if they were looking for a curry and should head to the Silver Bowl.

A rammy broke out when a paralytically drunk guy spewed in the shop and Ahmed had come round the other side of the counter and booted the jakey up the hole, telling him he was a "dirty bastard" before kicking him to the kerb. Ahmed's wife had brought out the mop and the disinfectant and cleaned up the sick. The smell of bleach was on me after that.

I walked down Leith Walk, avoiding the drunks playing dodgems with the parked cars and zigzagging across the road as I passed Storries Bakery and watched two women fighting outside the Volunteer Arms, affectionately known as The Volley, which was apt given that one of the combatants had just booted the other one in the pus. I made my way along Duke Street, past the baked potato shop where I bought my tea most nights, to the front of Leith Links and approached the family home.

By this time, the snow was starting to fall, and the stars were out.

My mind had drifted to London and the people I would be working with, the nightlife and the massive opportunity that lay ahead. I had done well at the tabloid and loved the cut and thrust of deadlines and smashing the competition, but this was a chance to do something truly creative and, like most journos, I harboured ambitions to become a "serious writer". However, my immediate plan was to have another drink and stay up to watch All the President's Men which was the late-night film on BBC2, while polishing off the last of the selection boxes.

I approached our house and saw there were two police cars outside and every light in the house was on. My mind raced and I felt a heavy weight on my chest as I knew right away that something had happened to Michael. Dad saw me coming up the drive and ran out the front door. He came towards me with a look on his face that I'll never forget as I heard my mother sobbing loudly in the kitchen, a woman police officer trying to comfort her.

'It's your brother,' Dad said.

'What do you mean it's my fucking brother? What about my brother? Where is he?'

Dad said, 'He's gone, Frank.'

'Gone where?' I replied.

I was raging and asked him what the fuck he was talking about, not letting him off the hook and forcing him to say the unsayable.

'Michael is dead,' he said, eyes dropping to the ground as a wave of emotion shuddered through his body.

We then had that pointless one-way conversation where I told my father that my brother could not be dead, giving a myriad of reasons that ranged from him "being only nineteen" to him "having everything to live for" and rounding off with "but we had fish suppers together for our tea."

He kept saying, 'He's gone, son. He's gone. Gone.'

I felt the blood drain out of me and realised my drunkenness had completely evaporated as I stared transfixed at the blanket of snow that now covered Leith Links, which had never looked more beautiful. Little did I know then the pain that first snow of winter would bring me at the start of each new year.

But my instant reaction was to get angrier. Why was everyone lying to me? What kind of sick joke was being played here? I grabbed one of the police officers and shouted, 'What the fuck is going on?' refusing point-blank to accept what my father had just told me ten times.

I went into the kitchen and saw my mother with tears streaming down her face, grabbing tissues out of a black box with "Man-Size Tissues" written on the side, and thinking the serious tissues were out for this one. We clung on to each other for an eternity and I tried to push the tears into my eyes, but the alcohol was blocking the signals to my brain, and I couldn't cry. Was I trying to wing emotion? This thought would haunt me in my sleep for evermore.

But the tears would come later, floods of them, building up to a tsunami of tears, lasting forty days and forty nights. I remember the smell of my mum: the mix of L'Air du Temps perfume and Embassy Filter cigarettes – the ones in the white packet with the red stripe down the middle like the Ajax football strip. My aunty, uncle and cousins had arrived along with my mum's friend, Jean, who was pouring everyone large whiskies straight from the Scottish playbook titled, "101 Good Reasons to Crack out the Bevvy". The urge to drink had left me as my need for answers took hold.

The sergeant took me aside and told me there had been an accident and Michael had fallen off the top board at the derelict open-air pool in Portobello – a special place where we had spent long hot summers as kids. I couldn't comprehend what he was saying. Why had Michael been at the open-air pool on a freezing cold night? The place had shut in 1979 and had lain in ruins for the last nine years. The top board at the open-air pool? This held a significance in our family as I had jumped off there as a daredevil eight-year-old and Michael had watched me do it. Was he sending me a message? Had he killed himself?

I listened carefully to what the sergeant was telling me as my father looked on. He was being cagey, and I became aware that he was trying to avoid any mention of suicide but wasn't giving us proper answers.

'How exactly did my brother die?'

The sergeant, who was now joined by the female police officer, tried to palm me off with accident chat, telling me to have a drink, using phrases like "too soon" and "too early".

'Please, officer, cut the bullshit and give us the facts,' I pleaded.

He closed the door to the kitchen and sat my father and me down on the sofa. He said, 'Someone called 999 shortly before midnight to say there had been an accident and a person had fallen off the top board at the pool and could they send an ambulance right away. The operator told them to stay on the line until the ambulance crew arrived, but the male caller said, "It doesn't look good," before hanging up.'

Dad was silent, trying to process what the sergeant had told him. I noticed the sergeant was choosing his words very carefully and in doing so was making things worse. He was inferring something, and it didn't take a genius to work out where this was going. I pressed him for more facts on how Michael was now lying dead, steering him away from the homophobia that was emanating from his every pore like a queer-hating Ready Brek glow.

Dad asked if he fell into the water. The sergeant said, 'No, there was no water. The pool was drained years ago; if there was water there, he would still be alive. Your son landed on the concrete and the absence of any water added around four metres to his fall. You'd have to be really lucky to survive from that height.'

I said, 'Michael had nae luck then,' which sounded as harsh as I'd meant it to. I then said, 'Was he killed instantly from the fall? Can we speak to the ambulancemen? I want to see his body.'

The sergeant was looking glum and had the air of a man who had performed one too many of these duties and was longing for his kip.

He said, 'My understanding is that Michael died instantly from the fall. He was dead when the ambulance crew arrived, although I believe they carried out CPR in the form of chest compressions and mouth-to-mouth resuscitation, but they couldn't revive him. I'm truly sorry for your loss.'

Aunty Jean came through at that point with a tray of tea and the "good biscuits", which the sergeant was now giving his full attention. I felt a sense of hopelessness wash over me, like a footballer arguing with the referee who has just awarded a penalty kick in the last minute of the cup final.

I said, 'Have you been able to trace the man who called 999? Was it a teenager? Or an adult? Maybe this guy murdered my brother.'

I stopped there, having hit the sergeant – who was taking the wrapper off a caramel wafer – with a quick hat-trick of questions, none of which he was prepared to answer. He dipped the end of the biscuit into the tea and effected his everyman persona.

He said, 'We're as anxious to find answers as you are and will be carrying out a thorough investigation into the circumstances of this tragedy.'

Yeah, just as soon as you've finished your biscuit, *I thought*.

'An appeal will be launched for information and anyone who was in the area will be asked to come forward. I know from experience that the derelict pool is often used by youths who go there to sniff glue and get up to all kinds of nonsense, so we'll be bringing in a few of the usual suspects for questioning and we aren't ruling anything out at this stage.'

I was starting to lose patience with this Masonic oaf. I shouted, 'Michael wasn't a glue sniffer. He was going to art college to study printed textiles. He was always scared to go into the pool.'

I contemplated this for a moment. That was right; my brother had shat out of breaking into the pool through the hole in the wall a couple of times, years ago when Bobby and I had gone there with him for a nosey. What had changed his mind? Or, more to the point, who had changed his mind?

The sergeant said, 'Apologies. I didn't mean to offend anyone.'

Dad reassured him he hadn't in that pathetically Scottish way of deferring to authority, any kind of authority. The sergeant got up to leave, nodding to the female officer to join him. This was the cue for Aunty Jean to ask them if they wanted more tea or "something stronger", not quite registering that the police weren't the ones doing the mourning. I remember the sergeant rounded off proceedings in a businesslike fashion.

He said, 'A death of this nature will likely be referred to the coroner for a post-mortem examination. You should contact the family doctor in the morning. One of the detectives might want to ask you some questions as part of their investigation. Once again, I'm sorry for your loss.'

The police officers left. I remember looking at the carriage clock in our living room and thinking that in the space of an hour I'd gone from eating a kebab without a care in the world to losing the person I loved the most, who I would now never see again. The cops hadn't left a physical smell, but their presence had polluted our family home and clung to the place. How dare they come here and ruin our family? How dare they come here with their "phone-it-in" procedure for breaking bad news and ham-fisted attempt at providing comfort?

Dad was now attempting to carry out his own post-mortem, one where Michael's "lifestyle" was the main cause of death. I knew this was in the post. But I never imagined it would come first class as a signed for special delivery, less than two hours after his son had perished.

'I told you, Rita. I told you something like this would happen. Some bloody poof has gone and killed our Michael. Christ knows what he was up to in that pool,' he said.

I shook my head but felt drained of all energy and didn't have the strength to have a go at the old man. 'He wasn't your Michael,' I said. 'He was his own man.'

I hit the whisky after that and decided to sleep on the living-room couch – my bed for the next fortnight. The thought of going into the room I shared with Michael was too hellish for words. The Betty Blue *poster hanging on his side of the room, next to his pile of magazines,* The Face, *that mum was always threatening to throw out.*

'Get rid of those bloody magazines.'

His clothes. The weekend staples: white T-shirt, Levi 501s, Doc Martens and a black leather jacket that he got from Armstrongs, the vintage clothing shop in the Grassmarket. Memories of playing "Bizarre Love Triangle" by New Order before I headed to Buster's with the footballers and Michael would go to trendier places like Oblomov up the Mound, then The Hooch. His entourage was cooler; the art students and young women who looked pale and interesting with bright-red lipstick. I was due to move out at the weekend and had been looking forward to us spending our last night together, having shared a room for the last nineteen years. Now it dawned on me that last night was the final time we would sleep in the same room.

I said goodnight to Mum and gave Dad a pass for his outburst as I settled into the living room. I never slept a wink and watched the dawn rise over the Links, letting the enormity of the loss sink in. The only person I wanted to think about was my brother, but a shadow was lingering at the back of my mind, a cancerous thought that was making its way to my frontal lobe. Brewster and his cronies had chased Michael along Portobello promenade on Christmas Eve and had been hanging around the pool. I remembered how they boasted of poof-bashing up Calton Hill and around the toilets on London Road where cottaging took place. A couple of gay guys had been put in intensive care and it was only a matter of time before the inevitable happened and someone got murdered.

Things were different in Edinburgh back in the 1980s. Being gay was a life choice where you literally took your life in your hands. There were no rainbow flags or pink triangle area around Greenside back in the bad old days when the gay scene was barely above ground and the thought of a gay village encompassing Broughton Street was but a pipe dream. Michael told me about his first trip to a gay bar called Chaps next to The Playhouse and how he would sit on the steps outside St Mary's Catholic Cathedral working up the courage to go in. Heaven or Hell? Things were more covert then and you knocked on the door and a flap opened whereby the doorman decided if you were in with the "in crowd" or out on the pavement. Michael was buzzing to have finally made it across the threshold of Chaps and Frank recalled how he never looked back, having had a great time being with like-minded people from his own tribe. He grew in confidence and became a regular at Chaps, The Laughing Duck and the nightclub, Fire Island.

Was Brewster involved in my brother's death? That thought would plague me for the next thirty-five years.

22

Naomi got the call from Bobby saying Frank was in the hospital after passing out, at the same time as a text dropped from the Wise One that read: *Afternoon Tea, Balmoral Hotel, 2pm today.* Although her immediate concern was for her father, she knew better than to miss the meeting. She quizzed Bobby on the details, knowing full well Frank had gone to see Brewster with the ransom money but not wanting to let on she knew.

'So, when did this happen, Bobby?' Silence on the other end of the line.

'Eh? Last night,' Bobby replied after an age.

'Last night. Where, Bobby? What were the pair of you up to last night, because you're sounding cagey as fuck.'

'No! No! There's nothing to worry about, Naomi. Honestly.'

'Normally when people say "honestly", they're lying, Bobby – that's my experience. My dad is in the hospital which is something to worry about and I need an explanation as to how he got there.'

'Okay, Okay, I get it. I'll tell you but please promise me you won't go mad.'

Naomi felt like she was now talking to a child. 'I promise I won't go mad.'

'Well...' Bobby said before clamming up.

'Well what, Bobby? I'm all ears here.'

'Well, to cut a long story short, returning the dog to Brewster never went quite as I'd planned and they ended up kidnapping me. Brewster wanted Frank to pay double the ransom that I was asking for Waffle to let me go, that's ten grand, which your dad got and gave to Brewster last night.' Bobby paused for breath as Naomi listened on.

'So, as I was saying, Frank gave Brewster the ten grand and they released me, but Brewster said something to wind your dad up as we were leaving and… Frank being Frank, well…'

'Well what, Bobby? What did Frank do?'

'Well, Frank stuck the head on him a beauty, then elbowed one of those Northern Irish pricks in the face and the other one pulled a gun and threatened to blow his brains out, but there's nothing to worry about, Naomi. Honestly.'

'What did Brewster say to my dad?'

'He said, "Tell Naomi I said hi", which I didn't think was that offensive, but Frank went ballistic.'

Naomi bent double, the contents of her stomach threatening to explode onto the carpet.

'Are you sure that's what he said, Bobby?'

'Yip, certain, as God is my witness, he said, "Tell Naomi I said hi." To be fair, Brewster was the one that eventually got us out of there without getting shot. That Billy Two character would have killed the pair of us. No doubt about it.'

'Jesus wept,' Naomi cried, a phrase she'd picked up from her dad.

'So, what happened after you left? You still haven't told me how Dad ended up in the hospital.'

'Well,' Bobby replied, 'we got a taxi and went back to Ramsay Tech for a stiff drink. Frank didn't say a word in the cab and was sweating and breathing heavily. We got to the flat and he pressed the button for the lift, then he fell to his knees and passed out. I thought he was having a heart attack, so I phoned the ambulance, and they came right away.'

Naomi listened intently as she ran into the bathroom to be sick.

'Naomi, are you all right?' Bobby asked, after hearing her retch.

'Yeah, yeah. I'm fine, carry on, carry on. Was my dad still unconscious when the ambulance came?'

'No. He came round after I put him on his side. It wasn't a heart attack, more of a funny turn. Anyway, he wasn't for going in the ambulance, but the paramedics were having none of it. I went to the hospital, but Frank sent me away after the doctor said they were keeping him in overnight for observation and were running tests. He called me this morning to say he was getting out later today and had been diagnosed with heart arrhythmia – an irregular heartbeat. They're putting him on beta blockers and he's to make lifestyle changes that the doctor said, "were not up for debate".'

Naomi told Bobby she'd pick her dad up from the hospital later that day before giving up on trying to talk sense into him and hanging up. Her mind raced as she thought about contacting Brewster to warn him to keep the fuck away from Frank but decided it was best to stay in lane and act professionally. All this stuff with her dad, Bobby and Brewster was a sideshow. Frank's health was the priority and she felt guilty for adding to his general stress levels, knowing he was onto her and didn't believe a word she had said. Naomi knew she'd have to come clean with him about her real job sooner rather than later.

The long-term plan wasn't under threat. Brewster had done the business for the Syndicate and Naomi realised she would have to cement her status as an asset to stay in the game. Any goodwill the Wise One had towards her would be trumped by the need to make the cinema a success and ultimately see the London mob take control of Scotland's capital. The Wise One was seeking an update on the cinema project, and Brewster could fill him in on the details. He had, after all, told her everything was going smoothly, and the councillors' votes were in the bag when the motion to approve would be put before the planning committee on 5th January. Naomi was more than a little apprehensive to be meeting her former Uncle Ray, now her boss. She realised the dynamic of their relationship had changed since she was a teenager and was now strictly business. Given the news from Bobby, she was dreading having to get dressed up and go for afternoon tea with the biggest drug dealer in the UK, who, by any standards, also fit the definition of a serial killer. Naomi tried to focus on the positive.

She was loving Portobello and her new flat, which was fifty yards from the seafront. The furnishings had been kept to a minimum; a sofa, comfy chair, coffee table and medium-sized TV in the living room where the picture from Frank of her mother took pride of place. A trip to IKEA had sorted her out with everything else she needed and the extra payment for assembly of the drawers was money well spent. A new Golf GTI was parked outside the flat; a decent runaround and not too flash.

Naomi's phone rang. It was Brewster.

'It's me,' he said.

'Who's me?' she replied, looking to piss him off.

'Me, you fucking know who me is, don't come the cunt. I'm not saying my fucking name on this phone. Did you get a message from the Cockney?'

Naomi weighed up her answer, then decided to play the daft lassie.

'No. He's not due up till tomorrow.'

Brewster said, 'Well, it looks like there's been a change of plan and he's here now. I got a text message saying I've to meet him at the top of Arthur's Seat at 2pm today. Christ knows what the fuck that's all about. I thought we were supposed to brief him tomorrow about the cinema project.'

Naomi quickly weighed up all the angles before replying.

'Yes, that's the instruction. To my knowledge, there's been no change of plan. He's extremely careful and probably wants to meet you beforehand to have a chat. Out in the open, away from prying eyes and security cameras. You can't get more open than the top of Arthur's Seat. A kind of meeting before the meeting, if you like. He hasn't met you before, right?' Naomi asked, resisting the urge to bring up Frank.

'No, I don't know him from Adam. We've always communicated through my Dutch contact and now you.'

'Don't worry. This is how he operates. He likes to keep people on their toes.'

Brewster sounded flummoxed, said he didn't like it and would be taking his own precautions.

'Quite right, it would be daft not to,' Naomi said, before adding, 'Is there anything else you want to tell me?'

Brewster snapped, 'Aye, you've probably heard about the run-in I had with your cunt of a dad and his rocket of a mate. I'll deal with them later.'

Now it was Naomi's turn to get angry. 'You'll do no such thing. We'll discuss this face-to-face.'

Brewster told her to let him know if she got word from the Wise One and hung up. Naomi's first thought was that the Syndicate were going to take care of him there and then. But why would they give him warning of what looked like an obvious set-up for a hit? No, she reckoned the Wise One was just having a bit of fun at Brewster's expense by making him climb Arthur's Seat. She pulled the top drawer of her bedside cabinet to look at the Glock 43. Naomi thought about taking it to the hotel, then decided against it.

The Wise One scared the living shit out of her. A ruthless boss who wouldn't let sentiment stand in the way of having her done in and chopped into a thousand little pieces if she didn't deliver on his plans. Naomi had heard all the rumours. How Armstrong got the nickname "Stretch" and it certainly wasn't after the action figure. No, this Armstrong was a connoisseur of medieval torture instruments, with a vast array of devices designed to cause maximum pain before dislocating then eventually separating hip, knee, shoulder, and elbow joints. His favourite toy was a wooden-framed rack. JJ had witnessed a Turkish rival to the Syndicate being placed on the rack and had filled Naomi in on the gory details. The guy was screaming for his mother by the end of his ordeal and was literally in bits before Uncle Ray put him out of his misery with two to the back of the head. The Wise One was now officially "off the tools" according to JJ, with his last hurrah being to crucify one of his own men suspected of being a grass, with a wooden cross he had built himself.

The Wise One had come up in the music business through the seventies up to the early nineties. He then moved into Soho and ran sex shops, spotting the potential of the internet on the smut trade way before anyone else in the UK outside the tech sphere. By the early 2000s, Armstrong was a key player in the online sex trade, setting up hundreds of sites, making a fortune from the sale of adverts and products with protected paywalls linking punters to the spicier content. This, combined with his ongoing drug, prostitution and protection rackets, provided him with the money to move into property redevelopment around the East End. By the time of the 2012 London Olympics, the Wise One's personal wealth was valued at around five hundred million and was set to double after the games, once the sweeteners kicked in on a variety of so-called "legacy" projects including a cycling velodrome that was now gathering dust.

Naomi approached the Balmoral Hotel which looked splendid against the backdrop of the Christmas decorations and rapidly fading daylight. She struggled to get her head round how it got dark so quickly in Scotland during December and had started going to bed at 9pm. Walking in, she was greeted by a member of staff resplendent in tartan trousers, waistcoat and wearing a hat with a feather on the side who held the door open. She made her way through to a glass-domed upmarket champagne bar with palm trees, where she spotted the Wise One who was getting up to greet her and appeared to be wearing the same outfit as the doorman. Was he moonlighting? He gave her a big hug and any feelings of awkwardness quickly evaporated. The Wise One was beaming and gestured for her to sit down.

'Well, Naomi, what do you think of the get-up?'

'You look great, Uncle Ray.'

Her heart skipped a beat as the Wise One paused two seconds for effect, just enough to put the fear of death in Naomi, before he burst into laughter and started to pour the tea.

'The trousers are from the Armstrong ancient clan and the badge I'm wearing has our motto on it, *Invictus Maneo*.' He held up his label to show Naomi. 'That means "I Remain Unvanquished" and I plan to keep it that way.'

Naomi nodded in agreement.

The Wise One said, 'I've been doing my homework, and it turns out I'm quite the little Jock, twice removed. Did you know that Neil Armstrong took a piece of this tartan with him onto the moon? We're probably related, Neil and I.'

He passed Naomi a plate of cucumber sandwiches and she shoved a whole one in her mouth. They exchanged more pleasantries and the Wise One reminisced about Maxine's 'voice of an angel' before he turned to business.

'So, what do you make of this Brewster?'

Naomi took a beat to think this one through. Did Armstrong already know about the dognapping and fight with her dad? He would see through any sitting on the fence and certainly wouldn't appreciate a fudged answer, so she decided to give him it straight.

'He's a toerag of the highest order.'

The Wise One sat back and took a moment to contemplate what she was saying. 'Expand.'

'Well, he seems to have delivered on the councillors and tells me the cinema project is in the bag. And he has got the women's football team and the youth theatre up and running, so he gets some marks on his report card. On the downside, he's skimmed one hundred thousand pounds from the money to pay the councillors off, has already tortured a couple of drug dealers, is running a car wash on the side and has two goons over from Northern Ireland dealing without your say-so. He's racist, borderline psychotic, hates Catholics and Jews; in fact, he probably hates everyone apart from his mother, dog and the Nazis. He loves the Nazis.'

The Wise One contemplated what she had said, savouring a tiny piece of carrot cake. 'I know this already. Unfortunately, he's the standard type of nutter we do business with these days. Is it just a matter of time before he goes? There's plenty more racists in the sea.'

The Wise One had put her on the spot – a test. Naomi thought carefully about her reply as she picked up a strawberry tart, feeling like Brewster's life was in her sticky hands.

'Eventually he might have to go, but I can control him for now. I don't think he's stupid enough to try anything directly against you, but I'm sure his plan is to muscle in and take over the drugs trade in Edinburgh. He knows the terrain and has contacts all over the city from his hooligan days. He'll have his own supply chain with the Dutch and the Northern Irish. So, he's well worth the watching.'

The Wise One nodded and seemed placated by Naomi's answer. Then he threw her a curveball that knocked her for six. 'So, all this bother with him and your old man. Has that been sorted?'

Naomi knew the Wise One's tentacles stretched far and wide but was shocked he had the skinny on the recent shitstorm involving her dad, Bobby and Brewster. Who had filled him in so quickly on that? Had he been watching them?

She sighed, clasping her hands behind her head, and leaning back in the chair. 'Yeah. I'm sorry about all of that. My dad is quite the celebrity up here, as you're no doubt aware, but I reckon he could help us promote the cinema in the long run. He's got some kind of grudge against Brewster, and they were at school together. Him appearing back on the scene has triggered my old boy, and his daft mate, Bobby, kidnapped Brewster's dog after a fight at the opening of the youth theatre. A mess, if truth be told, but it's quietened down for now,' she said, lying through her teeth.

'Get it under control, Naomi.'

She didn't need to be told twice.

The Wise One took a sip of champagne. 'I know your old man from way back. A good guy; I've got a lot of time for him. He stood up when Maxine was getting hassle from some drug dealer who was trying to get her on the smack. Sorted the guy out, he did. Frank was a bit wild back in the nineties but great for a night out. Tell him I said hi.'

'Yeah, my dad hasn't grown up.'

Armstrong returned to business.

'We're having a proper look at this Brewster as we speak to see if our guys recognise these ex-paramilitaries and if we've come across them before. Right, now tuck into some cake and enjoy the ambience. You could do with putting on a few pounds.'

Just as Naomi was processing that last comment, Falco appeared with Olga, both dressed up to the nines, and approached the Wise One, greeting him like a long-lost brother.

'Ray Armstrong, the one and only. What's it been, twenty years? That time I supported *The Waterboys* at the Roundhouse.'

The Wise One appeared completely unflustered as he got up and kissed Olga on the cheek, with a familiarity that made Naomi think they hadn't just met.

'That was in 1990, so you're at least ten years out, my Yankee friend.'

Falco laughed theatrically and grabbed a glass of champagne off the next table, downing it in a oner.

'Some things never change,' the Wise One said. 'I believe you three already know each other,' he added.

Falco kept up the theatrics. 'Of course, the lovely Naomi. I'm friends with her father, sold him the Shadow. You know, the one you always had your eye on, Ray.'

Something about the way Falco and Olga were acting around the Wise One didn't sit right with Naomi but she couldn't put her finger on it.

'Right, I better be going,' she said. 'It looks like you lot have a lot of catching up to do.'

Falco got up to see her off, giving her a big hug. 'Tell Frank I'm asking for him. Your pater is one mad cat.'

The Wise One got up to escort Naomi to the front entrance, taking her firmly by the arm.

'Good to see you, my love. You're doing well, so keep your chin up. This project is vital and I've every faith in you to keep things running smoothly. I want you to sit Brewster and your dad down in the same room and spell it out to them. This shit ends. Make sure Brewster is aware this comes from me.'

Naomi's stomach rumbled and she felt weak, knowing this would blow her cover with Frank.

'Yes. That's a great idea. I'll sit them down and warn them they must behave.'

The Wise One, bringing his voice down to a whisper, said, 'You'll get a message tomorrow to come up to Arthur's Seat to meet me and we'll see what Brewster has to say for himself. Take care, Naomi.'

The last sentence did little to quell the rising bile in her throat as she headed out into Princes Street.

Naomi arrived at the hospital to find her father outside smoking a cigarette. She grabbed it from his mouth and stubbed it out, with Frank offering little by way of resistance.

'Look at the nick of you, Dad,' she cried, giving him a big hug.

Frank had tears in his eyes. 'What a fucking mess, Naomi. I need to sort my life out and this is the wake-up call I need.'

'Smoking isn't going to help you, Dad.'

'No, no, the snout's going. It's on the list, and it's a very big list of lifestyle changes.'

Naomi was torn between giving him a row and wanting to give him another hug. At that moment she'd never felt closer or further away from him at the same time and longed to put things right. Stop the lies and come clean. They walked back into the hospital where the nurses were waiting on Frank.

'Can we get a selfie?' two of the younger nurses asked, putting their arms round Frank before a senior nurse told them off.

'Quite the celebrity, aren't we?' Naomi said as the nurse consultant handed him an envelope that contained a diet sheet along with his beta blockers and a host of leaflets about heart arrhythmias.

'Okay, Mr Savage, be sure to take on board what we discussed and make those changes. Take the tablets regularly and stay off the alcohol. You make sure he does what he's been told,' the nurse said to Naomi, who thought, *That'll be the first time,* as Frank nodded like a naughty schoolboy. Back in the car and everything that needed to be said was left unsaid, replaced by constipated small talk with them both skirting around the pressing issues. Finally, Naomi broke the silence.

'You'll never guess who I bumped into at the Balmoral Hotel today, Dad.'

'Barack Obama...' Frank replied, staring out across the Forth.

Naomi laughed nervously.

'No, Dad. Ray Armstrong, my old Uncle Ray. The guy who helped launch Maxine's career.'

Naomi looked across at Frank to read his expression but all she got was the back of his head as he continued to stare out across the Forth.

Finally, he said, 'Christ, that's a blast from the past, Naomi. Did he recognise you or did you speak to him?'

'No, we were introduced by someone from my firm. His wife is our chief exec. He twigged as soon as he heard my name. He's up here for Hogmanay. Looks well, was asking for you.'

'I bet he was,' Frank replied, finally turning round to face her. 'I bet he was.'

23

Brewster, sporting a bruised nose and two black eyes courtesy of Frank's head, dressed up in his new hillwalking gear in preparation for climbing Arthur's Seat to meet the Wise One. He'd dropped the best part of a "bag of sand" in that posh camping shop and was now decked head-to-toe in North Face gear like a cross between a drug dealer and someone auditioning for *SAS: Are You Daft Enough?* He'd struggled with the laces on his hiking boots and cursed why there were no holes to thread them through, only little tent peg things, that he eventually got the hang of. Brewster had climbed Arthur's Seat once before in the early nineties to beat up a couple of ravers who had gone there to watch the sun come up and bathe in the early May dew. He'd ended up letting them off with the money they owed him, having been caught up in the sheer beauty of the view, deciding to join them in taking one of his own E's, then going for a bevvy with his new pals and a bunch of students at the Moo Bar in Buccleuch Street. Despite getting on great, the ravers got their legs broken later in the week when the inevitable comedown kicked in and he changed his mind over the outstanding dosh.

It had only taken him about an hour to climb the hill, but he felt anxious on the ascent, not because he was meeting the Wise One but because he'd done a bit of research about Arthur's Seat and discovered it was a "distinct volcano", which meant, in his eyes, it could erupt again. Although unlikely, Brewster could not rule out the possibility that the fucking thing would erupt like that Mount Edna while he was on top of it waiting for this Cockney prick to show up. None of the so-called experts could be sure what dormant, distinct or active even meant.

Brewster was feeling sick to the teeth of being a gangster by this point and wished he could hand his notice in, perhaps working on for a month before having a leaving do.

'Who has a meeting on top of a fucking volcano?' he asked the gorse bushes on the way up, feet killing him, with the beginnings of a blister taking shape on his heel.

He contemplated why the Wise One was pulling this stunt and realised it was about control and showing Brewster who was boss. *No bother*, he thought, *I'll bide my time with him.* He had sent the Two Billys on ahead to suss out the lie of the land and hide in the bushes to see who appeared. He had also bought them some hillwalking gear but a cheaper make than North Face and hadn't provided the boots. The Two Billys, bedecked in waterproofs and trainers, were carrying Škorpion machine pistols and Billy Two had brought along a grenade for luck. *By failing to prepare, you are preparing to fail.* Brewster was not packing a weapon in case he got searched. He reached the summit, only to be met by the Two Billys, who said there was nowhere for them to hide. Brewster, now in the midst of a full-blown panic attack, stamped on the volcanic rock and knelt down, putting his ear to the ground, convinced he could hear the molten lava bubbling up under the surface. He swore if he made it back down alive he would stay off the bingo and cut down on the booze. Raging, he sent the Two Billys down the hillside, ordering them to hide in the gorse bushes and see if anyone came up.

'Who are we looking for?' Billy One asked.

'A fucking old Cockney prick with grey hair and blue eyes, I think. You'll know if you see him,' he hoped. 'And darkies, pull any darkies. I wouldn't put it past him to send a couple of Feargals to do his bidding.'

Brewster, who now definitely had a blister to go with his throbbing nose, waited for an hour at the top of Arthur's Seat, but no one came. He had been joined by a steady stream of Australians, South Africans, New Zealanders and a couple of Gurkha-looking guys like that Bobby, but no Wise One. He took solace in the fact the volcano hadn't erupted, telling an Aussie couple that it was "distinct" but this didn't mean it couldn't still erupt. The Aussie guy had corrected Brewster, telling him the volcano was "extinct", before Brewster had erupted.

'What the fuck do you know about it, you fucking Aussie cunt? Don't try and get smart. There's no way I'm taking lectures on Arthur's Seat from an arsehole whose relatives were convicts. Why don't you tourists fuck off somewhere else for Hogmanay and leave Scottish people alone? Edinburgh's Hogmanay, Edinburgh's Hogmanay?'

The couple looked on, bemused, barely understanding a word Brewster was saying but there was no doubting his tone. He continued, rant in full swing now.

'Used to be we went up the Tron for Hogmanay with a carry-oot, few cans of McEwan's Export, the Red Death, Tartan Special, half bottle of voddy, way before all this commercial, corporate shite. Then back to some cunt's house for a party. Hogmanay in Edinburgh was brilliant back then. Then you pricks and the English appeared and spoilt it. It's all fucking wristbands and street passes now.'

The couple grinned, not prepared to accept that a Scotsman could be so unfriendly and thinking it was an act.

'Look, mate, be a sport and take our picture, with the city in the background?'

This had the effect of placating Brewster, who agreed to take the picture, noticing the Two Billys had appeared and were milling about with the tourists. He told the couple to say "lesbian", then hit the red button on the mobile numerous times before throwing the phone as far as he could into the nearest gorse bush.

'Shame, that was a cracking picture,' he said.

The Aussie guy, who Brewster now noticed was built like a brick shithouse, made to go for him just as Billy One blocked his path and gave him a flash of the machine pistol. The raging Aussie took another step forwards as Billy One cocked the gun, before grabbing his fiancée and performing a quick about-turn. Brewster shouted after him in his best Australian accent.

'Tie your kangaroo down, sport. Kids and water, they love it… fucking Rolf Harris, pedo-loving cunts.'

A crowd of onlookers were by now doing their best not to onlook. Brewster decided it was time for a sharp exit and motioned for the Two Billys to make their way back down the volcano. He cursed the Wise One for the complete waste of time but wasn't too surprised as he'd been expecting some kind of wind-up to test him. He wandered over to his new bright-orange Ford Ranger pickup, a Christmas present to himself from the money he'd skimmed off the councillors. There, underneath the windscreen wipers, was an envelope. Brewster tore it open and pulled out a scrap of paper.

Tomorrow. Top of Arthur's Seat. 11am.
Leave the Two Billys and the guns in the house.

'Fuck's sake, not again,' he cried.

To Be Frank – Column #345

Should auld acquaintance be forgot, and never brought to mind?

Abso-feckin'-lutely and let me take this opportunity to wish you, my dear readers, my legion of fans, my trusted brethren, a Happy New Year or HNY as the kids and illiterate say, when it comes.

Give yourselves a giant pat on the back.

Top of my list of acquaintances to be forgotten is the whole sorry spectacle of Hogmanay in Edinburgh, or Edinburgh's Hogmanay as the old Etonians who run the city now call it. What was once a local affair for local people has become a global behemoth with street passes, wristbands and lanyard w*****s as far as the eye can see.

A once proud capital, the Athens of the North and epicentre of the Enlightenment, has turned into Blackpool, with funfairs, German markets and a portable ice rink taking pride of place in our beloved Princes Street Gardens. The days of a carry-out at the Tron and a bit of necking with the local lassies as the bottles rained down like Russian missiles are long gone. Sacrificed on the altar of political correctness and the corporate dollar as the council lined up to show the likes of Hoofers "world-leading live entertainment" company their fur coats with no knickers.

The influx of "sporty types" from Australia, New Zealand and South Africa over the years, with many claiming familial links to Scottish criminals, has ruined the event for us Edinburghers. No sooner has one Aussie rented a flat in Stockbridge to study sports science than it has appeared in the *Sydney Bugle* as a "must stay" destination, so they can tick Edinburgh's Hogmanay off their bucket list, next to drinking a pint of their own urine and bungee jumping off the Niagara Falls. Fifteen of them turn up, all wearing rugby shirts, to stay for a fortnight. The city makes no money on hotel rooms, they've brought their own food and one can of Foster's lager between four is their idea of a good night out.

To Be Frank, dear readers, this, like all bad things, must come to an end, which is why I'm calling for a blanket ban on foreign and English visitors to Auld Reekie during Hogmanay and New Year. A two-day ban, they can get back into the city from 2nd January onwards, but anyone found wishing someone a HNY after 4th January can get in the sea.

Right, that's the last column of the year sorted. Unfortunately, I've agreed to be a guest on BBC Scotland's *Hogmanay Special*, so you won't escape my giant pus just yet. The fragrant Deidre McAllister is the "hostess with the mostess" and I will be joining our Minister for Culture – now there's a misnomer for you – Albert Singh, along with such esteemed guests as serial bletherer, Chic McGrain and gambling footballer, Kyle Horsburgh, although I wouldn't bet on him turning up. The music will come from house husbands' favourite, Sharleen Spiteri and her band, Texas, with the Pictish Fairies providing some real Scots gobbledygook for all the little hobgoblins and Nat nutjobs out there. Then the pièce de résistance, a giant hologram of our very own Bay City Rollers, the Tartan Pimpernels, belting out a rousing rendition of their smash hit "Shan-A-Lang", beamed onto Edinburgh Castle as the clock strikes midnight. I wish you all the best from the bottom of my ice-cold heart. Keep in touch with yourselves.

Frank Savage

24

Brewster did as he was told and left the Two Billys and the shooters in the house for his real meeting with the Wise One and Naomi at the top of Arthur's Seat. The skin had come off his blister and he'd picked it to the point where his heel looked like a tasty piece of Parma ham, which Waffen was now showing a keen interest in. Changing the blister plaster for another one, he decided to ditch the hiking boots as he couldn't be arsed going through the agony of the breaking-in process. Brewster took a brand-new pair of burgundy New Balance 574s out of the box and laced them up no bother. 'Now you're talking,' he muttered to himself. He had been wearing the 574 for nigh on thirty-five years; an early adopter in the casual scene and considered himself to have invented New Balance. In fact, he remembered the first person he ever saw wearing them was Savage, who had matched the trainers with a cord jacket. Brewster instinctively touched his nose and checked his black eyes in the mirror. He was raging the shoe had become so popular in recent years as he always considered them to be under-the-radar cool and had heard them called "dad trainers", which he put down to ignorance. They fit like slippers and were ideal for a trek up Arthur's Seat, which he now thought was a bit overrated, having conquered his initial fear of the volcano erupting.

He decided to take Waffen with him – no doubt that would piss them off, but the beast would provide backup in the absence of a weapon, as he was heeding the warning to come unarmed. It was tempting to put two in the back of the Wise One's head and do away with that Naomi there and then, but Arthur's Seat would be crammed with tourists, and he didn't know what security the Syndicate would have in place. Brewster also thought Waffen could do with the exercise, having been spoilt rotten since his dognapping ordeal, gorging on sirloin steaks and a new-found love for mint chocolate-chip ice cream that he'd lick from his dad's pudding bowl. The dog therapist had said he was improving and would be back to normal in a couple of weeks, which pleased Brewster no end as he'd spent a small fortune on the sessions.

Although Waffen showed no physical signs of distress and Bobby had treated him well enough, Brewster wondered what was going on in the animal's head and reckoned he must be suffering from PTSD. He needed to send a message once and for all that "nobody fucks with the Brewster". He looked in the mirror and practised that line he loved from *48 Hours*, one of his favourite films.

'There's a new sheriff in town, and his name is Danny Brewster. Y'all be cool. Right on.'

Brewster wondered what Eddie Murphy was up to now, having loved the actor growing up – yet another black guy he admired.

He ran over what he was going to tell the Wise One. It was straightforward. The councillors' votes were guaranteed, and the cinema project would be granted approval on 5th January, building work would commence in February, which Brewster saw as an opportunity to skim even more cash, and the revamped picture house would be ready in time for a grand opening next Christmas.

In other news, his Dutch contact had paved the way for a large shipment of cocaine to come from Morocco through Spain and arrive by lorry in the UK, with its destination being The

Gypsy's compound. This was supposed to mark phase one of the Syndicate's plan to take over the drug trade in the capital. Brewster planned to throw a spanner in the works by keeping the drugs for himself and the Two Billys. He would do his own deal with The Gypsy, who he needed to keep onside, once the Wise One had been dealt with.

Brewster would take control of the cinema revamp and use it to launder their hard-earned profit from the drug trade and assorted other "side hustles". He had given his pet project a cuddly nickname: The Final Solution.

*

Naomi checked her social media accounts as she got ready for the meeting. She saw Frank had written the usual mad bollocks with a hint of truth in it and was calling for all tourists including the English to be banned from Edinburgh during Hogmanay. This was doing a solid trade on Twitter and the likes, attracting the usual suspects. Naomi thought it was just as well she'd moved here, as her own father would've banned her from Hogmanay. She took the Glock 43 from the drawer and placed it in the waistband of her jogging bottoms, having gone for a look that could best be described as Top Boy meets Sporty Spice. She decided to take the weapon in case Brewster turned up mob-handed with the Two Billys and things got ugly. The time had come to get serious.

The Wise One had told her to arrive at the top of Arthur's Seat at 10.30am, half an hour earlier than Brewster, and she reckoned he wanted to brief her on the contents of a large envelope that was posted through her letterbox last night. It contained a detailed dossier of the Two Billys that made for some interesting bedtime reading. The rap sheet for Billy One was an impressive litany of murder and mayhem.

Name: William Fitzroy Campbell

Age: 52

Aliases: Billy One, Kill Bill, Meatballs

Place of Birth: Belfast

Distinguishing Marks: William of Orange tattoo on right arm, FTP on back of neck, Rangers FC tattoo on left calf, SS Panzer Division tattoo on right calf, teardrop tattoo under left eye, three-inch scar on right cheek, shaved head with numerous scars on scalp.

Criminal Record: Senior member of UVF loyalist paramilitary organisation 1987–2001. Released from the Maze Prison in 1999 under the terms of the Good Friday Agreement while serving consecutive life sentences for the murder of three Catholic men who were playing darts in a pub.

Previous convictions: Murder (three), manslaughter (three), directing terrorist organisation, hostage taking (twice), aggravated arson, kidnapping, actual bodily harm (five), making gunpowder to commit offences, assault with weapon (four), bomb hoax, aggravated burglary, dealing in firearms (twice), drug trafficking (four), failure to disclose information about terrorism (twice), failing to keep dogs under proper control resulting in injury, engaging in sexual activity in the presence (procured by inducement, threat or deception) of person with mental disorder, engaging in sexual activity in the presence of child.

Naomi had lingered on the last two offences and noted Billy One was a beast along with everything else. That wouldn't fly with the Wise One.

There was also a similar list for Billy Two, real name William Ferguson, fifty, a murderer (twice) who went by the nicknames Billy Two, Fergie and Mad Billy. He also had a teardrop tattooed under his left eye and various other works of art declaring his fuck for the Pope and love for the late Queen. While Billy One had the better of Billy Two for murder and violence, Billy Two certainly came into his own in the specialist category marked "absolute nonce". Naomi noted he, too, had been released by the Good Friday Agreement but had added a couple of other strings to his bow including: *Gross indecency between male of 21 or over and male under 16, inciting child family member to engage in sexual activity and inducing person with mental disorder to engage in sexual activity and indecency with children under 14, permitting girl under 13 to use premises for sexual intercourse.*

Brewster had assembled quite the *A-Team* of utterly charming individuals, and on this occasion, Naomi was all in favour of the Wise One using his medieval torture methods to end these fuckers.

The jaunt up Arthur's Seat was no bother to Naomi who had taken to running round the hill twice a week, alternating her route between starting in the car park near Meadowbank, therefore tackling the steepest part first, or heading towards the Commonwealth Pool and a slow, steady incline. She had ditched the vodka and Valium for now and was getting a buzz off the running. The promenade outside her flat along to Fisherrow in Musselburgh and back was another favourite route. Naomi had also started going to classes at Lochend Boxing Club and loved the camaraderie and sense of community the place inspired. She had noted the presence of a few salty characters, who could definitely "look after themselves" and were worth keeping onside, for future reference. The endometriosis was still causing no end of grief and her periods were a living hell, but Naomi was determined not to let it boss her life. This was often easier said than done and she had to fight the urge to curl up into a ball on the sofa and stay in her cosy flat.

Preparing herself a coffee from the two-cup stove on the hob, she drank it while eating a banana and taking her vitamin tablets. This meeting called to be well-caffeinated, and she was looking forward to finally getting down to some serious Syndicate business. Deciding to arrive at the summit of Arthur's Seat for 10am, to suss out the lie of the land, Naomi considered it good discipline to be the first at a meeting. She was taking on a new mindset, that of a corporate high-flyer, committed to a career trajectory that would see her leave the Syndicate and go legit. Now, she needed to get the compulsively-lying-to-her-father hurdle out the way and make amends to him. She dreaded to think how Frank would take the news that his eldest daughter was, to all intents and purposes, part of an organised crime gang, therefore a prominent criminal in her own right. That could go either way but one thing she was certain of: Frank wouldn't give her up to the law.

She marched up the hill, loving the feeling of the cold, crisp air on her face. Nothing could beat Edinburgh on days like this; a city that embraced the changing seasons and provided them with an epic stage on which to perform.

Arriving at the summit, Naomi was only half surprised to see the Wise One already there, talking to Falco and Olga. What was the deal with Falco and Olga? Were they going to play the coincidence card again? The Wise One came forward to shake her hand, more formal than their usual hug, and complimented Naomi on her promptness. She noticed the firmness of his grip, the type you normally only get from lifetime tradesmen like joiners and scaffolders – "old man strength", she'd heard her father call it. Naomi said hello to Falco and Olga but was reluctant to engage in the "fancy meeting you here" preamble. The Wise One beat her to the punch.

'I dragged Falco and Olga up here as they're doing a bit of work for us; call it insurance. Falco is my head of special projects, but don't worry, he won't step on your toes. They have a particular skill set, let's just say, in the fields of surveillance and waste disposal that have been useful to me over the years and it's on a strictly need-to-know basis, but rest assured the pair of them have your back.'

Falco, standing with his hands resting on his skull cane, tipped the brim of his cowboy hat towards her.

Olga said, 'You won't have to worry about that animal, Brewster. We have him covered.'

The Wise One patted her on the back and sent the pair of them on their way. Naomi noticed how Falco moved, slinking like a panther, swinging his skull cane with a level of dexterity that belied his years. He threw it high up in the air and caught it one-handed like an Orange Order marcher.

'See you around, Naomi,' he said, blowing her a kiss as Olga took his arm. The Wise One was certainly full of surprises and she half expected her father to arrive by parachute next. The top of Arthur's Seat was empty apart from a few tourists trying to walk off their hangovers. The Wise One motioned for Naomi to join him as he moved towards the sundial, looking out over a 360-degree view of the city in all its glory. He seemed to be conjuring up a distant memory and looked as craggy as the surroundings.

'I remember coming here to visit your mother, who was touring Scotland with the Two-Tone label and was getting hassle off a Jock promoter who was avoiding paying her. Your father wasn't on the scene then. Frank would arrive with a bang later. Anyway, I'll tell you a story about the Salisbury Crags,' he said, pointing down towards the cliff face with the city centre in the background. 'They've always haunted me.

'A young Dutchman called Ernest Dumoulin eloped with his eighteen-year-old sweetheart, a German Fräulein called Helga Konrad, against the wishes of her parents who were very strict. The couple moved into lodgings and Ernest paid three weeks' rent in advance, allowing him to apply to be married at a registrar's office. They were married on Friday 13th October, 1972 – Friday 13th, Naomi.'

The Wise One let that sink in and Naomi immediately thought of that horror film she'd watched with Frank one night as a young girl, about that guy called Jason.

'So, Ernest, who was telling Helga about his plans to become a financial adviser, decided that instead of consummating their marriage, it would be a good idea to go for a stroll along the top of Salisbury Crags, the very same crags that you see over there. A merchant seaman, strolling along the foot of Salisbury Crags, discovered the body of a young woman and contacted the local plod who attended at the scene and they were met by a distraught and rather dishevelled-looking Ernie. He told the cops that him and Helga had gone for a stroll to watch the beautiful lights of Auld Reekie, but she had slipped and fell. They never arrested him, and he spent the night in the honeymoon suite playing the theme from *Love Story* over and over again. The tagline was *Love means never having to say you're sorry*.'

The Wise One was now humming a tune that Naomi vaguely recognised.

'To cut a long story short, the cops took him in for questioning on the Monday and the owner of the guesthouse discovered a letter in his room along with receipts for a four-hundred-grand insurance policy taken out on Helga's life the day before she died. That would be around four million pounds in today's money. Cheeky bar steward tried to claim the loot on the very morning poor Helga met her maker. Turned out he was a failed financial adviser and had met her through a lonely-hearts advert placed in a German newspaper. He turned up at her father's farm and asked if he could marry Helga, but the old man said he wanted to wait and see if this joker had any real dosh. Next thing, they've fucked off to Scotland and, well, the rest is history.'

Naomi shook her head. 'Poor woman, so vulnerable,' she said. 'This city is full of nasty surprises.'

The Wise One contemplated this for a while.

'Ernest denied it all, of course, insisting Helga had slipped and fallen, but the forensic experts showed she hadn't. He then had the audacity to claim Helga had plotted to con an insurance company by faking his death and he said *she* had tried to kill *him* on Salisbury Crags but had fallen when he put his hands up to save himself. The judge and jury saw that for the load of old cobblers it was, and Ernest went down for life. He served his sentence and is now living in Germany, working as a minister and conducting weddings. You've got to laugh. I've always fancied paying him a visit. Still, he gave me the idea for sorting out that promoter who was hassling your poor mother.'

Naomi felt a chill in her bones at the implication. She remembered what her grandmother had said about Maxine being on drugs and wondered what the Wise One's involvement had been. She'd always been told her mum had died of a heart attack and that was the reason why she'd gone to live with her Aunty Jane. But what if the Wise One had something to do with her death? Naomi parked her thoughts as Brewster arrived, approaching them warily and keeping a steady grip on his dog.

'Hello, Mr Wise One. I'm Danny Brewster but you can call me Brewster. Everyone else does, like Madonna or Prince.'

The Wise one said, 'Madonna calls you Brewster?'

'No, no, I haven't met Madonna. I meant like her name is one word and everyone calls me Brewster like one word instead of calling me Danny or Danny Brewster. Anyway, it's great to be up here and to finally meet you.' He held out his hand, which the Wise One stared at like someone was handing him a rotting fish.

The Wise One looked at Naomi, subtly prompting her to move things on.

'Can you brief us on the latest developments with the cinema project and current situation in Edinburgh?'

'Us?' Brewster was speechless for a second, as he felt his hackles rise. Who the fuck did this Naomi think she was? Grandstanding in front of the boss. Well, two can play that game. Brewster switched into what he imagined was business mode and gave the presentation he had been practising in front of the bedroom mirror earlier that morning.

He said, 'Well, Mr Wise One, I can inform you that everything is going smoothly. The councillors' votes are in the bag, so to speak, and the cinema revamp will be granted approval on 5th January, building work will commence in February, which I can keep an eye on for you, and the cinema will be ready in time for a grand opening next Christmas, all being well.'

He paused to let what he'd said sink in, but there was no response from the Wise One, who was stretching his arms above his head. Brewster thought, *This cunt doesn't say a lot*, and then he continued, looking round furtively to make sure no one was listening.

'My Dutch contact, who you know about, has arranged with our Moroccan supplier for fifty kilos of co... caine...'

Brewster stopped talking as he noticed the red dot was moving up from his groin region towards his chest.

'What the fuck is that?' he screamed. Brewster turned to Waffen and saw the dog had a similar red dot stationed on its torso.

Finally, it was the Wise One's turn to speak. He stepped forwards, giving Brewster a little slap on the cheek, as he bent down to stroke a now silent Waffen, who was shaking like a leaf, the dog having cottoned on to the severity of the situation way before its owner.

'Naomi will run the cinema project and you'll report to her. Your Dutch contact is a tout for the National Crime Agency and had his throat slit in Rotterdam last night. The Moroccans are still delivering the drugs but to our guys. Your Northern Irish pals are a couple of beasts and the Ferguson one worked with the RUC and British intelligence back in the day, fingering his loyalist chums. You've skimmed one hundred thousand pounds of my money from the councillors, which you'll pay back to Naomi in full, along with another one hundred thousand pounds in tax.'

Brewster looked shocked before trying to make a case for the defence.

'But, but… the guys are in the UVF. Where will I get one hundred thousand pounds?'

The Wise One cut him short, placing his finger in front of his lips.

'I don't care. Just get it or you're dead. We'll meet in a few days at South Queensferry for the Loony Dook, where I'll lay out phase two of our plans. Bring your Speedos and be in the water for twelve noon sharp. Don't dare wear a woolly hat. I want to see you get your hair wet.'

Brewster tried to take all this in, thinking it unlikely he'd be whacked in front of hundreds of Loony Dookers celebrating the first day of the New Year.

The Wise One laid out his plans. 'You'll look after our dealers and supply our product to the good denizens of Edinburgh, passing the money to JJ every Friday. He'll tell you the amount of product you're to shift and expected profit required to hit your weekly target. Failure is not an option and if you've a problem with any of that… well, I can turn those little red dots into nasty arterial blood spurts just by waving my left hand in the air.'

He let this sink in, before raising his left hand halfway above his head, causing Brewster to crumple to the ground, screaming, 'I agree! I agree, no problem, no problem, you're the boss.'

The Wise One looked at him with utter contempt.

'And another thing. All these shenanigans with Naomi's dad must end. I want you and Frank Savage to sort out your differences. That's not up for debate. Okay, nice meeting with you, Danny. Off you fuck now.'

The Wise One took Naomi by the arm and led her down the hill to have a look at Helga's memorial bench.

25

ogmanay morning and Frank was contemplating the wholesale lifestyle changes he'd be making as a result of his heart scare. He had already cut down on the booze and was now contemplating giving up the fags, perhaps trying one of those vape things that looked fucking awful. Frank always thought he was the embodiment of dishevelled cool with a cigarette hanging from his mouth, like Humphrey Bogart or Steve McQueen. It might have lessened their cultural impact and iconic status if they'd been vaping strawberry and watermelon bubblegum instead. He had already decided he was going to take it easy tonight, just a few drinks; it was Hogmanay after all and the trip through to BBC Scotland might be a little stressful. The start of the year was the perfect time to make changes and he'd vowed to smoke his last cigarette after the Bells so he could say that he quit on New Year's Day. Frank realised he was enabling himself and had been warned not to smoke or drink at all, but he was determined to do better. Having got to number seven on his list of changes, which was "only eat between noon and 8pm", he was interrupted by the buzzer sounding. It was Naomi. He buzzed her in and waited. It went again.

She said, 'I'm not coming up, Dad. I thought we could go for a walk along the prom. Have a talk.'

'Okay, love, give me five and I'll shove on my jogging bottoms and trainers,' Frank replied, already feeling more of an athlete just by saying the words "jogging bottoms and trainers" with the Crocs left in the cupboard. He detected anxiety in his daughter's voice and wondered if she was finally going to tell him the truth, or at least her version of it.

The two of them headed arm-in-arm towards the promenade, with Frank unlocking arms after thirty seconds to cross the road. He never felt very comfortable walking arm-in-arm with anyone and didn't think it was practical.

It was a lovely crisp morning, the sort that did Portobello proud – a free facial that was also good for the soul. The morning of Hogmanay was a strange time; the calm before the drunken storm. Frank wasn't prepared to let the elephant stay in the room, deciding to cut the small talk and get down to matters in hand. He guided her to the promenade wall and they both sat down with their backs to the water.

'Okay, time for this chat, Naomi,' he said, putting his daughter on the spot and watching a pained expression appear on her face.

'How about I tell you what I think, and you can fill me in on the blanks?' Frank said. Naomi bristled and he noticed that her shoulders and neck were gripped with tension.

'On you go, Dad,' she replied.

Frank wasn't for holding back, preparing to give her both barrels. To his mind, whatever Naomi was up to trumped any concerns she had about his erratic behaviour and declining health. He cleared his throat.

'I think you've been lying to me since you arrived. I think you're involved with this Syndicate crime gang run by Ray Armstrong and are about to help them launder millions of pounds of drug money through the cinema. I also think Brewster is involved and you lied to me about him approaching you in Daisy Park.'

Naomi made to speak, 'I haven't lied—' Not making it to the end of the sentence before Frank cut her off.

'I'm not finished, Naomi. You'll get your turn. I think you've been lying to me for years now and have been groomed by the so-called Wise One – a complete cunt of the highest order, by the way – to help him with his criminal empire.'

Naomi put her hands on her hips in a defiant manner as Frank carried on.

'Those are just the big lies; there's a whole host of little ones in there as well. I think you've reached the stage where every fucking word that comes out of your mouth is a lie, to the extent that you don't know what the truth is any more. Which must be pretty fucking stressful. On you go. Your turn to speak.'

Naomi got up off the wall and thought about walking away, but it was her who had wanted the chat and Frank had just covered most of what she was about to tell him. She now had the opportunity to come clean with her father and decided to take it, fighting back the urge to cry which Frank would think were nothing more than crocodile tears.

'You're right, Dad. I am involved with the Syndicate, and they are planning to launder money through the cinema. The project was my idea. And yes, Brewster is involved in the supply and distribution of drugs as part of Ray Armstrong's plan to take over in Edinburgh.'

Frank shook his head. 'You must think I'm daft, Naomi. DI Hope had already mentioned Armstrong to me and then you go and confirm it by saying you – surprise, surprise! – "bumped into him" at the Balmoral Hotel. Jesus wept.'

Naomi now felt like a teenager who had stayed out all night without permission and was nervously biting her thumbnail.

'I'm so sorry, Dad. I shouldn't have lied to you, but it's been hard to tell the truth. I've done it to protect you. Things were never meant to get out of hand, but I didn't know anything about your past with Brewster when I arrived. It all turned to shit after the opening of the youth theatre, and then Bobby kidnapped his dog.'

She started to sob a little and pulled a tissue out of her pocket. Frank didn't move to comfort her.

'It's not easy choosing the right time to tell your dad you're involved with an international crime syndicate.'

Frank blew out air and shook his head again. 'Protect me? Protect me! That's a good one, Naomi. In fact, it's a fucking belter. You've brought nothing but danger to our family and friends since you rocked up in Portobello. I know I haven't been the best dad, but I don't think we deserve this. You do know the police are onto you? You do realise that, don't you? You could be looking at serious jail time.'

Naomi's stomach churned but she felt a modicum of relief by finally having this heart-to-heart with Frank.

'I don't have to worry about the police up here. They're fucking amateurs. There are layers of protection that insulate me from any criminal activity. As far as my work goes, I'm handling legitimate government grants. Not a penny of drug money has passed through my hands. I haven't committed any acts of violence; at the very worst, I can plead complete ignorance.'

At that moment, Naomi realised she sounded like a hardened criminal.

'Is there any part of this shitshow that isn't a lie?' Frank asked.

'My job is a real job, Dad. My firm is a real firm. All the stuff about them being a FTSE 250 blue-chip company is true. I got my master's degree and I'm really fucking good at what I do.'

Frank was raging. He didn't like this hard veneer-coated Naomi and wanted his real daughter back. Everything was arse-over-tit. He never thought he'd have cause to worry about her as, to his mind, she was bright, clever and up till now was proving to be, most importantly, morally sound.

'When did Ray Armstrong approach you? Tell me how that happened,' Frank asked.

'I bumped into him after I got a job working at a nightclub in the West End that he owned when I was studying for my master's degree. I had no idea he owned it; we got talking about the Uncle Ray times and kind of rekindled our friendship. He loves maths and figures, like me. We spoke a lot about my mum, and he told me how talented she was. He promoted me. Had me looking after the accounts and things like the layout of the club, the best way to get maximum profit. Ray put a lot of faith in me and believed in my ability.'

'And eventually, after Uncle Ray had gained your trust, bit by bit, feeding you pieces of not quite legit work here and there, he offered you the icing on the cake. The chance to set up a new life in sleepy old Portobello, where your old man, sister, gran and fucking grandad live. How fucking sweet. Can you not see you're being played, Naomi? Like a fucking fiddle.'

She moved on from the thumbnail and was now biting her knuckles.

'He's been really good to me,' Naomi pleaded, instantly regretting how pathetic those words sounded. That was all the trigger Frank needed.

'Shall I tell you a few home truths about your so-called Uncle Ray? He's responsible for Maxine's death for starters.'

'How?' she replied. 'What do you mean, Dad?'

Frank felt his heart flutter but didn't care. He wanted to grab his daughter and shake some sense into her.

'That bastard was the one who got her back onto the smack. It all started after he stole a song your mother wrote and gave it to another artist. A huge fucking hit, Naomi. One you've no doubt heard of: "Camden Sunrise" – number one in fourteen different countries, went on to sell two million copies, won a string of awards including an Ivor fucking Novello.'

Naomi looked shocked, trying to comprehend what Frank was saying. Her mind flashed back to what Rita had said about her mother on Boxing Day, '… before the drugs took hold.'

'Mum wrote that? I love that song.'

Frank sighed. 'That's just the start of it, my love.' He hesitated as he prepared to unburden himself of the past with Maxine; a past that came a close second to Michael's death.

'After Armstrong stole the song, which he claimed his daughter wrote, Maxine hit a real downward spiral. She talked about a demo tape that she'd recorded but couldn't find it. Maxine had planned to send it to a music publisher along with the lyrics that she'd scribbled down – but the drugs kicked in. She'd been on the heroin as a teenager but had managed to kick her habit. A bit of recreational speed and coke when we could afford it was our bag, strictly no needles and I always preferred the bevvy. But like I said, that wanker got your mum back on the hard stuff.'

Frank felt the anger rise in his shoulders and wanted to lash out. He got up and kicked the bin, then instantly regretted it as a bolt of pain connected with his gout, doubling the agony.

'Bastard!' he shouted, before swearing at a passing jogger. 'Fuck you looking at, cunt?'

Naomi sought to placate him. 'Calm down, Dad, you'll set your heart off again.'

But her words fell on deaf ears as he was in full flow now.

'Maxine confronted Armstrong loads of times over that song, and I even had a word with him, but he always told us a pack of lies. He would "gaslight" her about it, although that wasn't really a term back then, saying the heroin was playing tricks with her mind. He denied she had written it, saying all she'd done was copy the words down on a bit of paper so she could learn them after he asked her to sing it. All bollocks and, surprise, surprise, the bit of paper that proved Maxine wrote the words went missing. He gave the song to Stella fucking Hart and the rest is history. I reckon Armstrong has made at least three million quid off the back of your mother and the bastard will still be getting royalties.'

Naomi tried to make sense of it all. 'Was the stress of this what caused Mum to have a heart attack?'

Frank pressed his forehead, reluctant to go on, straining against telling his daughter the awful truth but eventually relenting as time caught up with him.

'Your mother died of a heroin overdose, my love. She never had a heart attack.'

Naomi's eyes filled with tears and Frank fought against his emotions that were threatening to overwhelm him.

'Armstrong fed her the smack that killed her. I confronted him at Maxine's funeral, and he denied it. I told him I'd fucking have him and that I didn't give a fuck about his men. I took a swing and connected with his jaw. His heavies carted me off and gave me a bad doing. After that, I was told to get the fuck out of London. I was a wreck. A single dad with a five-year-old daughter who'd just started school. That's when your Aunty Jane stepped in and offered to look after you. It was only meant to be temporary, but she did such a good job and you were thriving. I decided it was for the best if she brought you up. I paid her well. Never missed a monthly payment and you came up to Scotland every summer for the holidays, but I couldn't set foot in London or I was a dead man.'

'Is that still the case, Frank?'

'No, I got word about five years ago that the Wise One had lifted my banning order. Very kind of him, I must say.' He rolled his eyes. 'Must have been around the time he came back into your life. I know he gave you things when you were growing up and hung around the school gates, taking you for trips in his Roller. Aunty Jane told me but there was nothing I could do from up here. It was your Aunty Jane who told him to stay the fuck away when you started secondary school. She was a great woman, just like her sister.'

Naomi tried to process what Frank had just told her. She felt a sense of revulsion towards the Wise One and knew she had to escape his clutches. Frank read her mind.

'You need to get away from him, Naomi. He'll bring you down. The guy is incapable of human emotion. He's a fucking psychopath.'

'I know, Dad. I know,' she replied, coming in for a hug.

Now it was her turn to question Frank.

'Right, Dad, why don't you tell me what you've been up to? I know you're skint, haven't got a bolt, but you managed to pay for the Shadow which must have set you back about forty grand, and there's the small matter of the ten grand you had to find for Bobby's release. So, I dread to think what state the rest of your finances are in.'

Frank shuffled uneasily. Naomi had been straight with him, so he owed it to her to tell the truth. Trouble was his finances were a clusterfuck of epic proportions.

'I'm not going to lie, Naomi. My finances are a fucking disaster. I borrowed money for the Shadow and then borrowed another ten grand from the same person to pay Bobby's ransom money.'

'Who did you borrow the money off, Dad?'

Frank hesitated. 'Oh, for fuck's sake, don't ask me that.'

'I need to know, Dad. If I'm going to help you, then I need to know who you borrowed cash off.'

'I don't want you to help me, love. That's the last thing I want,' he implored, losing the moral high ground that he'd briefly enjoyed.

'Look, you've no choice and no say in the matter,' Naomi said.

Frank put his hand to his forehead and felt his heartbeat had travelled down to his gouty toe, which was suddenly throbbing.

'I borrowed the money off a guy I know. He's called The Gypsy.'

'Fuck's sake, Frank! You borrowed money from The Gypsy? That fucker cuts people's ears off.'

'I take it you know him, then?'

'Of course I know him. He's our main contact in Edinburgh. The Wise One brokered a deal with The Gypsy to sell Syndicate product up here. Forget Brewster, it's The Gypsy who runs the show. How much are you into him for?'

Frank said, 'I'm fucking mortified, my love, this is really embarrassing.'

Now it was Naomi's turn to get angry. 'Cut the crap, Dad. How much have you borrowed from The Gypsy and how much interest is he charging?'

'I asked him for an initial fifty thousand pounds to buy the Shadow with, another ten thousand pounds for incidentals.'

'I take it by "incidentals", you mean money to gamble,' she asked matter-of-factly.

'Correct.'

'And?'

'Eh? I lost, not the whole ten grand, mind. I managed to pay for the repairs to the car.'

'Every cloud,' Naomi replied with extra sarcasm, before adding, 'and the interest?'

Frank hesitated, trying to remember. 'Initially, he was going to charge me ten thousand pounds interest on the fifty thousand pounds I borrowed, and I was to pay that back over a year at five thousand pounds each month starting tomorrow.'

Naomi let out a whistle. 'Fuck me,' she exclaimed. 'And after that?'

Frank rubbed his forehead, trying to massage the details of the new arrangement with The Gypsy from his brain to his mouth. He had done a good job of blanking out this nightmare.

'I went back to see him on Boxing Day and said I needed to borrow another ten grand. He already knew that Bobby had kidnapped Brewster's dog, and that Brewster had grabbed Bobby. He said taking a man's dog was a death sentence in his eyes.'

'Go on,' she urged.

'Anyway, to cut a long story short, he gave me another ten thousand pounds, no bother, and said I now owed him thirty grand in interest, on top of the sixty thousand pounds in total that I'd borrowed. He's given me six months to pay back the ninety thousand pounds or it goes up to one hundred and twenty thousand pounds and, after that, he says he'll be coming for my flat and my lugs,' Frank said, instinctively pulling his earlobes.

'Oh well, look on the bright side, at least you won't be needing a hearing aid,' Naomi replied.

They both laughed, a momentary respite from the pain.

Naomi took charge. All business.

'Look, Dad. I can help now that I at least know about the trouble you're in. I'll speak to The Gypsy and sort this out. I can make it go away.'

'Jesus wept, Naomi. I don't want you to get involved, not with a nutter like him.'

'Like I said, you've no say in the matter. I'm used to dealing with nutters. It's part of my job description. You're having a fucking mid-life crisis, Dad. Played out in the full glare of publicity and your behaviour is becoming more erratic. This health scare is the icing on the cake.'

Frank smiled wryly, shaking his head.

'Your columns are now the deranged rantings of a lunatic. You're being exploited by those bastards at the paper who don't give a flying fuck about your physical and mental health. Just as long as the digital hits keep coming. You're on the verge of being "cancelled" every week and have a following made up of right-wing nutters who think they're storm troopers in this stupid ongoing culture war against the "woke brigade".

Frank started biting his thumbnail, seemingly lost for words.

'Thing is, they don't know you, Dad. None of them have twigged you're a dyed-in-the-wool lefty, whose principal hobby alongside drinking, smoking and betting is winding folk up, which you now seem to be doing for a living.'

Frank put his head in his hands, then made to change the subject.

'Do you know it's been a dream of Bobby and mine to have the Regency restored and for us to work there? That's what I'd really love to do. Manage the place. I'd play old classics and have special themes like "Hitchcock Week". But I suppose it'll be mainly indie stuff for the hipsters, Marvel shite and cartoons for the bairns. Probably have a run of 007 films starring our very own Big Tam the Ham for the happy clappers. *From Porty with Love.'*

Naomi smiled as her dad laid out his vision, before bringing him back down to earth with a bump.

'I need you to do me a favour. And it's not up for debate.'

Frank, now resigned to his fate, gestured for her to continue.

'You're not going to like this, but I need you to sit down with Brewster and sort out your differences.'

26

Frank was far from happy with Naomi's suggestion that he meet with Brewster, and it was all he could think about as he picked up the Shadow to drive through to Glasgow for "BBC Scotland's Hogmanay shindig". The car had been repaired at a cost of two grand but still bore marks from the acid attack and a faint trace of the word "*Peedayfil*" could be made out on the passenger's side. Naomi had made it clear the sit-down had to happen and was "non-negotiable". Frank had determined he was going to try and enjoy himself. He would be picking up Bobby, Falco and Olga from The Haddonfield at 4pm, along with Naomi, who had agreed to drive them back from the Pacific Quay studio in Glasgow after the Bells. Four access-all-areas guest passes had been secured, with Naomi taking Bella's place as she had to stay and run the pub on the busiest night of the year. The plan was to head back to The Haddonfield after the show where Bella would host the traditional 'lock-in' reserved for regulars and assorted other Porty reprobates of questionable character, which would go on until midday. Frank had been dreading the gig, but the one thousand five hundred pounds appearance fee, plus five hundred pounds expenses and free bar Richard had promised sweetened the deal. He wasn't supposed to be drinking on the new tablets, so had decided not to take them, ignoring the little voice in his head reminding him he was an irresponsible cunt.

Secretly, he was looking forward to seeing Bridget who had been on his mind constantly since the opening of the youth theatre, and Plunkett had given him the heads-up on her marital strife. Frank had decided he was wearing the Savile Row, chalk-stripe suit, with crisp white shirt and pink tie (Windsor knot), to add a bit of colour to proceedings, with the obligatory Church's brogues – spit 'n' polished as per. He scooshed on some Eau Sauvage Extrême and remembered the old joke about looking like a million lira. Naomi had come over for lunch and he made some lentil soup. Things felt better between them now that everything was out in the open, and Frank was running a million scenarios in his head where his daughter escaped the clutches of the Wise One unharmed. There was no mention of Brewster and Frank listened enthralled as she filled him in on the work being done to revamp the cinema, which he considered a brilliant idea if they could just drop the nasty organised crime part. He was forever banging on about the place now and what it meant to him, while not so subtly hinting that he wanted a job there.

They drove the car to The Haddonfield and picked up their guests, who were well along the road to oblivion. Bobby said he'd started drinking at midday and was planning on being a "twenty-four-hour party person", boasting that he'd procured a bit of bingo for the journey.

Falco, wearing his Dior tux, had brought along two bottles of vintage Dom Pérignon for the trip and sat in the middle of the back seat between Bobby and Olga, who was resplendent in a black Chanel dress. He poured the champagne into plastic cups, then passed the bottle to Frank who took a healthy swig, joking that he "drove better drunk anyway". Naomi declined the offer of a cup, staying resolutely focused on making it through the next few hours. The traffic was quiet as the Shadow purred along the M8 heading towards the bright lights of the Glasgow high-rises. Frank felt good to be back in the driver's seat and was wearing his special driving gloves for the occasion, giving the steering wheel the odd pat and mouthing, 'Good girl, good girl.' He and Bobby led the group in a merry sing-song as they entered "the Weeg".

'In yer Glesgae slums, in yer Glesgae slums,
'You rake in the buckets for something tae eat,
'You find a deid rat and you think it's a treat,
'In yer Glesgae slums.'

By the time they pulled up outside the BBC studios, Falco, Olga and Bobby were half-pissed, and Bobby had already dipped into his stash of white powder.

'Jesus wept,' Frank said. 'It's only 6pm. The run-through before the show is not till 10pm and the thing doesn't start until 11. This will end in tears.'

They stumbled into the reception area of the studios and were escorted to the green room – which resembled the waiting room at a doctor's surgery – by a beaming bearded thirty-something wearing a Sonic Youth T-shirt, combat shorts and a white pair of Nike Air Force 1 trainers. Falco was by now swigging the remains of the second bottle of Dom and Bobby was attacking the six cans of Tennent's lager and box of sour cream and onion Pringles that passed as the Hogmanay rider. Olga had already raided the cupboards and sequestered a bottle of Jack Daniels and four small cans of Diet Coke; the kind you'd get flying cattle class to Majorca.

Deidre McAllister stuck her head round the door; head in curlers and wearing a pink dressing gown, she welcomed Frank like a long-lost sleazy uncle.

'My, my, Mr Savage and entourage. How the devil are you, Frank? All set for the show?'

'Fuck me, Deidre, you look like a young Elizabeth Taylor. Yes, absolutely buzzing for the show, can't wait, just the three hours to go.'

Deidre checked the time, then grimaced and asked the Sonic Youth to take care of Frank and friends, giving them "anything they want, within reason".

She then made a beeline for Falco. 'Mr Falco, what a pleasure it is to meet you. I loved your performance at the opening of the youth theatre in Portobello and haven't stopped singing "Big Chair, Little Stool" since then. It's my Christmas cracker.'

Falco took her hand and bent to kiss it. 'Charmed to finally meet you, Miss *Dial Deidre*, I'm a big fan of your show. Huge.'

Deidre was blushing now, as Olga gave her a look that could only be described as "I'll tear you a new arsehole".

At that point, two burly security guards entered the green room, casing the joint, ahead of Albert Singh, the Minister for Culture, and Chic McGrain, lead singer with Glaswegian soul boys, Token Gesture, who had come together. It was a straight toss as to who Frank detested more, Chic McGrain or Annie Lennox, but Bobby beat him to the punch, proclaiming, 'Oh no! Not that prick from Token Gesture, we'll be getting Annie Lennox doing her *Christmas Cornucopia* next.'

Bobby went straight up to Chic McGrain and asked him if he wanted a Pringle before greeting the Minister for Culture with a pat on the back, shouting, 'All right, Bert? I knew your father.'

Naomi, who had gone to help the assistant source more booze, arrived in the green room at the same time as Shelby St. George and footballer Kyle Horsburgh, who had his hand on the actor's arse. This was too much excitement for a coked-up Bobby, who was struggling to contain himself. He shouted across the room, 'Shelby St. George – or Sharon Henderson, Hendo's wee sister as we knew you at Leith Academy – how's it going? Mind that time I poked you in the music cupboard?'

Shelby looked at Bobby with disgust. 'Gurkha Bobby, are you still washing the dishes at that Indian in Lothian Road?'

'Nah, I've been promoted. I'm now the guy who makes the tea for the guy who makes the coffee.' Bobby laughed loudly at his own joke, then added, 'You've done well for yourself,' as Shelby smiled coyly, warming to the compliment.

She turned to Frank. 'Hello. Good to see you've recovered from the youth theatre.'

Frank nodded in Shelby's direction as he poured himself a double vodka on the rocks. 'Hello, Sharon, you're looking well, like a million lira.'

'Nice of you to say, Frank. Are we using Sunday names?'

Frank felt a wave of boredom sweep over him and had no desire to get into another slagging match with Sharon that had been going on since they were in second year, after he moved her hand off his testicles in French class.

Bert Singh and Chic McGrain tried their best to sit away from the rest of the group on the corner sofa, deep in conversation, but Frank decided to plank himself down in the middle, placing an arm around each of them. One of Bert's bodyguards moved forward but was given the nod that everything was okay, for now.

Frank said, 'Do you travel everywhere with them then, Bert? Bit sad that you've got to go about with minders, but that's the way of the world, I suppose, seeing as you've polarised the country with this never-ending Independence bollocks that you keep spouting.'

Bert was taken aback that Frank had gone straight for the jugular at an event like this, but Chic McGrain was quick to step in and rescue his new "bestie", the Minister for Culture.

'At least Albert is striving to make our culture automated and is not dabbling in the kind of primevalism with a strong hint of the populism you go in for, Savage, to appease your Unionist paymasters. Mr Singh is embracing Scotland as a progressive, multicultural society, which promotes self-identity and gender fluidity. He's certainly not pandering to "inferiorists" like yourself, who promote the emergence of "brandscaping" as a mode of order in neo-liberal capitalist society, thus relying on neologism to deconstruct semiotic idioms.'

Frank got up off the sofa to get himself a can of lager.

'No one understands a word you say, Chic McGrain, and that includes you. You talk in fucking riddles, man.'

'Watch your language in front of the minister, Savage. Have some respect,' Chic McGrain chided, but Frank wasn't in the mood for being lectured.

'"Have some respect", have some bastarding respect,' he replied. 'You're a disgrace, Chic McGrain. Hanging out this guy's arse, constantly talking shite on any television show that will have you and that's when you're not doing a bad impersonation of a guy covering a Luther Vandross song in the British Legion.'

Chic McGrain's bottom lip dropped in a sulky pout.

'At least I'm not a Unionist-supporting hooligan like you, Savage. Belt the bairns. Ban the babies, the dogs and now the tourists.'

Frank roared back, 'I support Independence, ya fanny, but I don't support political parties!'

He laughed, giving his can a wee shake before opening it and spraying it all over Chic McGrain's suit and ironic kipper tie, with a bit landing on the Minister for Culture. Chic McGrain made to go for him, but the Minister's bodyguards intervened, pushing Frank back, which did nothing to calm the situation as Bobby went into Pit Bull terrier mode, relishing the prospect of a "square go". Falco banged his skull cane on the floor and shouted, 'Bobby,' which had the desired effect of bringing him to heel. The bodyguards ushered Albert Singh out with Chic McGrain trailing in their wake.

'Come back and see me when your digital hits top four million, you blethering halfwit,' Frank taunted, then felt his heart flutter.

Deidre McAllister appeared and started to scold Frank and Bobby, with Richard and Bridget following in behind her. Perfect timing.

'And if this continues, Frank, we'll have to pull you from the show. I already have The Krankies waiting in the wings. So please behave yourself. This is your final warning. I'll keep you and Chic apart on the sofa, but you must promise me you won't start on him.'

Frank sheepishly said, 'I promise,' as Deidre told Richard to keep an eye on *his* columnist.

'I appear to have missed something,' Richard replied, pleading ignorance, 'but you have my word, Deidre, Frank will be on his best behaviour.'

Bridget grabbed a can of lager before planking herself down next to Frank. 'This looks fun. All we need is Brewster and his devil dog, then we'll have the full Porty jet set.'

Frank said hello to Bridget and gave her a lingering hug in which he started to rub her back before her husband, his boss and editor, gave a loud cough. Bridget gave him one of her "What the fuck, Frank?" looks that made him feel tiny, so he quickly motioned for Bobby to join him outside, giving him the international "I need a fag" signal by taking a sideways V-sign from his lips. Outside in the corridor, the pair of them burst out laughing.

'I fucking hate that Chic McGrain prick,' Frank said, 'always have done.'

'Fuck him, they must have been really struggling for guests to book him. When do I get to meet Sharleen Spiteri? I love her,' Bobby replied.

Frank took two puffs of his cigarette, then threw it away, mindful of his approaching health kick.

'Bit of bad news on the old Sharleen front, I'm afraid, Bobby. She recorded three songs for tonight's show two months ago. She ain't coming. We'll have to make do with the Pictish Fairies singing in "real Scots", whatever the fuck that is. Deidre told me they're letting Chic McGrain perform his one and only hit before the Bells.'

Bobby looked crestfallen. 'Don't tell me we've got to endure him singing, "Lager Haze". Are the rest of his dickhead band joining him? I'll need more Charlie if I'm going to make it through this. Do you fancy a nose beer, Frank?'

Frank considered this, then declined, miffed at how little his best friend understood about his recent health scare.

'My heart will explode if I touch that shit.'

Bobby headed to the toilet for a quick line, then emerged with white powder on his nose just as the Sonic Youth was walking by.

'All right, son?' Frank said. 'Love the T-shirt.' He gave the guy the thumbs up and vowed to get through the rest of the night without incident. He decided to try and lay off the booze until after the show as Richard took him to one side for a pep talk.

'Look, Frank, we can't have any repeat of events at the opening of the youth theatre. It's important that you represent the brand – obviously you've got a bit of leeway to give the odd controversial opinion, but for heaven's sake, man, keep it nice and light. A bit of gentle banter with Deidre and the rest of the guests. It's going to play badly for us if you antagonise the Minister for Culture. We get enough grief from the Independence supporters as it is and I'm constantly having to firefight on your behalf. I'm sure it's no surprise to you that you're not everyone's cup of char, Frank.'

Frank was angry but did his best to concentrate on his breathing as he counted to ten.

'Don't worry, Richard. I won't let the side down. It is Hogmanay after all.'

He really wanted to tell Dick Bell-end to go fuck himself but, for once, he was determined not to make a pure arse of himself. *Best behaviour from now on, Francois.*

He went over to Naomi, who was talking to Bridget, the two of them seeming to get on like a house on fire. This pleased Frank no end and he managed to grab a word with his ex-wife as Naomi worked the room.

'I'm so glad you and Naomi have hit it off. She looks up to you, Bridget.'

Bridget patted Frank on the arm. 'How are you, Frank? Naomi was telling me about your heart arrhythmia.'

'I'm fine, Bridget. It's nothing really, an irregular heartbeat. It's common in men of a certain vintage who perhaps should look after themselves a bit better.'

Bridget frowned. 'Well, you were always a bit of a hypochondriac, but this sounds serious. I hope you're going to make the necessary lifestyle changes, Frank.'

He quickly brushed that aside. 'Yes, yes, of course. Starting tomorrow, I'm off the booze and fags.'

Bridget said nothing but gave him a knowing look.

'Yeah, as I was saying, Naomi really looks up to you,' Frank said, breaking the silence.

Bridget replied, 'Aunty Jane did a good job with her; you should be proud of what she's achieved. She was telling me about the picture house in Porty, that sounds brilliant. I told her I'd be happy to have my name attached to it, as a patron.'

Frank felt the colour drain out of him as he thought of his ex-wife getting sucked into the vortex of crime Naomi had helped create. The Wise One would lap up her involvement; another celebrity endorsement providing another layer of respectability.

'Yip,' was all he could manage to say before swiftly changing the subject. 'How's things with you and Richard? You make a lovely couple.'

Bridget sighed, disappointed at Frank's attempt to goad her into slagging her husband.

'Look, Frank. Richard is a kind and considerate man. We have our ups and downs like any couple. Trust me, things are a lot calmer with him than they ever were with you.'

Frank felt the dagger pierce his heart. 'That's not fair, Bridge, I'm trying to sort myself out. The career's going well enough; it's everything else that's a bit of a mess.'

Bridget gave him another pat on the arm, which was starting to grate on Frank, who felt she was treating him like he had special needs. 'Ah yes, the career. Is that what you're calling it?'

'Fuck off, Bridget. I'm enjoying myself and finally making a bit of money to pay off my enormous debt. You know, divorce costs and all that. Anyway, I heard you've started taking Richard to Pilates.'

He was glad to have left a bit on her, but Bridget wasn't biting, playing it straight with a poker face.

'It helps to be flexible if you're married to me,' she said.

Frank decided he would have a drink, pouring himself what could only be described as a "hoose measure" of Jack Daniels with an afterthought of Diet Coke.

Plunkett had turned up, like an excited puppy. The plethora of Z-list Scottish celebs and Bridget, who was anything but, was too much for the news editor to handle and he looked on the verge of spontaneous combustion.

'All right, Plunkett?' Frank asked. 'You must have dreamt about being in the same room as Bridget and Shelby St. George all your life, mate.'

Plunkett laughed theatrically. 'Too right, Frank. This is absolutely brilliant. Hoggers at the Beeb, tree-fucking-mend-arse. A little bird told me you had a tête-à-tête with Chic McGrain – gutted I missed that. They tell me he's going to be playing before the Bells. I can't bloody wait.'

Frank stood speechless as Plunkett waxed lyrical.

'I love Token Gesture. Saw them perform their first gig at the student union back in '84 and I've got a signed twelve inch of "Lager Haze" and their first album, *Palms to the Sky*. I love Chic McGrain; the guy is a true maverick genius.'

'He's a bit of cunt, if you ask me,' Frank said.

'Why do you hate Scotland, Frank?' Plunkett replied.

27

Brewster read Frank's latest column online and couldn't believe how much he agreed with it. His arch-nemesis was making the same points as himself about all the Australian, South African and New Zealand wank stains coming over here to spoil Hogmanay. *Great minds think alike,* he thought. His nose and black eyes were starting to improve but the damage to his pride would take a little longer to repair. Naomi had yet to tell him the details of the meeting with Frank, and he was secretly glad at being given the chance to heal ancient wounds. Although he hated Savage, especially after the latest fiasco, a part of him would always hold a begrudging respect for his old school chum.

Brewster had invited the Two Billys over earlier to brief them on his plans for the Bells, which didn't involve paying back any money to the Syndicate, then sent them away to prepare. He was sick of dealing with these lunatics and longing more and more for the day he could lead a quiet life working with decent people in Portobello. The problem was finding a way to go legit and Brewster had been involved with criminals long enough to know that no one in "the life" retires. No, he would have to use all his cunning to find an escape route that wouldn't leave him six feet under. He stuck on the telly and started watching the usual Hogmanay shite, which he reckoned was a good twenty years past its sell-by date. An old episode of *Chewin' the Fat* was blaring in the background as he made a list of New Year's resolutions.

Meet Savage and take care of Cockney pooftah, who's no' getting paid.

Find new supplier (Irish, not Fenian).

Spend more time with Mum (take her to the chinky once a month, no puddings).

Hire personal trainer for man boobs, train for senior cage (check that's a thing).

Get another dog to keep Waffen company (XL Bully?).

Get tattoo of Mum on left calf and tattoo of Waffen on right (not at same time, recovery period).

Travel to New York to meet Pet Shop Boys (book same hotel for gig).

Coach women's football team (pervy?).

Write screenplay of my life (Gerard Butler?).

28

Back at the BBC studios, a by now half-pissed, belligerent Frank had finally made it to the sofa for the start of the show, having gone all of five minutes without taking a drink. After a frantic search, the producers had wheeled in the biggest couch they could find for the purposes of keeping Frank and Chic McGrain apart. Deidre was behind her desk but had been given licence to walk about and talk to randoms, which she was reluctant to do after a grinning idiot grabbed her arse last year. This had gone viral with the hashtag #Dialamilf which she didn't mind but was followed by the hashtag #Dialagilf which she found "downright offensive" once someone told her what it meant. Frank sat farthest away from Deidre with Kyle Horsburgh, Shelby St. George and Bert Singh between him and Chic McGrain.

The Pictish Fairies kicked off proceedings, their first number being sung in Scots Gaelic that featured a rousing ten-minute bodhrán drum solo by a bearded rugby player wearing a Jacobite ghillie shirt. Lead singer Flora MacDonald nodded along to the drum solo like a demented cult follower who still got the odd flashback of mouthing the lyrics to "Baby One More Time" dressed like Britney Spears in her school uniform while her parents attended the Free Presbyterian Sunday service. Frank felt his big toe throb as he sat side-saddle on the sofa and stole glances at Bridget, who was watching the band with Dick Bell-end and Plunkett. Chic McGrain and Bert Singh applauded at the end of the song like they'd just witnessed The Three Tenors performing "Nessun Dorma" during the 1990 World Cup. Flora then signalled to the band and the opening chords of the Prince classic "Raspberry Beret" sent the studio audience and half the sofa wild.

Three choruses later and Frank was laughing uncontrollably while trying to sing along in real Scots, as everyone on the sofa linked hands. The crowd went mental, cheering to the rafters as Flora and the boys soaked up the applause, while the bodhrán drummer pretended to lift his kilt for a flash of ginger nuts. Deidre then motioned for Flora to join them on the sofa, as Frank budged up to the point where he only had one arse cheek left sitting, as Chic McGrain shouted, 'Bravo, maestro! Bravo, maestro!' at the top of his voice.

Deidre stood to hug Flora, who then made her way along the sofa, hugging everyone until she finally made it to Frank who gave her a big hug, then impulsively rubbed her back, before he caught Bridget shaking her head and mouthing "No" at him.

'Fuck's sake,' Frank said, vowing to eschew all forms of physical greeting from now on. Flora moved nearest to Deidre and everyone else shuffled along the sofa with Frank being the odd one out in this game of musical chairs. He stood at the side, toe throbbing, back killing him, muttering, 'Beam me up, Scotty,' which was caught on the mic by Deidre who gave him a look that could strip paint. Chic McGrain was telling a blushing Flora she was a 'veritable tour de force' until Deidre attempted to regain control and get the show back on track.

'That was brilliant, Flora and the boys. Well done, the Pictish Fairies. What a way to bring the year to a close. I'm sure we'll be hearing a lot more from you in the coming months. Sláinte,' she said, raising a glass of Diet Coke to the sofa. The audience let out a big cheer and started chanting, 'Here we, here we, here we fucking go.' Deidre scolded them for their language, quickly realising she was fighting a losing battle.

Shelby St. George, with one eye on Deidre's gig, asked Flora, 'What made you choose to cover a Prince number?'

Flora started to answer, then broke off to say how much she loved Token Gesture and how it was an honour to be sitting on the same sofa as Chic McGrain and the Minister for Culture. She ignored Frank completely, heaping lavish praise on Shelby St. George, while Kyle Horsburgh appeared to grunt. Chic McGrain took this as his cue to launch into a spiel about how great it was to see indigenous Scots singing in their own dialect and how someone like Flora would be given a global platform to perform her songs when Scotland inevitably gains Independence, which according to Chic McGrain would happen in the next six months.

'I see the likes of Flora here as part of a nascent, effervescent, vibrant country, an eclectic mix of traditional music harking back to our Celtic roots merged with the smell and sounds of a multicultural modernist Scotland, represented by bands like Young Fathers, lo-fi fusing with avant-pop and indietronica to create a Scottish sensibility that focuses on a single paradigm where female voices are to the fore and othering is an anachronism left to swim alone on a sea of melancholy.'

Deidre then asked Kyle Horsburgh, who was surreptitiously checking his mobile phone, what he thought. Kyle scrambled to put the device back in his pocket but dropped it on the floor, before saying, 'Fuck,' followed by, 'Shit.' Deidre apologised for the language, saying that Kyle appeared to be having some "technical problems". Kyle sought to rescue the situation.

'I agree with Chic McGrain. I thought Florence was brilliant, really guid likes.'

'It's Flora,' said Flora.

Shelby St. George heaped some lavish praise back at Flora before Deidre reluctantly asked Frank what he thought.

'I thought it was hilarious. Funniest thing I've heard in years.

I love a bit of tatties 'n' mince,' he said, patting his belly before adding, 'Mind you, "Purple Rain" is my favourite.'

This was met with a stony silence from the sofa, with everyone turning to glare at Frank, except Kyle who was checking his phone.

Flora moaned, 'It's not meant to be funny,' before Chic McGrain jumped in to defend her honour, not missing an opportunity to hear the sound of his own voice.

'Don't bother with a heathen like him, Flora; pale, male and stale, that's all Frank Savage is. You are honey in a sea of gammon, whereas Savage is well past his sell-by date. Bloody yoon.'

Frank gave Chic McGrain the wanker sign before shouting, 'Don't listen to that wank, Flora. Chic Migraine. That's what they should call him – Chic bloody Migraine – because he gives everyone a sore heid.'

Deidre warned him, 'Enough, Frank. I know it's past the watershed, but can we limit the bad language, please.'

Frank gave her the thumbs up, then mimicked pulling a zipper over his mouth.

Deidre turned towards the crowd.

'Okay, we have a big treat for our audience and the viewers back home. Off you go and get ready, Chic.'

Chic McGrain got up off the sofa and gave the camera some jazz hands as he made his way backstage.

'We're going to have a song from Texas, then eighties heartthrobs Token Gesture will be performing their smash hit, "Lager Haze".'

Huge cheer.

'After that we'll bring in the Bells, then go straight to the Ross Bandstand in Princes Street Gardens for the moment you've all been waiting for, as the tartan teen sensations from Edinburgh, the Bay City Rollers, turn back the clock fifty-odd years to perform their smash hit "Shang-A-Lang" via a giant hologram that will see dearly departed singer Les McKeown beamed onto Edinburgh Castle.'

The pre-recorded Texas song played as Frank nipped to the green room to grab another large Jack 'n' Coke with Shelby St. George in hot pursuit.

'Pour me one, Frank. We better be quick, don't want to miss Chic McGrain singing.'

Frank handed her a drink, then grabbed a wee box of Pringles and shoved them in his pocket, along with a chicken leg wrapped in some toilet paper.

'I've always found the lyrics to that "Lager Haze" a bit rapey, if you ask me,' he said.

'Just as well no cunt is asking you then,' she replied.

They both laughed, then downed their drinks in a oner.

Chic McGrain and Token Gesture were now in full swing, with the singer gyrating his hips, white-soulboy-style, with a sprinkling of pound-shop Elvis. The crowd were going wild with middle-aged women close to throwing their knickers onto the stage as he held the mic their way, urging them to join him in the chorus.

'How I miss those endless days, we spent together in a lager haze,
'But please tell her I'm sorry,
'Please tell her that I'm all alone,
'Please tell her I'm sorry,
'Please tell her that I'm all alone.'

Deidre danced behind her desk, throwing her hands in the air, while the rest of the sofa, except for Kyle who was taking selfies, looked down on the stage and clapped like hungry sea lions.

Frank opened a can of lager and took the chicken leg from his jacket pocket. He admired the drumstick, waving it in time to the music like Bez in his pomp playing maracas for the Happy Mondays, while the rest of the guests now stood up to join him dancing.

Frank watched Bobby, standing three feet away from Chic McGrain at the front of the stage, completely still with his hands behind his back. He was staring hard at him, which had the desired effect of unnerving the singer, who moved across the stage, steering well clear of the nutter in the middle. Frank was well into his rhythm now, doing a gouty shuffle and shouting, 'Ya hoor, sir!' What happened next could only be described as a "Kennedy moment" with generations to come asking the tribal elders the burning question, 'Where were you when…?'

Frank studied the chicken drummer, which in his alcohol-fuelled mind was the mirror image of his throbbing big toe. Chic McGrain had finished his number and was now milking the applause, giving a little bow that said, "I have given you my all".

Bobby was pointing with both index fingers, arms extended, calling him fifty-seven varieties of "Fucking prick". Frank, lost in in the moment, decided to launch the chicken leg at the back of Bobby's head. Despite the gout and the alcohol, Frank hurled the projectile like a young Parisian hurling a petrol bomb at the gendarmes during the May '68 riots. His left hand made a fist as he pulled back his right arm and threw the chicken leg, managing to get a lot of shoulder, the required amount of follow-through and a lower body hip turn that would put Tiger Woods to shame – pre the shagging, the car crashing and the getting battered off the soon-to-be ex-missus shame. Old man strength. Bobby, the intended target, bent down to tie his shoelaces just as the chicken leg left the sofa area, glided across the Pacific Quay studio audience, before gaining momentum and striking Chic McGrain in the face.

A stunned Chic McGrain clutched his left eye and fell backwards into the drum kit with the hi-hat bouncing off his head. Frank, now frozen with horror, held his statuesque follow-through pose long enough for Deidre, all the guests, most of the studio audience, the millions viewing at home and the rest of Token Gesture to see who the culprit was. It was like Oswald had shot Kennedy, then announced by megaphone, "I'm over here in the Texas Depository Building!"

Frank, in full flight or fight mode, decided the decent thing would be to head down to the stage to make sure Chic McGrain hadn't lost an eye. This act of chivalry was ill-conceived, however, as hordes of adoring fans booed and hissed at Frank like Jimmy Savile had come back to life and was hosting a one-off *Jim'll Fix It* Christmas special. The Pictish Fairies mob joined in and soon Frank was surrounded, with the odds of him seeing in the New Year alive being slashed from evens to 1/8 against. Falco, who had been watching from the wings with Olga, moved forward to help his friend, casually clearing a path by dinking the likeliest of the lads to chin Frank over the head with his cane, while Olga took care of the perimenopausal Token Gesture fans.

The cameras cut back to Deidre, who was now beside the stage ignoring the melee and preparing for the big countdown to the Bells, which were only sixty seconds away. Deidre commenced the countdown, shouting to be heard over the baying mob, who were now lobbing plastic tumblers as Falco struggled to bat them away and Naomi, Olga and Bobby formed a protective cordon around Frank.

'Ten, nine, eight...' A dazed Chic McGrain had climbed down off the stage and was heading straight for Frank.

'Seven, six, five...' He pushed his way through the crowd until he was square in front of his attacker, breadcrumbs stuck to his forehead, leering like a demented Jack Nicholson at the close of *The Shining*.

'Bastard... fucking baaaaaastard!' Chic McGrain shouted, lurching forwards.

'Four, three, two...' Deidre said, into the mic, taking all of one second to do so.

'One.' Frank sidestepped Chic McGrain, who fell into Deidre, sending her crashing to the floor, mic in hand.

'Happy New Year,' Deidre shouted from underneath Chic

McGrain, who had Big-Daddy-splashed the presenter and was now going for a submission.

Punches were thrown as balloons and tinsel rained down on the revellers, with Falco adopting a Bruce Lee stance, cane in hand, daring anyone to come within two feet of him. Frank had the Token Gesture guitarist in a headlock and was using him to batter a way through the audience, while Bobby had headbutted the bodhrán drummer from the Pictish Fairies, who was now lying prone with his kilt round his waist, giving the watching millions a glimpse of his hairy ginger arse. Bert Singh had by this time been rushed out the building by his security detail who weren't taking any chances with the Minister for Culture, having gone into Defcon 1 as their *Poileas Alba* training kicked in. A groggy Deidre had escaped from beneath Chic McGrain and was screaming, 'Go to the Rollers! Go to the Rollers!' into the mic. The camera panned round to show Kyle Horsburgh necking Shelby St. George, before cutting away to a giant image of a young Les McKeown beaming down from the castle ramparts.

Frank made for the door, sweeping past a stunned Bridget and Richard, who was pleading with him to stop. The gang headed for the Shadow, with Frank not daring to look back in case he turned into a pillar of salt. Naomi reversed the Roller out of the guest parking space at top speed as Frank declared, 'I've well and truly fucked it this time.'

29

Frank entered The Haddonfield like the captain of a winning team bringing back the cup after a 102-year trophy drought, greeted by loud cheers and pats on the back from the assembled rabble. Bella, who was dressed in her Elvira costume, came from behind the bar and gave him a big kiss, before spraying a magnum of champagne in the air, soaking everyone in sight.

'Happy New Year, you fucking legend,' she said. 'It's about time someone sorted that gibbering arse Chic McGrain out. Did you see him land on top of Deidre? Call an ambulance! Operator! Operator! Get me the *Seirbheis Ambaileans na h-Alba* for one BBC presenter.'

Everyone laughed, but Frank felt a bit sheepish before deciding he would deal with the fallout tomorrow or the next day or the day after that while most likely looking for a new job. His mind wandered as he imagined working behind the bar in The Hadd, chatting to the afternoon punters while watching the racing on the telly. Not a bad life. Someone handed him a plate of chicken legs and he grabbed one, mimicking taking the pin out and rolling it underarm towards the bar, where the drinkers pretended to explode.

Naomi accepted a large glass of champagne, relieved to have delivered her dad in one piece to his local – a safe space for the next few hours where all thoughts of the Wise One, Brewster and the Syndicate could evaporate. She had a big meeting in the morning with The Gypsy where she would try to get her father out of his extortionate deal and on top of that she still had to arrange a sit-down between Brewster and Frank where they would iron out their differences. Naomi hadn't made any progress on that front. She was now having sleepless nights, playing the scenario over and over in her head, trying to work out when was the best time for the meeting and then choosing a suitable venue. Preferably somewhere they wouldn't kill each other.

Checking her phone, she saw that Frank, Deidre and Chic McGrain were trending across social media with various hashtags including #Chicastrophe #Chickendrummer #Piperdown #Savagebastard #FreeDeidre #SearchingforDeidre and #Chicsplash. Naomi had texted Bridget, asking her to join them, and, to her surprise, she turned up just as the party was in full flow.

Frank, who was sitting at the bar holding court with Bobby, Falco and Olga, felt a wave of longing wash over him as he spotted his ex-wife talking with his eldest daughter. He took his pint of lager and double rum with Coke across to join them as Bridget wished him a Happy New Year and gave him a kiss on the cheek. Frank caught a whiff of her perfume and smiled as his stomach churned. He asked Bridget where Richard was, and she gave him a resigned look and said he was tucked up in bed as he had work later today.

Frank said, 'I'm supposed to be in tomorrow, I mean today, but they can fuck that for a game of soldiers.'

'I can imagine what the top story is going to be for the next few days, Frank,' Bridget said. 'So, you don't need to worry about the news. You are the news.'

Frank stared off into the middle distance as Naomi got up, deciding to give them a bit of time together. Bridget asked her where she was going, a half-hearted plea not to be left with Frank, but she danced away, grabbing Bobby and spinning him round for a jig. Frank smiled at Bridget and felt a calmness descend. At that moment, he knew what was important to him and it wasn't his career, the column, Chic McGrain, Deidre McAllister or the thousand and one other distractions that he dealt with daily. Christ, even the booze and the betting could take a back seat. No, two of the three things Frank cared about the most were in the same pub, at the same time. Naomi and Bridget; his other daughter Katie being the third.

He took a sip of his rum and ran with his thoughts, convinced that through some kind of synergy the planets had aligned at that point to leave Bridget feeling exactly the same way, with the natural conclusion being her going home with him for make-up sex, followed by them renewing their wedding vows at some point in the New Year, probably summer or early autumn at the latest, followed by a second honeymoon on the island of Capri. Frank was sure that if he stared at Bridget's forehead long enough and hard enough, he could bend her mind, so they were both on the same thought pattern. Swept up in the emotion, he moved closer to her and decided to lay it all out, cards-on-the-table time – his true feelings, how he had never got over the split and what she meant to him. The pitch.

Among the list of things Frank hadn't considered at that exact moment were Bridget being married to his boss, Bridget witnessing him throwing a chicken leg at Chic McGrain, him being drunk and now wearing pink Crocs because his gout was "killing him", his breath, and, of course, any regard for how she might be feeling. To this you could add in Bridget having left him due to his – in no particular order of toxicity – alcoholism, drug-taking, betting, jealousy, cheating (although Frank had claimed going with a prostitute wasn't really cheating), smoking in the house when drunk, smoking in the house when sober, not doing any cleaning (woman's work), unreliability particularly with Katie, and assorted other sins that could be thrown into the pot marked "selfish bastard". Frank decided to waive any attempt at a preamble and go straight for the jugular, failure not being an option.

'I miss you, Bridget, and seeing you this last month has made me realise what a mistake I made in letting you go. If I think back, we got on great and, if the truth be told, I've never stopped loving you. Is there any way you would consider leaving Richard and us getting back together? Sure, we can take things slowly at the start, a step at a time, on your terms, of course.'

Bridget took a sip of her drink and stared blankly ahead, not quite the falling back into his arms that Frank had anticipated. He gave her a moment, then another one and another one after that, staring at her forehead, just to let her mind get in sync with his, but still no words came out of her mouth. Frank decided to fill the empty silence but had the feeling of the ice breaking and him plunging into the freezing water, unable to climb back to the surface.

'I know I'm a bit of a mess now but I'm going to clean up my act. I promise. Totally. Just seeing you get on so well with Naomi and the way you've brought Katie up has made me want to be with you, more than anything.'

Frank felt like a football manager whose team are down to nine men with an hour still left on the clock.

'And I know you're married to Dick Bell-end – in fact, fuck knows why you married Dick Bell-end, I mean Richard – but you surely can't be into that arsehole when you should be with me? We're made for each other, Bridge. It's a no-brainer.'

The slight shortening of her name to Bridge was a sure sign of Frank's increasing desperation. The stuff coming out his gob was a word soup; he felt like he was drowning, and Bridget was starting to fade away from him. Even though she still hadn't uttered a single word, there was no need; he'd starred in this movie before. The romantic comedy where the hero doesn't get the girl. *Love (not) Actually*, or *Love not even fucking close, pal.*

Finally, Bridget took a deep breath, preparing to bring down Madame Guillotine on her ex-husband's dreams.

'First off, I left you, Frank. You didn't let me go.'

'I know, I know, I never meant it like that.' Frank reckoned if this was a boxing match it, would have been stopped by a straight knockout in the first round.

Bridget continued. 'As you rightly point out, I am married to Richard, your boss, although that's got nothing to do with it. How Richard and I are getting on at any given moment and my feelings towards him are frankly none of your business, Frank. It's private. But for your information, I love him and we're happy.'

She took a sip of her drink and thought about not continuing, sparing Frank further hurt, but decided to plough on to save her having to go through the same spiel the next time they happened to see each other. Call it a mercy mission.

'I'd be even richer if I had a pound for every time you told me you'll clean up your act. From where I'm sitting, Frank, your life is a bigger mess and you're a bigger shambles than when we split up. Christ knows what this column nonsense is all about. Thing is, there's a bit of truth in the things you say but it gets lost in the ranting. You're the classic ultracrepidarian, Frank, and if you don't know what that means, look it up. The only person who comes close to spouting shite about things they know fuck all about and have no experience of is your new mate, Chic McGrain. Two peas from the same white, middle-aged, male pod. Take your "ban the dogs and babies" column, the one that kicked off this whole sorry mess. If ever there was an example of why the patriarchy shouldn't write about things they know nothing about, then that's it, right there.'

'Patriarchy?' Frank replied. 'We're not at the "smash the patriarchy" stage already? Are we?'

'Shut up, Frank. I don't talk to Richard about his work but it's obvious you're being exploited and you're happily playing along with this new-found fame like a drooling idiot. Get a grip, man.'

Frank felt like Bridget had him surrounded.

'I know, I know. I'm going to leave the paper, leave journalism altogether. I've had enough.'

Bridget shook her head in despair.

'Frank, you don't have a fucking job to go to and you've next to no transferable skills. You're no doubt still up to your eyeballs in debt. The drink and the drugs haven't gone away and that horse you bet is still running on Porty beach. Oh, did I mention your heart arrhythmia by chance?'

By this point, Frank knew he was fighting a lost cause and tried desperately to salvage some hope now that his pride had jumped out the window.

He cried, 'Do you not love me, Bridget? I know you love me.'

Bridget shook her head and gulped her wine down in a oner.

'You use the word love like a fourteen-year-old boy, Frank. What you really want is your hole. That would make you feel better, less alone, connected with another human being even if it was just for a few minutes.'

'Ouch,' Frank said, slumping down in his chair.

'I do love you, Frank. I really do and always will. But I'm not *in* love with you.'

Frank's head was spinning; this had all gotten a bit adult for him, and he was struggling to comprehend.

'What the fuck does that even mean? That's some shite you got out a woman's magazine. *I love you but I'm not in love with you.* Give me a fucking clue here – three across, anything. That's like those daft lassies who say they like bastards.'

Bridget sighed and rubbed her temples.

'In simple terms, I don't want to be with you. I have no desire to be with you and I don't want to be your friend either because that can't work. I care about you a lot, Frank; you're the father of my daughter, and I really hope that once and for all you do sort yourself out because, trust me, taking cocaine in your mid-fifties is not a good look. I'm keeping in touch with Naomi, and I'll be helping her with this cinema project, but that doesn't include seeing you. It's over, Frank. It was over years ago and deep down you know it. You need to move on with your life.'

Frank felt a rising anger in his belly but didn't want to lose it with Bridget. He got up and made for the door, motioning to Bobby that he was going outside for fresh air, with his friend following behind. Frank passed him a cigarette and Bobby asked how he was getting on with Bridget.

'She fucking patched me, Bobby. I asked her if she wanted to get back and she patched me. Gave me the old Spanish archer – El Bow. She custard-pied me, bumped, dinghied.'

Bobby shook his head, taking a deep pull on his fag. 'Fuck me, Frank, you've bumped into her, what, twice in the last month and before that you probably hadn't seen her for three years. Take it easy, for fuck's sake, man.'

Frank sighed. 'She said she loves me but she's not *in* love with me.'

'That's something women like to say. I interpret that as "I don't fancy you, you're a fucking mess" but you can put that right. Clean yourself up, then completely forget about her. Give it five years or so and you should have a chance. She'll have come around by then. Let's face it, there's no way she's going to stay with that Dick Bell-end fud. Bridget is a class act; your competition is more likely to be that Hollywood heartthrob, George Pittman.'

'Bridget knows George Pittman. He starred in an adaptation of one of her books. Says they got on like a house on fire.'

The pair watched the stars for a moment, drunk, enjoying the comfortable silence that comes with being friends for years.

'I still miss Michael,' Frank said. 'The pain hasn't gone away. If anything, it's just got worse; the older I get, the more sentimental I've become. I think about him more than ever, Bobby – what happened the night he died, what he would have gone on to achieve, if he'd have been happy. I'm sure he would have loved to see how things have turned out, how folk who are gay are treated better. Edinburgh's a different place now. The eighties feel like Victorian times.'

Bobby stared at the pavement for what seemed like an age before flicking his fag into the gutter.

'I was there the night Michael died, Frank.'

Frank looked stunned.

'What do you mean, Bobby? What the fuck are you saying?'

Bobby clammed up, forcing Frank to prod him, repeating, 'What do you mean, Bobby? Tell me. Fucking tell me.'

Bobby stepped away from Frank and started to speak quickly.

'I'd gotten drunk with Michael in The Haddonfield, and we'd gone for a walk along the prom. You were up the town, upstairs at the Café Royal. We saw a group of football casuals coming towards us at speed and reckoned it was Brewster's mob. As you know, Michael had been chased by them on Christmas Eve, so we cut up by the derelict pool and before I knew it, he had ducked under the fence and gone in. It must have been Dutch courage as he always said no when we went in there. The place gave him the heebies.'

Frank listened intently.

'Speak slower, Bobby, speak slower.'

A breathless Bobby bent over double, looking like he was about to vomit, before continuing.

'I followed him into the pool and the mob went by, or so we thought. We were both drunk and the moonlight made the place look beautiful and you could still make out some of the old Art Deco features. I got caught up in the moment. I had been toying with my sexuality since I hit puberty, Frank. I fancied your brother, and I knew he felt the same way. We were flirting, daring each other to climb the old staircase up to the diving boards which were still intact.'

Now it was Frank's turn to feel sick. He pinched his tongue between his teeth before barking an order.

'Keep going. I want the truth.'

Bobby continued to unburden himself of the pain he had carried for decades.

'Anyway, we heard voices at the fence and by this time we were on the top board staring out across the Firth of Forth.

It was Brewster and his cronies, so we hid, looking down on them, and they eventually left after about half an hour, when the cider and glue had run out. They must have been too wasted to climb up the staircase. I started to make my way back along the top board towards the steps and Michael came to follow me. I whispered to him that it was a bit slippy and he should take care on the way down. A fiver fell out of his pocket, and he turned back to get it. That's when he went flying on the ice and fell over the side.'

Bobby broke down, sobbing hysterically. Frank recoiled, not wanting to comfort him.

'Keep going, Bobby. Keep going.'

Bobby pleaded, 'I'm so sorry, Frank.'

Frank, like a dog with a bone, poked Bobby in the arm to continue.

'All of it, Bobby. I need to hear all of it.'

Bobby regained his passage of thought and started speaking, his voice choked with emotion.

'I heard a sickening thud and saw him lying on the ground, his legs were pointing the wrong way, and a pool of blood had formed at the back of his head. I knew he was dead. I ran back down to check on him, but he was a goner. He died instantly, Frank. I swear he wasn't breathing. I was completely panic stricken and took flight. I ran back through the fence and made it to a phone box. I dialled 999 and told the operator what had happened. I should have gone back, Frank. I left your brother, and I've lived with the pain ever since. I'm so sorry. It's taken me far too long to tell you.'

Frank was struggling to take it all in and felt a mixture of sympathy for this pathetic creature manifesting as his friend but also betrayal and revulsion.

'So, Brewster was there but had nothing to do with it? I wish you'd told me sooner, Bobby. Thirty years sooner would have been better, even twenty.'

Bobby sobbed gently. 'I'm sorry, Frank. I wish it was me that died that night. I really do.'

'So, are you gay, Bobby?'

Bobby pressed his thumbs deep into his temples.

'I guess so, but I don't have sex with anyone. I've been celibate for years. Back then, I was experimenting, if you like, trying to find my sexuality. Michael and I never did anything. I'm so ashamed, Frank. I should have stayed with him that night and I should have told you right away, then a month went by, and I still hadn't said anything. It kind of snowballed from there. I became scared to tell you and tried to push it to the back of my mind as I thought too much time had passed.'

Frank didn't know how to respond. A tiredness engulfed him the likes of which he had never experienced before, and the sadness was overwhelming. Not just a physical tiredness. Frank felt there and then he was tired of life. He felt like crying or lashing out at Bobby but didn't have the energy and the tears wouldn't come.

30

Naomi replayed what Frank had said about her mother's death on a constant loop in her mind as she headed to The Gypsy's compound at 7am on New Year's Day, determined to put her father's financial problems to bed. The hatred she now felt towards the Wise One was all-consuming and Naomi had to dig deep to stay professional. No doubt his time would come. She just had to be patient. Either a rival would take him out – and they were starting to line up – or the law would finally get their shit together and lock him up for good. Naomi had the brains to work out that putting a bullet in the old prick's head herself was a bad idea. She hadn't given up on the hope of settling down one day, perhaps having children and, if the endometriosis prevented that, there was always the option of adopting. But one thing was certain – she was no murderer.

Naomi had met The Gypsy a few times on Syndicate business, always finding him charming and easy to deal with. It was obvious to her the crime lord had control of Brewster and was the real brains behind the lucrative drug scene in the "festival city". She knew the Wise One also respected him and he'd told her The Gypsy had over a thousand men across the travelling community with strong links to crime families in Dublin and Glasgow. In short, he was a serious player and someone not to be fucked with. Naomi had brought along seventy thousand pounds in her Louis Vuitton holdall; sixty grand to pay back the amount Frank had borrowed and an extra ten thousand pounds interest payment to sweeten the deal. She had well over a million stashed away in foreign bank accounts and this was small change that she held in a couple of ISAs.

She arrived at the compound and, after being thoroughly searched by the sturdy youth with the neck tattoo, was escorted through the courtyard, past the pig pen to The Gypsy's palace.

The Gypsy roared when he saw her, wrapping her in a giant bear hug.

'Naomi, my love. Good to see you and a Happy New Year to you. You never told me you were Frank Savage's daughter. It's a small world, my dear, a small world.'

Naomi felt tiny in his presence. She hadn't been this close to him before, and the strong smell of Aramis aftershave stuck in her throat and made her eyes water.

'No. I guess I'm full of surprises,' she said awkwardly, mindful of the XL Bullies that were at The Gypsy's side.

'Róisín!' he roared. 'Róisín, get us a cup of tea and bring the good biscuits for Naomi.'

Róisín came into the room.

'Hello, Naomi, grand to see you at this ungodly hour. Happy New Year and all that bollocks,' she said. 'Don't be taking any shite from this one.'

Naomi smiled; she had met Róisín before and they'd hit it off.

'I'll try not to,' she replied softly.

The Gypsy eyed the holdall. 'I take it you've brought me a nice present to see in the New Year, Naomi. That's very sweet of you, my love.'

Naomi brought the holdall between her feet and got to the point. 'You know why I'm here. I want to pay off Frank's debt. He's got himself into a right state and hasn't been thinking straight. I respect you. That's why I've brought the sixty thousand pounds he borrowed and an extra ten thousand pounds interest. He's a civilian, miles out of his depth and not from our world.'

The Gypsy said nothing but cracked his knuckles. 'Naomi, Naomi. You know the script. I appreciate your father has been a true friend to the Romani people and did us a turn. That's why I lent him the money in the first place. But to renege on the original deal. Well, that's not how it works. You know as well as I do that Frank now owes ninety thousand pounds.'

He paused as Róisín brought in the tea and the good biscuits, which were homemade. Naomi made sure to make a big fuss of saying how great they were which she knew would go a long way with The Gypsy. It now dawned on her that not bringing the full ninety thousand pounds was a stupid mistake. A schoolgirl error. But just as things were looking a bit sticky from Naomi's side of the isle, her guardian angel spoke up.

Róisín said, 'Now, Emmett, I hope you're not going to give Naomi any of your bollocks. Like you said, her dad did us a good turn and Naomi has always been upfront with us.'

The Gypsy bristled at being called by his real name and tried to get angry with his wife.

'You see what happens when women get together. You see! The feckin' sisterhood! Need I feckin' remind you how things are supposed to work, Róisín? I put the food on the table, and you cook it. Jesus, woman. How many times are you going to interfere in my feckin' business?'

Róisín was having none of it. 'You watch your language with me, Emmett. Don't be a feckin' gobshite. Stop trying to bleed Naomi dry for a few quid. It's not like we need it. Give her a break.'

'I'll give you a break,' he warned menacingly.

'You can try, but I'll cut your feckin' balls off.'

The Gypsy, seeing his young wife was serious, burst into laughter.

'I love this woman, Naomi. I swear to the Holy Father. I feckin' love her.'

He waited until Róisín had left the room before he laid it out for her. 'Look. I'll take the seventy thousand pounds as a gesture of goodwill and your old fella can keep his flat and his ears.'

'Thank you. You've no idea how much this means to me.'

'But, and there's a but, Naomi. There's always a but.'

Her face sank, dreading what was coming. She instinctively touched her earlobe and, for a dreadful minute, thought The Gypsy was about to bring out the garden shears and do his worst. He sensed what she was thinking and let out a hearty chuckle.

'Jesus, woman! I'm not going to cut your fucking ear off.'

Naomi slumped back into her chair and pushed the holdall towards him. She thought it was cute how The Gypsy said feckin' and not its angrier big brother when he was talking to his wife.

'Now, we're just talking here, right? Just talking hypothetically, like. Quid pro quo. I reckon I've done you a solid letting Frank off the hook and turning a blind eye to the rules. Your father and I shook on a deal and that means a lot, as you well know. But putting that to one side, the facts are that your gaffer, the Wise One, is on a sticky wicket. There's a lot of talk about him being a grass, as there always is, but one of our guys from across the water was talking to an intelligence officer and he alluded to the fact that Ray Armstrong has been on the Met payroll for fifty years.'

This hardly came as a surprise to Naomi. She'd worked out for herself that good old Uncle Ray had to be a police informant to achieve the longevity and freedom of movement he enjoyed. Plus, it was an obvious way to get rid of his rivals and she reckoned although he was "heavy", he wasn't that heavy when it came to the likes of the Russian Mafia or the new breed of criminal coming from Ireland, Holland and within London itself.

'Go on,' she said.

'So, what I'm saying, Naomi, is that the Wise One might not be long for this world and the inevitable – in terms of nature taking its course – may happen sooner than you think. A lot fucking sooner.'

Naomi knew he was marking her card and any loyalty she once had for the Wise One had disappeared.

'And if your boss was to go, then that would leave you up shit creek without a paddle, running a cinema that has next to no chance of turning a profit.' He paused to dip one of Róisín's biscuits into his tea.

'So, to summarise, if something happens to the Wise One – and I must stress it wouldn't be at my hand – I might be able to offer you a job, which would involve me buying the cinema and running it as a legitimate enterprise. I know for a fact there's a major film and television studio just been built at Leith Docks, and this would be a way for me to move into that world.'

Naomi admired his vision but shuddered at the thought of the Wise One being taken out.

The Gypsy finished by saying, 'You don't have to say a word. I like you, Naomi, and appreciate your talents. What I would be offering you is a way out. Legitimate. You know the craic. If you stick with the Wise One, he's going to turn on you one day. You'd end up taking the fall at best and, at worst, well, you know how it goes.'

Naomi got up to leave, not wanting to overstay her welcome. She said goodbye to Róisín, giving her a big hug and whispering, 'Thank you.' The Gypsy told her he'd be in touch and to tell Frank he said hi.

Back in her car, Naomi glanced in the rear-view mirror and saw Brewster arriving with the Two Billys in tow.

'That's some serious fucking canines you've got there, mate,' Brewster said to The Gypsy as they sat down in the bar area of the compound. The barman, a human version of an XL Bully, popped a couple of bottles of Cristal and they toasted, among other things, "making shitloads of filthy lucre". The Gypsy nodded towards Waffen, who was tied up outside, and said, 'I like the German shepherds, but these fuckers would have your dog as a starter.'

Brewster thought better than to disagree with this fact. 'Correct,' he said. The XL Bullies were next level. He brought The Gypsy up to speed with developments and gave him the lowdown on his plans for The Final Solution as the Two Billys played pool, listening intently while pretending to concentrate on their game.

'I'm meeting the Wise One at noon, for this fucking Loony Dook thing in South Queensferry. Thinks he can make an arse of me by having me wear my trunks and get into the water with him. But he's got another thing coming. I'm taking Billy One with me and we've a plan to take care of the Cockney ponce. Good and proper.'

The Gypsy made a face that said, "Expand", so Brewster did.

'Billy One here is a dab hand at the old sniping from back in the day. A real one-shot, one-kill merchant. A patient fucker, he'll sit for days on end in a bush eating nothing but grass and drinking his own piss. He's agreed to come out of retirement for one last job and I've given him the perfect tool for his swansong, haven't I, Billy?'

Billy One beamed with pride as Billy Two looked mightily perplexed.

Brewster said, 'Nothing less than the OSV-96 semi-automatic, specialised high-accuracy sniper rifle, as favoured by the Russian FSS, the Syrian government and numerous Jihadi raghead fuckers. A contact delivered it to me a few months back when I realised this so-called Wise One would need to be whacked. We've got something spectacular in mind for him, and let's just say there'll be no Loony Dook next year if what we're planning comes off.'

Billy Two's nose was out of joint. 'Where do I come into this? I take it he's getting a healthy wedge for this hit. Where's my piece of the pie?'

Brewster looked at him with contempt as Billy One chalked his cue. 'I'll come to you in a bit,' he said.

Brewster laid out his plans for the takeover of the Syndicate operation and how he'd work hand in hand with The Gypsy ahead of more men coming over from Northern Ireland to help distribute the influx of drugs into the capital. He stressed how the arrangement would be "very much a partnership", knowing The Gypsy could muster a small army of travellers at the drop of a hat. Brewster reckoned that with the Wise One out of the way, the Syndicate didn't have any real foothold in Scotland, with Naomi and JJ not having the capability to put up a fight. He knew they had contacts in Glasgow, but Brewster reckoned his relationship with the Lafferty family, who ran the show on the west coast, trumped any loose business ties the London mob had up here. He also had no intention of paying back any money taken from the councillors and was still smarting from the humiliation he had suffered on Arthur's Seat.

Brewster would give Naomi a "take it or leave it" offer she couldn't refuse, to work for him and run the cinema project. Although he hated her guts, he recognised that she had a talent for figures that could prove useful.

He told The Gypsy, who hadn't uttered a word, that the fifty kilogram shipment of quality cocaine would enter Leith Docks next Friday on a cargo ship coming from Tangier. It would be held at an industrial unit in Granton ready to be distributed initially across the sink estates of west Edinburgh when the time was right. With the Wise One out of the way, it would simply be a case of helping themselves to the drugs and taking care of anyone who dared to stand in their path.

'A piece of piss,' Brewster said, bringing the curtain down on his grand scheme.

The Gypsy remained silent as Billy Two aired his grievance at Billy One.

'I'm not fucking happy about this at all. How many jobs

did we do together back in the day, killing the Taigs? And now you've decided to go freelance, a one-man band. The One Billy, that doesn't fucking work. How can we be the Two Billys if you decide you want to be the One Billy, Billy One? Fucking Silly One, more like.

Billy One took two steps back and brought his pool cue crashing down on the side of Billy Two's head. The Gypsy smiled as Billy One moved quickly to smash the butt of the cue into Billy Two's face before grabbing a champagne flute and launching a frenzied attack on his former mate's neck. Billy One was there for what seemed like an eternity, stabbing the glass at Billy Two's open neck as a fountain of blood shot into the air.

He screamed, 'A fucking tout, Fergie, you're nothing but a dirty fucking tout! Stringing me along over there when you were working for the Peelers and the fucking Brits. I should have dealt with you when you were pimping out yer own daughter. Fucking beast.'

The blood spurting out of Billy Two's jugular hit Billy One in the eye, temporarily blinding him. Billy One responded by banging Billy Two's head off the floor as he gurgled, gasping for breath, a farting sound coming out of a gaping gash in his neck.

'Watch the carpet and don't get blood on the beige,' The Gypsy barked. 'I've not long had it reupholstered.'

Brewster watched the violence, a sense of elation sweeping over him as he knew Billy One was now under his control. His very own trained assassin. *Cheap at half the price, this bam kills people for fun,* he thought. *All you have to do is tell him they're Catholic and its job done. Result.*

Billy One collapsed in a heap on the couch before The Gypsy told him to go outside for fresh air.

'What a mess. What are we going to do with the body?'

The Gypsy was dialling a number on his mobile, pausing to tell Brewster, 'Don't worry. I'll take care of that; saves me having to prepare breakfast for the pigs.' He ordered someone to "come right away" before telling Brewster to bolt and take Billy One with him.

The Gypsy said, 'That was quite the audition. He certainly passed and I've every faith in him to take care of this Londoner. Good shooting. Give me a call when it's done.'

31

Naomi heard the knock at her door and knew it was the police. The dull thud could only be them as she let DI Hope and a young woman who introduced herself as Detective Sergeant Gibson into her flat. Hope was the epitome of dour Scottish Protestant politeness, wishing her a Happy New Year with a firm handshake, before saying he just wanted to ask her a few questions about a known criminal called Danny Brewster. She asked the officers if they wanted a cup of tea, which he gladly accepted, 'Milk and two, love,' with DS Gibson politely declining. Hope was playing the role of tired old cop having to work on New Year's Day, but Naomi wasn't at all fooled by his world-weariness as she put the kettle on in the open-plan kitchen and brought out the Tunnock's Tea Cakes. This comedian was a wily old fox who she felt was processing the entire make-up of her flat, looking for anything out of the ordinary that could connect her to "the life" while at the same time talking shite about the biscuits.

Naomi already knew from her father that Hope had Brewster under surveillance and was aware of the Syndicate's plans for the cinema project. She therefore planned to show him everything and tell him nothing, having been well-versed by Uncle Ray in dealing with the law. Take nothing for granted. Naomi had to assume they were tailing her every move and were aware of her meeting with Armstrong, who was likely under constant watch, at the Balmoral. If they had indeed spotted him in Edinburgh, the Serious Crime Squad would be liaising with their colleagues in London, the National Crime Agency and, no doubt, Interpol. Up and comers like DS Gibson would be dying to get involved. They all watched the same television programmes about Organised Crime Groups – or OCGs, abbreviating anything that moved – the likes of *The Detectives* or *24 Hours in Police Custody* – and probably expected Naomi to answer "no comment" to every question.

Hope got through the preamble. A bit of fluff about how he'd known Frank for years since her father's days on the crime beat. How they'd drank together and sometimes played golf.

Blah, fucking, blah, Naomi thought, while keeping her eyes sparkling and the smile firmly painted on her face. She waited for him to ask her how she was liking Portobello.

'And how are you liking being by the seaside?' Hope asked, right on cue.

'I love it,' she replied enthusiastically, before adding, 'It's a bit chilly but Edinburgh is so beautiful.' Talkative and friendly, that was the default setting Naomi had installed.

'Well, Naomi, I hope you don't mind but like I said the reason for our visit is to ask you a few questions about a meeting you had with Brewster.'

'No, I don't mind at all. Ask away. I hope I can help, DI Hope,' she replied in a soft voice.

Hope began like he was explaining things to a child.

'Well, this Brewster is a nasty character, who's served time for attempted murder and is now back in Portobello. He's on our radar and we've been watching his every move. Hence the reason I told your dad that you'd popped up in our surveillance photos.'

DS Gibson brought out the pictures of Naomi and Brewster

sitting on a bench in Daisy Park, spreading them on the coffee table.

Naomi clocked right away that Hope had called it a "meeting" with Brewster and sought to nip that narrative firmly in the bud before the games began.

'I wouldn't go so far as to call him bumping into me a "meeting".'

The detectives waited for her to fill in the blanks as Naomi studied the pictures, which did look a tad suss, like two spies meeting at the height of the Cold War.

'I go to Daisy Park a lot on my walks through Porty. This Brewster guy sat down next to me on the bench and told me we'd met at the town hall. I didn't recognise him at first, then he told me he'd been dressed as Santa and had given me a lollipop. I remembered his dog, a German shepherd, had a Santa suit on as well.'

Hope picked up one of the photographs and made a big deal of studying it.

'Yes, that would explain why the picture clearly shows you know each other. Did he say anything to you about your work, Naomi? Why you're up here? Frank mentioned something about a cinema project, plans to redevelop the old Regency. That sounds exciting. I loved that place as a kid.'

Naomi played along with the charade.

'Yeah, my dad was waxing lyrical about it as well. He told me he saw his first film there, *Snow White and the Seven Dwarfs*.' She paused to make Hope repeat his question.

'So, did Brewster say anything about that?'

Naomi pretended she'd been distracted.

'Oh yeah, right. He did, as a matter of fact,' she replied, staring off into the middle distance while rubbing her chin in thought. 'He said he'd heard I worked for the private equity firm involved in the restoration of the old cinema. Said he'd like to explore the possibility of a tie-in with the theatre group, using the new venue to put on shows, possibly a pantomime. Like my old man is fond of saying, "Edinburgh is a village".'

'It certainly is,' Hope said sagely, with Gibson nodding in agreement.

Naomi laughed.

'He's a bit of a blowhard, this Brewster. He boasted about how he'd dragged himself out the gutter to become a success story. He told me he'd set up the youth theatre with funding he helped secure from the Scottish government and local charities.'

Hope exchanged glances with Gibson.

'We're aware that your father and Brewster have an ongoing feud that stretches back over thirty-odd years, with Frank blaming him for the death of your Uncle Michael. I know for a fact your dad is barking up the wrong tree there but there's no denying Brewster is dangerous.'

Naomi made to look perplexed.

'What's this got to do with me?'

'Nothing, other than you're Frank's daughter and Brewster may seek to exploit this feud at some point. We know your father's recently acquired Rolls-Royce was vandalised with acid; an incident at the town hall involving Brewster, your father, his friend, Bobby Thapa, and several others including two former paramilitaries from Northern Ireland.'

Naomi smiled wryly, vowing to keep things polite and not come across as a smart arse in any way.

'Yes, I've heard how Dad and this Brewster guy don't get on, but I wouldn't go so far as to call it an "ongoing feud". My dad lived in London for years. You're right at there being a rammy at the opening of the youth theatre but I guess everyone had too much sherry that night.'

Naomi laughed and offered Hope another tea cake, which he gladly accepted.

'What is it you do again?' asked Gibson, who had been waiting patiently in the wings, killer question at the ready.

Naomi had been schooled by the Wise One and had her spiel well-rehearsed as she went into full business mode. 'I work as a venture associate for a firm in London called Upton Park Wealth Management. We specialise in financial advice, corporate pensions, discretionary fund management and I work as part of a small team in the private equity department.'

Naomi checked to make sure she was remembering to breathe and talk slowly.

'I'm up here to work on the development of the old Regency cinema in tandem with the Portobello Heritage Initiative and the council. Our firm are backing the project and are providing venture capital of around three million pounds to the preferred bidder. I'll stay on to provide management support in the first year and will help with everything from the hiring of staff to looking at ways we can fully monetise the space. We see this as a massive opportunity for a start-up company to get involved at ground level on a once-in-a-lifetime project that will bring real benefit to the community.'

DS Gibson was like a dog with a bone as Hope became engrossed in folding his tea-cake wrapper.

'So how come a firm based in the East End of London gets to be involved in a cinema project in Edinburgh?' Gibson asked.

Naomi had seen this one coming. 'We're always on the lookout for opportunities in the UK and have learnt from our ventures in Brighton how much people love the seaside, which in turn leads to urban renewal of previously run-down areas. Call it gentrification, if you like. As you know, I have family in Portobello, and I'm aware there's been a buzz about the place for the last decade or so. A real influx of new money, with wealthy middle-class families flocking to the area – you only need to look around to see the effect, the number of cafés and community projects on the go. My firm sees Portobello as the "Brighton of the North" and feel we can make a real difference up here. But like everything else, it's about the money. I'm not going to hide that; we're venture capitalists. However, I've been transparent in all my dealings with local community groups and the council. The injection of capital can kick-start things and enable Porty to become a premier UK destination in terms of arts and culture. That's got to be a good thing. Right?'

DS Gibson nodded in agreement, while her slight grin told Naomi she didn't believe a word of it.

DI Hope decided it was time to go in harder.

'Look, Naomi, that all sounds very plausible but we have reason to believe an organised crime group could also be involved in your cinema project and are planning to use the new Regency as a front to launder their ill-gotten gains from the proceeds of drug dealing in the capital. Our information would suggest they have a contact in your firm and our inquiries are at an early stage. Obviously, you are a person of interest to us in terms of providing information, but at this stage I'm prepared to give you the benefit of the doubt in respect to knowingly assisting criminals. The Serious Fraud Office have been alerted and will investigate. Any help you can provide would be greatly appreciated.'

Naomi stayed in corporate mode, knowing Hope was on a fishing expedition.

'Thanks for the heads-up. I must say I'm shocked to hear this and will be reporting your concerns to my supervisors. This is a matter for the firm's lawyers, and I'll have them contact you to discuss it further. I can assure you that you'll be my first port of call if I see or hear anything suspicious. Upton Wealth Management is investing a lot in this project and it's in everyone's best interest for it to be a resounding success.'

Hope resorted back to simple bobby-on-the-beat territory.

'I'm just giving you a heads-up, Naomi. I don't get involved with corporate lawyers, they're a bit out of my league.'

'Your bosses in London. Who are they again?' Gibson asked.

Naomi, unruffled, replied, 'Our owners are made up of an investment committee that stretches the globe with interests in Saudi Arabia and the US. Our chief executive is a woman called Patricia Bleasdale – she started the company ten years ago, having made her name in the City as an early adopter of technology funds.'

Naomi felt fine mentioning the Wise One's wife, who acted as head of the company and went by her maiden name. She was high profile, having given interviews to the *FT Weekend*, *Vanity Fair* and *The Times* over the years, with the bit about Patricia making her name during the tech boom being completely above board. However, she liked to keep her private life just that and there was never any mention of a husband.

DS Gibson had her notebook open, asking Naomi how she spelt Bleasdale, while Hope appeared flustered and had switched into concerned uncle mode.

He said, 'Let us know if you hear from Brewster again. I'll warn you now to tread very carefully around him. He may give the impression he's a reformed character, but we've reason to believe he's part of the same crime group trying to muscle their way in up here. He's already brought a couple of bad guys over from Northern Ireland and has links to these gangsters in London. Your neck of the woods.'

Naomi mellowed. 'Thanks. I'll try to avoid meeting him on my own.'

DI Hope made to leave, heaving his lumbering carcass off the sofa. 'One last thing before we go, Naomi. You don't happen to know a guy called Ray Armstrong, do you?'

Naomi thought they were done and wasn't expecting the curveball. She had to think fast and decided honesty was the best policy. 'Uncle Ray, yip, he was a friend of my mother. Worked in the music business, owned a record label, I think.'

'When was the last time you met him?'

Naomi took a beat to think, knowing that down the line a good lawyer could argue her bumping into Armstrong at the Balmoral was a coincidence.

'I can tell you exactly the last time I met with him. It was 10th

May 2016. Last game West Ham played at the Boleyn Ground; they beat Man Utd 3-2. Why do you ask?'

Hope made to walk out the door as Gibson thanked Naomi for her time and handed over a business card.

'Just curious, that's all. We'll be in touch.'

32

B rewster left The Gypsy's compound and went home for a couple of hours' kip before the Loony Dook. Marjorie had stayed the night and would prepare him a hearty breakfast before he braved the chilly waters of the Firth of Forth. The mother and son had laughed heartily at the stooshie on the BBC Hogmanay programme involving that guy, Frank Savage, who'd gone to school with Danny and who Marjorie read every week in the paper without fail. *To Be Frank*. She was a big fan of the stuff he wrote recently about belting the bairns and wholeheartedly agreed with every word he said. If only her neighbours listened to that Frank Savage on discipline, then their son's football wouldn't have kept coming into her garden, spoiling her precious geraniums. Then she wouldn't have had to warn the seven-year-old the next time that happened, she'd put a 'knife through it' and he wouldn't have run away, tears streaming down his face, and told his dad. That sparked a most unfortunate chain of events with her Danny getting involved and losing his temper at the father, sticking the head on him, before someone poured concrete onto his front lawn… by mistake. But to Marjorie's knowledge, they weren't keen gardeners anyway and she'd never seen the father out cutting the grass at any point. People didn't seem to be "house proud" any more and she thought that a sign of the times. At least the ball wasn't coming into her garden any more, so every cloud and all that.

Brewster scoffed the breakfast his mother had laid out for him. He loved how she still cut the toast into soldiers and gave him an egg to dip. He went over again what Marjorie was to tell the police if they came a-calling. Namely that they'd spent today together watching the films on BBC2 and having steak pie for tea as was their tradition on New Year's Day. She knew better than to question him on his movements and Danny had assured her that he was just attending to a business matter, and she wasn't to panic.

'Are the police still picking on you, son?' Marjorie asked.

'No, Mum, but my name always comes up and they like to check up on me. Force of habit.'

'I think that's out of order, son. Look at all the good you're doing for the community with the youth theatre and the lassies football team, plus there's all the stuff you've done for charity, the food banks and the boxing shows.'

Brewster sighed. 'I know, Mum. But don't worry, they'll soon leave me alone.'

He went through to his room and dug out the Union Jack swimming trunks he'd worn in Sitges last year. They'd proved to be a big hit with the locals and Brewster had lapped up the attention. There was no way he was going to risk Billy One hitting him with that monster of a rifle. No fucking danger. He'd see the Wise One a mile off because he'd be standing next to the guy in the Union Jack trunks. Genius.

Brewster, confident that Marjorie had been well prepped, left to go and pick Billy One up. He cuddled Waffen and gave him a meat treat. How could anyone kidnap his dog? The sheer fucking cheek of it. Brewster had slept fitfully and dreamt that Gurkha Bobby was a one-eyed zombie and had been chasing him with a golf club through the Figgate Park, where they'd all played as children. Brewster and Bobby had been friends a lifetime ago and had gone to Cub Scout camp together. Frank had been expelled from the Cubs after he got caught nicking badges that he'd then got his mum to sew onto his jumper. Everyone knew he hadn't passed his first-aid badge, couldn't swim and was shite at tying knots.

Brewster put his trunks on and admired himself in the mirror. He'd bought one of those "See You Jimmy" tartan hats and a pair of shades so he could make it to South Queensferry without having to worry about being stopped by Lothian and Borders' finest. He pulled on a pair of jogging bottoms and stuck the Beretta 9000 into the waistband, despite being warned by JJ not to bring any weapons to the meet, where he was to hand over the cash he'd skimmed from the councillors and pay a one hundred thousand pound fine for his cheek.

Brewster grabbed the holdall full of old *Edinburgh Evening News* papers, kissed his mother on the lips and left. He was being picked up by one of The Gypsy's taxi drivers before they collected Billy One for the hit. Brewster had decided to leave his Volvo at home as a safety measure. The rifle was already at the venue, with Billy One having done a thorough run-through after the meeting was announced, and Brewster had recognised a once-in-a-lifetime opportunity to free himself from Armstrong's clutches. The plan they had hatched was certainly audacious and didn't lack for ambition, but if the Orangeman could pull it off and take out the Wise One, then it would be the talk of the steamie for all eternity. Brewster hadn't bothered to tell Billy One that his chances of escape were slim to say the least, preferring to let him get carried away in the moment thinking about the massive payout he would likely never receive.

The taxi driver made endless small talk as they scooted through a near-deserted Edinburgh, save for the bin collectors and a few Aussie stragglers, some wearing "See You Jimmy" hats, doing the walk of shame.

'Cunts have probably never even heard of Russ Abbott,' Brewster said, gazing out the window.

They headed along Queensferry Road, past the old Barnton

Hotel that had been redeveloped, like everything else, into flats. Brewster reminisced about the countless drug deals he'd done in the car park, meeting there before heading through to watch the football with the box of toys. He asked Billy One how he was feeling, giving him a wee tap on the knee for reassurance. Brewster needn't have worried as Billy One looked to be well and truly in the kill zone.

He went over the details, telling Billy One how the signal to shoot the Wise One would be him removing the "See You Jimmy" hat, after that it was a simple bullet to the head. He gave Billy One the description of the Wise One again. Guy about seventy, cropped grey hair, five feet ten inches tall, slim, athletic build. The unknown unknown that Brewster hadn't told Billy One was that he had no idea if the Wise One would be wearing swimming trunks or, for that matter, fancy dress like the rest of the sad fuckers going to this Loony Dook shite.

He spelt it out again.

'You shoot the guy standing next to me after I give you the signal, which is me removing this daft fucking hat. All going to plan, you fire shortly after everyone enters the water at noon.'

Billy One nodded furiously. 'Grand, grand, you've nothing to worry about. I did a trial run yesterday morning; a bairn couldn't miss from that distance. I'm telling ya. Piece of piss, so it is. Like shelling peas.'

Brewster went over the escape plan, which consisted of Billy One getting off the Forth Rail Bridge, after ditching the rifle in the Firth of Forth, then being picked up by the same taxi driver at Dalmeny station, who would take him to The Gypsy's where they would crack open the champagne. There were no trains planned to run on New Year's Day and the station would be empty according to Brewster, who handed Billy One the Beretta 9000 which had been used in fifteen previous shootings, finally glad to be rid of the thing.

'Here's your insurance policy in case you bump into any

heroes on the way down. I don't think you'll have much to worry about. Everyone will be concentrating on the body in the water. Nothing will go wrong. They'll build a statue of you at the entrance to that bridge after this. Might even rename it the Billy One Rail Bridge.'

Brewster thought back to the meeting he'd had two days before with the Wise One at the top of Arthur's Seat that now seemed like a lifetime ago. It was clear to him Armstrong was just another bullying bastard like Norrie. *He'll see what happens to cunts who try to play the power game with me.*

What was it the Wise One had said? *Don't dare wear a woolly hat. I want to see you get your hair wet* – that was it. 'Well, there's only one fool who'll be getting his hair wet. Bloody wet! And it won't be me,' Brewster murmured under his breath.

They arrived at Dalmeny station, dropping the would-be assassin off, with Brewster wishing him 'Godspeed', which he heard someone say in a movie once and thought was appropriate given the enormity of the challenge. The taxi driver got as close to the main drag in South Queensferry as possible, where Brewster got out and joined hundreds of revellers heading down to the water for the Loony Dook.

You'd be hard pushed to find a sadder bunch, Brewster thought to himself as he counted three Harry Potters, a group dressed as the Loch Ness monster, a couple of semi-fit *Baywatch* birds, a priest, two nuns and an Alex Salmond lookalike. Brewster made his way down to the water's edge, accepting the offer of a swig from someone's hip flask, which hit the spot. He still had fifteen minutes to kill before the noon start – the allotted time for him to meet the Wise One. Unfortunately, this gave him plenty of time to worry and he played the other day's meeting over and over in his head, still traumatised from his red dotting. *What was the point of this again? To give the Wise One his cash back including the tax?* He was supposed to be briefed on phase two of the Syndicate's plans to take over the drugs trade and get the cinema up and running, but why the fuck were they meeting at the Loony Dook? Paranoia started to grip Brewster. What if the Syndicate were planning to whack him? What if the Wise One didn't turn up and sent one of his henchmen instead?

'Focus, Danny. Fucking focus, man,' he said out loud.

A guy was shouting into a megaphone, 'Welcome, Loony Dookers and a Happy New Year to each and every one of you.'

Brewster's mobile phone started to ring, and he desperately looked for a quiet spot, finding one beside a row of parked cars. A London accent said, 'Leave the holdall at the top of the steps next to the grey wheelie bin, then make your way down to the water and get in next to the five guys dressed as the Spice Girls.' The caller hung up, leaving Brewster panic-stricken. He saw the wheelie bin, then looked down towards the water and sure enough there were five guys dressed as the Spice Girls, with Sporty really looking the part, he thought. Brewster's mind raced. What if they looked inside the holdall and saw that it was full of papers? They might try and murder him there and then. What if the Spice Blokes were really Syndicate hitmen in disguise? He decided he had no choice but to take his chances. Billy One was in position and the signal had been agreed; if the Wise One so much as set foot in the water, they'd blow his brains out. Brewster had a lingering sense of dread as he made his way to the water's edge, shoving the Incredible Hulk and Amy Winehouse out the way.

'Take it easy, pal,' the Hulk said.

'Get tae fuck!' Brewster screamed. 'Fenian bastard.'

'And a Happy New Year to you as well,' the Hulk replied. 'What is it with some folk?' Brewster stepped into the water, wearing his jogging bottoms and New Balance 574s before realising he'd done so. He stepped back on shore and kicked off his trainers, before pulling down his jogging bottoms and unzipping his fleece, to reveal a Pet Shop Boys "It's a Sin" T-shirt featuring Neil and Chris on the front wearing tuxedos. A flock of seagulls were now swooping down at the water's edge, grabbing at the remains of discarded food cartons strewn on the beach, with one particularly brazen bird dive-bombing a small child eating some chips. Brewster got back into the water and waded towards the Spice Blokes. It was now 12.02pm and he knew Billy One would be in place on the bridge, looking down and waiting for the Wise One to appear in the crosshairs. Brewster looked around and saw no sign of the Wise One, the oldest guy being one of the priests who he'd passed on the way down. He was bursting for a pee and decided to squat down in the freezing water and move his trunks to one side to let his shrivelled penis do its business.

The priest decided at that point it would be hilarious to bless everyone in the immediate vicinity, splashing "holy water" in the general direction of various sinners including the Spice Blokes. He approached Brewster, who told him to fuck off in no uncertain terms, muttering 'Fenian bastard' under his breath. The bolshie priest, who had been on the communion wine, was having none of it and waded towards Brewster, lifting his cassock with one hand to avoid the splashes while shaking his fist with the other.

Meanwhile, Billy One took aim, waiting for the signal. The priest was now giving Brewster a level of dog's abuse that brought shame to the cloth.

'What did you fucking say?' said the priest. 'Hey, cunto, what did you say?'

Brewster, who was now looking towards the Rail Bridge, turned round to confront the holy man. 'Not now, pal. Seriously, get to fuck.'

Brewster looked past the priest and saw the Grim Reaper in the shape of the Wise One wading towards him, brandishing what appeared to be a very real-looking scythe. For a split second, he envisaged his own death and the image of him lying face down in a sea of blood flashed before his eyes. At that moment, a giant seagull swooped down, spraying shit all over the Spice Blokes with a large dollop hitting Brewster on the forehead before running down from his face into his eyes, finally coming to rest on the Pet Shop Boys. He stumbled towards the priest, falling head first into the freezing water. Brewster desperately splashed water in his eyes and, without giving it a moment's thought, removed the "See You Jimmy" hat. The priest, now two feet away, jolted back with the full force of the high velocity OSV-96 projectile striking him between the eyes as the back of his head exploded, throwing brain matter that resembled strawberry compote into the water.

The Wise One, who had now removed his death mask, was smiling at Brewster with the dead priest floating between them. A shite Pamela Anderson lookalike in a *Baywatch* swimsuit, who looked like she'd had a hard time on the crystal meth, let out a blood-curdling scream as the Dookers tried to take in the full horror unravelling before their eyes. Paramedics and lifeboat crew made for the body as everyone turned to look at the Forth Rail Bridge. Brewster stood rooted to the spot, covered in seagull shit, wondering how he could get Billy One to fire again, this time at the intended target. He looked back to the shore and saw the Wise One being spirited away by JJ and another two heavies. People were by now pointing at the bridge, watching two figures struggling before one of them plunged off the side and landed in the Firth of Forth. Seconds later, another body plunged off the side before a parachute opened and a powerboat appeared.

Brewster realised Billy One was most likely a goner and decided to get the fuck out of Dodge, scrambling to the shore, pulling his jogging bottoms over his wet legs, while trying to get his feet into his sandy trainers, one of which contained his mobile phone.

He sprinted into the high street and dialled the number for the taxi driver.

'Abort! Abort!' he shouted into the phone. 'Meet me outside the Hawes Inn in five minutes and forget Billy One.'

The taxi driver, who wasn't the brightest, struggled to comprehend. 'Is that you, Brewster?'

'Of course it's fucking me, you daft prick. Did you hear what I said? Get away from Dalmeny station pronto and pick me up at the Hawes Inn, down the road at the bottom of the Rail Bridge. Fucking hurry.'

'What about Billy One?'

'Never mind Billy fucking One; he's gone for a Burton.'

'He's gone to Burtons? Surely it's not open on New Year's Day?'

'He's dead, you fucking idiot, *morte*, swims with the fishes. Now, get a move on.'

*

Olga packed her BASE jump parachute into the container, removed her goggles and threw the newly acquired OSV-96 rifle into the powerboat, giving Falco, who was also wearing a wetsuit, the nod to accelerate away from the bridge down the Firth of Forth towards Crammond where the van was waiting. She joined him at the wheel and kissed him on the neck.

'Take me home, my king, and make love to me in the bottom.'

Falco broke into a broad smile. 'Certainly, my queen. I've just the tablet for that.'

33

Frank stared out the window at the grey sky that gave Portobello the feel of Berlin in 1945, with the Russians at the door. It was that grim. His mood had deteriorated, and if the first couple of days of January were anything to go by, then he was in for a long and miserable year. Bobby's revelation had hit him for six – a veritable boot in the balls. He was glad to have finally found out the truth about Michael's death and took consolation in the fact that his brother had died instantly without suffering. But he was a long way from accepting that it was an accident, and although he knew any right-thinking person would deem it one, the lead up to his death and the part Brewster played in it would not wash away easily. Deep down, Frank felt a strong sense of guilt for Michael's passing. He had failed the basic job as a big brother to protect his younger sibling, and he'd never shaken the feeling that he was the one ultimately responsible.

He put the kettle on the hob to prepare the first of his morning coffees, setting his mind to think positive thoughts. Frank ate a banana, took his beta blockers followed by an alphabet of vitamins and considered firing up the blood pressure machine. He hadn't had a cigarette in two days and had decided to quit the booze with both his body and his mind grieving for their long-lost friends. This was the start of New Frank, a reinvention like New Labour that would see him rise out of the ashes like his favourite band, New Order. But right this second, he preferred Old Frank and craved his company.

The buzzer sounded, jolting him out of his mind games. It was DI Hope. He thought about telling him to fuck off, before accepting the inevitable grief this chat would bring. It could only be bad news.

'Happy New Year, Frank,' Hope said, extending his hand.

'You're too late for that, Bob. It's the 3rd of January.'

Hope laughed. 'Never change, Frank, never change.'

Frank felt a heavy weight on his shoulders as he heard his heart beating. *Not too fast, though, so the tablets must be doing their job.* He knew the depression was on him again, sapping his energy and plunging him into despair. Normally, he would offer Bob a cup of tea, but he couldn't be arsed, and the DI appeared to read the room.

'Okay, Frank. I'll get to the point. I had a little chat with your daughter. This was before the shooting at the Loony Dook which we believe was an attempted hit on Armstrong.'

Frank was distracted by a loose hair sprouting out of Hope's eyebrow and said the words "Crazy brows" out loud. The cop looked momentarily confused.

'I saw that on the news. Two bodies floating in the water. Total fucking carnage. Not a great advert for Edinburgh's Hogmanay. I tell you what, Bob. Why don't I make us a nice cup of coffee?' Frank said, realising he now had the perfect opportunity to shift some of the tablet he'd been given for Christmas. 'Come through to the kitchen and we'll talk.'

They made their way through, and Hope sat himself down at the table.

'Like I was saying, Frank. I had a word with Naomi.'

Frank waited for the kettle to boil and motioned for him to continue.

'I had no choice, Frank. The grown-ups wanted me to have a chat with her about Brewster. Like I told you at the police station, there's intelligence come in that he's linked to your old friend, Armstrong, who is trying to muscle his way in up here through Naomi's firm where his wife happens to be the chief executive. I asked Naomi about her work and the Wise One's name came up. She told the truth about knowing him but gave us the usual corporate bullshit we expected about her company and the cinema. She also never mentioned her boss, Patricia Bleasdale, is married to Armstrong and lied about the last time she met him, which was a few days ago at the Balmoral.'

Frank remembered Hope marking his card on the Wise One when he returned to Edinburgh, not long after punching Armstrong at Maxine's funeral. The cop had warned him to stay alert as the gangster's tentacles were just starting to stretch into Scotland.

He decided to cloud the issue, cast a bit of doubt on the proceedings in a bid to lessen his daughter's culpability.

'I'll do everything I can to help, Bob. If Naomi did bump into that vile, nasty fucker, then she hasn't got round to telling me. I can assure you she's not wittingly involved in any money laundering. I asked her about meeting Brewster, and she told me he approached her in Daisy Park after they met at the opening. They hardly know each other. Naomi is as passionate about the Regency as we both are. It's all she talks about, the plans for the interior, how they are restoring the proscenium stage, what films they'll be showing. She's a bit of a geek about it.'

Hope sighed, before taking a big bit of tablet from the box Frank had put in front of him.

'I don't suppose they'll be playing any of John Ford's *Cavalry Trilogy*. I'd love a bit of John Wayne. That's another thing Naomi lied to us about, Frank, meeting Brewster at Daisy Park. We know they're working together on the cinema.'

Frank wasn't in the mood for movie chat and Bob's patter was starting to grate. He cut to the chase.

'So where do we stand in terms of her committing a crime, Bob?'

'Technically, she's probably all right for now but that could change in a heartbeat. We could pull her in on conspiracy to commit fraud and money laundering charges but they're unlikely to stick. She's not involved in the heavy stuff, the violence, and we've no proof of drug dealing. But Naomi's in danger from Syndicate rivals if she turns out to be the brains behind the move into Porty.'

'Naomi, the brains. That's your best yet, Bob.'

Frank paced the kitchen, letting the silence linger like a Chernobyl cloud.

'So, what's the solution, Bob?'

Hope made a play of considering her options, to the point where Frank got tired waiting on him to answer. He caught sight of his reflection in the hallway mirror. A deathly grey pallor stared back at him, the face of a ghost. Frank was nearing rock bottom but had a few steps left to descend on the way down. Returning to the kettle, he wanted it all off his chest.

'Well?' Frank asked, growing impatient.

'Well, if Naomi were to testify against the Syndicate, she would go on the witness protection programme, which would mean a new identity and relocation. It's unlikely you'd see her again for at least five years.'

Frank stared blankly at Hope.

'But the trouble with that is even if Naomi were to turn states, there's no guarantee a jury would convict Armstrong. They've been tampered with before.'

'Is there any chance of you arresting Armstrong?' Frank asked sarcastically, already knowing the answer.

'Not as it stands, Frank. He's served the sum total of two years in the last fifty and that was for hitting a Millwall fan with an ashtray in a pub back in 1974. He's a criminal informant; a protected asset with the full weight of the Home Office behind him. I can keep Naomi under surveillance and provide her with a modicum of security for now. And it would help if she could feed me the odd scrap once the cinema opens. Failing that, she could always do a runner but it's not really an option given the Syndicate's reach. There's still the possibility a rival firm will take Armstrong out and whoever was behind the shooting at the Loony Dook came within a ball hair but missed their chance. He'd gone there to meet Brewster, but we don't know if Danny Boy was behind the attempted hit. Armstrong won't be taking any chances and it's unlikely he'll be seen out in the open now.'

Frank winced at the mention of Brewster and wondered if he had the balls or the wherewithal to assassinate the Wise One.

'I was waiting for you to get round to that prick, Brewster.'

Hope replied. 'I know, Frank. I've been dealing with Danny Boy for most of my career. From the time he accidentally killed his half-brother, to the death of his stepfather – he was a right bastard, mind, who gave him a terrible time – right through the casual days to the poof-bashing up Calton Hill and his graduation into organised crime. He's gone to ground since the Loony Dook. The paranoia must be bad.'

Frank clenched his fists and opened the kitchen window, letting the cold air in. He reached into the drawer and pulled out a pack of Marlboro Red and his lighter. He lit up and sat on the ledge, staring out across the Forth.

'That prick caused my brother's death. You forgot to mention that, Bob. Seems odd that it would slip your mind.'

Hope stared into the box of tablet at the little rocks of joy.

'For fuck's sake, Frank. We've been over this a million times. Brewster wasn't at the open-air pool at the time your brother fell. As you well know, two of our officers stopped him and his mates at the toilets in Joppa around the time of Michael's accident. You have to let this go, mate.'

Frank took a deep draw on the fag and welcomed the dizziness. He was past caring about his sodding health and at that precise moment welcomed the thought of death. At least he'd get a decent kip.

'But I can't let it go, Bob. There was a fucking reason Michael went into the open-air pool that night and it was to escape Brewster. I know for a fact my brother was shit scared of that place and would never in a million years have gone up the top diving board. Brewster has Michael's blood on his hands.'

Hope dabbed his finger into the box of tablet.

'I'm sorry, Frank. I don't mean to open old wounds.'

Frank threw his cigarette out the window.

'I want this to end, Bob. I want Naomi to stay in Portobello and work on the cinema, but I want it all to be above board. That's my dream. These cunts Brewster and Armstrong should be behind bars and you know it, or better still, dead.'

Bob drained his cup. 'I hope you're not making death threats, Frank.'

Frank appeared to contemplate the possibility.

'I'm too fucking old, Bob. I'm knackered and my heart doesn't know if it's New Year or New York, plus I'm not a murderer like them. But I'll keep my ear to the ground and talk to Naomi. I'll tell you if I hear anything about Brewster or the so-called Wise One.'

Hope got to his feet. 'Thanks, Frank, much appreciated,' before pointing at the packet of cigarettes. 'Those things will kill you.'

34

The next day, Frank made his way to Fusion Brew where Naomi had asked to meet him for a coffee. He had decided to go into work later that day and face the music. He was the talk of the steamie since the "Battle of Pacific Quay" and felt it was better to have a chat with Richard and see what his career prospects were "going forward", as he would no doubt say. But regardless of what the editor told him, Frank was ready to walk. He felt completely fucked and knew he'd reached the end of his career. He'd now had time to digest what Naomi had told him about her job as a money launderer and to say he was disappointed was an understatement.

My Naomi is doing great, he imagined telling his neighbours. *She's working for an international crime syndicate who specialise in drug dealing, murder and extortion.*

Frank walked into the busy café to find his daughter already sitting at a window seat with a flat white and German biscuit waiting for him. He gave her a hug and sat down, breaking the biscuit in two and dunking it in his coffee.

Naomi said, 'I've squared your debt with The Gypsy. I gave him seventy thousand pounds and he accepted. He wants to buy the cinema and run it as a legitimate enterprise, which sounds great on paper, but we don't play on paper. I told him I'd be in if he can make it work.'

Frank was conflicted at this development. He was delighted

to be free of The Gypsy but deep down he felt ashamed that he'd got himself into such a perilous financial state in the first place.

'I never told you to do that, Naomi. No fucker listens to me. I'll pay you back. I promise,' he said, mouth full of biscuit. 'But you shouldn't have gone behind my back.'

'Look, Dad. I told you I was going to do it. The situation with The Gypsy was out of hand and you were in danger because you couldn't afford to pay him. The interest was extortionate. News flash: you were being extorted.'

Frank smiled meekly.

'Are you sure, my love? Seventy grand is a hell of a lot of poppy.'

'Yes. I'm sure. In fact, I'm positive. The debt is cleared. We both know you can't pay me back. Consider this money to be the proceeds of crime but put to good use. The Gypsy is one of the better psychos out there, but I wouldn't push it. All I want is for you to get better, Dad, get some help for your addictions and clean up your act.'

Frank was rocked at Naomi mentioning addictions so blatantly. His gambling problem was something that could be added to his alcoholism and he knew that the time to sort out his addictions was long overdue. He thought about protesting but felt completely defeated.

'Wish I could add sex addiction to the list, but I'm too addicted to the booze and betting to find the time.'

Naomi gave him a disappointed look, which made Frank instantly regret trying to make light of his situation. *Always with the crap jokes,* he thought.

'I know. I know. I'm already thinking of going back to the meetings. Day at a time and all that.'

'Thinking about going to AA is not good enough, Dad. You need to step back through the doors. There's nothing stopping you.'

Frank drained his coffee and made to leave.

'I'm really grateful for your help, my love, and I will try to do better.'

He kissed her on the cheek, then glanced back before walking out the door. He loved his daughter more than anything in the world and felt a pang of regret that she and his brother had never met.

Frank headed for work, having decided if there was any possibility of voluntary redundancy, he would take it and be happy to pour pints in The Haddonfield if Bella would let him. He'd save himself a small fortune if he managed to quit the betting, booze, fags, recreational drug use and takeaways. If that failed, then he could always sell a kidney, although it probably wasn't in that good nick. Perhaps he'd ask Naomi if there were any openings in her line of work; perhaps a wee part-time delivery job.

He popped into Roasters of Stockbridge for a flat white to keep his engine running. Frank's favourite Baader-Meinhof sleeper cell member, who doubled up as a barista, wished him a "HNY". They said, 'I saw you on the television the other night. Absolutely brilliant. I detest that Chic McGrain guy. Scottish intelligentsia, my arse. He's just another pig with his nose in the trough.'

Frank laughed and cheered up as they handed him his coffee.

'Aye, "Lager Haze" indeed. HNY to yerself, pal, HNY,' he said, leaving the shop and sparking up a Marlboro Red, deciding he would quit tomorrow or the day after or the day after that. He knew Day Zero for both his health and mental health was fast approaching.

Frank arrived at the office just after 1pm to be met by Ronnie, who scolded him as he'd forgot his pass for the electronic barrier again.

'HNY to you, Ronnie, HNY. I see you've broken your resolution not to be a prick again this year. Oh well, there's always next year, mate.'

'Takes one to know one, Savage. I doubt you'll be needing your pass soon anyway.'

Frank made his way to the seventh floor in the lift, a combination of dizziness and throbbing toe stopping him from taking things further with Ronnie the Rocket. He nipped into the canteen to buy a can of fat Coke before taking a deep breath and striding through the open-plan newsroom shouting his daily greeting of 'I'm not dying for these bastards.' But his heart wasn't in it. A couple of young faces he didn't recognise stared back at him. *Probably Yifters in for the festive period,* he thought. Frank arrived at his bank of desks, staffed by the misfits and socially awkward that, in this moment, he was proud to call his colleagues. Deep down, he was fond of the lot of them.

Plunkett, whose gammon face now resembled a giant Ribena berry after the festive excess, came forward to shake Frank's hand. Frank told him to back off.

'Stay away, man. I don't do Happy New Year handshakes past the 2nd of January; we went over this last year and the year before that. Anyway, have you been hanging upside down again? You look like you've slept in a hedge. I take it you've been on a gin drip over Christmas, with the After Eights on tap.'

'Where do I start? I've had Chic McGrain on speed dial since the "Battle of Pacific Quay" and the Pictish Fairies are up in arms. Chic says he's traumatised and keeps having flashbacks of a chicken leg flying through the air; says it follows him everywhere, even when he's on the bog reading his well-thumbed copy of *Lanark*. Bert Singh's people have been calling for you to be sacked and the Scottish government media officers are campaigning to have your head on a platter, Frank. Dick Bell-end is crumbling under the pressure, what with the Loony Dook massacre, and the Swedes are close to taking over the whole shebang. Could be curtains for all of us. News Space of the Past.'

'Seriously, Plunkett. Try telling all of that to someone who gives a fuck. I'm past caring and haven't looked at a paper or a website in ages. I want out and if voluntary redundancy or any fucking redundancy is on the table, I'll snap their fucking hands off. That's if they don't give me the tin tack first.'

Carol came round to wish him a "HNY" and offer him a piece of her legendary homemade Stollen cake.

'Thanks, Carol. HNY to you, hen.'

Frank browsed his emails with a sense of dread, clicking on the weekly update from the deputy editor.

Happy New Year, News Hounds!

Last week was truly the icing on the cake in terms of us almost doubling the previous record and smashing through the hallowed eight million digital hits mark. Yes, folks, count them, that's eight million, an unbelievable effort down in no small part to our dedicated team of online reporters who gathered the breaking coverage from various news sites of the tragic shooting and death plunge at the Loony Dook. Special mention to Cara Crotchett who trawled through social media to provide live updates and gather pictures from Loony Dookers at the scene.

Our condolences also go out to the family of William Puller, the delivery driver with the bionic penis who tragically died of a heart attack in circumstances that won't be repeated in a family newspaper. Give yourselves a giant pat on the back, the Milky Bars are on me!

Alasdair Stewart (BA Hons)
Deputy Digital Editor News Content
Twitter: @futurenews

**FIRTH OF BLOOD: LOONY DOOK DOUBLE MURDER HUNT LAUNCHED:
2,333,419
"SPICE GIRLS" GIVE EYEWITNESS ACCOUNT OF SHOOTING HORROR:
1,867,322**

BATTLE OF PACIFIC QUAY: MINISTER CALLS FOR SAVAGE TO GO:
850,989
TRANENT MAN WITH BIONIC PENIS DIES OF HEART ATTACK:
799,591
EIGHTIES CROONER CHIC MCGRAIN: 'I FEARED ANOTHER HILLSBOROUGH':
560,808

Frank noticed that Alasdair had made no mention of his "star columnist" or any of the stories that featured said "star columnist" becoming the news. On any other day, the combined total of more than 1.4 million hits for the debacle at Pacific Quay would have had the deputy editor licking raspberry doughnut jam off his own nipples. But no doubt the sheer embarrassment felt by the bosses upstairs and political pressure brought to bear by the Scottish government had the senior management at the paper hiding behind the couch. *Shitebags.*

Frank noted that none of the reporters working on New Year's Day had considered jumping in their cars and driving the seven miles to South Queensferry and the Loony Dook – a journey that, given it was a public holiday, would have taken the best part of twelve minutes. He despaired they were trained to immediately look online – like this Cara woman – rather than encourage her to head to the scene, leaving the heavy lifting to someone else, in this case the general public. No eyewitness accounts, no colour; in fact, no photographs given the staff snapper had been and gone from the Loony Dook fifteen minutes after the priest's head exploded and Billy One had crashed onto the rocks. He had been urgently called to St. James Quarter to take pictures of teenage fuckwits queuing out the door for the latest in a line of trainers brought out by an American rapper who named them "Jesus Trumps".

All of this served as the final nail in the coffin of Frank's journalistic career. There was no going back, he was leaving. He thought now was as good a time as any to tell Richard – who seemed to be hiding in his office – that the end was nigh. He barged in without knocking to find a tearful Richard, dressed in a Lycra T-shirt and cycling shorts that made him look like a sack of tits, picking out the mini Bounty bars from a massive tin of Celebrations. At that moment, Frank felt nothing but pity for his editor. He saw before him another middle-aged man, battling to survive while trying desperately to keep the twin plates of career and family life spinning, all the while fighting to stay relevant in a world where the younger, the fitter and the better-looking ruled.

'Happy New Year to you, Richard,' he said tentatively.

'Oh, hello Frank, Happy New Year. Come in and take a pew. Do you want a mini Bounty bar? They're my favourites.'

Frank replied, 'I'll pass. Doctor, Doctor, I feel like a coconut… aye, you're Bounty,' he joked.

Richard ignored the gag; a beaten Napoleon facing exile after the Battle of Waterloo.

'It's been some few days for you, Frank. How are you feeling? Are you okay?'

Frank appreciated that Richard was the only person to have asked about his well-being. 'All right, all things considered. The old ticker is working and I'm operating at my normal levels of stress and heightened anxiety. Much the same as yourself, I imagine.'

Richard rubbed the tears from his eyes.

'Sometimes I wonder if it's still worth it, Frank. Journalism has changed so much since we started. No one I know buys a paper. I'm starting to think it's not worth losing our health over.'

'I want to take redundancy, Richard.'

Richard continued to play with the chocolates, picking out a Malteser and unwrapping it, before trying to flick it into his mouth and missing.

'I'm really sorry to hear that, Frank, but I totally get it. The events of the last few days have pushed everyone to breaking point and it's probably for the best. You'd be saving me the indignity of having to sack you. They held an emergency meeting last night to go over the events at Pacific Quay and the Scottish government have been screaming for your head. I told them to go and fuck themselves but that won't hold for long.'

For the first time, Frank looked at his editor with a modicum of respect. He was noticing the similarities between them instead of the differences. There was no doubt Richard loved journalism in a way he once did, a long time ago. He felt a bit chicken-hearted towards his boss and regretted christening him Dick Bell-end.

Richard continued, 'The decision taken by the grown-ups was to suspend you until the heat subsided. They know you're a major asset in terms of digital hits and it won't come as a surprise that your own personal welfare hardly tops the list of their priorities. It's all short-term anyway. The Swedes are close to completing a deal for the paper and they plan to go fully digital. They're going to call it "Capital Alive" and employ loads of fresh-faced graduates for a pittance, focus on something called "hyper-local news" with the emphasis on citizen journalism.'

Frank took a few seconds to let what Richard had told him sink in, then quickly decided he still didn't give two fucks. 'How are things with you, Richard?' When Richard took a long inhalation, Frank realised he wasn't going to get a short answer, so added, 'Just the bullet points will do.'

Richard let out a sigh. 'They're going to replace me, Frank. It's common practice for the editor to get the sack when there's a takeover. The new owners will want their own people in, likely some cereal-munching, digital whizzkid who's never done a death knock and wears trainers to work.'

Frank was about to reply, *You've never done a death knock,* but decided to let him off the hook. He knew Richard had actually done a death knock but never got the all-important picture of the victim, known as "the collect". That job wasn't for everyone.

'To make matters worse, I was at Pilates with Bridget this morning and she's told me she wants a divorce. Says she needs room to breathe, her own personal space. Told me she loves me but she's not *in* love with me.'

'Heard it,' Frank replied, instantly regretting saying it. 'I'm sorry about that, Richard. I mean it. Bridget broke my heart, but I deserved to lose her. There's no need for her to treat you like this. I appreciate everything you've done for my daughter. You've been more of a dad to her than I ever was and I know she loves you. Katie told me that.'

Richard was bursting with pride.

'Thanks, Frank. That means so much coming from you. I know we've had our ups and downs, but I still consider you a friend and I'll try to get you the redundancy payment. I'll play to their "new broom" philosophy, telling them I've purged the paper of the so-called "legacy staff". They'll probably have you replaced with a free-diving correspondent. Work the rest of the day, then go off on full pay. I'll tell the grown-ups you're not fit to work anyway. That should keep Bert Singh's people and Chic McGrain off our backs for now.'

Frank got up to leave as Richard came round the desk to shake his hand.

'We've had a good innings, Frank, and it's been a blast. You certainly shook things up a bit and I'm proud to say I was your editor during this period.'

Frank shook his hand.

'I used to resent you, Richard, because I thought I should have been given the editor's job instead of you. But you're a miles better editor – not reporter, mind – but a better editor than I could ever have been. I appreciate everything you've done for me.'

Frank walked through the newsroom, knowing he would be doing it for the last time. Tradition was a journalist leaving a paper was "banged out" but Frank didn't care about missing out on that ritual. He took the lift down to the designated smoking shelter – a post-apocalyptic chillout zone for the tobacco-addicted, where he saw a vaguely familiar face who was out having a fly vape. He nodded, hoping to forego the small talk with the young person – a digital journalist who might as well have been from another planet – but she opened the conversation.

'Happy New Year, Frank. How are you doing?'

She added that her name was Cara to save Frank the embarrassment of not knowing it. Frank decided he was going to engage in a bit of chat – buoyed by being nice to Richard, he sought to capitalise on this new era of personal *glasnost*.

'Happy New Year to you, Cara. I'm doing all right. I had a bit of a heart scare but I'm on the tablets and trying to cut down on the fags.'

'That's awful, I'm so sorry to hear that.' Cara looked genuinely concerned and took a long draw on the vape.

'Are those things any good?' Frank asked. 'I've been on the Marlboro Reds for so long I think what's left of my lungs are immune to them.'

'They're all right; this one is watermelon flavour. Should you be smoking after being in hospital?'

Frank was about to ask Cara if she was his mother but felt momentarily touched by her compassion.

'To answer your question, I shouldn't be smoking at all. Thanks for asking.'

Cara was all smiles as she asked, 'Do you remember coming to Napier University about five years ago and giving the students a talk on print journalism? I was there and it was brilliant, the best module on the course, and what you told us has always stuck with me.'

Frank took a while to engage his brain. 'Yes, I remember that,' he lied.

'You told us that being a journalist was the best job in the world and it was ten times easier if you liked people and were genuinely interested in them. You also said journalists shouldn't sit in offices all day and would be better spending their time in the pub. That's where contacts were made and stories were found. I never forgot that.'

'Thanks, Cara. I'm not sure that theory holds much water these days. It's all about the digital hits and the art of conversation seems to be dying out. Working conditions are deteriorating and half the staff still make out it's the best place in the world to work and not a digital sweatshop. Not that I need to worry any more. I'm taking redundancy. I'm done, had enough, pal.' Frank brought his cigarettes out of his pocket and thought about chaining another.

'I'm sorry to hear that, Frank. We need people like you to help the younger reporters. I don't think you realise what it means to us to get a wee bit of praise. You hit the nail on the head when you said at that talk you still get a thrill from seeing your name in print. You've no idea how much it meant to me when I saw my byline on the front page for the first time, on an exclusive story that was all my own work, or when I wrote my first column and showed the paper to my folks.'

Frank felt genuinely touched by what Cara was saying. Perhaps he had always underestimated his younger colleagues.

'Don't be fooled, Cara. I remember my first job at the *Daily Ranger*. It had a hotline to a rehab clinic, the reporters drank that much. A time of huge expenses and unreadable copy. The old guard from back then have left their mark on the current crop of editors, who are tarnished by the learnt behaviour they picked up from the tyrants of the past. Big characters, larger-than-life, basically code for misogynistic, racist, bullying drunks.'

Cara laughed. 'Most of us younger reporters suffer from imposter syndrome and don't feel like real journalists. It doesn't help when we're under constant attack getting called woke or snowflake every two minutes. I'm not daft. I can see that the bosses don't give a fuck about us and I'm not defending their shite website that's covered in stupid ads and takes an age to load up.'

Frank studied Cara with awe, admiring her passion and sense of outrage. *The Force is strong,* he thought.

She added, 'Take that Loony Dook massacre. I was desperate to go out to South Queensferry, but Alasdair and Richard wouldn't let me go. They said I'd be of more use anchoring the website and taking updates from other news sources. Told me the BBC and Press Association would be all over it and plenty of Loony Dookers would post pictures online. I felt like quitting there and then. We haven't even followed it up. The biggest story to hit town in years, a double murder at the Loony Dook and we've moved on already. I've six stories lined up today for the website ranging from a new boutique hotel being built to three "iconic" pubs closing. I'm sick of it.'

Frank stubbed out his cigarette.

'Can I have a try of that vape thing?' he asked and she handed him it.

Frank took a draw.

'Not bad, not bad at all. Watermelon, you say.'

Cara laughed as Frank signed off.

'Aye, the game's a bogey, Cara. Trouble is there's only about a few places left for journos to work in Scotland and it's the same dickheads who've been doing the rounds for years in charge. But stick at it, make things better from the inside and, whatever you do, don't get a job in fucking PR.'

35

Brewster had spent the last four days since the failed assassination attempt at the Loony Dook holed up in a static caravan near Burntisland, gazing wistfully across the Forth to Edinburgh. He was binging on energy drinks in a bid to stay alert and had orange powder all down his white Lacoste polo shirt from the giant bag of cheese puffs he was munching. He was in the process of opening his fifth can of "caffeine frenzy" when the idea struck him like a lightning bolt between the eyes. He would voluntarily hand himself in to the police and tell DI Hope that he was the intended target at the Loony Dook; the gunman had missed and hit the innocent pretendy priest by mistake. He would claim the Ulsterman wanted him dead as a loyalist gang were planning to take over the drug scene in Edinburgh and were labouring under the misapprehension that he, Danny Brewster, was still involved in that racket. He would claim complete ignorance of the subsequent killing of Billy One, which was in part true, although he strongly suspected that mad Falco bastard and his nutty Russian burd were to blame.

He texted The Gypsy to assure him that his plan to nick the fifty kilos of cocaine from the Syndicate was still a goer, but in truth Brewster had no idea if the drugs had been delivered. The Gypsy replied cryptically, *Bigger fish to fry*, which led him to automatically tug at his earlobes. He needed The Gypsy more than ever now, for protection after the fiasco at the Loony Dook, and the UVF would be raging over the death of Billy One, demanding answers. On top of that he would have to reach out to Naomi at some point. Get her to explain to the Wise One that he hadn't been set up for a hit and smooth things over. Brewster was finding this web of deceit exhausting and knew Armstrong would smell a rat but at least he'd be able to create an element of doubt that might just keep him alive until he worked out his next move.

He dialled an Uber to take him to Leith police station for a rendezvous with DI Hope. Brewster stared out the window as the taxi trundled over the Queensferry Crossing at a snail's pace. Normally, he would have given the Pakistani driver a piece of his mind but decided to give the racism a miss today. He contemplated the possibility of turning Supergrass and blowing the lid on the whole shebang.

Brewster let his mind drift towards a hot country in South America where he would have plastic surgery and a gain a new identity, like a top-ranking Nazi after the war. Friends with the local junta, a man of considerable influence, hookers on tap. He quite fancied Argentina or Uruguay; anywhere that had right-leaning tendencies, decent football hoolies and nice steaks. He was sure the serious crime guys would provide him with some top-notch accommodation and perhaps even be able to get decent seats for Pet Shop Boys gigs in return for giving up the Wise One and the Syndicate. Waffen would join him later, flown out first class in a container after he had got settled into the new life. The dog could have plastic surgery as well or at least dye its fur and would also need a new handle. Marjorie could meet them at some point; maybe he could travel to Florida and take her to Disney World like he'd always promised.

On the other hand, he was loving being back in Portobello and didn't want to leave. He'd been having these weird thoughts more and more where he went straight and didn't hurt people. Christ, half of the racist shit was an act, a by-product of his childhood with Norrie, and he desperately wanted to purge himself of the past. He wasn't getting any younger and the drink, drugs, gambling and violence was taking its toll. At some point, he'd have to pay the ferryman.

'Think, Danny, think.'

He stared out the window as the Skoda made its way down Ferry Road, reliving the memories of childhood where Norrie would scream, 'You killed my boy!' in Brewster's face before demanding half the wages from his milk round. This always occurred when Marjorie was working nightshift at the hospital and Norrie had been drinking. He'd boast how he "took care of your father" and how he'd take care of him if he dared to grass.

Brewster thought back to Norrie's death, which was etched in his memory. His stepdad, recently put on tablets for angina, had returned home steaming from an afternoon's drinking at The Central Bar at the bottom of Leith Walk. He'd bought fish in the pub for his tea like he did every Friday, despite hating Catholics, and was giving Brewster the usual dog's abuse in between cracking his new favourite joke about having "acute angina and a nice pair of tits".

While sitting in "his chair", he barked at his stepson to put on the videotape of *The World at War* episode, *Inside the Reich: Germany (1940–1944)*. The physical violence had stopped by now as Brewster had grown into a strapping sixteen-year-old, working as an apprentice scaffolder and running with the football hooligans at the weekend. Norrie was giving it the usual "You're treating this place like a hotel" spiel to the teenager when Albert Speer's handsome yet smarmy face appeared on the screen. To say Norrie was triggered was something of an understatement, screaming at the telly in between taking draws on his Embassy Regal Filter and sips from his can of Tartan Special.

'That fucking cunt. That smarmy bastard. He sold our glorious Führer down the river. Bastard. Albert fucking Speer. I know where I'd like to shove my spear – up that cunt's fucking arse… aaaaargh!!'

Brewster watched as Norrie clutched at his left arm, then his chest, wheezing while jumping to his feet and spinning round in a circle, panic-stricken, not knowing what to do.

'My meds, get me... ma fucking meds!!' he cried, voice getting croakier, face getting redder. Brewster remembered looking on in amazement, feeling like all his Christmases had come at once as it became apparent his tormentor might die right there on the frayed burgundy wool carpet. This was a beat the keeper, slot it into an empty net, open-goal opportunity that Brewster had cried himself to sleep dreaming about.

'What meds, Norrie?' he asked the now dying man, with his hand in the air grasping for the tablets that would never come. 'Oh, these ones, the beta blockers for your "acute angina and nice pair of tits", Norrie? The ones that provide instant relief? Well, I've got a bit of bad news for you on that front, old boy, you're not getting them,' a grinning Brewster taunted.

Norrie, by now gasping for air, pleaded for his stepson to phone an ambulance as a pish-stain enveloped the front of his beige Farah slacks. Brewster plonked himself down in Norrie's chair and helped himself to a fag, while taking a swig of warm beer. At that moment he'd never felt happier, watching Norrie, staring at the image of Albert Speer as he let out the final death rattle, which was music to the young man's ears. Brewster checked him over for any signs of life, then watched the rest of the documentary before heading to bed for the best night's kip he'd had in years. In the morning, Brewster gave his stepdad's corpse a kick before asking, 'Are you still dead, Norrie?' He finally dialled 999 as the body was starting to smell a bit.

Brewster entered Leith police station with his hands placed theatrically behind his head. The desk sergeant gave him a bemused look before calling for DI Hope to come down.

DI Hope welcomed Brewster like a long-lost son.

'Broadsword calling Danny Boy! Broadsword calling Danny Boy!' His familiar greeting.

Brewster cringed but played along.

'I want to have a chat, Bob. Just me and you; there's a few things I need to get off my chest.'

'Certainly, Danny. We've had an all-points bulletin out with the order for you to be arrested on sight. You've done well making it this far without some beat bobby slapping the bracelets on you.'

DI Hope took him up the stairs to an interview room, asking the duty officer to bring them tea and biscuits. Brewster relaxed with the veteran detective, who'd proved something of a father figure to him ever since he'd accidentally wedged his nine-iron into his brother's skull all those years ago.

'You know what this is about, Bob. That carry-on at the Loony Dook. The bullet had my name on it, not the poor guy dressed as a priest.'

Hope nodded sagely. 'Look, Danny. Do you want to call your lawyer, son? I'd like to get this on tape; a statement for the record.'

'I don't want my fucking lawyer involved, Bob. He's a crooked prick and I don't want to make an official statement. I just want someone I can talk to in confidence. They tried to kill me for fuck's sake.'

'Okay, okay,' Hope replied, 'but keep your language down, Danny. You're swearing like a trooper.'

'Sorry, Bob.'

Brewster's paranoia kicked in. He felt scared and lost, taking little comfort from the fact no one was likely to shoot him in the police station.

'Why don't we start with you telling me why you were at South Queensferry?' Hope asked.

Brewster took a deep breath but felt his heart racing. Too much caffeine.

'Well, Bob, I'd planned to take part in the Loony Dook to raise money for the Portobello Bluebells women's football team.

319

I do a lot of work for charity these days and I'm also involved with the youth theatre in Portobello. You know, give a bit back to the community.'

Bob laughed. 'That's very good of you, Danny, giving back some of the money you've taken from the poor helpless drug addicts over the last thirty years.'

'That's what I thought,' Brewster replied. 'Anyway, I'd gone to the Loony Dook in my "See You Jimmy" hat to fit in with all the other Dookers. Fancy dress, like. And I remember the seagull shitting on my head before I heard a couple of cracks which I knew were bullets whizzing past me. Must have just missed my head. That's when I turned round and saw the Fenian priest had been shot with half his brains falling into the water. I also saw a couple of folk wrestling on the Rail Bridge, then one of them fell into the Forth. It was carnage.'

Hope cracked a biscuit and dipped it in his tea before opening a thick manila folder.

He said, 'The shooter died from the fall. He was a real nasty piece of work. Former UVF man called William Fitzroy Campbell, aliases Billy One, Kill Bill amongst others, murdered three Catholic men in a pub, four murders to his name now including the one at the Loony Dook. His latest victim was Patrick Meikle, father of three, retired printer from Linlithgow.'

Brewster nodded like a nodding dog in heat.

'That's the bit I'm getting to, Bob. I was his intended target. These loyalist nutters want to move back into Edinburgh to run the drugs trade. Remember about twenty years ago they came over and caused mayhem in Wester Hailes, setting dealers on fire and that? Well, they're back.'

Hope's interest was piqued.

'Go on, Danny,' he urged.

Brewster was warming to his task, buzzing that things seemed to be going to plan.

'So, someone has told the UVF that I'm still the main man in the toon when it comes to the drugs. But – and I must stress this, Bob – I'm retired from all that shite, long gone. Things are going great for me in Porty what with the theatre group, the football team and the sculpting. The community have really taken me to heart, given me a second chance, a shot at redemption.'

Hope said, 'So why do you think the loyalist hoods think you're still involved, Danny?'

Brewster feigned bemusement.

'Well, Bob, there are a lot of jealous folks out there, envious of my success and how I've managed to turn my life around. Become a force for good. You know how chippy some people in Edinburgh are and they hate to see anyone get on. I wouldn't put it past one of my colleagues from the bad ole days to have put my name out there, provided a bit of disinformation to seek advantage.'

Brewster let that sink in before adding, 'It's a diabolical liberty, Bob, these bastards taking a pot shot at me like that when I'm trying to raise cash for the kids. I demand the same level of protection that an ordinary member of the public would get. I don't want to be walking around for the rest of my days in fear for my life.'

Hope slammed shut the file.

'Look, Danny, I've known you since you were a bairn. Right through from when you were a snotty football hooligan, but not a bad boy, to becoming a nasty, homophobic, racist, attempted-murdering prick. That story is absolute pish and you know it.'

Brewster feigned both hurt and surprise, with Hope in full flow.

'Isn't it about time you gave Marjorie a break and stopped playing the cardboard gangster? This is all a bit out of your league, son, running with the big boys, and it's only going to end in tears. You know that. I know you know that.'

Brewster lost his rag.

'Who the fuck are you calling son! I am not your fucking son, Bob! I'm fifty-six years old, for fuck's sake. I'm trying to turn my life around.'

'Look, Danny, we know all about the London firm. Armstrong and the Syndicate. We know they're muscling a way in up here and the cinema project they're involved in and all the other shite you've got going is a front for money laundering. Give us some credit. We also know that it was you who invited those nutters over from Belfast.'

Brewster sat back in his chair, resigned to the fact Bob was onto him. He knew the pitch was coming and a part of him welcomed it.

'All you've got to do, Danny, is co-operate, give us names and details of these London guys. You don't owe them anything. Armstrong is a snitch, has been for years. He'd throw you under the bus in a heartbeat. We already know Savage's daughter, Naomi, is involved. Do yourself a favour for once, Danny; you're still a relatively young man. Do you really want to end up with a bullet in the back of your head? Think what that would do to your poor mother, and who'd look after your dog? It would be the kennels for him.'

Brewster stared into space.

'What's the dog's name again? Waffle, is it, or Waffen, like the SS unit?'

'No comment.'

Hope wasn't having that.

'Come on, Danny. Don't give it the no comment crap here. The tape isn't on and it's only me and you. Will you at least think about what I'm saying? For old times' sake. I think you deserve a better life, mate.'

'I'm not your mate,' Brewster replied, turning back the clock to his teenage self being asked by Hope if he stole the church collection.

He felt deflated. Bob had been good to him over the years.

All right, he was still a cop, but Brewster had grown weary of "the code" which no one else seemed to be following. Even though Hope was right when he said the Porty projects were a front, Brewster genuinely loved being involved. He'd met new people at the youth theatre – Christ, he even quite fancied the drama teacher – and the women at the football team had welcomed him with open arms. If there was a way out of this mess, he would take it.

'Whatever it is you want me to do, Bob, I'll do it,' he said.

*

Naomi met the Wise One in a packed Easter Road outside Middletons Bar before the Hibs v Hearts match. A load of Hearts Ultras were milling about outside giving it the big one to their Hibs rivals. Although the police presence was large, his idea to meet among the crowd meant Naomi felt they were safe, effectively hiding in plain sight.

But this did nothing to deter the deep loathing she now felt towards Uncle Ray after learning the details of her mother's death. She wanted revenge. He had to pay for stealing Maxine's song and feeding her with smack. Naomi would do the preparation; it was just a question of getting the opportunity to put things right.

'I'll keep it brief, Naomi,' the Wise One said. 'You're to concentrate on the cinema and don't initiate any contact with Brewster. Final approval has gone through today on the project and the building work will commence in two weeks. Chances are he'll contact you anyway with some cock-and-bull story about the Loony Dook that he's dreamt up.'

Naomi nodded, listening intently while a Hearts fan banged a drum near her ear.

Armstrong continued. 'Play daft and go along if Brewster wants to meet you but make sure you take JJ. We need to get as much information from him as possible. It was a mistake to trust that prick in the first place. The Gypsy will run the distribution side of things for us up here from now on. He's tight with the Glasgow families and has an army of travellers at his fingertips.'

Naomi nodded, absorbing every word.

'You're doing good work, girl, but keep an eye out for the Old Bill. They're sniffing but they're miles away. Don't underestimate them though, that Bob Hope is a clever old soak.'

He outlined how a consignment of cocaine due into Leith would be moved through to Glasgow by the Gypsy for 'safekeeping' until things quietened down in Edinburgh. The Wise One said he would return to London and would be keeping his distance from 'chilly Jockoland' for the foreseeable future, as the police surveillance was on top.

'Take care, my lovely,' he said, before giving her a quick peck on the cheek and vanishing into the crowd.

Naomi headed in the opposite direction. Her mind was clear in terms of work, but she was concerned that the Brewster problem had landed on her plate. Surely the Wise One wasn't going to let him away with a free hit at the Loony Dook? What kind of message would that send to rivals? That he'd gone soft and lost his bottle. Naomi's instinct told her that wasn't the case but for once she was struggling to solve the equation.

36

Frank spiralled rapidly downhill in the days after leaving the paper. His mood deteriorated further after he got the call from Richard saying he'd been knocked back for redundancy and thus wouldn't be receiving the much-needed payment. His farewell column to journalism, which he'd already completed, would likely be the last time his byline appeared in print. He now had no source of regular income and was dipping into his pension, which was under twenty thousand pounds and unlikely to see him through the year, never mind retirement. On the plus side, Naomi had squared his debt with The Gypsy, so he no longer had to worry about getting his ears chopped off, but he hadn't taken her advice to return to the AA meetings. Plans for a Day Zero reawakening in the form of a health kick had gotten as far as him still eating a banana before going to the pub and hitting the deck on one occasion where he managed a measly seven press-ups. His gout had reached the stage where he'd volunteer for amputation, even offering to cut his own foot off if they let him and had taken to always wearing Crocs. A former regular at the doctor's, he now kept away from the place, crossing the road as he walked past in case Dr Khan spotted him and demanded he come in for a check-up. The blood pressure machine was hiding in the cupboard, and he'd "forgotten" to take the beta blockers since Hogmanay should they interfere with the drinking and smoking. Yes, he was back on the fags.

Days crept slowly by with Frank spending an inordinate amount of time in the boozer to the point where he was boring himself, never mind Bella and the punters. There was only so much "they should make tennis one serve" and "ban dogs from cafés" chat people could take. He would turn up around noon, order a pint of lager and sit hogging the pub's papers, defacing the racing pages with his selections for the televised races. Frank had taken to carrying his own marker pens for this purpose, highlighting the "certainties" in green and the "possibles" in yellow. Despite a horrendous track record, he fancied himself as something of a tipster, telling all and sundry that backing his chosen horse was "buying money". To date, no one including Bella had "bought money" but some had lost a small fortune betting on Frank's tips, most of whom were still running on Portobello beach.

To add to the misery, Bella had kiboshed his idea to become the "star" barman, telling him he'd be doing a proper worker out of a job, and she needed someone who would commit to working full time. In truth, she thought Frank would be hopeless and was doing him a favour. She'd already had a lifetime of him smashing glasses while steaming and didn't think things would improve much if he managed to stay sober for an eight-hour shift. His clumsy attempts at trying to unhook her bra straps over the years convinced Bella that his "butter fingers" were better suited on the other side of the gantry.

In between going to The Haddonfield and taking drives in the Shadow with Falco, where they'd get high on weed, Frank was visiting his mother who was in hospital after suffering a stroke. Arthur had recently moved into care and the family home in Leith Links, where Frank had shared a room with Michael, was in the process of being sold. All these arrangements were too much for him to deal with, so Naomi had stepped in as the responsible adult while Frank continued to behave like a delinquent child.

He still wasn't talking to Bobby, having decided not to forgive him for being there the night Michael died and then keeping quiet about it for nigh on thirty-five years. This manifested in the form of ridiculous three-way conversations, with Bobby sitting at the bar talking to Bella while Frank sat at a nearby table pretending to read the papers.

'What did he say?' Frank would ask Bella.

'I'm right here, Frank; you don't need to go through Bella,' an exasperated Bobby would implore.

'Can you ask him if he's finished with that *Daily Record*?' Frank would say.

'Ask him yourself. I'm sick of this shite,' was Bella's standard reply.

Frank's mood improved the day Plunkett popped in for a pint and told him Bridget had divorced Richard, but this was tempered with pictures of her on holiday with George Pittman on the island of Capri. There was an attempt at a date with a lovely woman called Nicola but she left before dessert after listening to a thirty-minute Frank diatribe about how people who watch television with the big light on should be fined, that inevitably escalated to them being shot after he'd sunk a couple or three double Bacardi's. Nicola told him to "bore off" before announcing she was away home to watch *The Crown* with the big light on.

Against this backdrop, Frank found himself drunk and the last man standing in The Haddonfield on a Monday night. He'd lost a small fortune in the afternoon and had hit the strawberry daiquiris early followed by white Russians, claiming they helped settle his stomach. Bella eschewed his ham-fisted attempt to come back to hers for a 'shot on the swings' and told him in no uncertain terms to go home, threatening to impose a one-month banning order.

'I'm telling you, Frank, you're this close to being Scotland Yard.'

He told her to "fuck off", then slammed the door on the way out and headed towards the prom. It was a nice night as he staggered along, eventually coming to rest on the steps leading up to the swimming baths. The full moon lit up the Firth of Forth and Frank fumbled to light up a cigarette, squinting to look at the various messages he had sent Bridget throughout the course of the day, which had become more frequent the drunker he'd become. There wasn't a single reply. He texted the word *sorry* to Bella but deep down he knew he'd crossed the line and was becoming a pest. He also sent *sorry* messages to Naomi, Bridget, then Bobby.

He made his way down to the promenade wall and stared back at the swimming baths. A happy place where he'd gone as a kid, diving for a black brick in his pyjamas and completing his first length. He remembered trying to play water polo and the girls from the swimming club in their Arena costumes. Frank thought about getting a chittery-bite after the baths, usually chips from the van outside. Michael was with him and Bobby, hair wet, digging out their fifty-pence pieces with Britannia on the front.

He turned to face the water and realised it was all bollocks. Frank was trying to insert thoughts into his brain, but the truth was he wasn't feeling any of it. He'd become the dreaded Replicant, mimicking human emotions, an empty vessel, hollow. He slipped down off the wall onto the beach, flicked his Marlboro Red and started to take his clothes off.

Frank felt the cold hit his thighs as he stepped out of his Crocs, placing them neatly on the sand before pulling down his jogging bottoms and pink Calvin Klein pants that he'd been wearing for two days and had turned inside out. Next came his overcoat and hoodie, laying them in a neat pile. He was completely naked, just the water and the moonlight for company. Frank felt an overwhelming sadness mixed with shame and crippling fatigue. He'd reached the point where he dreaded his own thoughts; the fear he felt for Naomi, being shunned by Bridget, falling out with Bobby – it was all getting on top of him. He now had no job, little prospects and his health was failing, physically and mentally. It would be easier to just make it all go away as he waded out, sobbing, into the ocean. His last thought was of Michael as he plunged under the water, then he felt a flash... right across his groin... that sent him running from the sea, screaming in terror.

To Be Frank - Column #346

So long, farewell, auf Wiedersehen, goodnight,
I have to go and leave this pile of s***e.

Alas, dear readers, the moment we have all been dreading has arrived, for the time has come for one to pen one's own career obituary. The final nail in the coffin. After two-score years and ten of residing at the pleasure of the Fourth Estate, I have decided to leave journalism to spend more time in my local pub where you will find me pouring pints for various dipsomaniacs and degenerate alcoholics who I sometimes call my friends.

I would still recommend a career in journalism to all you fresh-faced graduates who don't read this column as, trust me, it beats working for a living, just don't expect to make any money. The words of the great Australian journalist, novelist and adventurer, Murray Sayle, still ring in my ears when he proclaimed, 'The only qualities essential for real success in journalism are rat-like cunning, a plausible manner and a little literary ability.'

But seriously it's the best job in the world.

I know from a recent conversation I had with a young up-and-coming reporter that passions run high among Generation Z and Millennials who seek the truth and are sick to death of being spoon-fed second-rate digital content. They get the same buzz as we once did to see their name in print for the first time. A tangible record of their efforts. Perhaps, like those who came before, I am guilty of underestimating their abilities and reports of the death of journalism are greatly exaggerated.

I was told on my first job at the red top not to worry about the writing, "as we have plenty of people who can write", just get the stories. That still holds true today where the standard of literacy is in the gutter, but the message remains the same – all that's changed is the delivery method, with print on the way to becoming obsolete. "Write so your granny understands it" was always the advice, but now that's only if Granny can sign into her computer and remember the password.

Social media was but a glimmer in its mother's eye back then and no one surfed the net for stories. You were encouraged to leave your desk and find tales, with rich pickings to be found down the boozer. I would say the job is harder – fewer resources, longer hours and a reading public who have the attention span of a gnat. To counter that there are more opportunities, particularly for younger women, although we've still got a way to go before people of colour are gainfully employed in the Scottish media.

It's been a privilege to work with some lovely folk who I'm now proud to call my lifelong… former work colleagues. I recall my first "death knock", an eleven-year-old boy who had died on Christmas Eve after an asthma attack. His dad was rightly going to rip my head off after I came calling the next day until Bert the snapper, who had been in military intelligence at the height of "The Troubles", calmed him down. I drowned my sorrows to drink away the pain and toughened up.

But all in all, I've had a blast and look back on long, hot summers spent in Fife with Bert, hot on the heels of the Kennoway cat poisoner, and the time a fellow hack had a dead mouse thrown at him on a doorstep in Methil.

'Ya hoor, sir!'

To Be Frank, dear readers, as mentioned in a previous column, no one wants to hear from a white middle-aged man riddled with gout. Like the fishmonger's daughter, I know my plaice, and the time has come to pass the baton of truth on to the next generation.

I bid you fond adieu.

37

Frank applied the cream he'd been given to his nether regions, still aching from where the giant Portuguese man o' war jellyfish had stung him in the balls, forcing him to run out of the water, afraid his body was about to go into spasm. This divine intervention from mother nature had acted as an epiphany for Frank, who decided he wanted to live and vowed from that day on to lead a better life. The – *Here lies Frank Savage. He made life difficult for himself* epitaph that he had planned for his gravestone was on hold. Thus, the jellyfish was the catalyst that would propel him to health and happiness. The sting had left him with a peach of a scar spreading across his nut sack to the inner thigh. He'd been embarrassed at the A&E department but the doctor who treated him referred him on to Dr Khan and Frank had finally bitten the bullet and entered the GP's surgery. Dr Khan was kind and considerate but spelt it out to him in no uncertain terms that he was drinking non-alcoholic lager in the last chance saloon. After prescribing antidepressants to go with the beta blockers, he gave Frank a diet sheet and told him to lose weight. Dr Khan also advised seeing a counsellor and made an appointment for him to have his first session in a week's time. Frank had already stepped back through the doors of AA with a visit to Gamblers Anonymous to follow. He didn't think he needed to go to NA as the coke was only ever a by-product of the alcohol.

His phone rang and he answered on the first ring. It was Bobby. The pair were back on speaking terms after Frank had met him for a coffee and finally forgiven him.

'Hi, Frank. I'm feeling rough as fuck today. I went out and got rat-arsed yesterday. Bella had to kick me out The Hadd.'

Frank smiled and felt sympathy tinged with the merest hint of sober superiority.

'Well, the old Frank would say get yourself back in the boozer for a hair of the dog, my Nepalese friend, but you'd probably be better off making a fruit smoothie.'

'I wouldn't know where to start,' Bobby replied.

'Maybe buy some fruit. Listen, Bobby, I meant every word of what I said about forgiving you for Michael. You didn't do anything wrong, pal, and our friendship means the world to me.'

'Thanks, Frank. That means the earth. It really does.'

'We've both had to live with Michael's death hanging over us for too long. We need to move on. He would have wanted that, for us to make the best of our lives. It's still not too late. We owe it to him to do the right thing. So, don't be having the fear, Bobby. I know what that's like.'

'I know, Frank, nowt worse than the F.E.A.R. What you up to today?'

'Well, Bobby, I'm lacing up my new trainers as we speak and I'm about to head up Holyrood Park for a stroll, bit of a gander. Get the steps in. I'm nailing ten thousand per day,' Frank replied smugly.

'Oh well, have fun. I hope to join you one day soon but might have to give it a miss this morning or I'll spew on your new kicks.'

38

Naomi finally got a call from a desperate Brewster two weeks after the shooting at the Loony Dook.

'Can you meet me today at 2pm, top of Salisbury Crags? I'll be alone. Naomi, I need your help. Please help me. I want to put things right between us.'

Naomi, who was taken aback at this new human-sounding Brewster, took a moment to weigh up the situation.

'Okay,' she said, then hung up.

Immediately, she played the angles in her brain. Where in the name of fuck had he been hiding? Should she phone the Wise One, now back in London, and tell him Brewster had come out of the shadows? He had told her to "play daft and go along" if he got in touch and glean as much information as possible out of him, and she was sticking to that instruction. She had a nagging feeling in the pit of her stomach that contacting the Wise One could spell curtains for Danny Boy, and she wasn't prepared to send this lamb to the slaughter before she heard what he had to say for himself.

The cinema renovation, now well underway, had taken up all of her time, relegating Brewster to the back of her mind. She was also trying to keep her distance from The Gypsy, who she knew was holding fifty kilograms of the purest Syndicate cocaine, the profits of which the Wise One would likely never see. The Gypsy had swung by the cinema last week in his pickup truck to remind her that the offer to work for him still stood. Legitimately. Change was coming and she knew to stay patient and let nature take its course. The Wise One's jacket was on a shoogly peg with every man and his dog suspecting him of being a grass and the time was ripe for The Gypsy to take over. Danny Brewster and the part he would play, if at all, was the missing piece of the jigsaw.

She phoned JJ again, but he still wasn't picking up, which was odd. He had been acting as her de facto bodyguard since the attempted hit at the Loony Dook but picked the wrong time to pull a disappearing act. It was reckless to meet Brewster without him and she remembered the Wise One telling her to take JJ, but Naomi had made up her mind to carry on regardless.

She made her way to Holyrood Park knowing Brewster had picked his day and time carefully – the place was heaving due to a ten kilometre run taking place. She wore jogging gear to mingle with the other runners, the only difference being the Glock 43 tucked inside her waistband. Arriving early, Naomi carried a little potted plant filled with edelweiss in her rucksack for the occasion – that had been in her mind since meeting the Wise One up on Arthur's Seat. The sky was battleship grey as she made her way past Holyrood Palace, walking towards the park with the Scottish Parliament across the road.

She saw the benches chained to the railing beside the gatehouse, with the imposing shadow of Salisbury Crags creating a stunning backdrop. Naomi stood away from Helga's wooden bench that was looking the worse for wear and wondered if any of the thousands of tourists who passed by here had any idea of the horror it bore testimony to. She placed the edelweiss in the middle of the bench and studied the plaque: *In loving memory of our daughter Helga Konrad Schwerbach, West Germany, born 16.6.54 died 13.10.72.* Naomi sat down and imagined Helga's parents doing the same, facing the Crags where their daughter perished at the hands of the man she loved and imagined as her future husband.

She had half an hour before meeting Brewster and decided to do a quick recce. Naomi was surprised by how steep the Crags were and was quickly out of breath just walking. She nervously made her way to the edge across from the Dumbiedykes flats, a stunning example of 1960s Brutalist architecture that replaced the crumbling tenement blocks. By now she was across from the old James Clark School building, looking up to Edinburgh Castle – a view straight out of the pages of a Hans Christian Andersen fairy tale. Naomi was struck by the sheer beauty of the view tempered with the sheer dread of the one-hundred-and-fifty-foot plunge to the bottom of the clifftops, with no safety fence or warning signs of note. It was no surprise this was a suicide hotspot.

This reminded her of Daisy Park, another place of beauty that hid a dark secret. She was reading Robert Louis Stevenson's *Strange Case of Dr Jekyll and Mr Hyde* and had stumbled upon the numerous studies relating to the duality of Edinburgh itself, the light and the dark. This had resonance with Naomi's own life, maintaining an air of respectability as a high-flying, venture capitalist who helped the local community, but she was really fronting for the Syndicate. Her mind wandered to how everyone she knew was living a double life. Even Brewster was a different person around his mother and his dog.

She began her descent and spotted Brewster at the bottom of the hill with Waffen in tow. He looked stressed. He was wearing a black Adidas tracksuit and a fur trapper's hat with ear flaps that made him look like a cross between a fat Ian Brown and a nineties acid casualty who no one told the rave had ended.

'All right, Naomi. Thanks for coming. I really appreciate it.'

Naomi gave a wry smile and said nothing, she was thrown off kilter by this new reasonable Brewster, turning to march back up the Crags with him following dutifully behind, transfixed on his mobile phone.

'Where the fuck have you been?' she asked.

Brewster stopped and bent down to stroke his dog. 'Good boy, good boy,' he said, ignoring her question while putting the phone back in his pocket.

'Hell-oh,' Naomi said sarcastically, stopping and turning to face him.

Finally, Brewster stood up, face on to Naomi, but with a respectable couple of yards between them.

Brewster said, 'You know Armstrong is a grass, don't you? He's got it coming.'

Naomi wasn't in the mood for deflection.

'Answer my question, Brewster, and take that daft hat off. Where the fuck have you been?'

Brewster removed the offending headgear.

'I've been on the lam. I shat the bed and ran for the hills. Well, a caravan park in Burntisland. Fife's not that hilly. I don't know where I stand with the Syndicate and what's happened to the drugs. I take it The Gypsy still has them?'

Naomi started walking again, felt the pistol under her waistband and assumed Brewster would be carrying as well. *Best tread carefully.*

'Don't worry about drugs. What happened at the Loony Dook?' she asked, ready for the smörgåsbord of excuses coming her way.

Brewster, walking with her, appeared to be playing with the phone in his pocket, and did not disappoint.

'What happened at the Loony Dook? I'll tell you what happened at the fucking Loony Dook. That Billy One tried to blow my fucking head off. Isn't that right, Waffle Pops, someone tried to blow your daddy's brains out?'

Naomi couldn't believe what she was seeing. Had this cunt found God or something?

'So, how do you explain the holdall full of newspapers and not the one hundred grand you were supposed to pay back? The one hundred grand that you skimmed from the Syndicate?'

'I was being careful, taking precautions. I had a driver

waiting nearby with the money for when JJ or whoever showed. I knew the Ulstermen were watching my every move and had an idea they might try something at the Loony Dook, attempt to execute the Wise One, so I was looking to warn him. I didn't want to risk losing one hundred grand of Syndicate money if it all kicked off and that proved to be a good move.'

Brewster was stalling now, out of breath, letting the dog off the lead to make its own way up the Crags.

'So, where's the money, Danny?'

'I've got it stashed away. I'm ready to give it back, help smooth the waters, for my return to the fold with the Wise One. Have you spoken to him about me? He must be happy the cinema project's been approved; does he want me to start moving product in the schemes? We can work together, Naomi, to launder the money; we make a great team.'

Naomi didn't know where to begin. Brewster was sounding like a naïve rookie, the desperation pouring out of him. Something was off. He was being too polite, the flurry of questions a bit too specific. Like he was reading them off a list. She walked towards the edge of the cliff not answering any of them. Her gut feeling told her he was recording their conversation on his phone. Naomi checked to see if anyone was coming before pulling the Glock out of her waistband and shoving it against Brewster's head.

'Don't shoot me! Don't fucking shoot me, Naomi, please.'

Naomi reached into Brewster's pocket for his mobile phone and saw the record button was switched on and he'd been taping their conversation. The modern-day equivalent of wearing a wire.

'You're a fucking grass!' she screamed, cocking the pistol.

Brewster cowered as Waffle ran past him with not a care in the world.

'You better start talking quickly, Brewster, because I'm three seconds away from blowing your tiny brains out. One... two... thr—'

'Okay! Okay! I'll talk, I'll talk.'

Naomi pulled the gun away from his head as she scanned the clifftop for passers-by. All clear but that wouldn't last.

'DI Hope made me an offer I couldn't refuse. He said they had enough to put me away for the rest of my life and told me Armstrong was a grass. The cunt's been working for the Met police for fifty-odd years, Naomi.'

'I know all about that,' Naomi replied. 'The dogs in the street know that. But that's Armstrong. Why the fuck are you trying to put me away?'

'I'm not, Naomi, I swear. This is the first time I've tried this. I swear I haven't given Hope anything yet. I just wanted to try out the equipment. A dummy run, if you like.'

Naomi moved towards him pointing the pistol in his face.

'Don't give me any more of your shite.'

Brewster squirmed.

'I want out, Naomi. I've had enough of the life. I can't take it any more. The violence, the constant dealing with psychopaths – my nerves are fucking shredded.'

'Listen, you racist cunt. I told you not to give me any more of your shite,' Naomi replied, lowering her voice for added menace.

Brewster sobbed, 'I'm sorry about all that, Naomi, I truly am. I'm not a racist anymore. I listen to Soul II Soul and I don't even like the Nazis. I swear. Hitler was a prick!'

Naomi felt pity for the poor wretch in front of her but was still on full alert. She smashed the phone off a nearby rock and threw it over the cliff.

Brewster winced. 'If you're going to shoot, just shoot. You'd be doing me a fucking favour.'

Naomi told him to get to his feet.

'I'm not going to kill you. I'm not a murderer. But I won't hesitate to blow your fucking knee out. Tell me exactly what it is DI Hope wants you to do, and don't fucking lie.'

Brewster wiped his eyes, appearing to have aged twenty years in the last two minutes.

'He wants me to get all the information I can on the Syndicate operation in Edinburgh. That puts you in the frame as they're concentrating on the cinema restoration and the stuff I've been doing with the youth theatre and the football team. He knows they're fronts to launder drug money. He doesn't have conclusive proof, and no one's been arrested yet, but they're building a case, working with the Met and the National Crime Agency. He also told me the Serious Fraud Office are investigating.'

'He told me the same thing,' Naomi said.

Brewster sensed she was softening towards him.

'Look, Naomi. I've come clean. We can use this to our advantage.'

Naomi slid the Glock back in her waistband as, out of nowhere, a familiar figure came ambling towards them.

39

Frank sauntered into Holyrood Park without a care in the world. The place was heaving as another ten kilometre run had just finished and lots of fit-looking project manager types were milling about the car park looking very pleased with themselves. He decided to leave the main route and head up the Crags for a bit of peace, escape the hordes. Frank hadn't been up there since he was a child and knew the view across to the castle was stunning. He made his way past a couple of walkers coming back in the direction of the road and kept his head down, ploughing up the path. This was a shift, and Frank was beginning to realise he'd bitten off more than he could chew. Still, the view would be worth it. He thought about Bobby as he ascended the Crags. How his friend had always been there for him through thick and thin. Frank remembered christening him Gurkha Bobby as he was Nepalese and always going on about how his old man was a Gurkha hero. Frank loved Bobby's father, Adesh; a right character who would show the boys his kukri knife and regale them with stories of how he'd seen combat in Borneo during the 1960s. Adesh met Bobby's mum, Agnes Robertson, up Arthur's Seat during the summer of 1966 when he was in Edinburgh for the Military Tattoo. Her friend had dared Agnes to talk to the Gurkhas, with her and Adesh hitting it off instantly. Love at first sight. They were married a year later with Adesh in full military uniform. He left the army and settled in Leith, then Portobello. Bobby, named after Bobby Charlton since Adesh was a big Man Utd fan, came along a year later.

Frank was breathing out his arse by now. *Christ. I need to work on my fitness,* he thought, approaching two figures, a man and a woman, in the distance. As he got closer, Frank recognised the woman as Naomi. 'Fuck me, Naomi! Naomi!' he shouted, quickening the pace. 'Brewster! Fucking Brewster!'

Brewster let out a groan.

'That's all I need,' he muttered, before Naomi moved to head Frank off at the pass as he made his way towards his arch-enemy.

'Dad, leave him alone. Don't go near him. It's okay. I'm in control here and he's not hurting me. We're talking business.'

Frank replied, 'I bet you fucking are,' confused and disgusted by the situation at the same time.

'Look, Dad,' Naomi cried, 'Brewster is helping the police. He's trying to get information on the Wise One and bring him down. We're all on the same side now.'

Frank eyed Brewster warily as Waffle ambled towards his owner. 'A likely story. Yip, we're all on the same side now. We're the fucking *A-Team*!'

'It's true, Frank,' Brewster said, his voice soft and without a trace of the old arrogance. 'Hope approached me to work for him and I've agreed. Obviously, I won't be broadcasting the fact, but I've had enough. I want out. I've had a taste of what life could be like since I moved back to Porty, and I want a piece of that.'

'And I want revenge on Armstrong, Dad. He robbed me of my mother growing up and I want him to pay. If no one puts a bullet in his head, then getting locked up for good is the best alternative. If Brewster is the man to do it, then so be it.'

Frank was flabbergasted at this criminal love-in. He wasn't prepared to forgive and forget that easily.

'What is this, you pair? Fucking *Cagney and Lacey*? Dare I remind you, Danny, of all the drama you've caused me and my family – I won't be meeting you for a flat white and pain au raisin anytime soon to talk about the old days at Leith Academy. As for you, Naomi, my pride and joy, you have taken your considerable talent for numbers and used them for criminal ends to line your own pockets. You both work for a *fucking* crime syndicate! Jesus wept! You'd be hard pushed to find a bigger pair of deluded arseholes in all of Christendom.'

Naomi wasn't about to be lectured by her dad.

'Says the alcoholic compulsive gambler. I paid your fucking debt off, Dad. So, don't fucking lecture me about lining my pockets. You're a walking disaster. Don't come across all high and mighty with me when the only reason you're out here is because you jumped into the Firth of Forth naked and got stung on the balls by a giant jellyfish. You couldn't even kill yourself properly.'

Brewster burst out laughing. 'Is that true, Savage? A jellyfish stung you on the nut sack. Ha! Ha! Ya fucking beauty. Go on the jellyfish.'

Frank smiled but inside he was raging.

'Yes. But I've turned a corner, Danny, unlike you. You're still a fucking football casual at heart, haven't grown up or moved on from your poof-bashing days. You still wear Stone Island for fuck's sake and your dog's got a Burberry collar.'

Brewster put the designer lead on Waffle.

'I remember you ran with the hoolies once, Frank. That mob from this side of town. Aberdeen, that's who you were playing, the esteemed Frank Savage rolling about on the pavement with the ASC. Heard you did all right as well. Why didn't you go back, Frank? Did you bottle it?'

Naomi looked over at her dad who was shifting uneasily.

'I went once forty years ago. I quickly realised that spending the weekend in a cell and appearing in court first thing on a Monday morning was for losers.'

Frank was starting to enjoy this tête-à-tête with his old school chum; a trip down memory lane.

'I saved your arse more than a couple of times, Brewster. That time the boys from the Fort wanted to carve you up. If it wasn't for me playing football with them, you'd have been walking about with even more Mars bars on your stupid pus.'

Brewster smiled and touched the scar on his cheek.

'Aye. I can't deny it, Naomi, your old fella was a bit handy back in the—'

Naomi and Frank saw Brewster's eyes widen, before he spun on his heel and ran full speed towards the cliff. Two blurs moved quickly past them and then, a deafening gunshot. The blast hit Brewster square in the chest, propelling him backwards and over the cliff. Waffle yelped, searching for a way down to be with his faithful owner.

Frank turned instinctively, placing his body between his daughter and the would-be assassins, both wearing hoodies with scarves up to their eyes. He waited for the gunshot but it never came. When Frank looked up, he saw Naomi with her hands outstretched holding a Glock 43. Steady as a rock. The men pulled down their scarves.

'All right, Naomi. All right, Frank, long time no see.' It was Armstrong. JJ gave them a nod.

'Stay the fuck away from me,' Naomi shouted, as the sound of police sirens drew closer.

'Best be off. I'll be in touch. Be seeing you, Frank. Come on, JJ.' The Wise One jogged up the Crags, lobbing his pistol over the cliff edge.

'Let's get the fuck out of here!' Frank screamed, dragging Naomi by the arm and heading towards the car park. But Naomi was having none of it, running in the direction of the cliff edge like an Olympic sprinter out of the blocks. Frank screamed after her, but she'd already stopped to look down below. He caught up and peered over the edge of the Crags. There was an eerie silence punctuated by the sound of the sirens getting closer.

Frank saw Brewster splayed on the stone path, like a

mannequin someone had arranged in a disco pose with the legs pointed the wrong way. He couldn't see the dog, then heard a bark and saw it trotting away with not a scratch on him. Naomi wiped the Glock clean with her sweatshirt and threw it down towards Brewster before grabbing her dad and heading for Arthur's Seat.

40

The Wise One and JJ were arrested outside The Gypsy's compound by armed police who were waiting on them. Armstrong was red-dotted and told to hit the deck. He managed to growl, 'Do you know who I am?' at the lead officer out of the side of his mouth, before he was unceremoniously pushed into a black Range Rover. The Gypsy was nowhere to be seen. The compound was silent with the curtains drawn and no dogs barking. Their plan to hide at The Gypsy's then be spirited away in the dead of night lay in tatters. The Wise One was held at Saughton Prison under twenty-four-hour surveillance with armed guards patrolling both the inside and the outside perimeter of the jail.

DI Hope was a happy man as he slicked back his hair and adjusted his tiepin for his big interview. He'd recently purchased a new overcoat, and his made-to-measure suit fit smartly under it. Shirt sitting nicely against the collar, plenty of room in the sleeves and no bunching. Perfect. He was chuffed to be finally getting the recognition all the hard graft and long hours over a thirty-five-year career had earned him. He would retire in a year's time a happy man, no matter the outcome of Armstrong's trial. Respect well and truly earned, pension with a little bonus on the side, finally getting what he was owed.

He waltzed into the interview room: the Alpha Male, Charlie Big Balls. This lasted all of three seconds as he came face-to-face with the devil incarnate. The Wise One was sitting there staring at Hope with a beatific smile on his face. No sooner had Hope started to read him his rights than Armstrong was off on one.

'Where did you get the suit, Bob? Fucking Top Man? I never knew they did made-to measure, and you've emptied a chip pan on your head, I see. You look like Dirty Den from EastEnders. I bet you've got a fucking semi under that table, interviewing me. This is the fucking big league, son. You don't belong here.'

Hope flushed red and swore he saw a smirk on the faces of DS Gibson and the uniformed officer guarding the door. He knew half the top brass were watching through the two-way mirror, ready to critique his performance.

Armstrong turned to address the mirror.

'Bob Hope. You've sent Bob Hope to interview me,' he said, before turning back to face his accuser. 'Well, let me tell you, Bob Hope, this ain't the Road to Bali or even the Road to Singapore, this is the "Road to Nowhere" and you're on it, my son.'

Hope managed to read the Wise One his rights before launching into his first question, which, like the twelve subsequent questions, were met with the same answer.

'No comment.'

Hope wrapped up his questions, saving the joker till last.

'We've found gunpowder residue on the hoodie you were wearing, Mr Armstrong, and have at least one, possibly two, maybe even three eyewitnesses who put you at the scene and can testify you shot Danny Brewster. Looks like you're on the Road to Perdition,' Bob said, finally regaining his nerve and a modicum of self-respect.

The Wise One nodded, then placed his hands behind his head. 'Are we done?'

Hope met The Gypsy in Daisy Park a week later, handing him a piece of paper with the details of a bank account he'd opened in Jersey. A down payment of fifty thousand pounds would follow.

'Bob, I think this is the beginning of a beautiful friendship,' The Gypsy said.

Hope instinctively touched his right earlobe.

41

Naomi unpacked her holiday clothes from Maxine's old suitcase that Frank had given her after she ditched the Louis Vuitton holdall that brought her nothing but bad luck and could likely be used as evidence if DI Hope ever got his hands on it. She loved the stickers on the side of the suitcase; a mixture of music ones from the 1980s along with holiday destinations and one for Pan Am Airways. It provided a sense of glamour and an insight into her mother's past. Naomi was looking forward to the short break with Frank, Bobby and Bella. A chance to let her hair down, eat some nice tapas and finally have a proper rest. They had chosen Sitges as their holiday destination at Bobby's suggestion, who described it as being "just like Portobello but better". Naomi suspected the real reason he wanted to go there was because the recently out-the-closet Gurkha wannabe had read it was the gay capital of Europe.

The Wise One was behind bars awaiting trial on an attempted murder charge. Brewster had miraculously survived the shooting and was now in an induced coma, with his chances of survival rated in the slim-to-none category. His death would leave Armstrong facing a murder rap with Frank and Naomi likely to be called as the star witnesses. Hope had interviewed them both separately and together but kept it to routine questions about events on the Crags with no more mention of any links between her and the Syndicate. The Gypsy had already given Naomi the lowdown on Hope and his love of a brown envelope. The boys from the Serious Crime Squad were gathering evidence to build a watertight case against Armstrong to prove he was the boss of an organised crime group and lock him away for good. Word around the campfire was three murder charges were pending along with extortion, torture, drug dealing, prostitution and a spot of people trafficking. Naomi expected a tug from the Serious Crime Squad at some point but so far there'd been no mention of the cinema project with the renovation work well underway.

She had seen a headline that morning in the Spanish edition of the *Daily Record* that read:

US FOLK SINGER AND RUSSIAN GIRLFRIEND QUIZZED OVER LOONY DOOK MURDER

Naomi knew the journos were behind the times with Falco and Olga being let go after providing watertight alibis and would join them in Sitges that evening. Falco had assured her that he wanted nothing more to do with the Wise One, who he'd worked for on a freelance basis over the years. The aging hippie was appalled at finding out Armstrong was a grass and assured Naomi that taking care of Billy One would be the couple's last hit for the Syndicate.

Naomi grabbed her dad's arm as they walked through the town browsing various knick-knacks.

'You're looking well, Frank,' she said.

'I've lost two stone in weight, my love, and I'm feeling ten years younger. I'm not missing the booze and this vape thing is much better than the Melvyn Braggs.'

Naomi smiled even though most of her dad's references were lost on her.

'I'm walking ten thousand steps each day and Bobby and I

have started playing shite golf again at the nine-hole course in Porty.'

'That's great, Dad. I'm so proud of you. It's brilliant that all the gang's here and you've patched things up with Bobby and Bella. Life's too short to be bearing grudges.' Naomi didn't believe this and knew she would harbour a grudge against the Wise One for evermore.

'Yeah, I was out of order telling Bella to fuck off that night the jellyfish stung me in the balls. Hopefully this wee holiday will help make amends.'

They wandered into a shop selling ceramics and Naomi bought some Mediterranean-style white tiles adorned with lemons that she thought would make a nice addition to her beachfront flat back in Porty. She thought now was a good time to gently probe Frank about his finances.

'How are you for money, Dad?'

Frank nodded his head with a fair degree of enthusiasm while pretending to study a ceramic plate.

'All good, my love. All good. The Gypsy's offered me twenty grand for the Shadow, and I've accepted, given the nick it's in since the acid attack and the fact it guzzles fuel like a Sherman tank. That should keep me going for a bit and I can dip into my remaining pension funds if I need a top-up. My priority is to get ninety days' sobriety under my belt and start working though the programme with my sponsor. I'll decide on my next career move at some point. I quite fancy doing a bit of restaurant reviewing but the dream ticket would be to work at the cinema. I'll do anything there, even strap on an usherette tray and sell ice cream.'

Naomi said nothing. Frank had been dropping not so subtle hints about working at the cinema for a while now and she wasn't keen on the idea given the amount of heat around the project. Maybe one day when things calmed down a bit.

They ambled down to the beach where Bobby and Bella

had already secured some sun loungers. Naomi pulled off her T-shirt and kicked off her flip-flops to reveal a flowery bikini before sprinting into the water and diving head first into the Med. She tasted the salt on her lips as she lay back floating with, at that precise moment, not a care in the world. Naomi watched as Frank changed into his pink flamingo swimming trunks behind a towel that Bella and Bobby were holding up to protect his modesty on the beach. She heard him warning Bella, 'No peeping,' as he pulled them up over his thighs which he would later burn to a crisp after sticking to his bonkers rule of "No suncream on the first day". He tied his trunks and pulled down the towel Bella and Bobby were holding. The three friends hugged, with Frank telling them both how much he loved them.

Bella, who was wearing a skull and crossbones bikini, scolded him. 'Stop being such a soppy cunt, Savage.'

Frank gave her a playful nudge as they made their way to the water's edge. He started to run before looking back and shouting, 'Last one in is a hairy kipper!'

Naomi watched as her dad ran into the clear blue waters. Bella, Bobby and Naomi joined him and they formed a huddle, jumping up and down, then splashing each other. Bella reached under the water and pulled Frank's trunks down. At that moment it was clear to Naomi that jellyfish were the last thing on his mind.

The group headed back to the villa they were renting and found Falco and Olga waiting for them. Falco was wearing a black leather waistcoat and denim shorts while Olga wore a white linen shirt over a micro bikini that wouldn't have looked out of place on Copacabana Beach. Falco brought Naomi up to speed with developments back home.

He said, 'Looks like our good friend, Mr Armstrong, may have reached the end of the line. The feds are hot for him and the witnesses are crawling out of the woodwork. It all depends how much credit that rat fuck has in the bank with the authorities.'

Naomi kept her own counsel giving a cursory nod. She wasn't quite for trusting Falco and Olga just yet, seeing as they'd been acting as an on/off husband and wife hit team for the Syndicate. God knows how many executions this pair had carried out over the years.

'Yip, I suppose a lot will come down to whether or not Brewster lives or dies,' she finally replied.

'Well, Naomi. I can tell you that cat is putting up one helluva fight to stay alive. He's got shattered vertebrae and broken nearly every bone in his body. There's no chance he'll walk again but the key thing for Armstrong is whether he can communicate and there's more chance of me topping the Billboard chart than that happening at present.'

'What about the Serious Crime Squad and the case they've built against him?' she asked.

'Between you and me, Naomi, there's more holes in that than the Mojave Desert. Witnesses have a habit of disappearing around the Syndicate. I should know.'

Naomi felt a sudden urge to get away from Falco. The novelty had worn a bit thin and the "singing serial killer" had made her come over queasy.

'I'm away for a lie down. My dad and the rest of them are out the back. Good to see you.' Falco beckoned her in for a hug and whispered, 'Take care' as the smell of patchouli oil lingered in her nostrils. Naomi went into her room and lay on the bed. The owner of the villa was a friend of Falco, a music producer who had made a fortune from Hi-NRG disco hits in the eighties. It was classic Mediterranean style with a smattering of Eurotrash décor in the shape of marble busts and homoerotic pictures. There was a large swimming pool with sun loungers and a bamboo bar hatch. Naomi dozed for a while, then came to and wondered where she was. Maxine had come to her in a half dream, standing by the side of a swimming pool holding Naomi's hand while a younger, suntanned, muscular Frank swam lengths. She stared at the ceiling and had no recollection of ever being at a lido with her mum and dad, although the setting for her dream was London. Naomi glanced over at her mother's suitcase, wanting to touch something that would provide a tangible connection to Maxine. She pulled it up onto the bed and touched the stickers; one for Paris with a picture of the Eiffel Tower and another with the "Welcome to Fabulous Las Vegas" signage. Opening the case, Naomi smelt inside, hoping to catch some long-lost scent of the woman who brought her into the world. For some reason, she put her hand under the bottom insert of the case but found nothing. No remnants of a smuggled drug consignment or even a grain of sand from a holiday past. She made to close the suitcase, then saw the outline of an envelope in the lining attached to the inside of the lid. Naomi stuck her hand in the lining where the envelope had dropped down and pulled it out. The envelope was sealed and although the address on the front had faded, she could make out the second line in her mother's handwriting which read, *17 Denmark Street,* followed by a scrawled *London* and the first part of the postcode *WC2*. Only two words were legible in the first line, *Sounds of,* then a smudge. Naomi ran a finger along the edge of the envelope, then picked it up and shook it. There was something inside that rattled and felt hard. She rubbed the envelope in her hands, feeling it, unconsciously trying to connect with the essence of her mother. Her inclination was to rip it open, but a sense of guilt prevented her desecrating this relic from Maxine's past. No. The right thing to do was take the envelope to Frank, then they could open it together, uncover the mysterious contents and provide a sense of ceremony to the occasion. A million thoughts raced through Naomi's mind. What if this letter held a secret that could damage her dad? Maybe it was best just to throw it away. Naomi knew that was never going to happen as she shook the envelope up and down trying to gauge the contents that felt like they were in some kind of box. Take it to her dad. That was the best course of action but find the right time to do it as the last thing Naomi wanted to do was ruin his holiday.

42

The remainder of the holiday flew by with Naomi desperate to make it to the last day without discussing the envelope with Frank. Her father was on brilliant form, like the weight of the world had lifted from his shoulders. Naomi noticed how Frank was a better laugh when he was off the booze, gentler, less bitter, with a childish sense of humour as opposed to his default setting of telling every joke with a jab. He suddenly looked ten years younger with a bit of a tan coming through the lobster red – a welcome change from the deathly pallor he wore back in Porty. The group had gravitated towards the many bars with The Piano Bar (El Piano) a favourite. Falco had commandeered a guitar one night and "treated" the locals to a few Bob Dylan numbers with Olga on backing vocals. Bobby had taken to disappearing towards the end of an evening, heading towards the gay clubs to explore this new world at his fingertips. Naomi had caught Frank and Bella snogging outside the villa on the last night and told them to "get a room" in between making a play of sticking her fingers down her throat and shouting, 'Stop it, Dad, you're giving me the boke.'

On the morning of their departure, Naomi asked Frank if he wanted to grab a coffee and go for a stroll along the promenade; a chance to take in the beauty of Sitges for one last time. She had fallen in love with the place – a warmer version of Portobello with a promenade that wasn't taken up with dog walkers and angry cyclists. Naomi vowed she'd be back next year, all going well with the cinema. The Wise One behind bars had given her a bit of breathing space but she knew it would come "on top" in the coming year with a potential show trial where she'd no doubt be cited as a star witness. Armstrong would attempt to run things from behind bars, but it was debatable whether his trusted lieutenants down south would stay trusted, and a power vacuum would ensue if he went away for good. Naomi realised that keeping in with The Gypsy was a good move, but her life would be in danger if she testified against the Wise One. This latest worry was compounded by the start of her period and a trip to the hospital in two days for an ultrasound to check her endometriosis. She felt completely knackered and was popping Ibuprofen like they were Tic Tac mints.

Against this backdrop, she set off arm-in-arm with Frank, who unlocked arms after one hundred yards, saying he wasn't comfortable. This was her opportunity to present him with the envelope and open it together. Naomi had made up her mind that they needed to see what was inside and felt a mixture of excitement and dread as to the contents. A range of possibilities had played on her mind, including the possibility it could be a letter from Maxine ending the relationship with Frank. But Naomi had managed to convince herself it was something positive and parked the negativity to enjoy the walk with her dad.

'How have you enjoyed the holiday, Frank?' she asked as they glanced out over the Med.

'I fucking love it, my love. It's been bloody brilliant. Sitges is my new spiritual home, and Bobby seems to have fitted in well with the locals.'

Naomi laughed. 'Yip, he's taken to the place like a duck to water. Maybe we'll be able to buy our own place and move out here one day.'

Frank pondered this for a moment.

'Aye, that would be great, but you know I'd get homesick for Porty and the horizontal rain, plus it's harder to get into arguments over here as everyone on the prom behaves themselves.'

'I thought you were putting all that behind you, Dad. Live and let live.'

'Or *Live and Let Die,* my love – great movie, 1973, one of Roger's finest. No, you're right, the meetings seem to be helping and having a sponsor is working. It feels different in AA this time as opposed to the fifty-seven other times I walked through the doors to the "tea and biscuits".'

They walked on a bit, climbing the steps up to the Church of Sant Bartomeu and Santa Tecla that overlooked the town. Naomi guided Frank over to a wall with a drop down to the sandy beach and sparkling early morning sea. They sat down and she furtively brought the envelope out of her tote bag.

'What you got there?' Frank asked.

'It's an envelope from Mum, with a box of some sort inside. I found it in the lining of her old suitcase.'

Frank stared at the envelope and instinctively tried to grab it. Naomi pulled it away, turning to guard it with her shoulder.

'No, Dad! I want us to open this together.'

Frank jumped off the wall and was pacing up and down, rubbing his hands, then putting them behind his head. A bag of nerves.

'Okay, okay! Let's do it,' he said, clapping his hands. 'But I've no fucking idea what's in there, Naomi.'

Naomi held it in her hands and studied the stamp. A picture of a flower that she recognised as an Autumn crocus or "naked lady" as her Aunty Jane had called them in her garden. The flower hadn't bloomed and was pale lilac with a yellowish stem. The word *Colchicum* was written on the side underneath a picture of the Queen and 34p. She handed the envelope over to Frank, who shook it side to side, then held it up against his ear.

'It's not a fucking shell, Dad,' Naomi chided.

Frank placed it down on the wall, then grabbed it quickly as a gust of wind hit them square in the face.

'Right, I'm opening this fucker before it ends up in the water.'

'Do it,' Naomi replied.

'No, you do it,' Frank said, handing it back to his daughter, who carefully slipped a fingernail under the seal and peeled the envelope open. She made a big play of carefully reaching inside before slowly bringing out two pages of yellowing lined paper and a cassette box that had D-C90 TDK written on the side.

'Read the letter,' Frank said.

'It's not really a letter, Dad,' Naomi replied, peering at the handwriting.

> To whom it may concern.
>
> I, Maxine Lamont-Savage, do declare that the enclosed demo tape and lyrics have been created by myself and are therefore my sole property. I enclose the lyrics to the song 'Camden Sunrise' that I have written. Please treat this as notice of my registration submission for the aforementioned song, with attached copyright.

Frank held the demo tape in his hands, then turned it on its side to see the words 'Camden Sunrise' written on the side. He opened the box and brought out a tape that also had 'Camden Sunrise' written on it along with *Copyright © 1987 Maxine Lamont-Savage "all rights reserved"*. Frank studied the envelope and appeared to be racking his brains over the address. Naomi swore she could see the wheels turning in his brain.

'Fuck me. I think this was meant for the *Sounds of London* music publishers. They were based in Denmark Street, half the music business was based in Denmark Street.'

Naomi looked at her dad quizzically. 'What does it mean?'

'Give me the rest, love.'

Naomi handed over the bits of paper to her dad, who squinted at them in the sunlight.

'I haven't got my reading specs but if this is what I think it is, then we have proof that Maxine wrote "Camden Sunrise" and we could go after the royalties.'

Naomi said, 'Really, Dad? This proves Mum wrote that song.'

'There's no doubt your mother wrote that song before that bastard Armstrong stole it. Proving it in court will be a bastard but we owe it to Maxine's legacy to make things right.'

The pair turned to face the sea and silently looked out over the clear blue waters of the Mediterranean as Frank put an arm around his daughter's shoulder and hummed the tune to his favourite song.

One Year Later

T he stars turned out in force for the opening night of the new Regency cinema in Portobello, with queues stretching down the street and hordes of fans hoping to get a glimpse of George Pittman with his new fiancée, the author, Bridget McGreevy, formerly Bridget Bell, formerly Bridget Savage. A giant vintage poster accompanied the cinema hoardings, proclaiming: "James Bond 007, *The Spy Who Loved Me*". Scotland's power couple, Shelby St. George and new Rangers signing, Kyle Horsburgh, were there along with Deidre McAllister and Chic McGrain, who pumped his fist at the crowd, making his way towards the Art Deco entrance. Frank, who had a loan of the Shadow for the night from The Gypsy, got out of the car to open the back passenger seat as Naomi, who looked stunning in a black Chanel dress, emerged. The old lady of British motoring was gleaming and added a touch of glamour to the proceedings. Falco arrived, tipping his hat towards the well-wishers, with Olga towering over him in her patent-leather Louboutin heels.

Naomi and Frank nodded towards The Gypsy, who was pushing Brewster in a wheelchair with Waffle in tow. Brewster had miraculously survived the shooting and subsequent fall, spending six months in the induced coma after suffering fourteen broken bones including two vertebrae. The doctors said he had brain damage, would never walk again and crucially for the Wise One had lost the power of speech, thus rendering him next to useless as a witness in the coming attempted murder trial. The daily sessions with the speech therapist had proved fruitless and Brewster had shown zero recollection of the events on the Crags. He was wearing the top half of a Burberry tux and had turned out to receive the best wishes of the local community, who acknowledged the part he played in bringing the cinema project to fruition.

Champagne flutes were handed out and each of the guests was handed a box of either fruit gums or fruit pastilles as they settled in for the opening feature. Bobby, resplendent in a black penguin suit, and Bella, working a look best described as "scrubbed-up Goth at the school prom", handed out the commemorative programmes that featured a picture of the old Regency on the cover.

The audience settled down as the Pearl & Dean theme tune played with George Pittman and Bridget entering the back of the auditorium as the lights dimmed. Frank slowly made his way to the stage to introduce the main sponsor – a well-known brand of non-alcoholic lager. He couldn't wait to get stuck into his new role as cinema manager, with Bobby as his assistant, now that The Gypsy had bought out the council and owned the ninety-nine-year lease on the A-listed building. Strictly legit. Frank thanked everyone for attending and ran through the list of dignitaries who had helped get the new Regency off the ground. *The Spy Who Loved Me* had been Frank's choice for the opener but they would show more modern fayre and champion independent cinema. He sat down beside Naomi and Bobby as the curtain rose. Naomi winced as Roger Moore plunged off a snow-covered clifftop in the opening sequence only to release a Union Jack parachute. Frank glowed with delight and grabbed Bobby's hand as Carly Simon sang the first words to the theme tune, "Nobody Does It Better".

Halfway through the film, Naomi nipped outside for a

cigarette. She needed a break from Roger Moore battling with Jaws and wanted to stand back and admire the building. At that moment, ensuring the safety of everyone was uppermost on her mind. She'd effectively left the Syndicate and was now working for The Gypsy but, to her knowledge, Armstrong still thought he controlled the cinema. It was likely the Wise One would escape justice as the Crown case hinged on Brewster, who was in no fit state to testify. Naomi feared being in the middle of a power struggle between the Syndicate and The Gypsy that would see bodies strewn in the streets. There was also the ongoing quest to have Maxine recognised as the originator of "Camden Sunrise" that was tied up with the lawyers. They planned to "play the joker" at some point by releasing the demo tape, and Frank had tentatively reached out to a documentary filmmaker who had shown interest in a project about Maxine's life.

No sooner had she lit up than The Gypsy emerged with Brewster.

'I thought he needed some fresh air,' The Gypsy said, patting Brewster on the shoulder, who was staring into space. 'Can you keep an eye on him for a minute, Naomi, while I get some water? He's got white bits round his mouth.'

He went back inside, leaving Naomi alone with Brewster. She moved round to the front of his wheelchair to stand face on with her former tormentor.

Brewster had a demonic grin on his face that belied his vegetative state. He beckoned Naomi to crouch down before grabbing her by the arm.

He whispered softly, 'I remember everything, Naomi. That bastard is going down.'